DRAWN

QUEEN OF ZAZZAU

Afrocentric Books
St. Paul, Minnesota

Published in the United States of America by Afrocentric Books, an imprint of Mugwump Press, LLC, St. Paul, Minnesota.

Printed in the United States of America

First Printing, November 2018

Library of Congress Control Number: 2018956458

ISBN 978-1946595065

Queen of Zazzau is a work of historical fiction. Names, characters, places, and incidents are either the product of the author's imagination or are used fictitiously. Any resemblance to actual persons, living or dead—aside from historical public figures—is purely coincidental.

Afrocentric Books | Mugwump Press
2136 Ford Parkway, #8018
Saint Paul, MN 55116

www.afrocentricbooks.com
www.mugwumppress.com

For my mother, for giving me imagination.

For my father, for giving me the words to express my imagination.

For my children, for giving me the space to write the words.

And for my husband, for giving me the courage to put my words in print.

GLOSSARY

The Pantheon

Dawatsu............The god of thunder
Gajere............ The god of forests
Inna............ The Earth Mother
Kogi-Ayu............ The god of rivers
Mafarki............ The goddess of dreams
Mak'esuwa............ The goddess of fire
Nakada............ The trickster god of the Crossroads
Ruhun Yak'i............ The god of war
Ubangiji............ The Supreme God

Titles

Alkali............Judge
Dylala............Book/receipt keeper
Etsu............King (Nupe)
Fagaci............A Hausa royal official
Galadima............A Hausa royal official
Gimbiya............Princess
Kaura............Army general
Kuturun Mahayi............Mounted bowmen
Madawaki............Calvary commander
Mai............King
Mai Tasuniya............Storyteller/King of stories
Makama............A Hausa royal official
Mallam/Mallamai (pl) ....Learned man (sing)
Sarakunan Karaga............Kingmakers
Sarauniya............Queen
Sarki............King
Ummal............Titled military officer
Uwar Soro............"Lady of the House"
Waziri............Vizier

Ethnic Groups
Edo
Hausa
Kanuri
Kwararafa
Nupe
Oyo (Yoruba)
Songhai
Tuareg

Other Words and Phrases
-awa (suffix) ....In reference to a people
Babariga............Type of traditional West African menswear
Bature............Foreigner (of the "white" persuasion)
Bori............A Hausa traditional religious sect
Diwan............Divan
Ga ta ga ta nan ....Customary introduction of a fable
                                    ("here it is"), by storyteller
Gani............New Year
Ganuwar Amina............Amina's Wall
Gidan Bakwa............House of Bakwa
Gyatuma............old woman
Hausa Bakwai............Seven Hausa States
Jigida ....Waist beads
Karya ....Female dog
Koboko ....Rawhide whip
Ku zo, mu ji ta ....Audience response to storyteller's
                                    introduction ("come, let's hear it")
Kungurus kan bera ....Customary conclusion to a fable
                                    ("The rat's head is off")
Ranka ya dade ....May you live long
Takouba ....Type of straight sword
Tuwo ....Steamed balls of millet
Wallahi ....An oath ("By God!")
Yan Tauri ....One who is impervious to metal
Zazzagawa............People of Zazzau

PART I

QUEEN OF ZAZZAU

Woman

ONE

Rizga, Eastern Mountain Kingdoms, Southern Hausaland, circa 1557 CE

The smell of smoke wafted toward us like a malicious spirit. Burning grass—a field or thatched roofs—and something else that I did not recognize. When at last the city gates came into view, they were sundered, ripped from the wall and crumpled on the ground like tattered mats. Grey pillars of smoke rose from the city beyond. The odor, growing stronger as we neared, stoked revulsion in me. Its sharp taste constricted my throat.

"Bodies." Jaruma turned to me. She was my personal guard and companion. "The smell is burning flesh."

Aghast, I covered my mouth with my hand.

The *madawaki*, commander of my mother's cavalry, raised a fist above his head, and the steady clop of a thousand mounted bowmen—Kuturun Mahayi—drew to a halt behind us. Vultures' calls pierced the silence.

"Stay with Gimbiya Amina," the madawaki commanded Jaruma. Turning to his troop, he gave additional orders.

Twenty warriors galloped into the smoldering city, leaving the rest behind with Jaruma and me. They formed a living wall around us, each man alert on his mount, bow at the ready. And we waited. All was quiet but for the sounds of scavengers.

Jaruma peered out from between the men.

"What's happening?" I asked.

She didn't answer. Her fingers tapped impatiently on her thigh, as though aching to have a weapon in their grip. Over and over, she drummed a nervous rhythm while straining to see past the Kuturun Mahayi blocking her view.

After an interminable time, the madawaki and his men exited the shattered city gates.

"Rizga is devastated," he said, his horse fidgeting. "Survivors are mostly the aged and infirm."

"Who has done this?" I choked back the mounting fear.

"You must be taken to safety, Gimbiya."

"Who did it?"

"The Kwararafa."

My heart dropped. "Kwararafa?" I couldn't keep the quaver from my voice.

A newly risen plague on the savanna, Kwararafa was a kingdom built on the methodical subjugation of nations. They plundered city upon city to increase their empire. None who stood against them in battle lived on as a people.

Something evasive in the madawaki's manner, the way he looked past me, his eyes scanning the distant peaks, told me that he'd not been entirely forthcoming.

"What are you not saying?" I asked.

He ignored my question. "Jaruma, take the gimbiya to safety."

"Tell me!" I grabbed his horse's bridle.

His quiet scrutiny, which was difficult to endure at the best of times, fell on me. During my tenure as one of a scant few female soldiers in his cavalry, before my mother, Queen Bakwa, cut short my training, I had been subject to his orders. That was evident by the way he looked at me now. Although I traveled this day as the queen's representative, I wilted under the intense gaze of his coal-black eyes.

Subdued, I said, "Please, Madawaki."

An internal debate played across his dark face, deepening the furrow in his brow. Unlike most of the Kuturun Mahayi, he wore no headwrap, only a small white cap. After more than a week of travel, a layer of bristle covered his usually smooth head and face—black hair, interspersed with grey.

At length, he said, "They've made for Zazzau."

"What?" I had heard, but the words did not make sense.

"Go with Jaruma."

"But how can that be?" I asked. "We would have seen signs of a war band on our way here. Who told you this?"

"A man dying in the streets."

The man must have been mistaken. Or the madawaki had misunderstood. *They couldn't possibly be going to Zazzau.*

I said, "Where is he? Let him tell me himself."

"He is dead, Gimbiya."

Feeling my tension, my horse drew back. The madawaki's horse, its bridle still firmly in my grip, also shifted.

"They must be moving across the hills," he said, casting his eyes to the distant peaks. "And they possess powers we've never encountered."

"What powers?" My eyebrows rose. "You mean *magic*?"

"Call it what you will. The Kwararafa attack like biting flies— invisible until they strike. They came down on Rizga without warning. No one saw them before the raid. No one knew they were near."

Cold panic formed in the pit of my stomach, but I kept it under control. "Then I must return to Zazzau."

"You will not." The madawaki and Jaruma spoke as one.

"But—"

"No!" Even the tall savanna grass bowed at the madawaki's voice. "You will be kept safe."

I stiffened. "You no longer command me, Madawaki."

"The queen commands *me*, and I am commanded to protect you. You'll not return to Zazzau."

My hand flew from the bridle to his arm. "I will not linger amidst this carnage!"

My mother had sent me to Rizga on a mission of friendship. I was the chief administrator of two provinces in Zazzau and well versed in conflict and diplomacy, but I wasn't prepared for this. My role here was to extend a hand to our neighbor in the east, to negotiate fair tariffs and the exchange of goods. Thanks to the Kwararafa, our neighbor no longer existed.

"You will not leave me here," I said.

"The city is safe," he replied. "You and Jaruma, along with the men I can spare, will go into the city. The Kwararafa have finished their business." His nostrils flared in disgust. "You're safer here."

"No."

Without a care for whom he was manhandling, he seized my fingers and wrested them from his arm. "Do as I command."

The tone of his words and the intensity in his eyes forced my obedience. As I looked on in impotent dismay, the madawaki doled out orders. If my time serving under him had taught me nothing else, it had taught me that once he made a decision, he would not be swayed. He would never allow me to ride back with him, and now I dared not go on my own.

He huddled with Jaruma, lips moving, forehead pressed against hers. Even on horseback, his height made Jaruma's six feet look small. Despite their age difference, her dark skin and features mirrored his and lent them both a strange beauty. Seeing them together like that, I realized that my own sibling was in danger. Zariya and I were not close like Jaruma and her brother, but we were fond of one another. Zariya was my blood, a part of me. I needed to protect her, yet here I was. Powerless.

The madawaki pulled away from Jaruma. I thought I should say something more, offer him a prayer, wish him all speed back to our people . . . anything. But I did nothing, merely hung back as the bowmen rode off, kicking up stones and dirt.

"Come, Gimbiya." Jaruma rode toward me. "Let's go into the city. There are people who need our aid."

"My mother needs my aid," I said dully. "Who will help her?"

"The Kwararafa are on foot. The Kuturun Mahayi will soon intercept them."

"Intercept them?" I looked at her, incredulous.

The Kwararafa Empire lay beyond the impassable mountain ranges, but clearly they had found a way to march an army through them. Not only had they mastered the treacherous mountain passage, they managed to travel unseen by the plains dwellers in open savanna.

"They crept out of those peaks and decimated the city without so much as a whisper," I said.

"But now we know they're coming." Her voice was steady, but I knew her well enough to see the misgiving in her eyes.

I let out a shaky breath, my gaze darting westward to Zazzau.

When rumors of the Kwararafa first surfaced, I had wanted to expand our forces, but my mother had refused. She believed that because we had pushed back the mighty Songhai, we had no reason to fear the Kwararafa. And what evidence did I have to support my assertions? Besides, calling in the mere one thousand bowmen that had accompanied me on this journey had raised the council's ire. They would have expressed an even deeper dissatisfaction had the queen been inclined to recall the entire army back to the city. During peacetime, no less.

But peace was a fickle thing. And while my mother made every effort to meet hostility with diplomacy, the Kwararafa met diplomacy with slaughter.

"You must have faith, Gimbiya," Jaruma said firmly. "My brother has never failed me. He has never failed Zazzau. The Kuturun Mahayi will stop them."

I prayed she was right.

❋

The madawaki had left me fifty mounted bowmen and Jaruma, who now took command. We advanced into the city at her order, smoke billowing thick around us, the odor more acrid than before. Even with my veil pulled tight over my nose and mouth, the smoke coated my throat. Every cough burned. The others, similarly veiled, did not appear so afflicted. They moved quietly through the smoke, past burning houses, past the dead, who lay scattered, flies buzzing about their corpses. The bodies of children, small children, lay motionless among the adults. My stomach retched at the sight, but nothing came up.

"They killed the children," I murmured to myself.

I tried to avert my gaze from the tiny, lifeless forms, but death surrounded me. Men and women struck down, fear forever frozen on their faces. I looked upon the dead bodies and remembered Zariya's prediction—the oracular dream that had compelled my mother to end my military training: *The carcasses of men litter the fields.* Had she been referring to these carcasses? If so, she had failed to mention the women and children.

"They kill everyone," said Danladi, the soldier who rode to my left.

The stories that preceded the Kwararafa claimed that those who survived an attack were either too old to be bothered with or too well hidden when the enemy swept through their lands. Picking our way through the massacre at Rizga, I saw that the stories were true. To have believed that the people capable of such horror would hesitate to bring this butchery to Zazzau had been nothing short of folly.

Danladi looked around in disgust. "They've neither the need nor the desire for prisoners. They kill everyone."

"Not everyone," Jaruma said as a woman's wailing cut the air. She raised her voice. "I need five of you. The rest, find the survivors and bring them to the palace. Gimbiya, come with me."

I rode through the smoke, telling myself that my people would be safe, that my family would be unharmed. After all, nine hundred and fifty Kuturun Mahayi would be there in a matter of days. But it had taken us *eight* days to reach here from Zazzau. The men and their horses were travel weary. What if the Kwararafa, riding whatever power they rode, reached Zazzau first? What if the enemy made it to the capital? What then?

"There." Jaruma interrupted my anxious thoughts before they roamed too deeply into darkness. "Palace compound."

❋

The royal palace stood at the center of the city, much of it destroyed. From what remained, I saw that it had been a marvelous structure built with large adobe blocks. The outer walls were not high, but they looked about two meters thick. On this side of the compound, two walls overlapped so that, although there was no gate, the gap between adjacent walls was only wide enough for a single person to enter at a time. We dismounted here, securing our horses to iron pegs set into the wall, before entering the compound.

Though I'd known what to expect, I was unprepared for the sight of yet more slaughtered people. This time, when my abdomen clenched, I doubled over and vomited onto the scorched ground.

"Find the wells," Jaruma shouted over the roar of the fire, and five men rushed to do her bidding. Her hand dropped to my shoulder. "It will pass."

It did pass, as my revulsion turned to anger then back to fear for Zazzau. After removing the bodies and dousing the flames, we saw the full extent of the devastation. The iron gate at the main entrance, opposite the way we'd entered, lay partially atop the smashed gatehouse. The Kwararafa had set fires inside each of the cylindrical dwellings. The largest dwelling—presumably the king's quarters—at the center consisted of several conjoined buildings. The front-middle building was smallest, followed in size by the two flanking buildings, then the rear-middle. Having never traveled more than a day's ride from the borders of Zazzau, I had never seen such irregular architecture. The lack of conformity may once have imparted an exotic beauty to the overall structure; but today, it too had burned from the inside out, and—like the gatehouse—its walls were smashed. Only the king's pavilion, a large three-walled structure with a heavy thatched roof, remained intact.

❁

By late day, the survivors of Rizga—silent as the dead, frightened, and in shock—clung to each other in the pavilion.

"Who among you is of able body?" Jaruma asked.

A few people looked up at her with empty eyes, but no one replied. Then several young boys came forward. The tallest spoke.

"We were in the fields when they came." Tracks of tears streaked through the soot covering his face. "Had we known, we would have returned." He lowered his head. "Before it was too late."

"If you had returned," Jaruma said, "you'd be among the dead."

"I'd have died honorably, fighting alongside my father."

"There's no shame in your survival. The Creator has other plans for you."

"What plan does Ubangiji have that my whole family should die? My sister was only a baby. Did the Creator not have a plan for her? And my brothers?"

"It's not for us to question the ways of gods. For now, we must bury the fallen."

She spoke privately with a handful of soldiers, who gathered up the young boys and led them out of the palace compound.

"What of me?" I asked. Worry for my people would drive me mad. Pulling well water had done nothing to refocus my thoughts. I needed to set my mind and idle hands to a more challenging task.

"You and I will attend the living," she said. "See to their wounds. Prepare food."

I nodded and went about my assigned duty.

Among the wounded, only a few had minor injuries, and these were quickly addressed. The rest were beyond our help; we did what we could to keep them comfortable.

For food, some chickens roamed the city, but the process of feather plucking proved too onerous a task for that day. Although a few market stalls still stood, the Kwararafa had made off with the best edibles. So, we raided what remained of the Rizgawa grain stores and made a meal of cooked millet. It was not a satisfying dinner, but fatigue and despair didn't let anyone complain.

After eating, we took turns washing with water from the palace wells. Then, one by one, we crashed onto the earthen floor of the pavilion. Sleep came quickly.

TWO

I heard my name and opened my eyes to darkness.

"Amina." The voice was like a stream bubbling over a bed of stones.

Looking this way and that, I saw nothing but the blackness beyond. "Who calls?" I asked.

"It is me."

Grey light filtered through the darkness like the first rays of dawn dispersing a fog. I sat in a forest unlike any I had ever seen. Dark tree trunks rose like giants around me, their canopy lost in the heavens.

"Here." The voice came from somewhere near my foot.

I looked down and saw a tiny spring gurgling from the earth.

"Do you not recognize me?" the voice asked, but there was no one present. The words had come from the spring.

I stared intently at the water. Small bubbles floated from the bottom, increasing in size as they ascended and broke through the surface. From each bursting bubble came the sound of cascading laughter.

"Kogi-Ayu?" I said uneasily.

Stories abounded of the temperamental rivergod. As Kogi, he provided life water to the soil and to the people who toiled it; but as Ayu, he was wicked and drowned any who entered his demesne. Cautious, I scooted away from the water.

"You know me now, Amina?"

"I know you." I glanced around for higher ground. "Why have you come to me?"

"The Kuturun Mahayi have overtaken your enemy."

My head fell forward in relief. "Then Zazzau is saved."

"Your enemy is unseen and will come upon your people under shroud of darkness and cloak of magic," he said. "Zazzau is doomed."

My breath caught.

"Unless . . ." Kogi-Ayu paused and the babbling spring went still.

"Unless?" I exhaled.

"Unless you, Amina, save them."

"Me?"

"Destiny demands it."

The Oracle had decreed that I travel to Rizga instead of my mother's usual representatives. That same Oracle had then demanded that I travel with one thousand Kuturun Mahayi.

"What does the Oracle say I should do?" I asked.

"Destiny," Kogi-Ayu corrected. "They are not one and the same."

"What?"

"Destiny and the Oracle are not the same." The tight, deliberate flow of words indicated the rivergod's impatience.

I moved farther away from the spring. "What does *Destiny* say I should do?"

"Destiny says you should save your people."

How could I save them? The closest I had ever come to battle was a fight with Jaruma. I could spar with and had sometimes beaten some of Zazzau's finest warriors, but good swordsmanship didn't make me a savior.

Because of prophecies and predictions that said I would be the cause of war and untold death, my mother had since banned me from the war council and any battle preparations. Indeed, she'd banned me from *everything* pertaining to war. I was twenty-three years old. My training wasn't complete and my skills were untested. What could a single, half-trained woman do that an army could not?

"Destiny brought you here," he said. "Trust her to show you the way."

Trust? I didn't trust anything the gods offered. But if the Kwararafa went unchecked, they would destroy my people.

Holding my faith together by the thinnest thread, I rose. "I will go to my people." *Madawaki's command be damned.* Then I hesitated. The dark forest spread as far as the eye could see. "How do I leave this place?"

And how will I save Zazzau?

"You will leave here when you wake. As to saving your people? That is the domain of War. Ask him."

I'd not realized I had spoken my thought aloud.

I said, "I would not disturb Ruhun Yak'i with the paltry affairs of men."

The rivergod's laughter brought the bubbles in the spring to a boil. "Ruhun Yak'i, indeed." He laughed again. "I do not blame you for not wanting to be in my brother's debt. But hear me, Gimbiya Amina. Zazzau is in danger. If you cannot do what must be done, no one will."

The spring began to dwindle into itself, growing smaller and smaller until it was but a trickle twisting between greenish-black tufts of grass.

"Wait," I called. "What must be done?"

From the diminishing stream came the bubbling voice, "Keep the hills close on your right and follow the flowing water. Now you are in *my* debt."

The forest dissolved into blackness.

❀

I woke in an unfamiliar place. Rubbing my eyes, I sat up and attempted to get my bearings.

"What is it?" Jaruma sat with her back against the wall. She had removed her headwrap. The length of red cloth, a dark contrast to the undyed linen of her trousers, lay draped across her knees.

"Where—" I began and then remembered. I was in Rizga. We had taken shelter in the pavilion with the city's survivors.

"Are you all right?" She leaned closer to peer at me in the darkness.

"I had a dream," I said, trying to recall what remained on the edge of my consciousness. "About a river."

"A river?"

"No." I pressed my knuckles against my temples to jog the memory hiding in the mist. "No. Not a river." The memory came clear. "It was the river*god*."

"You dreamed of Kogi-Ayu?" Along with weariness, her voice conveyed a distinct lack of interest.

"Yes." More of the dream came through. I raised my head sharply as the memory surfaced. "He said Zazzau is in danger. That we are doomed."

"It was a dream." She leaned her head back against the wall.

"It was more than a dream," I said tersely.

She angled her head downward to look at me again.

"He spoke to me," I said. "It was more than a dream."

The continued tone of disinterest belied her next question. "Did he tell you nothing more?"

"He said I, alone, could save Zazzau."

"You?" Her response reflected my own doubt.

"So he said."

"And how did he suggest you do it?" Irritation now seeped into her words.

"He didn't. Not precisely." Grabbing the bunched-up cloth of the headwrap upon which I had rested, I climbed to my feet. "He said to follow the flowing water and keep the hills to my right."

"What?"

My eyes searched the night for hers. "Jaruma, we must wake the others. If we remain here, the Zazzagawa are as good as dead."

"Wait." She rose, clutching her sheathed straight-sword in her left hand. "Wait, Gimbiya. It was only a dream. A dream born from worry over Zazzau."

"It was more than a dream." My loud words stirred some of the sleeping Rizgawa. Lowering my voice, I repeated, "More than a dream." I shook out the cloth and began clumsily tying my headwrap into place. Several turns around my head, then I pulled the cloth over my face to create a loose veil before taking it around my head a few more times.

She continued to look doubtful.

"I know what I know, and I'm going." Tucking the trailing end of my headwrap into one of its many folds, I tried to walk past her, but she stepped into my path. I pulled down the veil and said in a harsh tone, "Either help me or get out of my way."

"We were ordered to stay here."

"*You* were ordered. Your brother has no authority over me. Step aside."

"No."

"Obey me, Jaruma, and move. *I will not repeat myself.*"

She held her ground for several breaths, her expression an empty threat of violence. Without a word, she slung her headwrap around her neck, undid the thick, red sash at her waist, and knotted her scabbard onto it. Turning, she began to rouse the soldiers. "Up," she commanded, and added snidely, "We ride."

Those who had been standing sentry were already up and moving. After she gave them their new directives, they filed out of the compound.

Some of the Rizgawa woke as we were leaving, but only one approached us. It was the young boy from before.

"I want to come with you," he said. "I can fight."

I looked at Jaruma, who shrugged.

"What's your name?" I asked.

"Zuma."

"How old are you?"

"Fifteen."

Fifteen was old enough to fight. It was even old enough to marry and have children, as I should have done were I a dutiful daughter. The lean-muscled boy was around my height—a few inches short of six feet. He may even have proven adept with a weapon, but I didn't intend to make the child into a warrior when I was hardly battle ready myself.

I said, "Zuma, your responsibility is here with your people."

"But I have no one," he protested.

"Those who destroyed your city are on their way to destroy mine. We'll defeat them, and when we do, we'll come for you. All of you. Until then, you and those who are able must care for your people. Keep them safe. Keep them fed. Help them regain their strength. It's many days' journey to Zazzau."

"But how will I avenge my family?" he asked, looking so downtrodden that I wanted to put my arms around him.

"Your time will come. But in times of despair, there can be no greater honor than putting aside your own desires to do what is right for your people. The spirits of your ancestors will not find fault with you."

The boy didn't look convinced. His disappointment, his grief, swirled like a thick cloak around him, but we could do nothing for his family. They were dead and he had to accept new responsibilities. My family yet lived; my responsibility was elsewhere.

❋

We moved out on horseback, with me leading the procession of fifty bowmen. Jaruma rode at my side. Had we bothered with protocol, the ranking officer and a select few would have ridden ahead of me. In the previous eight days of travel from Zazzau to Rizga, Jaruma had gibed without end that I was gazing *wistfully* at her brother's back. Now I'd welcome any gibe to have him with me as I rode toward the dark mass of hills in the east.

Within minutes of setting off from Rizga, the tall grass of the savanna gave way to dry, rocky ground. The terrain made the going rough and worsened as we traveled farther. By the time we reached the peaks and turned northward, the rocks had grown to boulders around which we navigated our horses in near silence. Every now and then, conversation broke out, but our somber mood kept talk to a minimum.

After more than three hours of riding, we stopped to investigate on foot. The barren ground had the consistency of pulverized stone. High in the hills, however, spotty patches of green gave evidence of water somewhere. I considered climbing the peak, but the rivergod had said to keep the hills to the right, not underfoot.

Jaruma cleared her throat.

"What?" I snapped, turning back toward the group.

She stood between my grey horse and her dark bay, tying the wrap that she had until now worn as a loose scarf over her head. The undyed tunic and trousers of her uniform, stained with soot in Rizga, were now covered with dust. So were her feet in their stiff leather sandals. No doubt I was also filthy, though my light indigo held up better than white.

The bay shook its head, jangling the triangular amulets that Jaruma had woven into its mane. It was beyond me why she didn't hang the devices from the horse's bridle, as did the other horsemen. My horse, untouched by battle, had never needed a protective amulet; perhaps it was time he had one. The amulet my sister had given me hung around my neck. Removing it, I approached the horse.

"Gimbiya," Jaruma said, wiping her forehead with her sleeve.

It was an inopportune time to envy her smooth skin, as dark as the darkest soil. But I did. Mine was neither dark nor fair and glowed bronze in sunlight, betraying those few drops of Arab blood running through my veins.

"Are you certain we're meant to keep to the hills? Perhaps we came too far eastward," she said.

The thought had crossed my mind. Our current northeasterly route took us away from Zazzau's capital of Kufena, which lay northwest of here. We had already ridden out the night and come across no running water. On this desolate terrain, we were unlikely to find any.

"Perhaps," I replied uncertainly as I looped the amulet's string through the horse's bridle. "But I think this is where we're meant to be."

"You *think*?" She fell silent.

I tied the amulet in place and looked at her. Black eyes regarded me down the length of her unusually narrow nose, thoughts playing openly on her face. Perhaps she believed the prior day's strain had driven me mad. In truth, my own thoughts toyed with that idea. Jaruma followed me because she knew I was stubborn enough to go without her, but *I* knew she'd never let me go on my own.

"It was no dream, Jaruma."

✸

Another three hours passed. Maybe less, but time was dragging. The earlier smatterings of conversation had died down to silence and the sound of gravel crunching under hoof. Every now and then, Jaruma threw me a sideways look.

She turned to me now. "Gimbiya, the sun has long since risen, and there's still no sign of flowing water. Not a river, not a stream, not even a puddle. Either we turn back to Rizga or head to Zazzau. Regardless," she muttered, "my brother will kill me."

"The madawaki answers only to my mother, but *you* answer to me," I said. "We will not turn back."

"But, how can you—"

"Don't question me, Jaruma." I feigned a confidence I didn't feel.

"I'm not questioning you. It's just—"

"Enough."

"Amina . . ."

"Enough!"

She shut her mouth.

"You may turn back if you wish," I said.

She glared at me, her mouth twitching as though she intended to say something nasty. But she held her tongue. The soldiers closest to us exchanged looks with one another. They, too, likely thought me mad. A large part of me even doubted my sanity at this point, but something in my heart told me to persist. Of course, that was the sort of thing a mad person would believe, was it not? It didn't matter. We continued forward.

We rode for what felt like ages, but judging from the position of the sun, perhaps only a little more than another hour had gone by. I tried to mask my disappointment as we traveled, keeping my eyes open for even the slightest sign of water, but the soil was so dry, not a blade of grass grew. I debated admitting the error in my judgment and had begun formulating words of apology when I heard something.

I brought my horse to a stop. The others halted as well.

"Do you hear it?" I asked no one in particular.

Jaruma, who generally had the keenest ears, listened for a moment. Once the horses stilled, the splashing sound of water came clear.

"Not a dream." I said it more for myself than for her.

She rolled her eyes and looked toward the green of distant peaks. "It's probably runoff from a mountain forest. After nine hours, it's only natural that we find some sign of life on this barren plain."

"Where is your faith, Jaruma?"

Belly churning with anxiety, I dismounted and went in search of the rivergod's sign.

Jaruma joined me, looking thoroughly exasperated. The source of water, when we found it, was not what anyone would have expected.

A puddle of water bubbled from a small hole in the stony ground. When we came near, it rose straight up then fell back to the ground. It rose again, the column higher this time, before falling. The waterspout continued to rise and fall, its base thicker than its tip. Like dripstone growing from a cave floor, except its surface rippled with the water flowing through it. The column stretched higher and higher with each repetition. And higher still, until it was man height, before collapsing back into a puddle, now twentyfold its original size. Then it streamed forward.

"Do you believe now?" I asked and headed back to my horse.

Falling in step beside me, Jaruma said dryly, "Humblest apologies, Gimbiya."

❋

We rode after the stream, following it across the uneven ground, through clefts in the mountain, and up narrow defiles. If anyone doubted the handiwork of Kogi-Ayu, the fact that the stream flowed from low ground to high made the rivergod's involvement clear. The higher we went, the steeper the incline. In due course, we found ourselves ascending a craggy mountain path. Our horses, better suited to even terrain, had a difficult time of it. We dismounted.

"Gather your weapons," Jaruma said.

The Kuturun Mahayi wore their bows and quivers whenever they rode. Mine were hanging from my horse's saddle, along with my sword and the rest of my travel supplies. Despite cavalry training, I was not a titled officer, as the title of *ummal* was earned in battle. Still, I was Zazzagawa; my archery skills surpassed most. I grabbed my bow and arrows and started up the path.

"No," Jaruma said, a hand on my shoulder. "Danladi, Gambo, you're at the head."

The two soldiers—Danladi and Gambo—took the lead, followed by ten more before she finally put me in position, with herself on my left. Another twelve came behind, each identical to the other in his simple tunic and trousers, bow and two quivers slung across his back, scabbard hanging from a red sash.

Not all of the Kuturun Mahayi wore swords. Some of the men who remained with the horses doubled as lancers. These had unfastened their spears from their travel supplies and stood ready for whatever battle might reach them on this uninhabited slope.

"I'm the one who brought us here," I said to Jaruma as started up the path. "Why am I not leading?"

"Count yourself fortunate that I didn't make you stay with the horses." The scowl affixed to her face was entirely too reminiscent of her brother. "I thought nothing would come of this ride, but you've proven me wrong. There may be danger ahead."

I was aware of that, aware of the nervous excitement crawling up my spine, all too aware that this was precisely the sort of situation from which my mother had protected me my entire life. The sort of situation I'd promised to avoid.

"Why would I send soldiers to face an enemy that I cannot face myself?" I said.

Brow furrowed by an ever-deepening scowl, Jaruma glared at me. "First and foremost, you're the queen's daughter. I am ordered to keep you safe. You think I enjoy commanding from the rear?" Her eyes narrowed. "Don't look at me like that, Amina. I'll push you off this mountain myself."

"Oh? Is that how you keep me safe?"

The scowl grew deeper still. *Impressive.* "If you insist on riding the path of danger, Gimbiya, the least I can do is finish you off quickly."

"*Karya.*"

Most women took great offense to being called a female dog.

"Pfft." Jaruma couldn't be bothered.

We climbed only a short distance before the forward motion of the tiny stream slowed then stopped. The stream itself appeared to have joined with another, natural, stream, but the water was unnaturally still.

"Stop," I said.

Jaruma halted the troop. "Why are we stopping?"

"The water isn't flowing."

I stared down at the narrow line of water. The Arabs brought many tales of travel to lands so cold that water froze, but I had never seen such a thing. The smooth surface of the rivergod's stream looked like a pane of glass set into the ground. A flawless pane imported from the far north, because no glass produced in Zazzau ever looked quite so perfect. The smoothness of it befuddled the senses. I reached out to touch it, to see if it had somehow solidified.

Without warning or sound, the glass exploded upward. In the ensuing commotion, it took a few moments to realize that the exploding shards were still liquid. They sprayed into our faces, past our heads, and settled into mist above us before floating into the sky. My eyes followed the receding water droplets.

And I saw them.

Above us, about four hundred meters ahead, a column of men marched steadily through the peaks.

THREE

"How many?" I asked.

Jaruma crouched behind a wall of rock and shrubbery. We hoped this shelter would keep us hidden from the war band filing across the far peak and separated from us by a steep chasm.

"Two thousand?" she said. "Maybe more. They're marching three abreast; I can't see where they begin and end. What does it matter? We're badly outnumbered."

As many of us as would fit had crammed into this shallow mountain cleft, the main body of the mountain behind us and a jagged outcropping serving as a barricade in front. The twelve who could not pile into the crevasse crouched in tall patches of faded green grass. The shrubbery provided some cover, but the red of their headwraps was impossible to camouflage.

Danladi rose to get a better look at the column of men marching through the pass. "Whether there are two thousand soldiers or more, that peak is a good fifty meters higher than this one, and they are on foot. If they are traveling through the mountains, how could they have crossed from this ridge to that so quickly?"

"You saw what they did to the city we left behind," I said. "They're strong and they're fast. They had nearly a full day's lead on us."

"Apologies, Gimbiya." He dropped back down. "But they are more than forty times our number and traveling on foot. Even on horseback, it took *us* the better part of this day. It should have taken them no less than two days."

I remembered the madawaki's words and said, "They possess powers we cannot fathom."

Silence fell, each soldier looking to the other. Each one reluctant to accept such a prospect until a tentative voice said, "Magic?"

To my recollection, Gambo had never spoken a word in my presence. Now his deep voice all but echoed in my skull. He looked at me, then lowered his eyes. Any other time, it might have been comical to see such shyness in a man who appeared as though he could wrestle a lion.

When no one responded but continued to glance askance at one another, he said without looking up, "It is the most reasonable explanation."

"Whatever the explanation, they don't need magic to see us." Danladi gestured at the ridge.

True enough, a number of half-clad warriors had stopped marching and were pointing in our direction. A few more joined them. There was some obvious shouting, then the entire troop halted.

Oh, gods of Jangare.

Surely, Kogi-Ayu hadn't led us here to be killed? Then again, he had never claimed to know how to defeat the enemy. That was his brother's purview, and I had no intention of calling on the wargod. Not when I knew what such action portended. *Damn Zariya and her oracular dreams.* I tried to think but couldn't focus.

"They haven't seen us." Shy Gambo broke my disjointed train of thought. "They've seen the men and horses below. We should attack now."

Everyone turned to stare at him. Perhaps he was addled as well as shy.

"We attack," he said again, more confidently. "We can't escape without being seen, and the Kwararafa won't let us walk away."

Danladi scratched his scraggly beard and nodded. "He's right. Better to attack now and attempt escape while they're confused. Before they reorganize."

Inexperience didn't make me entirely ignorant of the logic in the plan, but it seemed prudent to state the obvious. "There are too many of them, and they have the higher ground."

Gambo spoke again. "From what we know, the Kwararafa fight best in close quarters. They have short-range bowmen, but not many, and no long-range. Any one of us is more than a match for ten of them."

The Kuturun Mahayi were, indeed, legendary marksmen, but Gambo's words couldn't be anything other than bravado. The balance was so decisively tipped against us that the likelihood of our survival was virtually nonexistent.

"There are only twenty-eight of us," I argued. "Assuming they have three hundred *blind* bowmen, they are still up there and we're down here."

"Forgive my audacity, Gimbiya." The big man looked me in the eye. This time, he did not lower his gaze. "*We* have the range."

"We'll be hit." Perhaps it was fear talking rather than caution. Had I faced death as many times as these soldiers, the idea of dying in these hills might not have caused such sharp pains in my gut.

"Some of us may die," Jaruma said. "But not you."

Now they were staring at me.

She said, "Your life is worth more than all of ours put together. We'll do what we must to keep you alive."

Horrified, I looked at the faces around me. "No, Jaruma. I won't ask anyone to die for me."

"Do you think you have to ask?"

The coolness of her tone, coupled with stern black eyes, once again brought the madawaki to mind. He was the coldest, sternest, most disdainful man I had ever met, and if we died here, he would never know it.

Before premonitions and prophecies had halted my military aspirations, I had dreamed of a warrior's glory. Where was the glory in allowing fifty good men to die when it was me who had brought them here in the first place?

"If they fight, *I* fight," I said.

"You can't," Jaruma said.

"I don't need your permission."

Rather than waste more time arguing, she conceded. "Very well. Get in formation."

I didn't know what "formation" was, so I stayed put, while the soldiers, still crouching, spread out so they were nearly shoulder to shoulder with one another. Following suit, I moved slightly to Jaruma's left, positioning myself between her and another soldier. Surely, the Kwararafa saw all of us now.

"All right then," Jaruma said. "Ready yourself. You stand, aim, and shoot. The commands will be quick. Empty your quivers fast. We need to take down as many as we can."

I nodded, my heartbeat pounding in my ears. The excitement, which, earlier, had risen up my spine, now trickled down as apprehension. I nocked the first arrow. After years of target practice, this was the true test of my ability. Closing my eyes, I took several long breaths to steady my hands and prayed that my arrows would fly true.

"May Allah be with us," Jaruma muttered.

"Aim!" The command came from Danladi.

Focusing on a target—any target within the ranks of the enemy war band—I rose to my feet and drew back the bowstring.

"Fire!"

Danladi had not finished speaking the word before the collective twang of strings drowned out his voice. Twenty-eight arrows whizzed through the air, immediately followed by twenty-four more— somehow the signal had made its way to the men below.

As Gambo had noted, we had the range. Even the arrows from the men below reached the opposite peak. Nothing less than a score of the bare-chested warriors fell, a few crashing down the mountainside.

Without pause, we nocked again and fired. More men fell. Then again. And yet again. The enemy scurried for cover. We loosed volley after volley, taking out dozens of their men before the Kwararafa regrouped. Then a throng of arrows poured from the sky.

Wind rushed from my chest, as Gambo pinned me to the ground with his hulking body. Metal arrowheads clattered against the rocky edge of our mountain cover. I heard Jaruma's panicked cry.

"Gimbiya!"

Gambo rose off me, shouting, "Take her."

"Gimbiya," Jaruma cried again. She grasped my forearm, hauling me off the ground.

"Go!" Gambo yelled.

I hesitated.

The Kwararafa did, in fact, have poor long-range capabilities. Many of their arrows either fell short or overshot the Kuturun Mahayi to shatter against the rock above our heads. Those that found their marks, however, were deadly accurate. A soldier crumpled beside me, the shaft of an arrow jutting from his throat.

"Move!" Gambo said and let another arrow fly.

Jaruma yanked me down the path, behind the row of Kuturun Mahayi who continued to shoot without pause. These men were here because of me, and soon their quivers would be empty. How could I leave them to die? I dug in my heels.

Jaruma turned. "What are you doing!"

A crippling guilt gnawed at my insides. "I can't leave them."

When her hand came up, I thought, for a moment, she would strike me.

Instead, she clutched my jaw and gave my head a rough shake. "They will die for you today! Honor their sacrifice and live!"

Another Zazzagawa soldier fell. Another. And another. Each death chipped a new notch in my heart. Though I was afraid to die, seeing the men fall around me, I was too ashamed to live. Fifty brave men were paying for my life with theirs. But as Jaruma said, I had to honor them. Their sacrifices needed to count for something. Impelled by this reality, I voiced no more protests and scrambled down the mountain path.

We reached our horses and climbed into the saddles. The ascent had been tricky on horseback; the descent was no less so. The two horses tripped and stumbled down the path, kicking up stones in their wake, until we were back on level ground. Hugging the base of the hills, my companion and I rode south to put distance between us and the Kwararafa before finally turning westward toward the open plains. Jaruma and I rode until nightfall, the full moon illuminating us like glowworms in the dark. Anyone with eyes could see us out there on the savanna. Whether it was paranoia from our open position or heightened sensitivity from the danger we had left behind, I couldn't shake the feeling that someone was following us. Perhaps it was the shades of the fallen Kuturun Mahayi.

When we eventually stopped, my heart raced at every sound, jumped at every shadow. An ominous trepidation filled me. It bordered on outright terror.

"I'm uncomfortable stopping here," I said.

Jaruma was on her knees, filling her water gourd from a small creek. "The horses need rest." She gestured for my gourd. "They'll founder if we push them much more today."

Looking over my shoulder for heaven-knew-what, I absently handed her the gourd. The sooner we reached the madawaki and safety, the better. But Jaruma was right. The horses had been moving for most of the day. If we didn't give them time to recover, they would go lame or die.

Nodding reluctant agreement, I rubbed my horse's muzzle. "You've done well, Galadima."

Our dire situation notwithstanding, Jaruma chuckled. "Galadima, indeed. Only you would give a horse such a lofty title. "

He who rides before the queen. I tried to ignore the heavy feeling of dread settling in my core.

My horse, once a hot-blooded, poorly behaved ninny of a gelding, had grown into a fine warrior. He handled as though he shared my thoughts. His step seldom faltered. On the rare occasion that I fell from his back, he came to a complete halt rather than running blindly into the distance. Now he stood patiently while I unhooked my supplies from his saddle, before leading him to the water's edge.

After the horses had their fill, we moved to drier terrain, away from thirsty predators. The contents of Jaruma's pack clattered when she tossed it to the ground.

"You should sleep, Gimbiya." She unslung her bow and quivers and laid them beside the pack. Her sword followed, then her sleeping mat, and she sat down.

The place looked as though it had once been a village. If one gazed hard enough, one could just make out mounds of earth that looked like the remnants of walls. The harsh soil of the area must have driven the villagers away. Small fissures in the ground told of fallow land.

Retrieving my arm-knife from among the supplies, I strapped it to the inside of my left forearm. The hard leather of the sheath irritated my skin, but going without a weapon tonight was out of the question. Scratching my arm, I looked at the dark outline of the mountain range and wondered if any of my Kuturun Mahayi had survived. Of those who had not, were they at peace? Had their souls drifted to the Crossroads or would they linger forever on that desolate peak?

"I cannot sleep." The dried-grass scent of raffia rose into the air as I unrolled and shook out my sleeping mat. "You close your eyes and I'll take first watch."

She started to say something but instead shrugged and began rummaging through her pack. "We have little left in provisions." She pulled a piece of dried meat from a pouch, tore the meat in two, put one half back, and nibbled slowly on the other.

"Eating it like that won't fill your belly any better."

She swallowed. "The slower you eat, the slower you starve." Digging in her bag again, she pulled out a small sack of groundnuts. These she did not nibble. She poured out a handful and threw them all into her mouth at once. "You're not going to eat?"

The dark feeling in the pit of my belly abolished any hunger I might have felt. Besides, the idea of food reminded me of the vultures at Rizga, which turned my thoughts back to the dead Zazzagawa I had left in the hills.

"I'm not hungry." My eyes remained focused on the mountains, my fingers absently undoing my headwrap, but I felt her gaze on me. After several breaths, she said, "All right." Then, past a mouthful of whatever she was eating now, added, "Wake me in two hours."

※

I didn't wake her in two hours. Overcome by sudden fatigue, and despite my trepidation, I fell asleep during my watch. It was a troubled sleep. Full of nightmares in which I was suffocating, drowning under a pile of dead Zazzagawa soldiers. Even so, I didn't wake until a hyena's howl drew me from the depths.

Sleep vanished in a rush of nerves. I jumped to my feet just in time to see the dark figure of a man running toward me. The figure was upon me. I veered to the side, just avoiding the edge of a large battle-axe. The half-clad man swung the axe again, and I jumped away from its upward arc. The axe's momentum pulled him off balance. Before he could readjust, I charged forward, arm-knife in hand. The man gave a grunt and fell backward as the six-inch blade pierced his abdomen. I went down with him, pushing the blade deeper. We hit the ground. I extracted the blade and jabbed again. This time into his throat.

Something heavy crashed into the back of my skull. I cried out, my body tipping sideways, and fell hard. Dazed, I opened my eyes, then rolled away as another rock slammed into the earth beside me. In the corner of my eye, Jaruma and a second figure tussled. Without a sound, the other man doubled over, dead on the end of her sword.

A third rock catapulted through the air, narrowly missing her. Cursing, she released the sword, let it fall with the dead man, and stooped to pick up her bow. There came the twang of the bowstring, followed by a heavy thud. Another twang, another thud. Silence.

"Four of them," Jaruma said. I *thought* she said. She sounded as though she were speaking through a gag. She stepped over me, an arrow positioned in her bow. "Were there only four?" She looked down at me and spat out the arrow she was holding between her teeth. "Are you all right?"

I took hold of her proffered hand, jerked myself upright, and was immediately dizzy. Half expecting to find my skull smashed to bits, I touched the back of my head. It was dry. No blood, only a massive lump.

"Did you see them?" Jaruma asked. "Were there only four?"

"I—I don't know. Didn't see them until they were here." In fact, I had seen only the two. I glanced down at the dead men, whose dark trousers and bare chests marked them as Kwararafa warriors. My feeling of foreboding was gone, replaced by yet more guilt. If not for the call of the hyena . . . "I think that was all of them."

She yanked my blade out of the dead man's neck and wiped both our weapons on his trousers. "Can you stand?"

"I believe so." I got to my feet without assistance, but my legs were liquid under me.

"You can't walk." She took my arm to steady me and helped me into my saddle before gathering up our things and climbing onto her horse. "We have to move, in case there are more of them. We'll ride at whatever pace you can manage. We've covered much distance already and should reach Zazzagawa territory in the next three or four days. Rest," she said, tying my reins to her saddle.

❀

After we'd ridden for a while, I spoke. "You saved my life." My head was pounding. The pain made me hazy, and I could scarcely hold myself upright.

"Of course I did. I'm your protection, no?"

True. She had done her duty. My mistakes, on the other hand, continued to pile up. "I fell asleep," I said, though she probably already knew.

"It happens to the best of us, Gimbiya. We're still alive, eh? I'm more experienced than you. I should have been more alert."

I had almost gotten her killed. Her flawless reactions had saved us where my watchkeeping had failed so miserably.

"The folly was mine," I said.

"Don't worry yourself. I told you, it happens to the best of us."

I acknowledged her words but said nothing more. We rode through the rest of the night in silence.

❀

At dawn, we stopped for a short time, then again around midday, after crossing a wide spring. Having regained my stability, I went, unaided, to the water and plunged my head inside. The water ran cool against my throbbing skull. It trickled down my neck and into my tunic when I came up for air. It was a refreshing respite under the hot sun.

"Let me see." Jaruma knelt beside me and looked at my swollen head. She ran her fingers over the lump in a gentle, almost soothing manner. "It's a nasty bump." She removed her hand.

I touched it. It felt bigger than it had during the night.

She bent over the stream to splash some water on her face and shivered. The water's temperature was a steep contrast to the afternoon heat.

"Cold," she said.

"Quite."

We cleaned the last traces of blood from our weapons, washed our hands, ate from our provisions, and let the horses be. When the time came to resume our journey, we filled our water gourds then packed up. We were climbing back into the saddles when an arrow whizzed over our heads and buried itself in the ground behind us. Midway to the stirrup, I froze, my foot motionless in the air, terror draining the blood from my heart. I looked down at the shaft protruding from the earth.

Vaulting from her horse, Jaruma made for the arrow in a dead sprint. She dropped to her knees when she reached it and yanked it out of the ground. The long feather of a peacock was bound to its shaft. She gave a breathless exclamation, relief evident in the sound, and threw her head back with a loud, jubilant whoop. Tearing the plume away, she turned to me, brandishing the arrow. "It's the madawaki's scout."

FOUR

Jaruma sent the scout ahead while she and I rode at a pace more manageable for my splitting skull. According to the scout, we were less than a day's ride from the madawaki's last bivouac. If fortune held, we would rejoin them soon.

By nightfall, I was half dead on my horse, so we made camp beneath a massive baobab tree.

"How are you?" Jaruma asked.

"I'll survive," I replied, slowly unloading my supplies.

"Let me help." She shooed me away and took over, unloading my sleeping mat and laying it on the ground, end to end with hers.

Abruptly, she straightened and looked out to the savanna. Pulling an arrow from the quiver still strapped to her back, she bent to pick up the bow she had laid beside her mat and aimed toward the sound of galloping hooves.

Five men rode into view. Stumbling around my horse, I reached for my own bow but doubted my legs would hold steady long enough for me to shoot.

"Oh no." Jaruma lowered her weapon and dropped the arrow back into its quiver.

"What is it?"

"My brother."

My heart leapt then fell when he drew close and the obtrusive moonlight showed the grim set of his jaw. He gestured for his men to ride the perimeter. Two went in one direction, the other two in another. His frothing, snorting horse had scarcely come to a stop before he jumped from its back.

His eyes swept over Jaruma then me, searching my body. "My rider says you're injured." He stepped into my space, chest heaving. "Show me."

I lowered my swimming head and raised my hand to the lump. Battle-rough fingers found mine, but they were gentle as he drew my hand away and felt the tender spot at the back of my skull. It was immensely comforting to have him near, and I closed my eyes at his touch, trying not to weep into his chest.

"Thank the gods you're all right," he said almost imperceptibly. A loud exhale and he stepped away.

I looked up at him. His face now stiff with anger, he strode to his sister.

"I gave you a simple order." He crossed his arms over his chest.

Jaruma bowed her head. "Yes, sir."

"Keep Gimbiya Amina in Rizga. Did I not speak clearly?"

"Yes, sir."

"Then why is she here?" A look of concern fell on me and turned to steel. "Injured, no less."

He moved back toward me. The closer he came, the more willpower it took to stay on my feet. I hooked a hand in the horse's reins and held tight.

"I left you fifty men. Where are they?" His eyes drilled into me.

Jaruma replied before I could form the words, "Sir, it was—"

"I wasn't talking to you."

"No, sir. But we had reason to believe you might overtake the Kwararafa and—"

He turned and was on her in three steps. "Open your mouth again, and I will beat you bloody."

Her eyes widened, and she ceased speaking, but her rigid stance screamed defiance.

He returned to me. "Where are my men?"

I looked toward the eastern horizon. "In the hills."

"Why"—his exaggerated control bit off each word—"are they in the hills?"

"They are dead." Unable to meet the fire in his eyes, I cast my gaze to his feet and weakly added, "Because of me." Tears of guilt and fatigue and pain and fear welled in my eyes but did not fall.

"It wasn't your fault, Gimbiya. They did their duty," Jaruma interjected.

He stormed back to her before she finished speaking. I feared he would carry out his threat right then, but Jaruma merely stood, defiant as ever.

"What the hell is she talking about?" he asked her.

Maybe the scout hadn't repeated everything we'd told him.

When Jaruma did nothing but glare at her brother in silence, he bellowed, "Speak!"

"The Kwararafa," she said. "They were in the hills. Northeast of Rizga. East of here."

He looked eastward. "Why, in the name of all the gods, were you in the hills when I told you to stay in Rizga?" His voice grew louder with each word.

"Because of me," I said again.

"Explain." He was still looking at Jaruma.

I replied, "I knew you wouldn't find them. You said yourself they possessed power—"

"And so you went in search of them? Yourself? With only fifty men?" He strode back to me.

"No. I meant only to . . . to . . ." *Save my people by whatever means Destiny planned for me.*

"It doesn't matter what you meant to do."

He stood so close now that I could feel the anger radiating off his rigid body.

He continued, "I knew you were reckless, Gimbiya, but this is by far the stupidest thing you could have done. What if you had died? Or Jaruma? What would you expect me to do then?"

"I didn't intend—"

"What? You didn't intend to die?"

"No. I mean—"

"Did you think it through? Did you stop, for one moment, to consider the consequences? *You could have died!*" The force of his words shook me to the core. He took hold of my face, grasping my jaw the way Jaruma had recently done. "Do you understand that?"

My heart raced as he encroached upon my personal territory. I nodded, speechless. He had never touched me in so familiar a manner before. My head grew foggy, and when my knees buckled, I wasn't sure the injury was entirely to blame.

One strong arm slid across my back, the other across my belly to grasp my waist, and he caught me before I fell. As I swayed backward, he shifted his hold to lift me off the ground.

Oh Great Creator God!

The look of concern that had flashed in his eyes returned in full. He peered at me, his face so close that, even in the dark, I could see the flecks of grey in his scruffy beard.

"Have you slept?" His voice echoed some of the concern in his eyes as he carried me toward the sleeping mats.

My breath was trapped in my throat. All I could do was shake my head, which brought my face to his chest. His heart beat against my cheek.

He lowered me onto the mat. "Rest. We leave at first light."

For a few moments, I could still feel the warmth of his hands on my body. A soft wind blew through the tree, the leaves rustling a quiet lullaby. As I drifted into sleep, I heard the madawaki's voice.

"Jaruma, I will beat you senseless for this."

❋

City of Kufena, Kingdom of Zazzau, Central Hausaland, circa 1557 CE

Four uneventful days passed on the road back to Kufena. Four days beside Jaruma who simmered in anger at her brother and barely spoke to me. Four days marked only by the periodic attention of the madawaki as he confirmed that I was still upright on my horse and my wits were still intact, after which he always returned to sullen silence. He tried to mask his concern every time he asked if I needed rest, or whenever he felt my forehead for fever or helped me off my horse, but I saw through it. Even as he showed Jaruma the brunt of his ire, I saw the love and relief flooding his eyes when he looked at her. He was full of more kindness that I'd thought.

When we finally arrived in Kufena, he sent me immediately to the medicine man, who prodded at the lump on my head until I threatened to cut his throat. Sputtering curse words, he pushed a twisted grey root into my hand and told me to chew it whenever I felt pain. He didn't bother to inform me of the bitter herb's potency or I would have waited before taking it. That afternoon, when Jaruma and I stood in the war chamber like oddities on display, my entire face was numb. My tongue felt as though it had grown to twice its size, and I began slurring my words like a drunkard.

The five members of the royal council—along with the madawaki, my uncle, and my mother—sat before us on plain wooden chairs. Jaruma and I stood against the wall of the circular room, facing them. Aside from the chairs and a small table on the far side, the room was empty of any furnishings. The packed-earth floor, swept to a hard shine, was bare. Unlike many of the other buildings in the palace compound, this one had a wooden door and wooden shutters on its two windows. The closed door added to the heat even though both windows were open.

While the madawaki knew most of what had occurred after I had led my troop out of Rizga, neither Jaruma nor I had mentioned the visit from the rivergod. So now, in the war chamber, when we retold the story from start to finish—beginning with my visit from the rivergod and ending with the madawaki's scout on the savanna—the madawaki eyed me with both astonishment and suspicion.

The *kaura*, our war leader, exhibited no interest in the denizen of my dream world. He leaned forward in his chair, about to speak.

The *fagaci* spoke first. "Then it's possible you've destroyed their commanders?"

"Unlikely," the kaura said.

"Even so, it will only delay them," Jaruma interjected, her hand on my back in case I grew dizzy.

"What of their magic man?" The *waziri*, or vizier as the Arabs said it, was more interested in the supernatural aspect of the Kwararafa than their collective brutality. "What of Kogi-Ayu? Did he say nothing more?"

"We know nothing of a magic man," Jaruma said.

With a meaningful look at my mother, I added, "Kogi-Ayu said I should consult Ruhun Yak'i."

Bakwa gasped and immediately recomposed herself. She looked from the madawaki to the kaura. "Are you not men of war? Are you unable to do battle without personal guidance from the god of mayhem?"

The heat of this day was unusually damp. It draped me like a heavy cloth, made my tunic stick to my back beneath Jaruma's hand, and left me increasingly uncomfortable.

Sweat beaded on the kaura's forehead. "Great Bakwa, we're more than capable of stemming this crisis."

"Then what is your plan?" she asked.

The kaura looked at the madawaki, who was less effective at hiding his agitation, and said, "The Kwararafa chose a circuitous path. If we assume they move at the same speed as one-tenth their number on horseback, they will reach our territory in ten days, but they may reach us sooner. Or considerably later. We've plotted the most likely and *un*likely routes they could take from their most recently known location and sent scouts in eight different directions."

The fagaci spoke again. Historically, he was the royal rug bearer or something of that nature, but in recent times the title bore the responsibility of maintaining royal protocols. To me, he was simply the royal burr-in-my-hair. Whenever he attended my provincial council meetings, he stayed after to chide me on the impropriety of one decision or another.

With a frantic twinge in his voice, he said, "But if they're invisible, what does it matter if you send scouts in a *hundred* different directions? The Kwararafa won't be found."

"Gimbiya Amina found them," the madawaki said, momentarily turning his agitation on me. "Evidently, they are *not* invisible—merely difficult to see."

"On top of that," the waziri said, "the gods wouldn't have led her to the enemy for no reason. It was the Oracle who sent her to Rizga in the first place. Or have we all forgotten?"

A deep crease lined the madawaki's brow. "We've forgotten nothing, Waziri. Gimbiya Amina and one thousand Kuturun Mahayi. Fifty of whom are now presumed dead."

"Death in battle is the way of the warrior, is it not?" the waziri said.

Anger further darkened the madawaki's features, but he gave no response. There was nothing to say. The Kuturun Mahayi so lived for battle that few remained in the city during times of peace. Instead, they hired themselves out to trading caravans or grew rich on state-sanctioned slave raids. Still, I knew the weight he carried for those fifty men; I carried it myself tenfold.

The waziri continued, "The Oracle requested Gimbiya Amina and one thousand mounted bowmen for a diplomatic mission that should have called for one or two members of the council and no more than thirty common guards. Do we continue to doubt the will of the gods?"

The madawaki's ire grew yet more apparent. "Your point, Waziri."

"Whatever else she may have done, Gimbiya Amina has most certainly eliminated the power our enemies used to conceal themselves. I believe they'll be easy to follow now."

"What makes you sure of it?" The fagaci's nervousness raised my own anxiety level. "Or you?" He gestured at the madawaki. "What makes either of you certain that, in light of our people coming upon them, the enemy has not redoubled their efforts at stealth?"

"Calm yourself, Fagaci," Bakwa said. In this torpid heat, my mother sat regal and stoic, wearing a plain, blue, long-sleeved dress that reached her ankles. Her lustrous black hair was loosely wrapped in matching cloth, yet not so much as the sheen of perspiration showed on her brow. "Excess worry doesn't alter the situation. We play the pieces laid before us." The light of the early evening sun streamed through the window, lending her fair skin a reddish hue and accentuating the warm brown color of her eyes.

She faced the madawaki. "In ten days, the Kwararafa, concealed or no, will break through our gates. What becomes of us then?"

All focus shifted to him. I took measure of the man, who sat rigid as stone beside the kaura. The madawaki was the leaner of the two. He was taller, his skin darker and face sterner than the other man. Had I only just met them, I would have thought the madawaki was the war leader here.

He spoke in a voice much deeper than the kaura's. "Thanks to Amina's one thousand-man guard, our bowmen are already assembled."

Calling one thousand Kuturun Mahayi back to the city had taken a full month. Had the Oracle not insisted on it, those men would yet be scattered. The madawaki's tight face gave evidence to his displeasure at having to concede the Oracle's accuracy.

He continued, "Once the scouts confirm their position, we'll ride out to meet the enemy and engage them on our own terms."

"And what are your terms, Madawaki?" Bakwa asked.

"Our strategy is being finalized. But I assure you that we will defeat the enemy."

"Or die," said old Makama. As the man who coordinated activities between the many provinces and allies of Zazzau, the *makama* had an intimate understanding of what was at stake. Our defeat would send disaster rippling across the savanna like grassfire.

"This isn't the time for your pessimism, Makama." Frustration flashed in the eyes of the queen's enforcer of law, *he who rides before her*, the *galadima*.

"This is not pessimism." The makama showed no sign of annoyance. "Merely pragmatism. Is it words we use to fight the Kwararafa? The madawaki proclaims victory before battle and *that* is our assurance?" The makama's utterances only increased the high tension in the room.

The waziri said, "It's far better to proclaim premature victory than to weep in defeat at first sight of the enemy."

"The Kwararafa don't rely so heavily on magic," the makama retorted. "They're mighty warriors. As great as any of you has ever been."

"We don't underestimate their might," the madawaki said, growing ever more impatient.

The makama's brow rose. "Don't you?"

"Makama, I assure you that we're familiar with Kwararafa warfare. We *can* defeat them. However, the more time we spend arguing whether words can slay a dragon, the less time we spend finalizing our battle plans."

"Then we should leave you to it, eh?" The makama set his walking stick into the ground and made as if to rise from his seat. "Ah, My Queen." He eased back onto the chair. "These two women should be hailed for what they've done." He gestured at Jaruma and me, then glanced at the madawaki.

Bakwa's spirits lifted. "Yes, it's true. If not for Kogi-Ayu, we would not have known where the enemy came down from the hills. My daughter is blessed that the gods speak through her." She looked at me. "It is proof of your courage that Kogi-Ayu chose you, no?"

Groaning internally, I prayed the earth would swallow me.

"Now you can give her rank," she said, nodding in the kaura's direction.

Oh, Mama. No!

The entire room fell silent. Even the crickets outside ceased their carefree chirping.

Other than what information she needed to send them into battle, my mother knew nothing of soldiers. Rank was not merely a symbol of a warrior's ability but also a mark of respect. Especially for the mounted bowmen. Theirs was initiation through blood. A warrior did not earn the right to be called ummal until he—*she*—proved to be of sufficient caliber. There would be no honor in bestowing such a rank upon me. Certainly not now. Not after losing my entire troop.

Desperately wishing I could shrink into Jaruma's shadow, I cast a mortified glance around the room. The kaura's mouth opened and closed, but no sound escaped. The galadima coughed. Even the makama, who had instigated the situation, looked astonished—though his expression bordered on amusement. I hazarded a glance at the madawaki and wished I had not.

There was no amusement in his eyes. Already vexed by the makama, his ill humor took on a darker hue. "Advance rank because she talks with spirits?" he asked coldly.

I hoped my mother would leave it be. The taut nerves in the room needed no additional fraying.

"Talks with spirits?" Bakwa said indignantly. "She led a group of your best men to the enemy. Together, they have managed to slow them, possibly even slay their commanding officers."

"How many did you slay?" the kaura asked, as though he were actually considering the mad proposal.

Everyone looked at me. I tried to say something, but my frozen tongue refused to move.

Jaruma said, "Many fell to our arrows, Kaura."

"It is of no consequence how many died on the points of Amina's arrows." The madawaki rose from his chair, his tone carrying a great deal of threat. "She fled like a demon in the night."

"Madawaki, sir," Jaruma began.

I didn't give her the opportunity to explain, again, the circumstances surrounding the encounter in the hills. Stepping out of her shadow, I said as evenly as was feasible, considering my swollen tongue, "We did what was necessary." *Necessary.* An impossible word to speak when one has no feeling in one's mouth.

The madawaki was far more annoyed than he had any right to be. My mother's absurd notion of rank advancement aside, his response made light of what we had done in those mountains. Of what the men had sacrificed. We'd not fled out of cowardice; we'd ridden home to give warning lest the Kwararafa meet us at our door. Regardless, there were thousands of enemy soldiers with eyes across the savanna. The odds of survival had *not* been in our favor.

"Without diminishing what Gimbiya Amina accomplished," the kaura cut in, as though he had heard my thoughts, "what the madawaki is saying is that a true warrior proves herself under the pressure of battle, not in distant ambush."

"Any man, or *woman*, can kill like an assassin," the madawaki added. Eyes fixed on me, he drew himself to his full height and folded his arms across his chest. "Only a true warrior can stand and face the enemy."

"Kaura. Madawaki. Are you saying that I'm *not* a warrior?" The words staggered around my wooden tongue, making me sound more comical than stern.

No one laughed.

Jaruma tugged my tunic in warning. Across the room, my uncle shook his head, silently telling me to desist. The madawaki narrowed his eyes and took a few steps in my direction.

"Pray you mind yourself in my war chamber, Madawaki," Bakwa said, though she made no other effort to control her cavalry leader.

He continued to stride toward me, a dangerous glint in his eye. When he was within inches of me, he stopped. "Would you prove your mettle or have glory handed to you?"

I too drew myself to my full height, which was almost a head shorter than his. "I can earn my own name. *Sir.*"

At the last word, which came out of my mouth in a garbled slurry, the madawaki backed down.

"May I go?" *Damn those bitter roots and my wooden tongue.*

Bakwa rebuked the madawaki with a frown and faced me. "Go, my daughter."

I gave my mother a quick bow. Snatching Jaruma's arm, I dragged her out of the room with me.

Outside, as we walked away from the war chamber, she nudged me and said, "You've proven your mettle to me, Ummal."

Choking back the tears of anger and humiliation that had threatened in the war chamber, I flung my arms around her neck in a rough embrace. Then I remembered we were in full view of the palace staff and courtiers and hastily released her. Taken aback by the open display of affection, Jaruma looked discomfited.

Feeling no less awkward, I said, "Let us go and fill our bellies with something other than groundnuts and stale meat."

FIVE

That evening's bath was by far the most satisfying I'd ever had. I washed my hair and scrubbed away days of filth. Immersing myself in an oversized tin basin, I rinsed off the tension of enemy threat, though no amount of water could rinse off the guilt for fifty men. When my body was pristine, I tied a wrapper at my chest and slipped on my sandals.

My wet hair, dark brown rather than the black of my mother and sister, fell in matted clumps. I combed through it with my fingers. Navigating around the rowdy children of courtiers, I meandered past the conjoined cluster of three identically sized huts that made up the queen's private quarters. A massive mango tree, which spanned the fifteen paces from my mother's abode to mine, was not yet in full bloom, but its sweet musky odor laced the air.

I reached my modest abode and drew back the palm bark curtain covering the doorway.

"I feared you had drowned," Jaruma said as I entered my chamber.

I removed my sandals at the tiled entrance. Strips of bark fell back into place with a rustling sound.

Two steps into the room, a thick raffia mat replaced the red clay tiles. Unless one took my weapons bin and the various cushions strewn about the floor into account, there were only two pieces of furniture: a three-legged stool and a pallet bed.

Jaruma sat cross-legged on the floor, water droplets shining in her closely cropped black hair. She took a drink from the gourd in her hand and grinned. Her sheathed sword lay on the ground at her feet, a burning oil lamp rested on the stool beside her, and the smell of palm wine floated to my nose. She had changed into a long kaftan. If not for the multicolored thread detail at neck and torso, the red sash of the Kuturun Mahayi, and the trousers beneath, she might well have blended in with the other women of the compound. She held the gourd up to me.

I glanced at it and frowned.

"Drink," she said. "For our fallen brothers."

I took the gourd and brought it to my lips then made a face. This batch was over fermented and not as sweet as I preferred. Swallowing the mouthful, I handed the gourd back to her.

"You need your own room." I doffed my wrapper and tossed it onto the bed, then sat down alongside her, gesturing toward the chest.

"You're tired of me already? Has it even been a year?" She passed the gourd to me and leaned back to grab the clay jar sitting atop the chest.

"It's been more than a year." I turned my back to her as I took another sip of wine. "A woman needs privacy."

The scent of coconuts mingled with the palm wine aroma. Warm, oily hands pressed against my back, as a dejected sigh escaped me.

Her hands paused. "You're not to blame, Gimbiya. We all meet our ends at our appointed times." She squeezed my shoulders. "Those men deserve better than this melancholy. They deserve celebration. Celebrate them, Amina. They died as warriors."

I swallowed the lump that had formed in my throat and chased it down with more sour wine.

"If you like, I can always go and sleep where the sentries sleep," Jaruma said.

Glad for the return to lighter conversation, I said, "Only men sleep there, karya."

As always, the exceptionally cool-headed woman ignored the insult and retorted, "*Guards* sleep there. Is it my fault they're all men?"

She gestured for the gourd. I gave it to her, and she poured oil into my hand. I slathered the stuff onto my legs and arms.

"You know, Jaruma. You're exactly what they say you are."

Laughter did not so much burst as rolled from her throat in a sinister wave. "What do they say I am? And who says it?"

A wanton hussy was what they said, but I didn't put it like that. "They say you're . . . *free* with your love."

She laughed again. Less sinister, but wicked nonetheless. "Suleyman was too lenient in my upbringing."

"Who?"

"My brother."

I had almost forgotten the madawaki had a name. *Suleyman.* His image formed in my mind, warmth spreading over my cheeks. The wine was taking hold.

It was rare that family life came up in discussion between Jaruma and me. She was only three years older but had seen so many battles that our talk usually centered on warfare.

"Did he truly raise you all alone?" I turned to face her, my palm outstretched, and imagined the sort of upbringing she must have had with the madawaki as her guardian.

Had she grown up in that vast compound of his, or did he have property elsewhere? I scarcely saw the man attired in anything other than the soldier's tunic and trousers and found myself wondering what he wore at home. He was among the highest-ranking military men in the kingdom and submitted to no one, but he was such a surly fellow. Based on his behavior in the war chamber, it seemed not even my mother could keep the man under thumb.

As far as I could tell, nothing made him smile, let alone laugh. He sometimes looked at me as though he were inspecting a cow at market. It left me feeling not only naked but inadequate.

"Do you bind them when you fight?" Jaruma asked, eyeing my chest as she poured more oil into my hand and set down the jar.

"Have you ever seen me bind them?"

"They'd be less wieldy if you did."

"How would you know?" With raised eyebrows, I stared pointedly at the tiny mounds jutting out like small oranges under her gown.

"I may not have your endowments, Gimbiya. But such baggage must be a hindrance." The way she spoke, one might have thought a pair of colossal calabashes hung from my ribcage.

"Perhaps I'll bind them and see if it improves my spear aim."

"Ha! Only a miracle can improve your aim."

"We'll see about that." I rubbed the sweet-smelling unguent onto my belly and breasts.

Jaruma watched me, amusement dancing across her face. "You smell like coconuts." She took another sip of wine.

I rolled my eyes. "As if you've never rubbed with coconut oil."

"Such oils are for the pampered. I'm a warrior." Her brow fell. "I *was* a warrior until I became your wet nurse." She tilted the gourd to her lips, swallowed a long draught, and offered it back to me.

"You're still a warrior." I declined the proffered wine. The medicinal root had already made me tipsy; now I was adding the effects of overly strong wine.

Jaruma snatched back the gourd with a snort.

She was a fierce soldier, one of the most skilled Kuturun Mahayi Zazzau had ever seen. Slingshot, knife, or bow and arrow, she could hit a guinea fowl fleeing in the bush without her horse so much as breaking stride. She fought like a man and carried on like one outside of battle. Her name even translated to *courageous*.

"I truly despised you when I first came to the palace," she said.

"I felt much the same about you."

Our first meeting had not gone well. Nor had our second or third. She had not taken to reassignment as my personal guard, and I had not taken to *her*. For a long time, we had each done our best to frustrate the other.

"That's why you tried to kill me?" she asked.

"How many times must I apologize for that? It was an accident."

"Accident? Pfft. You are a dirty fighter. And it isn't as though I could have bashed *you* in the head with impunity."

"Stop complaining." I touched the receding lump at the back of my skull. "I'm now paying for that crack in your skull."

That "accident" had been a year ago. Since then, my adversary had become my truest friend.

"Jaruma, if you want to march with the madawaki against the Kwararafa, I'm sure I can do without you for a time."

"I belong here with you, Gimbiya. And you can't do without me." The lamplight flickered when she put the gourd on the stool. She sniffed her oily hands and rubbed her bare forearms. "Also, palace life has its benefits."

I didn't want her to go and—she was right—I wouldn't know what to do without her, but I doubted she preferred her role with me to her place in the cavalry. If she was content, though, I was more than happy to let things lie. Saying nothing further on the subject, I stood and crossed the tiny room to pull a long, green dress from a basket of folded clothes.

"Rub the oil on your feet," I said, sliding into the dress. The silklike kapok material flowed like cool water over my skin. "It keeps them soft."

"Soft feet?"

"See?" I pressed a foot to her cheek.

She yanked my leg and I toppled. If not for the cushions covering the floor, my backside would have suffered in the landing.

"Heh. You *do* have soft feet," she noted. "No wonder you don't like to walk."

Laughing, I crawled back over and laid my head on her lap, facing away from her. "You were telling me of your upbringing. Continue."

She resumed her storytelling. "Suleyman's mother was our father's first wife . . . Your hair is wet, Gimbiya."

I used my foot to snag the wrapper off my bed.

Jaruma took the wrapper from me. "She had three girls, then Suleyman. The girls were married early—thirteen or fourteen—and carried off to foreign lands before Baba married my mother. But you know this."

"Wait. You said thirteen? Truly? Why?" As far as I was concerned, there was nothing worse than being shackled to some man at the age of thirteen.

"Shall I finish? Or do you want to interrupt? Raise your head."

I raised my head. "Sorry. Continue."

She shoved the folded wrapper between my wet head and her lap. "Baba wanted more sons, so he married my mother. She was nineteen or so, already had her own mind." She laughed. "Difficult to train. *My* mother ran away before Baba died. I don't remember her. Suleyman's mother is the one I called 'Mama.'"

"Mm-hmm."

"Suleyman was away then. Fighting battles. He fought alongside your father even."

The thought of the madawaki and my father fighting side by side made me grin. Before my father had died, he had been much like the madawaki. Stern, dark-skinned, tall. Except my father had always had a ready smile for me. He'd put no stock in the prophetic warnings from my naming ceremony. He'd had no fear that my inherent nature—my fascination with war, as Bakwa put it—would draw undue notice from Ruhun Yak'i, the *god* of war. Papa used to call me his "little warrior" and promised that, when the time came, he would take me on campaign. The time never came. I was only seven when he left this world.

Taken by my father's memory, I missed some of Jaruma's tale but refocused in time to hear her say, "Joined the ancestors. This was before he had his own household, so after he collected me, I followed along wherever he went."

I already knew that her parents—the madawaki's parents—had died and left her alone at a young age, but I never understood why her brother had dragged her into battle with him.

"You had no other family?" I asked. Most people in Zazzau had extended families that included first, second, even third cousins who would take in an orphaned child.

"Do you?"

I shrugged. My father's father had loved only one woman and never sired another child after she died. He couldn't have known he'd survive his only heir.

"Mama was the child of Tuaregs, same as your mother, but mine didn't run off with the crown prince of Zazzau. Since those nomadic types never stay in one place, her family had moved on long before my own mother joined the household. And Baba was born Songhai."

Hence her odd surname. While every nation within a fortnight's ride from Zazzau spoke the common language, the name *Dongo* wasn't of Hausa origin.

"I suppose Baba had grown tired of living in sand caves," she continued. "He settled here."

"Sand caves, indeed." From what I had heard, the Songhai built cities like no others in the world.

"During wartime, I stayed in the army camps with Suleyman, doing whatever jobs they had for me. Cooking, mending battle dresses. Until I began attracting unwanted attention." A deep, throaty laugh accompanied the statement. "My brother taught me to fight with a knife. I was already learning sword. The men took their interest elsewhere. But by then"—she made a clucking sound—"they were more interesting to *me*."

"How old were you?"

"Fourteen."

I grimaced. "You were interested in men at fourteen?" My first tingle of awareness hadn't come until I was sixteen. Considering Jaruma's reputation, her early curiosity shouldn't have surprised me.

She said, "They're interesting, are they not?"

"I don't know," I replied, tartly.

"What?" Her words were heavy with disbelief. "You mean, you . . . *never?*"

"You were saying?" I steered her back to the story.

"There's nothing more to say." She bent forward to look at me. "Suleyman was too lenient with me; he isn't lenient with his sons. Maybe because they're boys."

"He seems a stiff man."

Perhaps she heard the wistfulness I had tried to keep out of my tone. Perhaps some underlying emotions showed on my face. Or perhaps Jaruma simply knew me better than I knew myself. She pressed hard on the lump at the back of my head.

When I sat up, cursing, she fixed me with a peculiar look and said, "Don't let him fool you, Amina. He's like a snail. Hard shell on the outside, soft rubbish on the inside."

"Karya," I murmured.

"So." Rising, she carried her scabbard to the weapons bin and placed it on the lid beside her arm-knife. "Twenty-three years old, and you've never been with a man. That's difficult to believe." Grabbing the wine gourd, she dropped back onto the floor.

"Why so difficult? You've never seen me with a man."

"I'm not with you every moment of every day. Most women of status are secretive about their dealings. I assumed you were stealthy. After all, you're the future queen. What man wouldn't want to get his dirty, callused hands on you?" She tossed the wrapper back onto the bed.

"That's why I avoid them. I know what they want."

"And what do *you* want?"

My eyebrows rose.

Smirking, she emptied the gourd and placed it on the tiled section of floor. With a loud yawn, she lay on her side, propping herself on one elbow, a cushion pulled to her bosom. "Out of your many suitors, none took your fancy? Not one sparked your curiosity?"

"Perhaps one," I admitted, grudgingly. "Tumsa. Stupid boy. When I was seventeen."

"And what happened to stupid Tumsa?"

"He stopped speaking to me when I refused to . . . to . . . *open* to him."

"If you fancied him, why didn't you open?"

"I won't surrender my birthright to any man."

"Virginity is not a birthright. It's merely a possession, which, once lost, you'll find was not so great a thing in the first place."

I gave her a dirty look. "I meant my kingdom. Any man who marries me will be the next king of Zazzau."

"You think all men chase you for your kingdom? Perhaps they desire it, but many would still desire you if you were a pauper in the streets."

"Name one," I said, tucking my legs beneath me.

"I can name two."

"Who?"

"That pretty one. The slender one with fair skin. What's his name? The makama's nephew."

"Siddhi? That boy who's always idling around the palace compound?"

"That boy is a man. He's as old as me."

"He has the face of a child."

"He's too young for you then? What about Danladi? On the journey to Rizga, he couldn't keep his eyes off you."

"Danladi?" I laughed but became quickly sober. "Do you think any of them survived?"

That sobered Jaruma as well. She shook her head. "We can only pray."

We fell silent then, in reflection on the comrades who had given their lives to ensure our survival. She inhaled and let out a loud breath.

"I'm sorry I took us there," I said after the long pause.

"Where? To the mountains?"

I nodded.

"You did the right thing."

"I killed fifty men."

"No, Amina. The Kwararafa killed fifty men." Sitting up, she clutched my jaw, much gentler than she had done on the mountain. "You listen well, Gimbiya. Death in service of Zazzau is an honorable death. Each of those men knew the warrior's risk." Though I tried to drop my chin, she refused to let go. "You saved Zazzau, just as the rivergod said."

"But the madawaki—"

Releasing me, she made a dismissive gesture. "Forget Suleyman. He worries like a mother hen."

"He said he would beat you."

That made her laugh. "If I tell you how many times he's threatened to beat me. Pfft. Don't mind what he said. You did the right thing."

Her words lifted some of the weight from my shoulders, though the responsibility for fifty deaths still tore at my heart.

After several breaths, I smiled weakly. "He was a handsome man, Danladi. Too much hair on his face. But handsome."

"Yes," Jaruma replied dreamily. "Well formed and *big*."

Her salacious response drew a giggle out of me.

A servant announced herself at the doorway.

"Enter," I said, still giggling.

The palm strips parted. A young girl took a step into the room and bowed. "The madawaki requests Gimbiya Amina in the war chamber."

Surprised, I looked at Jaruma.

"Does he?" The way Jaruma said it insinuated something lewd. She started laughing.

"Be silent, woman." Turning to the bewildered servant, I said, "Give the madawaki my apologies. I have a headache."

For some reason, that made Jaruma laugh even louder.

The girl bowed and, taking the empty gourd with her, retreated from the doorway.

Jaruma's laughter died down. She lay on her back, fingers interlaced beneath her head, and slanted me a knowing look. "Perhaps lowly Kuturun Mahayi aren't your type. Perhaps you find men with power more interesting?"

"If that were the case, the waziri would be fascinating." As my mother's closest advisor, the waziri was probably the most powerful man in Zazzau.

"But the waziri doesn't have the skill of a madawa—" A cushion to the face cut her short.

Certainly, the madawaki was well-endowed with military skill, his battle prowess widely touted. He was also mean, crass, and wholly unlikeable. The man treated me like camel dung. And he was old. At least forty.

So why did my palms sweat whenever he came near?

Jaruma pierced me with a gaze so sharp, I thanked the Lord of lords that my face didn't darken with heat like that of a lighter skinned northerner.

Her next words came without any hint of jest. "If you open your eyes, you may find what you desire."

"You know nothing of my desires," I replied haughtily.

"I know most men want whatever a woman is willing to offer." Dark eyes studied my face. "He wears his severity like a mask. You need only pry it off."

No response came to mind.

Her brow wrinkled in continued contemplation of my face. "You're young and you're attractive enough."

"Attractive *enough*?"

Perhaps it was vanity, but I always considered myself above average pretty. My brown hair shone with life. I disliked my scorched-bronze skin, but it was somewhat pretty. My full lips might have been on the large side, and my round nose lacked the aquiline line of my mother's, but it wasn't *ugly*. Despite her narrow hips, Jaruma never had any issue finding a man, so my more rounded figure couldn't be a bad thing.

She said, "Your beauty is a benefit, not a prerequisite." Leaning close, she added in a conspiratorial whisper, "The object of *your* desire requires only that your blood is warm in your veins."

Mortified, I gaped at her.

"I'm teasing you," she said between chortles.

I wasn't certain that she was. "Watch yourself, Jaruma."

"My apologies, Gimbiya." She rolled her eyes in a manner that was, decidedly, not apologetic. "You're the queen's daughter. If you want him, take him. I assure you, he won't protest."

Before I could return with a suitably indignant response, a deep voice announced the arrival of a man at my door.

SIX

"Gimbiya Amina?"

Jaruma and I looked at each other. When I remained frozen, she gestured at the doorway and got to her feet. Instinct told me to rise as well, but my stinging pride made me stay put.

I let out the breath I had been holding. "Enter."

The curtain rustled and Jaruma straightened her stance as the madawaki stepped onto the tile.

The man had been insufferable. *Demon in the night? Would I have glory handed to me?* My mother's request had been outlandish, but to belittle me in court? I intended to make certain he felt my displeasure.

"I need to speak with Gimbiya Amina." He too was washed, the stubble scraped from his face and bare head. He stood close to the door, looking uncomfortable. Out of uniform this night, he was in an undyed, sleeveless cotton tunic. The neck and torso of the tunic had the same pattern of colorful stitching as the hems of his white trousers. A sheathed long-knife hung from the brown leather sword belt at his waist.

Crossing to the chest, Jaruma retrieved her arm-knife and strapped the sheath to her forearm. With the weapon concealed under her sleeve, she moved toward the door.

As she passed, her brother grasped her hand. "In private," he said. "No need to stand outside."

She glanced at me, mischief twinkling in her eye.

Misinterpreting the exchange between his sister and me, he added, "No worries. She's safe."

"It's not *her* safety that concerns me." Flashing me one last conspiratorial grin, she said, "Remember, Gimbiya, soft rubbish on the inside." Then she left us alone.

The madawaki waited for the curtain to fall back into place before he faced me, looking uncharacteristically unsure of himself. "It is a breach of propriety for me to be in your room."

"It was a breach of propriety for you to send away my guard when entered my room."

He nodded. "I needed to speak with you, and you refused to come to the war chamber."

"Was it an order?"

"You know I cannot command you."

"You've been commanding me for two weeks now."

"It was necessary."

"So you are here now to do what's necessary? By all means, Madawaki, sit." Whether it was the wine, the roots, the conversation with his sister, or something else entirely, I felt strangely emboldened.

His eyes darted around the room. "I'll stand."

"Straining my neck to look at you aggravates my injury." In truth, the pain had dulled to a tolerable ache. The only aggravation now was the knot tying my stomach every time his eyes met mine.

Exasperation flashed across his face, but he removed his shoes and came farther into the room, lowering himself to his haunches. "Listen," he began.

"Gimbiya." If he planned to admonish me again, he could address me properly.

"*Gimbiya.*" He inhaled and exhaled before continuing. "If I bestow rank upon everyone that has spiritual insight, the waziri and his Bori priestesses would be commanding the army."

My eyes lingered on his mouth when he spoke, the knot in my stomach growing tighter and tighter. His lips, when not in their usual scowl, looked soft.

"You aren't a soldier anymore," his lips said. "You never finished your training."

The last comment drew my attention away from his mouth. I looked into the dark chasms of his eyes and said, "One can earn rank without training."

It was a frequent occurrence. Nobles or other well-equipped citizens without formal military training could distinguish themselves in battle. More often than not, those citizens received rank and all its trappings.

"True enough," he admitted. "But they earn it through blood."

I frowned.

"I'm charged with maintaining order," he said. "Even if I thought you deserved it, *which I do not*, giving you rank would dishonor those who breathe the heat of battle, those who have *died* in the heat of battle. You did what any soldier in that situation might have done. Jaruma was with you. She's not suddenly asking to be kaura." He took a deep breath and watched me, perhaps expecting a response. When I remained silent, he added gruffly, "I thought I should explain myself."

Under normal circumstances, keeping a clear head around him was difficult. Here in this small space, *breathing* was difficult.

"Explanation is unnecessary, Madawaki."

"Yes . . . well . . ." He appeared to be having some difficulty of his own. "I know you're a skilled warrior. Reckless, undisciplined, arrogant, but skilled."

My eyebrows drew together in another frown.

"I apologize, Gimbiya. For speaking to you as I did in the war chamber." He rose to his feet.

"I apologize as well." I stood too quickly. The change in elevation made me dizzy, and I put out a hand to steady myself. Realizing my hand was now pressed to his chest, I drew it quickly back. "I should have heeded your summons, rather than force you to come to me. Of course, I didn't expect you to come to me."

"Uh . . ." He looked even more discomfited. "Things needed saying."

"In the interest of saying things, I must also apologize for the fifty men who traded their lives for mine." Rubbing my face with both hands, I squeezed my eyes shut until the rising grief subsided. "I should have stayed in Rizga as you ordered."

"You should have, but you didn't."

Guilt settled back into my heart. I lowered my gaze.

"If the waziri's assertions are accurate, you and those fifty warriors were meant to find the enemy as you did," he offered, though I knew he didn't believe it. "In which case, it was all for the good. Regardless, any one of us would give his life for yours."

I shook my head. "No one should have to die for me." Raising my eyes, I met his intense gaze. "As you say, I did not earn rank and could not, in good conscience, have accepted it. But my mother isn't fully acquainted with military matters. She didn't know."

"Your father was Kuturun Mahayi. She understands more than you think. And she knows she was misguided. I have spoken to her on that count."

"She does? You did?"

"I explained the . . . *ramifications* of such a decision."

"Truly?" I gave a small laugh. "How many people would dare refuse Bakwa Turunku, much less reprimand her afterward?"

"I didn't say I reprimanded her."

His expression softened, but no smile broke the surface. Black eyes bored into me. They stripped me naked, made me want to confess all my sins, my darkest desires. At that moment, my darkest desire was him.

I said, "As long as you hold command, I am what you say I may be. I shall give you the respect due your rank."

He dropped his head in a bow. "Your understanding is appreciated." After a moment's hesitation, he turned to leave.

"Wait."

He turned back to face me. "Is there something more you wish to discuss?"

"Yes." I hesitated. "No."

He stood patiently, lamplight dancing in his eyes.

Finally, I said, "You sent my guard away."

"Jaruma?"

"She's the one you assigned."

"I'll send her back to you."

"Then you know where she's gone?"

"The compound is only so big, Gimbiya. She can't have gone far."

Jaruma never squandered an opportunity to spread her wings. The likelihood that she had remained within the compound walls was slim at best.

Realizing this himself, he said, "Right. Of course." He let out a sigh. "I'll send you another."

"And your guard will sleep in the room with me?"

He fixed me with an irate look. "Don't be absurd. He'll sleep outside."

"And if I don't want the man to sleep outside?"

"Excuse me?"

"I don't want your guard."

His brow furrowed. "What *do* you want, woman?"

To that point, my behavior had been bold. It now progressed to outright brazen. I stepped closer, took his hand, and rose onto my toes. With my lips brushing the smooth skin of his cheek, I whispered, "Gimbiya."

Drawing his hand out of mine, he took a step back. "Are you drunk?"

"Perhaps," I confessed.

Escaping death had shown me the fleeting nature of life. If I had died in those peaks, my intact chastity would have amounted to nothing. Now more than ever, here with him, my life was my own. I wouldn't give in to death or prophecies or the restrictions of propriety. There would be no shame if this man was mine to command by the end of the night.

I closed the distance he had created.

He seized my shoulders and held me at arm's length. "Gimbiya," he spoke slowly, pleading.

I could see the debate raging across his face but could not tell what he was thinking. My body burned with anxiety, but I held his gaze. Lamplight flickered on the surface of his eyes, but much fiercer flames burned in the depths of those dark pools. Seconds or minutes or days passed, and he stared at me, saying nothing, making no move.

"Am I . . ." My voice faltered. "Am I not pleasing?"

"By the gods, Gimbiya."

Disappointment welled within me. What a fool I was to think such a man would want me. I was untrained in the ways of a woman *and* the ways of a warrior. Certainly not a fitting consort to one so hardened. The heat in my body turned to shame. Dropping my gaze, I shook free of his grip and turned away.

"You may go."

He did not go, did not move. The curtains didn't rustle. I could feel his stillness behind me, smell the rich masculine scent of him.

The lightest touch grazed the nape of my neck. I closed my eyes, pulse quickening, as his fingers closed around my shoulder again. Without a word, he turned me to him, cupped my chin, and drew me forward. When he lowered his mouth to my lips, I stopped breathing entirely.

For a moment, we stood at the precipice. Then we plunged.

The feel of his lips against mine sent a thousand shudders snaking through my belly to explode in a heat that loosened the over-tight knots. He slid one arm low around my waist, and the other dropped to my back. He pulled me close. Ever more wanton, I rubbed myself against him.

Groaning, he moved both hands to my hips and pushed me gently away. "I think it's best I control myself."

"I don't want you to control yourself." I put an arm around his neck.

My free hand undid his sword belt. Knife and belt dropped to the floor. I slipped a hand under his tunic, skimming over the taut muscles of his abdomen and chest. He groaned again, his hands running over my backside before settling at my waist.

When he bent to kiss me, I inclined my head to meet him, my body vibrating with anticipation. He touched his lips lightly to my chin then pressed them to my mouth. His tongue traced the outline of my lips, parted them, and slipped inside. Gasping, I jerked away, eyes wide.

"You've never done this before?" The hasty manner in which he released me verged on panic.

My encounters with the likes of stupid Tumsa had never progressed this far. The kisses I'd shared with the boys of my youth, the ways they had handled me then, did not compare to the touch of this man. My body had not reacted to them with the desperate need I was feeling tonight. Despite a reluctance to admit it, my inexperience would be evident soon enough.

I shook my head.

Nonplussed, he pulled my hand from under his tunic. "I must go."

"No."

"What?"

"I forbid it."

"*What?*"

"I forbid you to leave."

He gave a gruff sigh and rubbed the back of his neck. "A man who lingers too long in your presence could lose his head."

"So could a man who excuses himself from my presence before he's dismissed."

I might have missed the subtle smile if he'd not followed it with a quiet chuckle.

"Please," I said. "Don't go."

"Gimbiya—"

"Amina."

"Make up your mind, woman."

Determined to do the kissing properly, I clutched his shirtfront with both hands and drew him close, pressing my body so tightly to his that he, no doubt, felt all of me through the flimsy material of my dress. I saw that he wanted to resist, saw him *trying* to resist, but his resolve was tenuous at best. It crumbled to dust.

Draping his arms around me, he brought his mouth down on mine. I rose onto my toes to snake my arms around his neck and, parting my lips, let him inside. The feel of that kiss, the intimacy of his tongue on mine, was inexplicably arousing. I sighed softly.

He drew back but didn't take his arms from around my body. "In my younger days, I wouldn't have hesitated to take what you offer. But I'm—"

I stifled his next words with another kiss. He made a pitiful attempt to pull away again, but I locked my arms around his neck. His hands rose to my face, and he tried to push me back. His efforts merely redirected my kisses from his lips to his neck. Tonight had taken all of my courage. I had opened my soul to him, made a wanton hussy of myself. I did not intend to let him go.

He let out another groan. "Amina, you make me very foolish."

He lowered us to the floor and laid me across a large cushion. With a light caress, he touched my breast through the cloth of my dress. A thrill of new sensations coursed through me, and I shuddered in his arms.

His mouth fell to my neck and trailed kisses the length of my collarbone. His caress moved from my breast slowly down the front of my body, over my hip, down my calf, until he reached my ankle. Grabbing a handful of dress, he pushed the garment up, over my knees where it settled in a pool at my thighs. Tenderly, he stroked the bare skin of my leg, his touch sending quakes to my core as his tongue traced circles on my throat.

"Are you sure about this?" His breath warmed the skin of my neck.

"I was sure of you long before this night, Suleyman." His given name rolled off my tongue without any of the anticipated awkwardness. "You don't want me?"

He stopped nuzzling my neck and looked at me, a small crease in his brow. "Who wouldn't want you?"

Smiling, I drew him down and kissed his forehead. He dropped his mouth to the hollow of my throat, to the mounds of my breasts.

I wrapped my arms around his head, crushing his face to my chest, and raised my hips so he could push the dress over them. Extricating himself from my grip, he undressed me altogether, then sat back on his knees and stared at my body in the lamplight.

"You're not pleased?" I asked, dismayed.

His focus never left my body. "No. It's not—"

"I'm too thin?"

Years of military training, particularly the two years of cavalry, had toned my body in a way that was more common to the laboring class. I lacked the lavish curves of a properly domesticated noblewoman.

He shook his head.

"What then?" My anxiety rose.

He finally raised his gaze to mine. "A body so perfect shouldn't be sullied by one such as me."

Exhaling in relief, I sat up and caressed his face. "I choose whom I please to sully me." I pushed his tunic up and jerked it over his head. Then *I* was the one staring.

The scars of battle were plain to see on the body of a perfect warrior. Lean muscles shaped contours under dark skin that glowed warm in the lamplight. Oblique striations of muscle along his ribs flexed when he leaned forward. Transfixed, I sat clutching the tunic until he took my hand and pried the garment loose.

He sat back on his heels and regarded me with those bottomless, black eyes. His fingers rose to stroke my cheek. "If we do this, I can never give back what I take from you tonight."

I spread my hand over his, pressing his palm into my face, and interwove our fingers. I kissed his open palm. The fingertips of my other hand traced the jagged line of a scar down his chest. "If I had died on the plains or in the hills, I would have died without having lived. What's mine to give is yours."

The hand against my face curved around the back of my neck. He drew me to him and kissed me again. He nibbled my lower lip then trailed kisses down my chin and to my throat. Lying me back down on the cushion, he kissed the valley between my breasts. I let out a tremulous breath as he moved progressively lower. My breathing grew ragged when his mouth reached my belly. He continued downward, his tongue sliding over the crest of my thigh. What he did then took me to the brink of madness.

I cried out from the sheer ecstasy of it. Unable to control my response to this wicked pleasure, I screamed his name and pushed his head away from me.

Flushed and embarrassed, I propped myself on my elbows to stare at him. Laughter lit his eyes. If he could make me feel like that without putting himself inside me, who would be commanding whom this night?

He stood and undid the drawstring of his trousers. My eyes widened as the rest of him came into view.

It wasn't that I had never seen a naked man before. I'd seen many naked men working the fields and rivers, but I'd never seen one like *that*. He stood fully erect, brandishing his manhood like a weapon before me. I put out the lamp, lest I lose my nerve. Even so, it remained visible in the moonlight.

He lowered himself onto me. "'You're trembling."

I shook my head.

"Are you frightened?"

I shook my head again, but that was a lie. I was petrified. All of a sudden, my seduction of Suleyman Dongo didn't seem like such a good idea.

"Don't be frightened," he said.

Heart pounding, I buried my face in his shoulder. He planted a kiss on my temple and drew me into him. I braced myself for what I knew came next.

It didn't happen as I expected. He was gentle and took his time, soothing, caressing, and easing my body into compliance. He moved his mouth down the column of my neck, and I shuddered in a pleasure that built with each kiss, each nibble, each touch. My body relaxed beneath him. Then I inhaled sharply as his fingers found my moisture.

Tiny shocks rippled over my skin. He suckled my breast, his fingers stroking my most sensitive place, driving me to greater heights. He snaked an arm around my waist and moved himself between my legs. I held his head to my chest, stroked his clean-shaven pate with my fingertips, shuddered and shuddered again. Through the tremors, I felt the pressure. He was pushing into me. I bit my lower lip and clutched his back, trying not to cry out at the stab of penetration.

Despite the preparation, the touching, the stroking, nothing could have readied me for this sharp pain. I cried out and clenched my teeth to bar the exit of more noise.

He went still. "I'm sorry. I don't want to hurt you."

"Don't stop," I whispered.

"You're certain?" He lifted his head to look at me.

The fine mingling of pleasure and pain was like nothing I'd ever experienced. It filled me, spread me to what seemed my limit, then spread even more. It was agony bordering on ecstasy.

I repeated, "Don't stop."

When his mouth dropped to my throat again, a tingling heat rose between my legs. He eased into me carefully, while he moved his mouth to the tender spot under my chin, beneath my jaw, below my ear. He paused, his mouth still pressed to my neck, and gave me time to adjust, to feel the pleasure wash over me. Clutching his arms, I bit my lip again, and he began the slow thrust of his hips, a careful ebb and flow of pressure.

I lay still beneath him until the pain washed away, leaving only pleasure. Slowly, uncertainly, I drove my hips upward to meet his. My hands slid down his back, fingers splayed over rigid muscles. I wrapped my legs around him, ankles locked at his waist. It hindered his movements but did not slow his thrusts. A deep groan sounded in his throat. His hands lifted my hips, and he pushed deeper in.

Quivering in his arms, I clung tightly to him, dug my nails into the flesh of his back.

A wave of ecstasy crashed down on me like hot rain on a warm evening. Floating on a cloud of bliss and blinded by the thrill, I saw only the man around whom I'd wrapped myself. The world might have moved on without me and I wouldn't have noticed.

Seized by the euphoria of it all, I moaned, gasped, and cried, "Sule—"

He clamped a hand over my mouth, muffling the rest of his name.

With one hand still pressed to my mouth, he rolled over so I was on top. I shrieked. Snatching his hand from my face, I fell away from him to lie panting on my back.

"It was painful," I said.

"Sorry."

Hooking an arm under my waist, he tugged me back into his embrace, climbed on top, and glided back inside. Intense pleasure racked my body. I draped my arms around his neck, kissed his chin, his chest.

Bracing himself on one arm, he rose to his knees with me straddling his lap. He moved his hands to my backside before sliding them around my waist. Holding me so tightly I could scarcely draw breath, he buried himself to the hilt. This time, it didn't hurt.

A long moan rolled from my throat, growing louder as the orgasm rose within me. My skin prickled. My body shook violently, jerking and spasming like a possessed Bori dancer, and I cried out, beyond caring who might hear. While I tumbled into a cloud of delirium, Suleyman groaned. He shuddered once, twice, and spilled into me. Breathing heavily, he unfurled his arms from around my body, and I slid to the floor where he collapsed beside me.

Even though I knew I wasn't the first to bring the man to a state of such release, I was glad for my private victory and kissed his neck. He shuddered again, sending a shudder through me as well. We lay like that for a while, breathing hard, shuddering, kissing, caressing.

After he caught his breath, he raised his head and said, "You realize this won't give you rank?"

I laughed, rolled onto him, and pressed my mouth to his. "Then I'll have to try harder."

SEVEN

The war council met every day for the next three days. From morning to evening, servants came and went with food while the council made battle preparations. Once or twice, I saw Suleyman, but he did not stop to speak. It drove me mad. Not only because he showed no emotion toward me, but because I received no word about the upcoming battle.

My sister never attended the war council, and I couldn't go to my uncle, Karama, lest my mother catch me "involving myself" in military affairs. Which left only Jaruma to pry whatever information she could from her brother during their brief meetings. He never imparted much.

However, on the morning of the fourth day, he paid a visit.

"Gimbiya Amina." The voice outside my door pushed my heart to a faster pace.

I rose from the floor and faced the doorway, making every attempt to mask my excitement. "Enter."

He did not enter, didn't even part the curtain. "Where is Jaruma?" The question didn't sound as though he'd been hoping to catch me alone for an early morning tryst.

Miffed by his standoffishness, I frowned. "She isn't here."

"Where is she?"

Was he deliberately going out of his way to pretend nothing had happened between us? Had our night together truly meant nothing to him?

"Am I *her* nursemaid or is she mine? I don't keep watch over Jaruma."

"Gimbiya, I must set out within the hour."

The curtain parted and he stepped through the doorway. He had on the heavy linen tunic and trousers meant to be worn beneath thick leather battle armor. His *takouba*—a one-handed, double-edged straight-sword—and a long-knife hung from his sword belt.

"Suleyman?" I was too stunned to say anything more.

"The Kwararafa are two days hence."

Two days? We had given them ten days to come through the mountain range. I knew there was a chance they would make it in less time, perhaps even seven days. But four? They were three days ahead of our most cautious estimate. If we had so drastically underestimated their speed, what else might we be underestimating? Raising a hand to my temple, I drew in a long breath to quell my anxiety and reached for the stool. Suleyman was at my side in the span of that single breath.

Sliding an arm around me, he asked, "Are you all right?"

For a moment, I wondered whether he was asking out of genuine concern or if he merely thought it his duty to ensure my welfare. I couldn't tell where his feelings lay or if he had any feelings at all.

I sank onto the stool. "Two days? Then we didn't slow them at all. Their speed. Such speed is unnatural."

"Perhaps." Releasing me, he dropped to one knee. "Or we miscalculated. But we can be thankful they no longer travel under stealth. The scout says they're plain as day. They won't creep upon us unawares." He examined my face, a querying gaze in his black eyes. "You *are* all right?"

I touched his face, then dropped my hand to his chest. Beneath the tunic, I felt the rough stitching of his last layer of protection—a tight, quilted vest. "I fear for your safety."

He grinned. "I'm flattered you care so deeply that you swoon in fear for me." Perhaps he made jest, but it was difficult to find humor in it.

"You don't share my affection?"

Looking out of sorts, he briefly lowered his gaze. A crease formed between his brows and he raised his eyes back to mine, searching my soul. I regretted the question. Steeling myself against rejection, I managed not to look away.

The intensity in his eyes softened and he kissed my forehead. "You've breathed new life into me, Amina. I loathe leaving you."

Buoyed by his response, I nearly threw my arms around his neck but held back for decorum's sake. Instead, I touched his face again. "You stayed away these past three days."

"You didn't send for me."

"Must I?"

"It's the way of things, is it not?"

"I wasn't aware." My gaze moved from his face to the bit of vest showing at the top of his tunic, and my heart wrenched at the thought of the danger awaiting him.

"You forget your status, love." He raised my chin with the crook of a finger. "I cannot call on you without your leave."

"Of course you have my leave." I pressed my lips to his and told myself it wasn't for the last time.

We broke apart at the sound of the curtain opening.

Jaruma stood in the doorway, an amused expression on her face. "Should I go?"

"No," I replied. "He was looking for you."

"In your mouth?" she asked but noticed either his garb or the somber atmosphere in the room. The smirk faded from her face. "Brother?"

Suleyman got up and embraced his sister. "We shall depart within the hour."

Her lips parted, but no sound came out.

He said, "We must reach them before they reach our borders."

"I should be at your side, Brother. I—"

"Don't say it. Don't tell me you're afraid for me." He took her hand and held it to his chest. He caressed her chin, kissed her cheek. "You, my sister, are fearless. You keep me strong. Do not succumb to the mad terror the Kwararafa instill in others. Or else it will defeat us. You know that."

She nodded, then looked to the doorway as Karama, also garbed in battle dress, entered without announcing himself.

I stood. "Uncle."

In my lifetime, there had never been a war the magnitude of what was coming. There had never been a threat as great as the Kwararafa. The Kwararafa fought without fear, without surrender. As far as I knew, they'd never been defeated. Pushed back—yes. But never *defeated*. Unlike the Songhai, who once ruled over us, the Kwararafa didn't integrate. They eradicated everything that wasn't theirs, eliminated any culture that might contaminate theirs. If our army could not hold them off, the Kwararafa would exterminate us. Seeing Suleyman and Karama prepared for battle drove that point deeper.

"May the mercies of Allah rain down on you, Uncle," I said, bowing in greeting.

Karama's eyes darted to Suleyman, who still clutched Jaruma's hand.

"Madawaki." He angled his head in acknowledgment.

Taking his leave, Suleyman stepped out of the room, Jaruma with him. They didn't go far—I heard their voices outside.

Karama turned a crooked smile on me. He held out his hands, and I put mine into them. Closing his fingers around me, he said, "The jackal is going into battle with the elephant." It was a tale he used to tell when I was a child. The jackal always won a resounding victory. He squeezed my fingers. "Your hands are cold."

I said nothing but stepped closer, laid my head on his chest, and wrapped my arms around his waist.

Scarcely ten years my senior, my mother's brother often related to me and my sister more as a sibling than an uncle. It was he who had taken my side when I had first begged my mother to let me join the army, he who had entreated the madawaki to put me in the cavalry. He had even bought me the gelding horse Galadima. Karama was my champion in all things. Hot tears rose to my eyes. Inhaling deeply, I kept the tears from falling.

His arms came around me, one hand resting on the back of my neck. "The madawaki speaks true. We must master our fear or be defeated. I'll return in one piece, eh?"

The lighthearted tone was meant to reassure me, but he wasn't going on a routine raid; he was going to face something far more brutal. Still, I looked up at him and nodded, struggling to swallow the fear that had formed a painful lump in my throat.

He kissed me lightly on the lips. "You'll see me to the gate?"

I nodded.

Jaruma and Suleyman were still there when Karama and I stepped out of the room, hand in hand. They fell into step with us as we made our way to the compound gate.

"Your mother cries," Karama said. "So we never say goodbye. No doubt she's watching."

"I don't blame her," I replied, resisting the need to cry myself.

When we reached the gatehouse, the three guards sitting outside rose to attention. Suleyman glanced at them and turned to me. "If we don't return . . ."

My breath caught, and I tried to steer my mind away from such a possibility.

"If the Kwararafa defeat us," he continued. "Take the people to the hills. Do not stay and defend the city. You hear me?" He looked from me to Jaruma.

She didn't answer.

"Do you hear me, Jaruma?" he asked, sounding every bit the cavalry leader.

She nodded and gave a reluctant "yes, sir."

"And you." He used the same tone on me. "With or without Jaruma, you go with the queen to Turunku."

"What?" Confused, I looked at my uncle.

"You should already be gone," Karama said. "But your mother is stubborn. She won't leave until she knows everyone is safe. The hills are the last resort for them."

"But there are too many. We can't get everyone there safely," I argued.

"You," Suleyman said, "are going to Turunku."

"No, I—"

"No discussion." His demeanor softened and he sighed. "Please."

I nodded, sick in my gut. Sick at the thought that these two men might not come back and the Kwararafa would enter my city. Sick with the fear I was supposed to master.

"Get the queen to safety. She is your priority, Gimbiya." He glanced at Karama.

Karama said, "If the enemy subdues us, they'll come directly here. You won't have the resources to defeat them. Flee, Amina. Bakwa has sense enough not to let pride lead her to folly. I'm sure your companion is more than capable of getting our people to the hills."

"Yes, Uncle."

Saying nothing more, the men turned to leave.

"Uncle." I grabbed Karama's wrist, which was wrapped in coarse linen to protect his flesh from the war bracelets he had not yet donned. "Come home."

He beamed. "Always." His fingertips brushed my cheek for just a moment before he turned again and followed Suleyman out the wooden gate.

Jaruma and I looked at one another.

"I can do nothing except watch him leave," she said, a barely noticeable tremor in her voice. In the ensuing silence, she fought back a host of emotions that crossed her face like clouds passing over the sun. "The most difficult part of war . . ." Her voice faltered. "Is being left behind."

Having just watched my own blood walk away, I agreed with that sentiment. "Is any part of war easy?" I wasn't expecting an answer.

She nodded. "Dying. Dying is easy."

❦

I dreamed. Not a dream of laughing brooks and water spirits; I dreamed of an empty plain. I stood in the field, yellow-green savanna grass swaying in the wind. As its soft whistle grew to a roar, the grass whipped my legs violently. But it wasn't the wind roaring; it was men. Hundreds, thousands, tens of thousands suddenly surrounded me. Each man fought the other with murder in his eyes. My uncle was among them. Sword in hand, he lunged at the nearest half-naked man and brought down his blade, cutting into the other man's shoulder. His enemy howled in pain but did not fall. The soldier rushed forward, still howling, pushing the sword deeper into his own flesh, and stabbed at Karama with a long-knife. Karama swept the knife away with a braceleted wrist. Then his wrist came down on the howling man's head, burying the raised, serrated edge of a war bracelet in his skull.

Dislodging his bracelet, my uncle pushed the corpse off his blade. He turned and saw me. Our eyes locked for only a moment before a spear sprouted from his chest. Screaming, I ran to him but was buffeted by a sea of men. The faster I tried to run, the farther away my uncle was.

"Uncle," I cried. "No!" But the wave of men pushed me to the ground. Curling into a ball, I tucked my head under my arms, closed my eyes, and screamed as the men stampeded over me.

Silence.

I opened my eyes, confused, sweat slick on my brow, tears still damp on my cheeks. The men were gone, but I could hear their cries. Climbing to my feet, I scanned the vast savanna ocean. A mud altar that hadn't been there before now stood beside me. Blood spilled from the edges of the altar like melting wax. The men's cries came from the structure. From the thousands of tiny figures piled upon it. At first, I thought they were living dolls, but they were the miniaturized bodies of men suffering myriad violent deaths. These were the casualties of war.

I stared at the mangled bodies, some of which were writhing in pain, and somehow knew these men had died—*were dying*—in the battle many leagues away. Frantic and nearly petrified by what I might find, I searched for my uncle among the bodies. There were so many

Zazzagawa and Kwararafa mingled in the pile; I couldn't tell one fallen soldier from another.

Wringing my hands, I backed away and reminded myself not to let fear subdue me, but terror pounded in my chest. The stink of death hung over the altar like a horrible fog that choked my lungs. Retreating from it, I came up against something hot and solid.

I froze.

The thing behind me shifted. It spoke.

"Look upon Death, Beloved. And know it for what it is."

I spun around, stumbling backward, to find myself staring at the chest of a very tall man. Still trying but failing to fully master my fear, I took another backward step and looked up at who stood before me.

Towering over seven feet, the man had skin like polished ebony. He wore a vivid red and gold kilt that hung to just above his knees and a black cloak so long it brushed the ground. Black leather bracers with gold clasps covered his forearms. The open cloak was slung back over his shoulders, exposing a lean, powerful torso that rippled with muscle under smooth, dark skin.

I followed the contours of his chest, his long neck, a proud jawline. Save for the pointed tuft of hair on his chin and the thick, black eyebrows, his face and head were bald. His gaze was not upon me, his chin raised, so I could not see his eyes. I didn't need to see them. I knew that once he looked at me, I'd be staring into the roiling red eyes of War.

"Ruhun Yak'i." The name came out of my dry throat in a nervous squeak. I bent my knees in deep genuflection without dropping my gaze.

Focusing those bloodred eyes on me, he bowed in return. "Are you mortals not aware that I have a name?" After a short pause, he added, "Dafaru."

"Lord Dafaru." I bowed again, then glanced about like a frightened rabbit for some means of escape. There was none.

He followed my gaze with a quirk of amusement. "You have done well."

I wanted to believe that this was all a construct of my imagination. But I knew this creature was real. His very presence overpowered me. And I stood spellbound in his snare. "I don't understand. What have I done well?"

"It was *your* arrow that killed the Kwararafa's magic man. Without him, they are an ordinary army. As wars go, you affected the outcome of this one rather well."

"I . . ."

"Of course, I guided the arrow. I am not supposed to lend such direct assistance, but how could I deny your prayer?"

"My—*what?*"

"You said a prayer before you loosed your first arrow, did you not?"

I expelled a loud burst of air as the realization struck: *I had prayed for my arrow to fly true.* Dread permeated every corner of my being, and I stared up at him in horror.

"Who did you expect to answer? Ubangiji?" He chuckled. "Your Creator has far more pressing concerns, and conflict *is* my realm, is it not?" His eyes flashed a brilliant red for a moment before settling into their previous supernatural hues.

Speechless, I gaped. His eyes, terrifying to look at, were too fascinating to ignore. The whites—what should have been white— were tinged with red, as if he had been drinking all night then roused from a perfect slumber. The darker parts of his eyes were at once the dark crimson color of clotting blood and the bright red of a fresh kill. The two colors, and every shade in-between, swirled together in a tumultuous pool.

He moved close. Caught in his gaze, I stood fixed to the spot and wondered how a single prayer had doomed me.

"Long have I awaited the pleasure of looking upon your beauty in the flesh," he said.

The air around me grew hot. The closer he came, the hotter it got because he was the fire. Heat radiated from his body like a lit furnace, and I was a moth spiraling helplessly into the inferno.

"I should thank your madawaki," he continued. "I would never have approached you in your innocence, but he has helped you do away with that."

His gaze dropped, releasing me from its spell. I took several hasty steps backward and bumped the mud altar. Doll men tumbled to the ground at my feet.

"You may not have earned rank by the laws of your land." He looked into my eyes, snaring me once again. "But in the eyes of War, you are a destroyer of armies."

He came suddenly forward. I jerked back, knocking more of the tiny figures to the ground. I felt his hand on my back. The metal clasps of his bracer pressed into my skin. Fingers splayed, he held me, kept me from leaning onto the altar. Heat crawled up my spine to my neck, where it hung heavy like an iron manacle. I didn't know when I began the rapid breathing, but I was panting, my chest heaving, trying to take in air that had become rarefied in the wargod's presence.

The inferno engulfed me when he put his mouth on mine. Stunned, I made no attempt to disengage. Excitement took hold, insipid in the way it smothered my senses. I let him pull me close and didn't recoil when he parted my lips. When our tongues met, I remembered my sister's dream. The dead lay scattered at my feet and the god of war was lying me on an altar of carcasses.

My wits crashed back into place. With a muffled sound, partway between grunt and scream, I wrenched myself free.

He stood unfazed, regarding me with a look that was difficult to decipher in the hazy red mists of his eyes. "Soon, Beloved." The tips of his teeth gleamed white in a fiendish leer. "You will be sweeter when you are ripe. The taste of you more *robust*." With those words, he turned away.

I came instantly and fully awake.

Shaking, I sat up, my eyes darting about the dim room to scan the shadows, afraid the wargod might slither out of them, and hoping to find Jaruma's sleeping figure bunched among the cushions. She was not there.

"It was a dream," I whispered to myself. "Just a dream." But the heat of his lips still smoldered on mine. My hand flew to my mouth to rub away any trace of him. "A dream."

As my visit from Kogi-Ayu had been more than a dream, this was also more than a dream. And the burnished-metal flavor of War lingered on my tongue.

❀

Fear didn't let me go back to sleep, and fatigue didn't let me stay awake. In compromise, I settled into uneasy slumber and woke often. The wargod did not make a second appearance.

Jaruma returned with the morning sun and immediately left again for the cookhouse. I lay staring at my thatched ceiling, trying to forget the heat of Dafaru's touch, when the curtain rustled.

"Sister?" Zariya's voice called from outside.

I'd not seen my sister since the day after my return from Rizga. She lived with her husband—a prominent nobleman—at his palatial compound on the city's edge. Two years my junior, she had been married for six months.

She entered the room behind a pregnant belly that was, most certainly, larger than six months along, and lowered herself unsteadily to sit beside me on the bed. "You look tired, Sister. Have you not slept?"

"I slept, but not well." Yawning, I sat up and stretched.

Zariya was the image of our mother. She had the same fair skin, the same warm eyes. They even shared the same mannerisms. When she reached over to take my hand, the manner in which she gave a commiserative nod, the way her small mouth turned down at the edges, I might have been looking at Bakwa herself.

She squeezed my hand. "The army will prevail."

I squeezed back.

Dafaru had already hinted at our victory, but I now wondered whether the wargod had been behind it from the start. Had he orchestrated this war to fulfill a prophecy that led me into his arms? Was this all just a game of the gods, a way to relieve their divine boredom? How was it that a small prayer, voiced only in my thoughts, had so profound an effect on the outcome of a battle?

And what of Karama? I saw him die in my dream. I wasn't cursed with my sister's oracular powers, but I had watched him die.

Zariya wrinkled her brow. "Are you well?"

I considered telling her of my dream and the wargod's visit, but she would likely have told our mother, who had taken great pains to shield me from the wargod's sight. She'd halted my military training, banned me from the war council, and hung a dozen protective amulets on my walls. None of it had mattered. In a single breath, with a single prayer, I'd undone it all. I didn't want to see the fear or disappointment in her eyes.

"Uncle promised he'd return," I said. "But . . ." I shook my head.

Zariya squeezed my hand again. "We're all afraid. All we can do is pray for the mercy of Allah."

Knowing that my prayers fell on the wargod's ears, I planned never to pray again.

A child's voice called from the doorway. "Gimbiya Amina?"

"Enter," I said, eager to have something other than wars and wargods to occupy my thoughts.

A well-dressed girl of about ten or so shuffled through the doorway. Her blouse, wrapper, and headdress were of an intricately woven design. Expensive. Certainly not the standard attire of a domestic servant. Yet, I was certain I recognized the child as the daughter of one of my slaves.

"Fatima?" I asked.

The girl flashed half a smile and nodded.

Other than the two administrators who ran the daily affairs in the provinces my mother had assigned me, I did not routinely utilize slaves and had only a few of my own. As such, I rarely saw any of them. Fatima's mother, if I recalled correctly, was payment for a debt I couldn't remember. From the look of her daughter, she must have found herself a rich benefactor.

"What is it?" I asked.

The girl dropped to her knees. "May you live long, Gimbiya." She handed me a rolled-up piece of parchment as she spoke the belated greeting. Realizing it was Zariya beside me, she dipped her head in another bow. "And you, Gimbiya. May you live long."

I took the parchment, unrolled it, and frowned at the Arabic script. Some of the words were easy to decipher, but too many were beyond my understanding. Zariya had demonstrated more aptitude for reading and writing, so I passed the parchment to her.

Tilting her head, she studied the document. "Yukubu wants to buy this girl and her mother."

Fatima nodded. "He says I should return with your answer."

Nothing prohibited slaves from roaming the city; it wasn't as though they could return to their families—our raids were thorough. But I wondered if, perhaps, the slaves had too much free rein. Clearly, Fatima and her mother spent a great deal of time with the weaver, Yukubu. In such cases, one always ran the risk of losing a slave to another master.

"I haven't time for this. Tell Yukubu he can wait until our soldiers return safely home."

"But he says I should bring your answer!" The girl blurted out, then quickly lowered her head and her voice. "He will be angry."

"At who?" I asked.

"At me."

"Does he beat you?" The question came out with more force than I had intended.

The girl shifted nervously, refusing to meet my eyes.

"Answer me," I said.

"Only one time," she said in a quiet voice. "With *koboko*."

Zariya let out a small gasp.

The rawhide whip was a vicious form of punishment. Intended for animals, the koboko was unsuitable for my horse, much less a child.

My eyes narrowed in anger. "Did he leave a mark?"

She gave a vigorous shake of the head.

I regarded the girl, debating whether to make her remove her clothing so I could see for myself whether the weaver had scarred her.

Zariya spoke. "Your mother is with Mallam Yukubu now?"

The girl nodded.

"Does he beat her?" Zariya asked.

While the weaver may have thought it acceptable to discipline the child, it was unlikely he would take such an approach with the mother. She belonged to me, after all; she could return to the palace at will.

The girl gaped. "Never."

"You'll not return to that man," I said and noted the look of relief on her face. "I'll send word to your mother. If she wants to remain with Mallam Yukubu until I'm ready to deal with him, that's her own palaver."

"Yes, Gimbiya." She rose.

"Go and find Uwar Soro," I said.

As head of the household staff, the *uwar soro* would ensure the child was taken care of.

"Yes, Gimbiya." Fatima bowed once more and left the room.

I glanced at my sister.

"So, Gimbiya," she said. "Will you sell them?"

"I can't think of that right now, Gimbiya."

She chuckled.

My thoughts—still twisted from the wargod's nocturnal visit—couldn't focus on much other than the battle with the Kwararafa. While my soul rejected it, my mind saw my uncle dead. Although I knew it wouldn't happen, my mind saw Zazzau ripped apart like the gates of Rizga, the land littered with the bodies of children. My mind saw my sister slaughtered, her unborn child dead in her womb, and the Kwararafa spilling into my city like specters of death.

One wayward slave was the least of my worries.

EIGHT

Eight long nights of troubled sleep, eight days watching the horizon before the first Zazzagawa soldiers began trickling into the city. Two thousand five hundred men, almost one thousand Kuturun Mahayi, another thousand infantry, and five hundred mounted spearmen had gone into battle. Less than half had made it home. Eight days dragged into nine. Neither my uncle nor Suleyman returned. We heard from the soldiers that the kaura had not survived. Some believed that Suleyman had died; others said he was alive. They all agreed that Karama still breathed. So I waited, hoping beyond hope, and afraid to utter another prayer.

Nine days crept past ten and into eleven, then Karama finally came home.

Upon hearing the news of his arrival, I rushed to the war chamber where my mother was holding a briefing. My heart dropped at Suleyman's conspicuous absence, but my uncle was alive. He approached and lifted me into a tight embrace.

Wrapping my arms about his neck, I inhaled the sweat-and-blood odor of battle and asked, "Where's the madawaki?"

"No greeting for me?" He lowered me to the ground.

"Welcome, Uncle." My relief at seeing him was evident in the kisses I planted on both cheeks before hugging him close again. "I know you warned against it, but I feared for you." And I was thankful that my dreams never predicted the future.

"I told you I'd return safely."

"I know."

He drew back, lips turning down in disappointment. "You doubted me?"

"Never." I stole my arms around his waist. "You're one of the last to arrive. I thought the madawaki might be with you." It was difficult to mask my growing trepidation.

"This concern for the madawaki is . . . unexpected." As though trying to see into my mind, he narrowed his eyes.

I blinked away the tears pricking mine. "He's Jaruma's family. Of course, I'm concerned."

Before my uncle could probe further, the makama spoke. "Let the council begin."

Karama took my hand and led me across the room. We sat next to each other on the wooden chairs now arranged in a circle. I looked around, desperate to see Suleyman enter. He did not. There were two faces, however, I'd thought never to see again.

Danladi and Gambo, bedraggled and bruised, sat beside the waziri. Shocked, I stared at them. As one, they turned to me, and I offered a tentative smile. Danladi smiled back while Gambo lowered his head in a bow.

"Karama," my mother said. "Give us the good tidings."

Karama stood, and we turned our attention to him.

"We met the enemy only two days north of here. Near Tsaroma. They had already ransacked the surrounding villages and were waiting for us. It was as if they had deliberately planned the time and place of our meeting. They had the advantage of numbers, nearly four thousand to our two thousand five hundred, and they had time to familiarize themselves with the lay of the land. What we lacked in numbers and optimal positioning, however, the bowmen made up in skill."

The expression on his face was both proud and rueful. War being what it was, a solid dose of misery would temper the high of victory.

"The Kuturun Mahayi took the vanguard and flanks," he continued. "We charged into enemy lines, expecting them to scatter, but they stood their ground."

A few quiet murmurs rose in the room with the realization of just how fierce the Kwararafa were. A group of infantrymen that faced down four hundred war chargers without breaking formation was a force that should never be underestimated.

Karama continued, "Despite the enemy's stand, the first offensive cut a gouge in their center. Our ground runners swelled to fill it. Kuturun Mahayi in the flanks weakened the enemy's rear guard. By evening, the tables had turned. *We* had the upper hand. The fight was brutal. The kaura was killed, the madawaki injured."

At the mention of the madawaki, I sat bolt upright. He was injured. But alive?

"I sustained minor injuries, but the madawaki's condition was grave."

I held my breath.

"The medicine men tended him as best they could, but he's still weak."

And I didn't know whether to breathe again.

Karama said no more on Suleyman's condition. "These men"—he indicated Gambo and Danladi—"joined us in battle. They were in the hills with Amina when she first found the Kwararafa. It's because of them and their comrades that my niece returned safely to us."

"Well done," the makama said to the men. "Well done."

Karama turned to Bakwa. "There were fifty-one Kuturun Mahayi with Amina that day. One returned with her. Most died in the hills. Eight did battle with us at Tsaroma. Only these two survive."

More talk ensued. I thought I heard land endowments to Danladi, Gambo, and the families of the other forty-eight Kuturun Mahayi who had accompanied me to the hills. But I had ceased listening after Karama had mentioned Suleyman's status. All that mattered now was that Suleyman was alive. But for how long? The medicine men had tended him, but was he healing? Would he recover? My hands squeezed together on my lap.

Through a fretful cloud of tension, I heard old Makama say, "We have no war leader."

That brought my focus back around.

The makama looked at my uncle. "You said the madawaki's injuries are not life-threatening?"

"No," Karama replied. "I didn't say that."

Every muscle in my body contracted.

"But I imagine they aren't," he continued. "I brought him to his compound myself. God willing, he should recover fully."

Unclasping my hands, I breathed.

The makama spoke again. "Then I recommend we name a new kaura while most of the council members are present. Madawaki Dongo is, of course, my selection."

"I agree," Karama said. If he had hoped the position would fall to him, there was no sign of it on his face or in his tone. "There's none more qualified. Except, perhaps, the galadima."

The galadima chuckled absently. "I have long put away my weapons, Karama. My blades have gone to rust. I second the nomination of Dongo."

"Amina?" My mother looked at me. "I would like to hear your thoughts on the matter. You have, as your uncle calls it, a warrior's heart. What does your heart tell you regarding the madawaki?"

Unprepared for Bakwa's question, I sat speechless.

"Do not hold us in suspense, child," Karama said, a devilish smirk on his face.

I gave him a dirty look then stuttered my response. "I—I'm sure Madawaki Dongo would make a fine kaura. He has a . . . uh . . . sharp mind. His prowess with . . . with weaponry is impressive." I could have kicked myself for the clumsy choice of wording.

Karama slanted me a baffled look, and I resolutely turned my face toward Bakwa. Once again, I thanked all things good that no one could see the heat flooding my cheeks.

"Then, unless I hear objections, kaura he is," Bakwa declared. "I'll have the proclamation documented and my daughter, Amina, will deliver the message personally." She beamed at Karama. "If there's nothing urgent to discuss, I'm sure my brother and these men would like to rest." She concluded the meeting and dismissed us.

"Prowess, eh?" Karama said as I rose excitedly to my feet. "Why the rush?"

"I'm going to find Jaruma."

"Don't bother. She's gone to him already." He stood slowly, wincing as he got out of his chair. "You look infinitely happier now than you were when you first saw me."

"I'm happy you're home, Uncle." I flung my arms around his neck.

He grimaced in pain. "Is all this exuberance for me or for our new kaura?"

I glared at him.

"My child." He stroked my back. "I'm happy to be home."

❋

Delivering the news of my mother's proclamation was only my second visit to Suleyman's compound, the first being when Karama had brought me to Suleyman for entry into the cavalry. The abode, which rivaled the palace in size, was a modern structure with a high mud-brick wall and arched entryway. Jaruma met me in the dark entry alcove and ushered me inside. The palace guards who had ridden with me remained outside.

Jaruma had been with her brother since the day of his return, bringing me regular news of his slow recovery. This was the first day he was well enough to receive me.

I had forgotten how green his compound was. Grass grew in the courtyard. Not the occasional tufts that generally sprouted in the compounds of Zazzau but a lush expanse that covered the ground from wall to wall. A single freshwater well fed the extensive irrigation system that nourished the grass and the fruiting trees dotting the landscape. Suleyman's eldest son was nearly my age. He stopped for a short and somewhat formal conversation, while other members of the household scurried about, pausing just long enough to acknowledge me with cursory greetings.

Jaruma led me to the central hut, a newly thatched, square structure with a window shuttered by palm bark. Before she could rap on the door, one of Suleyman's female servants stepped out of it. She bowed, gave a quick greeting, and continued on her way.

"Uwar Soro," Jaruma whispered.

"Her?"

I glanced back at Suleyman's head of household and suffered a pang of jealousy. She was the mother of his two eldest children and mistress of this property. While I had to wait until he was well enough to see me, she had been with him. He had a harem of slaves, but his uwar soro was his most treasured, a slave who, according to Jaruma, was the only one allowed to care for him on his sickbed.

My temples burned as I watched her recede from view.

"Brother." Jaruma stepped through the open doorway. "I've brought Amina." A breath later, she invited me in.

Other than Karama's quarters, I had never been inside a man's room. Such things were frowned upon. A glance around showed that one man's sanctuary wasn't much different from another's. Weapons, both battle ready and ornamental, hung from metal hooks on the walls. Clay tiles covered the floor, which was otherwise bare. His bed and furnishings were raised on thick, wooden legs, and there was only one cushion in the room. The man himself was reclined on a leather-upholstered diwan, one leg on the ground, the other propped upon that lone leather cushion. The thigh of his propped-up leg was bound in linen, as were his ribs. His face was drawn, but he looked otherwise well.

Overcome by relief and joy, I quickly crossed the room and dropped to the hard floor, kneeling beside him. I took his hand and kissed it. "You're well?"

He gave me slow nod.

Jaruma excused herself and left the room.

"I feared for you," I said. "I know I shouldn't have."

"I admit that I feared for myself." His voice was weary. "The battle was vicious." With his free hand, he pulled the cloth from my head. He stroked my hair and ran his fingers between the ridges of plaits traversing my scalp. "They knew we were coming. Somehow they knew Tsaroma would be the place. They waited for us there."

Caressing his face, I nodded. "Yes. Karama said so. I've come to deliver a message from my mother."

"And I thought you were here because you cared for me."

"You know I care." I leaned forward to kiss his lips. "But I have news."

"What news? I am the new kaura?"

My excitement, which had been bubbling over, drained. "Jaruma told you?"

"I saw Tariki die. I didn't think he'd be returning to claim the post." He tried to sit up, but the attempt caused him pain.

"Don't move." I kissed him again and sat back on my heels. "I thought you'd be more . . ." *Excited* wasn't a word one could ever associate with Suleyman. "Enthusiastic? Would you be less indifferent, if you knew there were other choices for kaura?" I asked, leaning forward to kiss him yet again.

He snorted. "What other choices? Galadima? He would turn it down. And Karama isn't ready." He tried again to raise himself higher on the diwan, winced, and gave up the effort. The battle still uppermost in his mind, he said, "They are fearless, those Kwararafa. As fierce as the stories claim. I wouldn't mind having men like that fighting *with* me instead of against."

"They had a magic man, but he died in the hills." Even as the words passed my lips, I knew I shouldn't have said them.

Silence settled on the room.

"How do you know this?" He fixed a piercing gaze on me.

I rebuked myself internally. "I was told. In a dream."

This revelation did not please him. "Kogi-Ayu again?"

"Let's not speak of it." The truth would have displeased him further. "You must rest."

He looked askance at me but said nothing.

"Do I have leave to call on you?" I asked in a mockingly stern voice.

Our next kiss lingered. He stroked the back of my head while I ran my fingers lightly down his stubbly cheek, his neck, to the linen covering his torso.

When we pulled apart, he said, "You are Amina of Zazzau. You need no permission to call on your servants."

"You are no one's servant, *Kaura*." I kissed his hand then gathered myself off the floor. He handed me my headwrap. As I tied it onto my head, I said, "I saw your son. The younger Suleyman is handsome."

"Yes." He settled into the diwan. "He looks like his mother."

And my temples burned anew.

NINE

City of Turunku, Kingdom of Zazzau, Central Hausaland, circa 1558 CE

In light of recent events, we reevaluated our city's defenses. Situated on open savanna, the capital city of Kufena was easy to invade from almost any direction. The only obstruction between a marauding army and my people was a line of low hills in the east. Considering the Kwararafa's skill at traversing the peaks, those few hills were hardly sufficient defense.

Kufena's lack of natural fortifications stood out as a liability. Amidst heavy protestation from certain members of the council and some of the nobility, we relocated our administrative seat from Kufena to the small town in which my mother was born, some forty-five kilometers to the south.

Surrounded by a range of rocky hills on three sides, Turunku was much easier to protect. Its extensive wall required reinforcement on the southern side only. Sentry stations, arranged at intervals, were our eyes in the hills, able to raise the alarm on any invaders before they could reach our walled city.

The physical move—uprooting everyone and everything that made Kufena the center of Zazzau's power—did not prove difficult, but the consequences blew through both cities like a sandstorm. In Kufena, trade began a precipitous decline, while the influx of people and the subsequent flood of commerce brought the chaos of metropolitan living into Turunku. In less than a year, the previously quiet town grew into one of the busiest trading hubs in the Sahel.

My sister, who had birthed a daughter and still lived in Kufena with her husband designed the palace compound in Turunku. Gidan Bakwa—Bakwa's house—was grander than the previous compound, and Bakwa set about filling it to brimming with residents and entertainment. Musicians, dancers, and storytellers were just the start. She opened her palace to puppeteers, acrobats, singers, and sundry other performers. And she did it all in time for the Gani Festival.

The Gani ceremonies were a celebration of the birth of our greatest hero, Bayajidda. The festivities began with a secret ritual that was hardly a secret. At midnight, the queen, the waziri, two temple singers, and a small group of nobles—including me—made their way to the city's central well. There, the singers sang a song to bless the water against Dodo, the evil snake of history.

As legend told, the snake had tormented the people of ancient Daura, refusing them access to their city's well, until the fugitive Persian prince Bayajidda killed it. Bayajidda's six sons from his second wife, the most grateful queen of Daura, and one son from his first wife fathered the Hausa Bakwai—the seven Hausa states, of which Zazzau was one.

After the ceremonial song of blessing, my mother drew a gourd of water from the well. We returned to the palace, sacred water in hand, and stood before the Traveler's Tree. Standing even prior to palace construction, the tree was considered a life-giving tree, blessed by Inna, the Earth Mother.

Though the crescent moon was weak, the stars dotting the sky sparkled so brightly one could almost hear them sing. It was a good night for folk magic.

In his lilting voice, the waziri said a prosperity prayer for the coming year. Ethereal humming accompanied him, the singers swaying side to side. The ground, parched by the dry harmattan season, sighed when Bakwa poured the blessed well water at the base of the tree. The waziri's prayer ended as the gourd emptied. He gave one last salutation to the New Year and sent us our respective ways.

The festival proper began the next day.

❋

Six fattened rams, eight goats, and basins full of chickens from the queen's livestock were killed, cooked, and served to the people of Turunku that evening. Storytellers entertained on the queen's pavilion. Dancers, with their suggestive movements, gyrated to the music of drums and woodwinds. Hyena men performed tricks with their trained animals—muzzled hyenas, baboons, and monkeys. It was a night of revelry, a night of overindulgence.

Jaruma, drunk on honey beer, wandered off to her new palace abode with Danladi, who I suspected was also drunk. Across the courtyard, the daughter of a rich nobleman, who had made no secret his desire to have the new kaura as a son-in-law, monopolized Suleyman's attention.

From my chair at the queen's table, I watched the woman giggle and touch his arm. He raised the sleeve of his blue kaftan, and she made a face of either amazement or indigestion—it was difficult to tell from where I sat. With one hand on her chest, drawing attention to her gratuitous bosom, she used her other hand to finger the hilt of Suleyman's arm-knife. I wanted to strangle her, loose one of the hyenas on her, stab her in the eye with the arm-knife that so fascinated her.

Annoyed, I left the table and headed toward the row of administrative huts that divided the compound into east and west. Suleyman looked up as I passed. He wasn't laughing with her, but he rarely laughed at anything, so I couldn't determine his interest in the clucking hen. When he returned his attention to her, however, my irritation doubled. I wanted to grab her by the hair, which she had done up in an elaborate style of beads and ivory pins, and fling her over twelve feet of palace wall.

Passing between two clusters of conjoined servants' quarters, I heard the cow giggle again and increased my pace to escape her aggravating voice. I reached my room and pushed open the wooden door. It swung inward on metal hinges.

My room at Gidan Bakwa was twice the size of my previous abode. Clay tiles covered the floor at the entrance, while several layers of mats and rugs softened the rest of the room. I no longer had only cushions as accoutrements. The diwan, an import from Arabia, stood on legs of heavy wood, which curved under at their bases. It was upholstered in green brocade and currently held a sleeping child.

Fatima stirred when the door swung shut behind me. The palace uwar soro had made the child my personal servant. Fatima was still too young to be very useful, but she was always eager to help. Earlier, she had been playing in the streets with the courtiers' children. I hadn't seen her return and didn't know why she was sleeping in my room, but I was too furious at Suleyman to care.

Muttering curses to strike Suleyman impotent, I unwrapped my hair from a lengthy swath of red brocade. Tiny braids fell from the tight headdress. The matching gown was next to go. I tossed it onto the heavily padded bed on the other side of the room. The bed was also an Arabian import. Carvings etched into its wooden frame and short legs depicted a desert caravan of shrouded men riding two-humped camels. The artistry was so fine that I was never quite sure whether to sleep on it or admire it.

Tonight, I tumbled naked to the floor and, because I had imbibed nearly as much as Jaruma, sleep came quickly.

❋

Voices called me back from oblivion.

"You will take me tomorrow?" It was Fatima.

Suleyman responded, "Only if your mistress allows it. I'll take you with me when I go." Having apparently bribed my slave with a journey to see her mother, he dismissed her. "Now, go to your own room."

Small feet padded softly across the floor. The door opened and shut. Suleyman latched it closed.

I opened my eyes a sliver to see him standing over me. I almost welcomed him but remembered the cackling hen with her oversized chest. Admittedly, I had never demanded exclusivity from him, but he was the only man that had ever touched me. The harem of four women he kept in his Kufena compound did not bother me. Particularly because they predated me. But it chafed my heart raw to think of him with yet another woman.

Stretching, I attempted a look of annoyance but was not awake enough to know if I succeeded.

He said, "I told your girl I'd take her to Kufena tomorrow. In exchange for her leaving us alone tonight. Is that acceptable?"

Of course he would assume I wanted to spend the night with him after he'd shared his evening with some other woman. Unfortunately for my pride, that was exactly what I wanted, but he didn't need to know.

I said, "Did your other woman turn you down?"

"Would you rather I leave?"

As if he would.

"What do you think?" I turned onto my side, rising just enough to rest on my elbow, and glared at him.

"One can never tell with women." Raising his sleeve, he unstrapped the sheath of his arm-knife and placed it into the alcove nearest the door. Then he began tugging his kaftan over his head.

"You presume too much, Kaura. I didn't say you could remove your clothing."

With a grunt, he dropped to hands and knees and leaned close. I breathed in the odor of sweet tobacco. He often smelled like sweet tobacco. The scent filled me with a familiar longing. He kissed me lightly, the taste of wine simmering on his lips.

"Do I have your permission to undress, Gimbiya?" His voice resonated through me like the caress of a hundred fingers.

I took back all my curses.

Shoring up my collapsing pride, I said, "Be quick about it."

Despite the order, he was not quick to undress. He stood and drew the kaftan slowly over his head, titillating me into fidgety madness.

"Did Mallam Usman offer you his daughter?" I asked with growing impatience.

"The Gani Festival isn't the place for such a transaction, Amina. Do you know nothing of propriety?"

"Nothing whatsoever, love."

His response didn't answer my question. While my body screamed for him, my heart squeezed tight with the thought that I might lose him.

He fumbled with the drawstring of his trousers, frowning slightly, as though he couldn't undo the knot, and said, "The offer of a wife is best done in the privacy of a man's home. We couldn't very well haggle over dowry during the festivities."

Our relationship was less than a year old, and we had never discussed marriage—a prospect that terrified me. But if he wanted to settle down with a woman, why hadn't he asked *me*? And why was he interested in a wife when he already had five sons with his four mistresses?

I made a rude, irritated sound. "I take no issue with you bedding your slaves, Suleyman, but—"

"But you're threatened by any woman with status to rival your own?"

My tone grew lofty. "Unless you're referring to my mother, no woman in Zazzau has status to rival mine."

"Then you have nothing to fear." Finally loose, the trousers fell. He stepped out of them.

"I will be second to no woman."

He chuckled. "You won't at that, will you?" He dropped back down onto his knees.

Fighting a strong desire to take him in my mouth, I instead took him in my hand. His body responded appropriately.

"You needn't concern yourself with Mallam Usman's daughter or any other man's daughter." He moved closer. "I already have enough."

"Suleyman!"

"Yes, Gimbiya?" He wore a mask of innocence.

Although I truly wanted to perform the obscenity he had in mind, I dropped my hand and rolled onto my back. "Move that *thing* away from my face."

He gave an exasperated sigh and kissed my collarbone. "Women have certain talents." With his finger, he traced the outline of my lips, parted them, and put the finger into my mouth. "Yours will go to waste if not adequately utilized."

With my tongue against his fingertip, I was more sorely tempted than ever to do that scurrilous thing he was urging me to do. I shuddered at the indecency of it and pulled his hand from my mouth.

"That is a talent for whores." I exhaled sharply at the gentle pinch of teeth on my nipple.

He muttered a response too garbled to comprehend and climbed onto me. "You, Amina, are selfish." His voice was muffled against my breastbone.

He kissed my body, moving his tongue haphazardly over my torso and in the general direction of *down*. When he reached my navel, his tongue flicked out. I exhaled, a quiver running through me.

Grinning up at me, he lifted my leg, kissing the inside of my thigh. Then he pushed my thighs apart and dove into my heated center. With a deep, noisy breath, I clutched his head. He deepened the intimate kiss. I exhaled slowly, savoring the sensations coursing through my body. When his tongue slid into me, a soft trill sounded in my throat.

The pleasure was intense. Too intense to keep under control. Battling my slipping composure, I tried to push his head from between my legs, but he didn't budge. Instead, he grabbed my wrists and held them down. Wriggling violently under him, I chewed my lower lip to keep from crying out my indignation, my pleasure, his name. Even so, he managed to elicit several loud moans from me before he surfaced.

"I could have you executed for that," I said after he released my arms.

"Then let me die a happy man." He kissed my belly and worked his way back up.

We made love that night as though we'd never see each other again. He quickly brought me to climax, then again, without reaching his.

"What's the matter?" I asked after my second release. "Am I not pleasing you?"

Laughing, he pulled out and turned me onto my stomach. He kissed my shoulders, my neck, nibbled my ear, and plunged back inside.

"No!" I lowered my voice to a harsh whisper. "No. This is how animals do it."

He chuckled, mocking my dismay, and gripped me firmly around the waist with one arm. His free hand cupped my breast. I struggled against him, but my struggles served only to heighten his excitement. He bored into me with increasing force. Shock gave way to pleasure and our bestial coupling carried me higher into ecstasy. In spite of my indignation, despite the fact that Suleyman chipped at my ego with every pelvic thrust, this was rapture.

My third release was strong. The wave of climax began somewhere deep in my soul. It radiated out to touch every centimeter of me and shrank back only to crash upon and shatter my self-possession like a clay pot struck with a mallet.

No longer attempting to suppress the sounds emanating from my lips, I moaned and grunted and crooned and whimpered, my body trembling from top to bottom. With a loud moan of his own, Suleyman spilled into me. Groaning, he slid out and fell onto his back.

We lay silent for a time. Suleyman recovering his breath, me still subjugated by this method of lovemaking. He started to speak, but before he finished the second word, I sat up and slapped him hard across the face.

"That is for defiling me like an animal." My glowering eyes dared him to strike me back. Then I fell on top of him and kissed him with unreserved passion. "This is for giving me more pleasure than I imagined possible."

"I'm forgiven then?" He rubbed his frowning face.

"Only if you promise to do it again."

He looked mortified. "What? Tonight?"

"Why not?"

"Because I'm too old and too drunk for that kind of performance twice in one night."

"How old *are* you?" In eight months, I'd not asked, because it seemed unimportant. But now, after seeing him wooed by another woman, everything mattered.

A grin came and went. "A soldier never reveals his true age."

"That's rubbish. You can't be much more than forty. I've had marriage proposed by men of sixty. I'm sure any of them would gladly do as I ask."

"I'm forty-six, and I shall be dead before I reach sixty." He laced his fingers under his head and closed his eyes. "But you're free to ask one of your aged admirers to service you."

"Don't say that."

"I'm teasing." He opened one eye. "I'd rather not share you with another man."

"No, Suleyman. Don't say you'll be dead by sixty." Such declarations of misfortune tended to come back and haunt those who declared them.

He opened both eyes and saw that I was serious. "Sorry, love." His arms slid around me. "I won't say it again."

Satisfied, I snuggled into his embrace.

❈

Suleyman didn't leave before cockcrow. He slept well past sunrise, waking to a soft rap on the door. There was no way he could leave now without drawing attention to the fact that he'd spent the night in my abode. I sat up as he got to his feet, his body a hard-muscled silhouette against the sunlight pouring through the open window.

The knocking came again. "Gimbiya?" Fatima called.

Suleyman donned his trousers and, tying the drawstring, went to the door. When he opened it, I saw Fatima's thin legs in the doorway. His back was to me, so I couldn't see his face but imagined his features softening, as they did whenever she was near. He turned his head to look at me over his shoulder, a question in his eyes.

"She may go," I said.

The child clapped her hands.

Yukubu, the weaver, had offered a good price for Fatima and her mother. I might have sold them, if not for the koboko beating. How he chose to discipline his own children was his business, but I wouldn't leave Fatima to his mercy. Fatima maintained that the man had never beaten her mother; the mother said the same. Nonetheless, I couldn't give him possession of the woman. He could keep her, but as long as she was my property, he could not harm her. A visit from Suleyman had pressed that point deep into Yukubu's head. It wouldn't hurt for the weaver to know Suleyman was still watching.

From the courtyard, the uwar soro called to Fatima.

"Yes, *gyatuma!*" Fatima shouted and ran to answer the call.

Suleyman chuckled and shut the door. "Gyatuma?"

I shrugged. The uwar soro was hardly an old woman, but to a ten-year-old child, even *I* was gyatuma.

As Suleyman strapped on his arm-knife, I rose from the floor and strode to the large alcove next to the bed. The alcove held the tools for my morning ablutions—several chewing sticks, a lump of black soap, a jar of coconut oil, and a jar of shea butter. I pulled an unused chewing stick from within and handed it to Suleyman, who was now fully dressed, save his sandals.

He put the stick into his mouth, stepped back, and folded his arms. His eyes swept slowly over my naked body.

Around the chewing stick, he said, "It's difficult enough not to ravish you when you're dressed. Cover up, else I'll never get that child to her mother today."

Heady from his words, I took my discarded dress off the bed and slid it over me.

He shook his head and came forward. "That doesn't help."

More rapping on the door and Fatima's cheerful voice called, "Gimbiya."

Groaning, Suleyman lifted his eyes to the heavens, crossed back to the door and opened it.

Earthenware clattered atop a wooden tray that Fatima was attempting to lift off the ground. Before she could spill the food, Suleyman took the tray.

Amused by her clumsy effort, I snorted while Suleyman placed the tray on the small round table beside the diwan. The wooden tabletop sat on three elephant tusks. Two stools with carved ivory legs sat partially beneath the table. He pulled one out for me.

"Are you ready?" he asked Fatima, the stick dangling from his mouth.

Large eyes bright with excitement, she nodded.

"Have you told Uwar Soro?" I asked, in case the woman had other tasks planned for the girl.

Again, she nodded.

"And you've eaten?" Suleyman asked, donning his sandals.

Another nod.

He took the bowl of honeyed meat from the tray, turned to Fatima, and gestured toward the door. She walked out ahead of him, and I accompanied them to the small, rust-colored iron gate in the southern wall.

Our morning procession drew intrigued looks from other palace inhabitants and vague indifference from the one guard sitting in the tiny gatehouse. Upon our approach, he rose, bowed, and opened the gate without so much as an eyebrow twitch. Several horses sheltered beneath a corrugated tin roof outside. Another guard stood against the wall, chatting with a Turunku local while the sound of continued revelry played in the streets beyond. When the second guard saw us, he quickly untied Suleyman's dark bay and led it over. Shiny new amulets clinked in its mane—Jaruma's work, no doubt.

Handing me the bowl of meat, Suleyman lifted Fatima into the saddle. She squealed with delight. During our move to Turunku, she had ridden in a cart; this was her first time on a horse. Suleyman climbed up behind her. I handed her the bowl. He took it from me, giving her the reins instead. She squealed again. I rolled my eyes. Their five-hour journey would now take twelve.

✳

The Gani festivities came and went. Weeks passed and life in Turunku eventually settled into a natural groove. The rumor of my affair with Suleyman spread quickly. Mallam Usman ceased trying to wed his daughter to my kaura, and my mother ceased asking me to find a man. As our relationship was now common knowledge, his visits were less surreptitious. He dined with me and my mother in her private quarters, escorted me to various official functions, and occasionally hunted with Karama—a thing he'd only done with Jaruma before.

Suleyman was passionate in love. He was generous, affectionate. Any number of sweet words could describe him, and my heart grew lighter whenever he looked at me. He all but adopted Fatima. She called him "Baba" and flung herself into his embrace when he visited, bringing toys that she would promptly break and an array of *jigida* beads that she strung around her waist. I could see what Jaruma had meant by "Suleyman was too lenient."

My work in the provinces kept me busy, although my two administrators handled things well. Mostly, I served as my mother's *alkali*, presiding over legal proceedings, passing judgment here, doling out punishment there. The wargod had not visited again, and so much time had passed that the initial visit seemed an inconvenient recollection, all but forgotten. In essence, life in Turunku was good.

Until one evening when, after I'd lain down to a concert of night birds and the fragrance of lilies, something pricked my awareness. I tried to ignore the feeling, to close my eyes and let sleep take me, but whatever it was niggled persistently at the edge of my perception—like someone standing just outside my field of view.

"Greetings, Beloved."

I bolted upright, eyes open. *That voice.*

"How long has it been since I looked upon you?" he asked.

My eyes swept the room as I scrambled to my feet. "Show yourself." I sounded bolder than I felt.

A shadow moved beside me, his appearance so sudden that I had to stifle a scream.

I'm dreaming, I thought. Or delusional. Perhaps I'd gone mad, because he couldn't really be here. Not in *this* world. Squeezing my eyes shut, I willed myself to wake.

"You are not asleep, Beloved."

I opened my eyes. He stood so close that I jumped backward.

"Do you fear me?" he asked. "But I have not harmed you."

"You startled me, my lord."

He'd done more than startle me. He blended into the night, with nothing but the faint glow of red eyes to give him away. That and the rapidly rising temperature in the room.

Belatedly, I bowed. "I didn't know you could—"

"You thought I was confined to your dreams?" He gave a snort of derisive laughter.

In wakefulness, Dafaru's presence was far more overpowering than the Dafaru of dreams. In wakefulness, he was more real, more menacing, altogether more terrifying. And that damnable heat rising from his body left me short of breath. I backed farther away.

He advanced. "Is that your wish? That I remain a construct of your sleeping mind?" He'd done away with the cloak and wore nothing but black trousers and the black leather bracers that blended with his ebony skin.

"What do you want from me?" I asked, though Zariya's visions had told me precisely what he wanted: love and loyalty. And, if the foretelling at my naming ceremony came to be, the deaths of thousands of my own people. All in the name of War.

"Only to look upon your beauty," he said.

I took another step back, and another, trying to maintain my composure. But tentative words trembled on my lips. "There are other women. More beautiful. Women who would die for your attentions." I backed into the wall.

He paused, a wistful thought curving the corners of his mouth. "Priestesses of the old magicks. Yes." The thought didn't hold him long; he resumed the advance. "They *are* beautiful and, as you say, would gladly die for my attentions." He halted again and considered. "Did you mean that as a figure of speech?"

They would *literally* die for him?

He started forward again. "It is of no consequence, Beloved. I do not want them. I have never wanted them." Reaching me, he caged me in with an arm to either side, his palms pressed against the wall. He moved closer, until the only thing between his chest and mine was the short, sleeveless shift I'd worn to bed.

"My lord, I—"

"I have waited longer than you could fathom," he said. "*My* dreams are of you. I dream of your touch." He trailed his fingers down my arms, and my skin tingled where his hands met bare flesh. "The scent of your neck." He bent and nuzzled the space between my ear and my neckline. "The taste of your mouth." His lips brushed against mine.

With several deep breaths, I urged my racing heart to slow, urged my mind to turn from the sensual feel of his lips against my skin. This was the god of destruction. Blood, pain, and suffering were his daily bread. I wanted no part of it. I wanted no part of *him*. Tens of thousands dead, Zariya had said. I'd do what it took to prevent such a future from coming to pass.

I said, "I belong to another."

His eyes glowed deep red, his cocksure expression faltering, but only for a moment. "You are refusing me?" The glow dimmed further. "In favor of a mortal man?"

Bolstered by this brief display of uncertainty, I nodded. "I've chosen. Yes."

The Mallamai—learned men of Zazzau and beyond—had said I must make a conscious decision, and I had. No foretelling would manifest unless I *chose* War. This was what the Mallamai had said and what I relied on now.

Moments of silence passed in which red embers studied me. "What does a mortal man offer that I cannot give?" He asked the question with calm curiosity, as though no logical answer could exist.

"He gives only himself, my lord."

His eyes dimmed even more, to a red that looked black in the darkness, and he continued to study me. Abruptly, he drew back and the room cooled like a bonfire doused. I shivered at the empty cold left in the wake of his body.

"You are mine, woman." His voice grated like stones against my heart. "No one else may claim you." He slipped into the shadows as insipidly as he had arrived.

Exhaling slowly to steady my flailing nerves, I sank to the ground, whispering, "Ubangiji Allah. Help me."

TEN

City of Turunku, Kingdom of Zazzau, Central Hausaland, circa 1563 CE

The wargod came every year before the first new moon. If I happened to be alone, he would intrude upon me in this world. If anyone was with me, he would invade my dreams. Each visit left me more shaken than the last. In his presence, I felt a sharp stab of need, which terrified me. He was, compared to ordinary men, what a stallion was to a goat. Whenever he came near, my body behaved as though it belonged to someone else. I couldn't control my stuttering heart or ignore the itch of longing at his touch.

I despised him for it.

It had been five years since the transition to the new capital, and five times I'd rejected the god of war. But what were five years to an immortal? A single breath?

The New Year was fast approaching. Its arrival would herald another visit from the deity. Already, I felt the stirring of anticipation, the vulgar tingle of desire that surged up my spine at the thought of his searing touch.

"Your mind is elsewhere, love." Suleyman slid his hand off mine.

Shutting down the memory of Dafaru's burnished-metal taste, I said, "I apologize. I was thinking."

"Of what?" The remnants of our supper were spread between us. He poured himself some wine and reached across the table to fill my earthen cup.

"Nothing."

Head cocked, he eyed me. "You were thinking of *nothing*?"

"Nothing of consequence. Merely wondering how long you'll be gone this time."

"This time?" He huffed and looked up when Fatima entered through the open door.

She had grown into an attractive young woman of sixteen. Her short hair shone midnight black against rich brown skin. Her large eyes gave her a look of innocence, though I knew she was hardly that—more than once, I'd seen her exiting one of the courtier's houses early in the morning. She had a slender figure with small breasts and a shockingly large backside. Suleyman watched her, always careful not to show his temper when she was near. He still thought of her as a child. Little did he know. Humming cheerfully to herself, she packed up the used earthenware, gave him a wide grin—which she generously shared with me—and left.

His attention mine again, Suleyman spoke. "I told you—"

"I know what you told me."

He threw a nasty look across the table. "Don't interrupt me." After several breaths, he continued, "Three days. I told you that. Just long enough to go and come. Then I'll be back."

"Then you'll go to Kufena."

"My house is in Kufena."

"You have a house here."

"My children are in Kufena."

"You have a child *here*." I gestured at the now closed door.

He chuckled.

Suleyman doted on my slave as though she were his own blood and often took her to Kufena to see her mother. Not too long ago, she had spilled an entire gourd of palm wine on my diwan, and he had scolded me for scolding her. Then he had replaced the ruined diwan with another. If Fatima were not a responsible girl by nature, he would have spoiled her to the core.

"Your harem sees more of you than I do," I muttered.

He fixed black eyes on me. "Is that what's upsetting you?" When I gave no response, he disregarded my comment. "Kufena is less than a half day's ride from you."

My hand dropped to the table, slamming the earthen cup against wood. His brow rose.

"Half a day's ride, Suleyman, is not close enough. Why can't you reside in your Turunku house?"

"What difference would it make if I stay in Kufena or Turunku? Short of marriage, we're as close as I can manage."

I groaned.

"You demand the comforts of a husband, but you refuse to be a wife. Do you think I'm interested in your kingdom? Keep it. I have enough to busy me."

Possession of Zazzau wasn't a concern, not when the scars on his body showed what Suleyman would sacrifice to protect our people. But, in marrying him, I would lose ownership of myself. It was giving up possession of *Amina* that did not sit well with me. Even without the bonds of marriage, Suleyman demonstrated a control over me that no one else could claim. Perhaps the self-ownership to which I clung had already been stripped from my grasp.

Then there was Dafaru.

If Suleyman knew of the wargod's visits, would he want me then?

I said, "You've gone this long without, why do you want a wife now?"

He shrugged. "Why does any man want a wife?"

"Children. You have them in abundance."

All boys, his five children ranged in age from eight to twenty-one.

His expression softened, and he put his hand back on top of mine. "Companionship, Amina."

"How can I be a companion to a man who's never here?" The accusation was more aggressive than I'd intended.

Frustration passed like a shadow over his face before he sighed and squeezed my hand. "Well, love. If you marry me, you'll be in my house on the occasions that I return. There's no impropriety there. Surely you would see more of me than you do now?"

Married or not, the affairs of state would keep me in Turunku. With him so committed to the household in Kufena, we would hardly be better off than we already were. *And there's Dafaru.* How long could I keep the wargod at bay?

Wrinkling my brow, I shook my head.

"Very well." He finished his wine, pushed back the ivory-legged stool, rose, and drew me to my feet. "I'll be back in three days."

"You're not staying tonight?" Irritation flooded my voice.

"No." He gave me a chaste kiss on the forehead, turned, and walked out the door.

Seething, I refilled my cup and drank. I downed a third cup and picked up the gourd, swirling the liquid around. *To hell with him.* Lifting the gourd to my lips, I drank what was left.

The fermented sediment was stronger at the bottom. It coursed through me with the usual speed but didn't dull my anger. I found myself cursing aloud as I paced back and forth. I even threw something across the room. A small brass figurine that Suleyman had brought from one of his many travels. The man spent more time on diplomatic missions than he spent soldiering. And he expected me to marry *him*? Stuffy in the head, I tossed myself onto the diwan and eventually fell asleep in a drunken haze.

I woke the next morning with a raging headache.

Groaning, I lay still, trying to muster enough willpower to get up. Achieving a sitting position took more than one attempt, and before I could rise off the chair entirely, a strong wave of nausea knocked me back down.

Careful not to further aggravate head or stomach, I eased myself off the diwan, sliding gently to the ground. My head pounded in angry protest and my stomach churned. Queasiness rushed upward. I clapped a hand over my mouth, retching as I dragged myself to my feet and out the door just in time to eject the bilious contents of my stomach.

That was how Fatima found me. On hands and knees, heaving at the door to my abode.

"Gimbiya?" Panicked, she dropped the basin of water she'd been carrying.

"I'm fine," I said, gruffly. "Too much wine last night."

Her panic transformed to disapproval—she had learned the palace airs well. Pressing her lips together, she allowed her eyes to do the admonishing while she looped an arm around my waist and helped me to my feet. She wrinkled her nose when I spat out the foul taste in my mouth.

The nausea subsided. "I'm going to bathe." A flash of dizziness struck when I pried her arm from my waist, but I remained upright. "I can manage."

She stepped back, mouth puckered into a frown. "I'll bring your wrapper and soap."

Nodding acknowledgment, I made my way to the bathing area.

❋

After washing, I returned to my hut. Both the queasiness and the mess outside my door were gone, but the headache sapped my strength. Rather than dressing, I sprawled face down onto the diwan, wrapper tied at my waist.

Fatima arrived with a breakfast that didn't look at all appetizing. Chunks of honeyed meat, goat cheese, sorghum bread—the usual fare. The mere thought of putting it in my mouth threatened to set my stomach off. I waved the food away and spent much of the day vowing never to drink again.

By the next morning, my headache had lost its tenacity. I sat up on the diwan just as Fatima pushed the door open with her gratuitous posterior. She entered and placed the breakfast tray on the table. As the aromas from the tray rose to my nose, heat began to bubble in my stomach, and I clenched my teeth. Fatima did not immediately leave but stood watching me. So I nibbled the bread and took a sip of the milk.

"Leave the milk and go," I said, willing my stomach to behave.

Suleyman's allegiance to her made Fatima overly bold. She leveled her disapproving eyes on me. "You must eat."

I wrinkled my nose but hadn't the energy to quarrel with a sixteen-year-old. The sooner I filled my belly, the sooner she would leave me in peace. Since the bread looked least formidable, I ate it. Grinning her approval, Fatima left.

After I finished the milk, I tried setting about my morning routine, but a wave of nausea swept over me as soon as I got to my feet. I barely made it out the door and to the latrine before spewing the entire meal. Through the noise of my violent vomiting, I heard running feet.

"Gimbiya!" Fatima's voice evinced none of the muted disapproval of the day before. "What's the matter?"

"Go and find Jaruma," I said in a strained voice before vomiting again.

She obeyed.

The smell of the pit-latrine worsened the nausea. My stomach twisted and screamed, fire burning in my tortured gut. With great effort of will, I gathered myself, spat and spat and spat, then shambled to my room to drop onto the diwan. When Jaruma arrived, I lay on my back with an arm over my eyes, wrapper again tied at my waist.

In a sardonic tone, she asked, "What is it, Your Magnificence? Do you not have slaves to cater to your every need?"

I peeked through the bend in my elbow. "You're supposed to be my guard, karya." But I hadn't the drive to insult her further.

"What's the matter with you?"

"Ill."

She raised an eyebrow. "I can see that, Gimbiya. What ails you?"

"I don't know."

I was hot, short of breath, and felt as though I was being squeezed on all sides. She sat on the edge of the diwan while Fatima stood in the doorway, wringing her hands in worry.

"Bring cold water and a cloth," Jaruma said, and Fatima scurried away. She put the back of her cool hand against my forehead. "You're sweating. You should go and see the medicine man."

"No."

"Why are you always so stubborn?"

"Why do you always question me?"

She scowled. "You're the one who called me. What did you expect me to do?" After a long pause, she asked, "Besides the vomiting, what else?"

"Yesterday, my head was beating like a drum."

"Yesterday, you drank a gourd of palm wine."

She glanced up as Fatima, who had obviously told of my overindulgent night, returned. Fatima handed the cloth to Jaruma and set the basin of water on the ground.

"I vomit every time I move, Jaruma. I can't breathe. Even the smell of roasting yam in the cookhouse is making me ill."

Jaruma dipped the rag in water, wrung it out, and ran the wet cloth along my forehead. "No other aches? Pain? Anywhere? Your breasts?" She scrutinized my bare chest.

"What type of question is that?"

Her black eyes met mine in silent inquisition.

"They're always painful before my monthly," I muttered.

"So it's yet to come?"

"It . . ." I paused. The damned thing was late. "I . . ." Slow realization took root.

"Well?"

"Well what?" I snapped, trying to remember when I'd last experienced my monthly flow.

She made a dismissive gesture. "Perhaps no medicine man is required after all. I imagine the sickness will pass after some months."

I rose onto my elbows. "Fatima, get out." Back at Jaruma. "What?"

How could I be pregnant? I was careful in planning the times for my interludes with Suleyman. He never spilled into me during my fertile days. Wracking my brain, I realized my last cycle was more than a month ago. Probably closer to two months. My cycle was occasionally unpredictable, but we were always careful.

Jovially, she said, "It seems I'm to be an aunt yet again, again . . ." She repeated the word "again" three more times, counting off the numbers with her fingers. After five, she grinned.

I let out an agonized moan and fell back onto the diwan.
Pregnancy was as much a hindrance to me as was marriage. If not
worse.

"Jaruma, what should I do?" I moaned again.

"What do you want to do?"

Unlike my sister, who nurtured those around her, my mothering
instinct extended only as far as tolerance. I tolerated the palace
children, tolerated Fatima. Fatima called Suleyman "Baba," but she
had never called me "Mama." Or even "Auntie," as she did Jaruma.
Because I didn't know how to be either of those things. I was
awkward around Zariya's children, whose temper tantrums made me
think koboko wasn't so harsh a punishment after all. The part of a
woman that craved motherhood didn't exist in me. What sort of
mother could I possibly be?

I said, "I don't want a baby."

She gazed at me, a small frown creasing her brow. "You don't?"

"What would I do with a wailing infant?"

"What everyone else does with them."

"I don't see *you* rushing to fill your womb with brats."

She met the comment with silence.

After a while, she said, "I never wanted children. They interfere
so completely with everything. But I'm alone. I'd consider changing
places with you, if I had a man who loved me the way my brother
loves you." She pressed her lips together. Looking pained, she added,
"If you don't want it, go to Laraba; she'll remove it."

"The medicine man's wife?"

She could remove it? But how? Was she a witch? The talk of
"removing it" made me uneasy. Was it that simple to pull a child from
its mother's belly?

I pondered. "Maybe I'm not with child. Maybe I'm poisoned?"

She shrugged, looking more like her usual belligerent self, and
dipped the rag back into the basin. "You can wait and find out, but
soon you'll either be dead or you'll be fat with child." She dragged the
wet cloth over my neck and chest.

I wanted no children, and Suleyman certainly didn't need more. The decision seemed easy enough, but it wasn't. I needed time to think, but how much time did I have? The decision had to be now.

"Can you go to her for me?" I asked.

Jaruma frowned. "Amina . . ."

"Please, Jaruma."

The frown deepened.

"Please."

"No."

"I can't do this." Tears rose in my eyes. "I can't have this baby, and I can't go to Laraba myself. People talk. I don't want Suleyman to know."

She made a frustrated groaning noise in her throat.

Desperate, I clutched her hand and held it to my chest. "Please, Jaruma. I beg you."

"Do you think I want Suleyman to know that *I* went?" she argued. "And why can't you have the baby?"

Because I'm afraid, I wanted to admit but couldn't. Because my life wasn't fully my own. Because, if the future came to pass as the prophecies foretold, what would become of the child?

Because of the wargod.

Though he came only once a year, he was determined. His every touch sent prickles of desire racing through me. What if he didn't relent? Would my child then be subject to the wargod's whim?

I told her none of this. Instead, I said, "Please, Jaruma."

"It's enough, Gimbiya." Snatching her hand away, she dropped the rag into the water and got up. "That"—she pointed at my belly—"is my flesh and blood."

It was selfish of me to ask her, but I couldn't go myself. Aside from Suleyman finding out, there was my mother. Pregnancy was only to be expected, but "removing" it was another thing entirely. I didn't want Bakwa to find out. I didn't want *anyone* to find out.

My eyes continued to plead.

Finally, she said, "I'll go. Don't ask for anything else." She stalked out of the room.

✻

I was asleep. Asleep but not asleep. Wrapped in a blanket of emptiness, I floated. My diwan was a raft adrift on a great river. I stretched out as the waves lulled me into content relaxation. My right arm fell over the side of the diwan. My hand trailed through the water. But the water wasn't wet and there was no resistance. I touched something firm. *Curious.* I dug my fingers into it. Earth? I opened my eyes to see clouds floating overhead.

"You awaken, my lovely queen-to-be." Dafaru stood above me, wearing a smile that was as disarming as it was disconcerting. "And you have changed." He put a hand on my belly.

My stomach tightened. At the same time, my heart fluttered.

He was almost four months too soon for his yearly visit. I had not expected to see him before the rainy season reached its final drizzle. Angling my head to look at him, I noticed that I lay upon his altar.

He put out a hand to help me up. "You are not to be sacrificed yet."

A single glance at the proffered hand and I tried to rise without his help. He cocked an eyebrow as I swooned back onto the altar.

"Your condition makes you weak." He extended the hand again. This time, I took it. Long, powerful fingers curled around mine. He pulled me upright and stepped closer, putting an arm around my waist. Before I could protest, he lifted me off the altar.

"You go too far, Gimbiya." It was shocking to hear him speak so clearly while maintaining so broad a grin. "You choose the depredation of pregnancy over the attentions of War?"

I cringed. He always had a malicious look about him, no matter what expression he plastered onto his face.

"Then you're no longer interested?" I asked, my feet touching ground.

"There are *some* advantages to you being with child." His red eyes blazed across my chest, and he pulled me close.

"Stop it." My voice quivered.

"Your mouth protests, but your body does not object."

His strong, slow heartbeat reverberated through me like a quiet storm. The hand on my back grew as hot as sun-beaten stones. I tried to push him away, but he was like granite. Immovable. Anger welled inside me. At him and at myself. At myself because refusing him was more difficult than it should have been. Because saying no took every scrap of my will. Because I wanted to say yes.

Gathering up those last grains of willpower, I raised my chin. "Release me, Dafaru. I've already said I'll not have you." But my imperious tone had no effect.

"Your words are like the howling wind—meaningless. You are mine."

"I am not yours."

I tore free of him and, in a streak of daring, slapped him across the face. His eyes narrowed, but he did not otherwise react. Drawing yet more foolish courage, I drew back my arm to strike again. He seized my throat. My hand flew to the fingers around my neck as he jerked me forward, bringing my face to his. I had to rise onto my toes to keep from choking. Nose to nose, we stood, his turbulent eyes a swirl of dirty blood.

When he spoke, his voice was like the cold winds gusting from the mountaintops.

"You cease to amuse me, Amina."

He released me and I stumbled away.

My tone matched his. "I'll never be yours." *Not willingly*, I added to myself.

"Willingly or unwillingly makes no difference, Beloved."

Nausea subdued, I shrank back. *He can hear my thoughts.* My knees grew weak with the knowledge. I reached out a trembling arm to steady myself, remembered Dafaru was the only solid structure in the vicinity, and dropped the arm to my side. Disoriented, I closed my eyes. When I opened them, I was back in my room, lying on the diwan, and thoroughly shaken.

Even my most private thoughts were his to take.

ELEVEN

Jaruma returned late that evening. She scarcely dressed like a woman but did today, wearing a wrapper and a matching short blouse that displayed her well-defined midsection. A headwrap draped over her head to fall on either side threw her face into shadow

"Are you feeling better?" she asked.

"No." Compounded by my other condition, the wargod's visit had inspired a new dread in me. I sat up.

She held out a small package. "You must put it in your food. Should I call Fatima to bring you something to eat?"

I shook my head.

"Laraba said it will spoil after two days, so you should take it before then." She gave me a contemplative look. "*If* you decide to take it."

"I already told you I want no part of childrearing."

Her hand closed around the package, and she sat down beside me. "Suleyman will be back tomorrow. Wait until he comes."

"This is not Suleyman's concern. He has five children. He won't miss this one."

"Amina, it's his right."

"It's no one's right but my own."

Her face grew taut.

"This child will never see the light of day," I said and thought, *it will never feel the warmth of its mother's breast.* Regret jabbed me, but I pushed it aside and held out my hand. "Thank you."

She gripped the package more firmly. "Amina—"

"Thank you."

Sighing, she dropped the package into my hand.

"Now go." I waved a negligent hand toward the door. "I'm tired."

After a moment's hesitation, she rose from the diwan and bowed. "As you command, Gimbiya."

I didn't take the medicine that night. I left it on the table, intending to take it in the morning. But when morning came, after nearly an hour of vomiting, I was disinclined to put anything in my mouth. Sick to my stomach, I avoided food—and the people who prepared it—until evening, when I managed some soaked cassava. Not much of a dinner, but my stomach didn't churn from it. Perhaps because soaked cassava was utterly tasteless.

The packet of medicine still sat on the table. I picked it up to examine it more closely. It was wrapped in a fragment of banana leaf and tied with a sliver of same. I turned it over in my hand. Such a small package for so great a decision. Careful not to spill its contents, I unwrapped it.

The yellowish paste crumbled when I rolled a small amount between my fingers. It had no smell, but my gut protested. I thought of the life growing inside me and wondered whether "removing it" would be painful. For the child, for me, or for both? The regret that had nagged me the night before returned to pierce my heart.

Some considered it a blessing, this miracle of life. A blessing from the highest God. Yet, I was tossing it back. Would the Creator forgive me for that? Would there still be guilt on my soul when I reached the Crossroads? I wanted to scream my frustration because there was no easy answer.

"Amina."

Startled from my ponderings, I looked up. Suleyman stood in the open doorway. So engrossed in thought, I'd not noticed the creak of the door when he pushed it open.

"You've returned." I quickly rewrapped the packet and dropped it onto the table.

"I told you three days." The door shut gently behind him as he entered the room.

"When did you arrive?"

"This morning. A little earlier than expected."

He crossed the room in several long strides. His face and head were scraped smooth. Wearing a plain white kaftan, he looked as though he had just washed. The smell of sweet tobacco reached me when he sank onto the diwan.

He took my hand and brushed his lips against my fingertips. "I heard you were ill, but you seem the picture of health." He spied the packet. "What's that?"

I hesitated. "Medicine."

"What ails you?" He furrowed his brow.

I leaned in and kissed his chin. "Tell me, love. How was your journey?"

"It was uneventful. Now you tell me. What ails you?"

From the suspicious look he leveled on me, I thought he already knew. Still, I was tempted to make up some benign ailment and put an end to the interrogation.

"I'm with child."

Disbelief registered on his face, and he regarded me for several drawn out seconds. Slowly, his eyes dropped to my waistline. He stared as if hoping to see some verification of what I had told him. The scrutiny, as always, left me feeling self-conscious.

He raised his eyes back to mine. "Is this by choice?"

What sort of response was that? I had expected happiness or anger or anything other than this taciturn reaction. Scrutinizing him as intensely as he had done me, I tried to gauge his emotions. Aside from the lingering incredulity, his eyes revealed nothing of his feelings.

I said, "If it were by choice, would it be a bad thing?"

"It's neither bad nor good," he replied. "Only surprising. I was unaware that children were on your agenda."

I shook my head. "It wasn't by choice."

"I see." He glanced again at the packet on the table and fell silent.

When the silence became unbearable, I said, "Say something, Suleyman."

He let out a breath. "Say what?"

"What do you want me to do?" I could not trust myself to make the right decision.

Irritation darkened his eyes but was quickly gone, his expression again unreadable. He glanced once more at the package on the table. "What do you think I want you to do?"

I studied his face again. Searched it for anger, disappointment, any outward sign of what he felt. Some hint at what he wanted.

His stony features cracked. Leaning close, he put a hand on my belly. "I want you to give me a girl."

I didn't know I was holding my breath until it came out in a loud sigh. The guilt, which previously had been a mere nudge, exploded into something harder to ignore. Suddenly, I was crying. It was pathetic really. I couldn't tell if Suleyman was appalled or bewildered.

"Or it can be a boy," he said quickly. "I'll be pleased either way."

Between sniffles, I said, "I was . . . going to . . . to . . ." I gestured at the packet on the table.

His eyes darted to it and back to me. He clenched his jaw.

"I'm sorry." I hung my head. "I didn't know what to do." My face was hot with shame and tears.

Cool fingers wiped the tears away. "You could marry me."

Lone women bearing children outside of marriage were not that uncommon. I could easily have had the child and left it in Zariya's care. Or Karama's—both his wives had children. Or even left it with Suleyman. Either the emotions of pregnancy had driven me mad or his persistent proposals had worn me down, because, in that moment, marriage seemed a fitting resolution to a worrisome state of affairs.

I raised my head. "I could try that. Yes."

"Are you agreeing to marriage?" The hopeful look on his face was endearing.

Smiling, I nodded. "Yes, love."

The rarest smile beamed from his face. "Then I'll bring the offer to your mother." Caressing my cheek, he added, "All that I own shall be yours." His pleasure swirled around him like a sweet breeze, but he maintained a steady outward demeanor. The only indication of his joy was the wild grin affixed to his habitually rigid face. He embraced me, kissed my temple, and stood. "Rest. I'll return in the morning."

I felt the tension slide off me like dewdrops from a blade of grass.

※

The next day began with more vomiting, but I pulled myself together and arrived at my mother's court as she stepped into the pavilion with Karama at her side. I followed on her heels, entering to a chorus of cries.

"*Ranka ya dade!*"

"May the gods shower down blessings upon you!"

"May Great Ubangiji preserve you!"

"Treachery to the south, My Queen!"

Halting midpace, I looked around the now silent pavilion. A man came forward. Despite the deep reds and yellows of his flowing robes and trousers, the man looked dingy, as though he had traveled a great distance through the desert with nothing but the clothes on his back. He bowed low and waited for us to take our seats.

"Great Bakwa Turunku, ruler of these fair lands," the man said. "There is a blight to our south."

"What blight?" Bakwa asked. "We are at peace with our neighbors."

He spoke in an urgent, agitated tone. "Our 'neighbors' waylaid my caravan and stole my wares. There is no safe passage to the south."

My mother studied the man. As did I. He wouldn't be the first merchant to go mad after a long and unprofitable journey. Nor would he be the first merchant to claim banditry to conceal his own shortcomings in the business of moneymaking.

"The word of a single man cannot be counted as reliable information." She swept her gaze across the pavilion. "Is there no one here who can confirm this man's accusation?"

Another man pushed through the silent crowd. It was Mallam Bello, a successful merchant who traded in goods from as far south as Edoland to the northernmost reaches of Fezzan. He was a man well known to my mother and a more reliable a source of information than most.

"Ranka ya dade, Your Excellency," he said with a small bow.

"And may your own life be long," Bakwa answered.

"It's true what Mallam Asma'u"—he indicated the other man—"says. I too lost merchandise on the return from the south. I also lost several good men when my caravan was ambushed. Perhaps I'd be lying dead on foreign soil had I been with them."

A significant murmur rose in the crowd, and Bakwa's face took on a much more troubled appearance. "When did news of this ambush come to you?"

"Only this morning."

"And you?" she asked of Mallam Asma'u. "When were you ambushed?"

"A day or two before Mallam Bello's caravan met the same fate. My caravan took heavier losses—most of my men and all my goods. What remained of Mallam Bello's caravan met us on the way. We arrived in Turunku together this morning."

Silent rage boiled in my mother's eyes, though her face remained placid. Keeping her voice steady, she asked, "Where is Kaura Dongo?"

"I am here." Suleyman appeared amidst a group of officers. He strode over and stood before my mother.

"You will take a convoy to the south and find the source of this blight. Any southern king who refuses safe passage for the traders of Zazzau will explain his actions."

He bowed. "As you command, Great Bakwa." Dismissed, he cast me a furtive glance—bride-price would have to wait—to which I responded with a slight nod. He retreated, followed by his officers.

It would take a month to contact all of our allies in the south, two months at the outside. The time apart from Suleyman would give me time to think things through more completely, because I must not have been thinking clearly the day before when I had accepted the marriage proposal.

Or perhaps I wasn't thinking clearly now. There was far too much confusion in the air. Not to mention the various emotions feuding inside me. Contemplating a future as Suleyman's wife, I chewed my lower lip and grasped the armrest of my chair.

Bakwa took a steadying breath, but anger still flickered in her gaze. She regarded the faces around her. The court kept silent, each citizen awaiting the monarch's next words, each citizen tensely assessing Bakwa's mood. The new Makama, however, was watching me. The old makama had passed away, leaving the once idle young man, Siddhi dan Musa in his place. He didn't even have the decency to avert his eyes when I caught him staring.

Trade routes—east, west, north, or south—tended to be dangerous. For this reason, trading caravans were heavily armed. Both Mallam Bello and Mallam Asma'u were veteran traders, born into families of traders. They were each wealthy enough to hire the most skilled men-at-arms. Perhaps even Kuturun Mahayi. It made no sense that bandits would attack such well-defended caravans.

But what if the attackers weren't bandits? What if they were trained military men? If that was the case, were these random attacks or were they somehow coordinated? But for what purpose? To disrupt Zazzau's trade? If the attacks were neither random nor the work of bandits, Suleyman's mission was anything but routine.

I grew hot and wanted to sit but could not while Bakwa remained standing. Several deep breaths quelled some of the nausea building with the dread in my belly. Once again, the emotions of pregnancy were clouding my thoughts, raising my anxiety. Suleyman and his soldiers could handle any "blight" from the south. They would resolve this quickly. Two months at most.

"Has no one brought news of a less distressing nature?" Bakwa asked.

There were some mutterings, but apparently no news that was good enough to offset the troubling information Mallam Asma'u had brought. Nobody came forward.

"Very well, then." Her disappointment manifested as a frown, and she lowered herself onto the mahogany throne. "Let us continue."

❋

At the conclusion of the morning's business, I made my way from the pavilion. The new makama approached me. Siddhi had generally shown no interest in State affairs, which made him an unexpected choice for the position. And most statesmen were considerably older than twenty-nine. From the courtly rumors floating about the palace, he'd been hand chosen to take up the mantle by the old makama. That didn't explain why no one had challenged the selection; many a non-successor was chosen by the previous titleholder. Of course, most weren't as wealthy as Siddhi. I wondered whom he had bribed to gain the title uncontested.

"Greetings, Gimbiya." He bowed. "Your radiance shines brighter each day."

As much as I wanted to ignore him, his charm edged stealthily past my defenses. I smiled. "Your flattery leaves one headier with each word, Makama." Then I chided myself for flirting with him. Was I flirting? I had never flirted with anyone before. No. We were simply exchanging niceties.

"It is a lovely day for riding, Gimbiya," he said at last. "Do you ride?"

I made no reply.

"Yes, it's a silly question," he admitted. A fine-featured man, Siddhi had slender fingers that always seemed to be doing something. Right now, they were scratching his earlobe. "You're cavalry trained, after all."

We walked in silence for a few paces before he spoke again. "I would like to take you riding."

I regarded him: his fair skin, narrow face, the tapered nose, thin lips. In total, these features gave him a somewhat effeminate look. He was a pretty man.

I said, "Riding is a pastime for you?"

"It's a pastime for many people, Gimbiya."

"For the *bature*, perhaps."

"Ah yes. But the bature certainly enjoy their pastimes, don't they?"

"They have more time for frivolity than I do," I said of the Arab traders who, after concluding their business for the season frolicked with the locals. "I'm busy."

He cast his eyes downward with an expression so heartbroken that I almost believed it. *Would have* believed it, had he not then looked up and grinned. "Then allow me to escort you to wherever you wish to go." He took me by the elbow.

Surprised by his touch, I stammered, "I—I wish only to return to my room."

"Then I shall escort you to your door."

I yanked my arm away.

"Only to your door, Gimbiya."

I considered. What harm in allowing him to escort me to my quarters? It wasn't as though the location of my abode was a secret.

"I envy any man who is allowed *through* your door," he said as we walked by the row of administrative buildings. "I especially envy the kaura."

There's the harm.

"Be careful what you covet," I said. "Kaura Dongo is not a tolerant man."

"So I've noticed." He slipped an arm around my waist, evidently harboring a death wish.

I unhooked his arm from around me. "Surely you've gone through the doors of many noblewomen?" The gossips claimed that he had affairs with the wives of some of our most prominent citizens.

"Never a door as beautifully constructed as yours."

Heat spread from my neck to my ears and slowly burned into my cheeks. "More flattery? Do you wish to intoxicate me?"

He laughed. "I daresay it's you who intoxicates."

Siddhi was not a soldier, so he had no true notion of peril. But he would learn soon enough if Suleyman caught wind of this foolhardy attempt to seduce me. *Was* he trying to seduce me? Whatever the case, Suleyman was as dangerous as he was intolerant. Still, when we reached my door and Siddhi faced me, Suleyman's potential wrath wasn't enough to keep me from reeling at Siddhi's dazzling smile. He was strikingly handsome.

He started to speak, but just as he opened his mouth, Jaruma sauntered into sight.

"Thank you for escorting me." I tried not to look like a child caught pulling the head off a chicken.

"I'm honored to have escorted you." He bowed slightly then turned his dazzling smile on Jaruma.

She gazed coolly at him.

A soft chuckle and Siddhi went on his way.

"Has Suleyman gone?" I asked nonchalantly and entered my room.

She entered behind me. "Yes. And count yourself fortunate that he wasn't here to see that."

I turned to meet one of her most penetrating stares.

The damned woman was right, no matter how innocent the exchange between me and Siddhi—and it wasn't entirely innocent. For the time being, it was best to stay away from the makama and his words that flowed like silk over my body.

Jaruma raised a brow as though awaiting some sordid confession. After a few unproductive moments, she delivered the message that had brought her to me in the first place. "My brother said he would do it on his return."

I nodded.

"Do what?" she asked. "He refused to tell."

"If he wouldn't tell, then why should I?"

"You're both keeping secrets, are you?"

"Speaking of secrets . . ." I eyed her. "Who told Suleyman I was ill?"

She tilted her head to one side, her face a paragon of innocence. "Were you ill, Gimbiya? I was not aware."

"I should take you outside and thrash you."

"Are you trying to pick a fight with me?" She laughed. "Now? When you're in no condition to take a beating? No more sparring for you, Your Magnificence."

"Get out."

With that wicked laughter rolling from her throat, she slipped out the door.

TWELVE

My uncle woke me with news that didn't take root in my mind. Suleyman had been gone a full month, and this was the first information we'd received from the convoy. I lay on the diwan, Karama seated on the low table before me, and stared unfocused at the space above his ear. Quiet words that I couldn't acknowledge fell from his mouth.

"Tell me again," I said.

"Amina."

"Again."

Resigned, he imparted the information a second time. "They traveled south without event. Until they reached Nupe territory and were forced to await an escort from Nupeland."

Karama's face was strained. He didn't want to repeat himself, but I regarded him steadily, my hand rubbing a small cramp that had formed in my belly.

Sighing, he continued, "Around twenty men made up the Nupe escort. They demanded tribute to ensure safe passage through Nupe demesnes. Your man refused."

As he should have. Zazzau was a sovereign state and paid tribute to no one.

Karama's flat tones grew quieter, his words more hesitant. "They . . . um . . . insulted your mother."

"What did he say?"

"In the name of heaven, Amina."

"What did he say?" I asked calmly.

My uncle gave another sigh. "He said Zazzau is ruled from a woman's gash."

"The man is a bastard," I said. When Karama remained silent, I prompted him onward. "What then, Uncle?"

"The kaura warned the Nupemen. He told them we don't desire war but will defend our position if need be."

The Nupemen had responded with more insults.

"They said only the most feckless of men allow a woman to rule over them." My uncle tilted his head upward, his gaze rising to the ceiling before falling on me. "They gave no warning, Amina, before the arrow flew." He began kneading his temple with the base of his palm. "Our people fought and sent the Nupe scurrying."

Of course they did. Eleven of Zazzau's finest warriors were in that convoy. Those eleven were more than a match for a mere twenty Nupemen.

My uncle dropped his hand from his temple and took mine in both of his. "They say he called your name."

He exhaled as though the telling had exhausted him.

I sat up, pulling my hands away. "You are mistaken, Uncle."

The story made even less sense the second time around. Karama was trying to tell me that Suleyman was dead. But Suleyman could not have died. Not like that. I glared defiantly at my uncle. "You are mistaken."

"Amina," he began in a regretful tone.

"It's not true."

How many times had Suleyman been wounded in battle and survived? Never, *not ever*, would he succumb to such an ignoble death. Death in battle was what a warrior craved. But to be cut down by unknown, *unseen* enemies? Slaughtered like a rabbit in the bush? It wasn't true. Suleyman was a warrior. The best of the best. He was kaura.

"I'm sorry, Amina," Karama said softly.

"You are mistaken, Uncle." I jumped to my feet. "Where are these fools who say the kaura is dead?" My voice rose in pitch. "Where are they?" I began moving toward the door.

Karama got to his feet. Before he could grab me, I darted outside. With my uncle on my heels, I ran past the administrative row and into the courtyard, where a small crowd had gathered, their attention focused on the ground. One by one, they looked at me. Tears glistened in Fatima's eyes. Her expression wrenched my heart, but I ignored it and strode into the parting crowd.

Until they made way, I'd not seen Jaruma. But there she knelt. A body—undeniably a body—wrapped in a white shroud, lay on the ground before her. Karama reached me, tried to pull me into his embrace. I broke free of him.

I stopped and stood, staring at the figure on the ground, as my head grew faint.

"It isn't true," I whispered.

It wasn't possible. Suleyman was stronger than any mere assassin. Jaruma looked up, eyes filled with tears. My body grew numb. Absently, my hand went to my belly, covering it, shielding the child from the reality now sinking into my core.

Suleyman is dead.

I would never again look into the light of his eyes or hear the rumble of his laughter. His arms would never again hold me, his lips never touch mine.

He was gone.

And my world fell to pieces. Grief surged outward like a monster ripping through my soul. Dropping to my knees, I let out a strangled cry.

Wailing uncontrollably, I rent my clothes, my hair, and flung myself onto Suleyman's lifeless form. Jaruma was speaking, but I couldn't understand the words. Her body wrapped around me. Convulsing with sobs, she tried to pull me away. A stronger set of arms surrounded me, lifting me off the ground. Kicking, screaming, and clawing at everything in my way, I struggled. Through the chaos, I heard my mother's voice but didn't care. I heard Karama's voice, Jaruma's, my own wild and frenzied screams. Still, I struggled.

Then pain wrenched my abdomen, twisted it into a knot. A loud, guttural cry tore from my lips, cramps slicing through me, searing my body. Clutching my belly, I doubled over and vomited. The ground tilted toward me. The voices were far away now. All but one. One voice, close to my ear, moaned in agony. An abject sound that I realized was coming from me.

"Mama," I heard myself say as I curled into a ball and fought off an obscene urge to move my bowels.

Something warm trickled from inside me. It dampened my thigh. The buzzing voices converged into a solid mass of noise pounding at my temples. I clenched my eyes shut, but tears streamed past them. Someone lifted me off the ground. In my mind, I was screaming, but only piteous moaning came from my mouth as excruciating pain plunged me into darkness.

❀

I awoke, head groggy and thoughts a jumbled mess. Jaruma and Fatima stood at my feet. My mother knelt on the ground beside my bed, head bowed, my hand clutched in both of hers. When I tried to sit up, a lance of pain shot through my midsection.

Bakwa glanced up. "Thank the Creator!" She got off her knees and sat on the bed, sliding another cushion under my head. "Leave us."

The others obeyed.

"Suleyman." His name crackled from my dry throat.

Bakwa brought a tin cup to my mouth.

Shaking my head, I waved it away. "Suleyman?" I said frantically, feeling the tears before they reached my eyes.

She put the cup on the table. "My daughter, he is—"

As the tears began to pour, she gathered me into her arms.

"My baby?" I asked, though I could feel the emptiness in the pit of my stomach.

"There was so much blood."

"My baby?" I repeated weakly. Were I not already lying down, I would have collapsed. Fighting to keep hysteria at bay, I clung tightly to her.

The gods were punishing me. I had not cherished the child. Not at first. But in the weeks following Suleyman's departure for southern lands, I had dreamed of holding it, longed for the day of its birth. The child was all that was left of Suleyman. Why did the gods take even that from me?

"He was bringing a bride-price." My voice racked with quiet sobs.

Holding me to her bosom, she rocked from side to side and said in an anguished tone, "I didn't know. I didn't know you were with child. I didn't know."

"Mama." It felt as though my heart was dying.

"Cry, my daughter."

They were gone. Suleyman and the child. Just *gone*. And I would never get them back. Held in my mother's embrace, I cried.

❋

Several days passed before Suleyman's funeral. Along with Jaruma, I dressed him in funeral linen. The ceremony at his compound in Kufena, befitted a king. As with many such occasions, it was a blend of Muslim and native Hausa customs.

When the night-long wake keeping began, I took my place in the courtyard, seated beside the bier. Throughout the evening, I watched the dignitaries and soldiers pay their respects in a shameless display of opulence. Women dripped with the finest jewelry, their attire made of brilliant-colored brocades imported from the far north. The men were no less dazzling. Rings glittered on their fingers, gold hung from their necks, corals rattled around their wrists, cowries around their ankles.

I kept my vigil into the night, keeping my mind empty, lest my thoughts wander into misery. Thus, I watched the mother of Suleyman's elder children light the torches scattered about the compound and saw Fatima trying to ward off a preening peacock of a drunken man. I considered leaving my betrothed, so I could defend his favorite daughter, but Jaruma settled the issue quickly. She broke the man's finger before tossing him to Suleyman's guards.

The uwar soro finished lighting the torches and came to join her son standing over the bier. Even now, having her near Suleyman fueled my jealousy. I had not let her near his body before I shrouded him but could not send her away this time.

The younger Suleyman turned from the bier and faced me. He had his father's eyes. I wanted to look away before my tears started again, but he dropped to one knee before me and reached into the folds of his voluminous robe. When his hand reemerged, it held a package of indigo cloth.

"My father's war bracelets." He gave me the package.

My eyes slid to his mother, who was now facing me. With tears glistening on her cheeks, she bowed low, and I suddenly regretted excluding her from dressing the body. As she walked away, I took the offering from her son, my own tears falling silently onto the cloth. He rose and followed his mother.

After much of the food was gone, the Bori cult arrived in their silken indigo and white dress. They formed a circle around the bier and began to sing. They danced as they sang, twisting, spinning, and gyrating to the beating drums. They moved their bodies in a manner that must have offended the more devout Muslims among us, but the Bori never claimed to be Muslim. They danced their spirit dance and sang their spirit song deep into the night. They summoned the god of the Crossroads to guide my Suleyman from this world to the next, and their song swirled around me like night mist, tingling with the presence of the spirits.

With voice and body, the Bori called upon their patron gods. The pitch and tempo of the drums rose higher, deeper, louder, until the sounds were heavy thuds penetrating my soul. Bori voices grew wild with ululations that seemed impossible to have issued from human throats. Feet pounded the ground. Dancers' bodies jerked as they were possessed, *ridden* by the gods they summoned. I stared. Horrified. Because *my* patron god stood across the courtyard, the gold clasps of his black bracers reflecting the torchlight.

I felt my body rise from the chair, felt it begin to sway with the Bori dance. I heard the Bori song in my voice. Then Dafaru's presence filled me. He was inside me. His fire burned in my veins, and I danced the spirit dance. My own inhuman cries mingled with those around me. I danced and danced and danced. Until the first crowing of the cock. Then I collapsed back onto my chair with the taste of burnished metal on my tongue.

✳

After Suleyman's entombment, I remained sequestered in my room, bathing but little, eating only when Fatima forced it on me. I refused all visitors, even my mother and sister—though they both came regardless. Jaruma, whom I did not ban, didn't come to see me at all.

Days and days of mourning turned into weeks and weeks. Though I swore I could not live through the pain, the agony refused to kill me. I wished it would; I prayed to the gods whom I'd vowed never to beseech again, begged for release from this life that meant nothing without Suleyman.

A god eventually answered, though I doubted he was here to end my misery. Looking up from where I lay curled on the floor, I found the wargod sitting cross-legged on the ground. Sunlight, slanting through the window, bounced off his ebony skin.

In broad daylight?

I might as well have spoken aloud because he replied, "I am not confined to dreams, Beloved. Why would I be confined to darkness?"

"Because you are the god of darkness," I muttered and dragged myself to sitting.

"Come now, Amina. I am the god of war. Darkness is another entity altogether."

Rubbing eyes that had cried themselves dry many days ago, I said bitterly, "Wasn't he a good servant to you? How much blood did Suleyman spill in the name of War?"

"He will have his reward at the Crossroads."

"You took him from me." A single tear managed to trickle from my eye.

Dafaru said nothing for a while. Then he leaned forward and touched my face, brushing away the tear with his thumb. Placid red eyes looked into mine. "This is not my doing, Beloved. Death comes when it will."

The wargod sounded sincere. But Suleyman had stood between Dafaru and the thing he desired. Gods did not abide by the same rules as the rest of us.

I jerked my head away. "I am not your beloved."

He sat back, regarding me coolly. "I hoped you would leave your mortal lover of your own accord. Then I would not have to suffer these tiresome sentiments of yours. Come to me when the man is well behind you."

My anger flared. "I will never come to you."

The tranquil pool of colors in his eyes turned turbulent—more in keeping with his usual demeanor. "Every warrior has her day, Amina. You will come." He appraised me with a look that was difficult to describe. Disgust, perhaps, and pity? "If you come crawling on your belly, you *will* come."

With a loud cry of frustration, I grabbed the stool by one of its ivory legs and swung it at him. A bracered arm shattered the wooden seat and sent two legs hurtling across the room. In a movement so fast that it seemed he'd not moved at all, he seized my hair. Twisting in his grip, I attempted a second assault with what remained of the stool. He snatched the makeshift ivory weapon from me, tossed it aside, and pulled my hair to yank my head back. With his other hand, he cupped my chin and drew me to him.

"Look into my eyes," he said. "What do you see?"

The red swirls cleared like smoke blown on the wind. For the first time, I saw my reflection in his eyes. A moment later, the reflection faded and was replaced with another image. An image of him and me nude, our bodies twined around one another. And the woman in his eyes was clearly willing.

I scrambled away when he released me. "It will never be."

"It already is." He rose to his feet. After another appraising look, he turned and walked out the door.

※

Jaruma finally came to visit.

The low sun cast my room into shadow. She lit the oil lamp and turned its blaze to full. Resentment burned across her face as brightly as the light from the lamp. I sat on the diwan, hugging my knees to my chest.

"You dishonor my brother," she said. "And the memory of your child. *His* child. Have you seen yourself?" She gestured toward me. "You've grown haggard. My brother is dead, and you would send yourself to the grave with him. You would leave me alone to avenge him."

High-pitched laughter rose hysterically in my throat. "Avenge him? Avenge him how, Jaruma? Eh?"

The light flickered as her hand shook with anger. She placed the lamp on a stool.

"The men who killed my brother are drinking wine and bedding whores without a care while you do nothing!" She glanced at my tray of uneaten food. "Except starve yourself. If you want to end your life, do it with honor." She pulled her arm-knife from its sheath and held it out to me, hilt first. "Take it and cut out your useless heart."

Bemused, I stared at the knife in her hand. Then my own anger erupted, and I jumped to my feet. "You will not speak to me in that manner!" I snatched the knife, inadvertently slicing into her fingers, and brought the tip to rest under her chin.

"There's still fire in your heart, is there?" She watched me warily.

Blinking as though waking from a trance, I lowered the blade. "Jaruma, I—" What could I say? I dropped the knife and fell onto the diwan.

She sat down beside me.

"Jaruma—"

"Don't speak of it, Gimbiya."

"But I—"

"Please don't."

Under a blanket of silence, we sat. Until I heard a sniffle and turned my head. She was crying.

"I'm sorry." I slid my arm around her shoulders. In my misery, I'd forgotten that she too mourned, that she grieved for a brother whom she loved.

Blood seeped from her fingers onto her lap.

Gathering up the hem of my dress, I pressed the garment to the wound. "I'm sorry."

"Please, Gimbiya." She quieted her sobs and tried to keep her bleeding hand off my dress. "I was out of order."

I took hold of her wrist. "No, my friend. You were right. I've wallowed in misery long enough."

She sniffed and wiped her eyes on her sleeve before dropping her head onto my shoulder. I held her hand, my dress bunched up around her fingers.

"There is no vengeance to be had," I said. "Nupeland covers too much territory; its army is vast. There's nothing we can do." But those words, I knew, were not entirely true.

THIRTEEN

City of Turunku, Kingdom of Zazzau, Central Hausaland, circa 1564 CE

The harmattan winds tore across Zazzau like a troop of rampaging baboons. At the height of the dry season, the winds brought so much desert dust that it all but blotted out the sun. During this time, the entire savanna stood still. As such, many months passed without any word to, from, or about Nupeland.

This extended period of inactivity stoked my temper ever hotter. I reserved most of my foul attitude for the likes of Jaruma and Siddhi, who were unperturbed by whatever verbal abuse I heaped upon them. In Jaruma's case, her attitude was scarcely any better, but Siddhi was something else.

Despite my poor treatment of him, he remained lighthearted and cordial, often presenting me with expensive gifts procured from the Arab traders with whom he associated. He accompanied me to the Gani festivities of the New Year, and I was glad because it kept other potential suitors at bay. Suleyman had been gone less than six months, and already, the vultures were circling. Certainly, Siddhi also hoped to woo me, but aside from gifts, he made no overt attempts.

As the end of the dry season drew near and the harmattan haze finally began to clear, we received word from Nupeland: the emissary was on his way. A dust-covered but officious-looking messenger on horseback brought the communication from Tsoede, the Nupe king, himself. Though I might have liked to drive a stake through the messenger's throat, rules of hospitality dictated that we welcome him.

We began preparations for the emissary's coming.

❀

The emissary arrived with a cavalcade that rivaled my thousand-soldier convoy to Rizga. Mirroring my displeasure at his arrival, the harmattan gasped its dying breath, darkening the sky once more with desert sand. By nightfall on the following day, however, the winds had abated. I readied myself to meet the convoy from Nupeland.

Fatima had braided cowrie shells into my hair, so I eschewed any headwrap and put on a long dress of red brocade. The neck and bodice were embroidered with black thread, as were the cuffs of the long, loose sleeves.

Jaruma accompanied me to my mother's quarters, her hand on the pommel of her takouba. After the messenger's arrival, she had taken to wearing the straight-sword at all times—a none-too-subtle show of protest.

"This is absurd," she muttered as we made our way to Bakwa's private rooms. "Why must we dine with them?"

"You aren't dining with them," I said.

The compound bore testament to the season. Sahara dust coated everything. Green shrubs were dusty brown from crown to stem, except for the flowers, which displayed their brilliant colors in defiance of the dry season.

I lifted the hem of my dress to keep it from brushing the ground. "It's a formality. They'll pretend they knew nothing of the attack, then they will apologize for the misunderstanding that led to Suleyman's death."

"Misunderstanding?" Her hand tightened around the pommel. "They expect us to swallow that horse sh—"

"Good evening, Mama."

Eyes front, Jaruma swallowed her words and bowed. "Ranka ya dade."

Bakwa nodded her acknowledgment. "We do what we must, child. To maintain peace."

"Yes, My Queen."

Similarly dressed in brocade, my mother's thick, upswept braids gathered into a roll on the top of her head. A headdress of coral beads hung in layers across her smooth forehead.

"But they expect us to submit," Bakwa said. "We will not. And I will demand retribution against those who slew your brother."

Jaruma nodded.

"You may join us tonight." Bakwa studied Jaruma's face. "If you wish."

"No, My Queen. The men responsible for my brother's death are at your table."

Bakwa smiled. "You have his candor."

"My apologies. It's a family trait."

My mother's smile widened. She turned from Jaruma, looped an arm through mine, and we started for the pavilion. Jaruma came a few paces behind us. When we reached the administrative row, Jaruma's footfalls turned toward her quarters.

❀

"The Etsu Nupe, Tsoede, offers abject apologies for the misunderstanding with your convoy." The emissary dipped his hands into the water bowl.

He sat in a place of prestige on my mother's right. I sat on her left with Karama on my other side. Members of the royal council and the rest of the Nupe party sat in random order at the long table.

It had been difficult for me to dine with these people. The knot of rage tightening my stomach had spoiled my appetite. Throughout the evening, I'd done little more than nibble at the food. Dinner was over now, and the servants were clearing the water bowls from the table.

"Apologies do not return the life that was taken," Bakwa said. "If the Etsu Nupe wants to show his sincerity, let him send forth the man who murdered my representative."

"Alas," the emissary said, "we do not know who killed your kaura."

"If you call it a misunderstanding, then you must have some inkling of what led to the misunderstanding. Who, but the men involved, could have told you?"

Showing a good deal more teeth than should have fit into his mouth, the emissary smiled. "Indeed. However, the men who brought us the news didn't kill your kaura, who I hear was betrothed to your daughter." He leaned forward on his chair and looked past my mother to face me.

For the first time this evening, he addressed me directly. "My condolences, Gimbiya."

I didn't trust my mouth not to speak the hateful words in my head, so my only response was a stiff nod, which he returned with his toothy grin.

He said, "Tonight we humbly share your hospitality. Let's wait until morning to dwell on unpleasantness."

"Unpleasantness?" Anger broke my silence. "A man was *murdered* in this unpleasantness, as you call it."

"Forgive my poor choice of words." His dismissive tone wasn't asking forgiveness.

Karama covered my trembling hand with his. He twined our fingers and squeezed. The emissary was fortunate that I didn't carry an arm-knife like other trained warriors, else I might not have resisted the temptation to reach across my mother and plunged it into his smiling mouth.

I was not mastering my anger, but managed to speak calmly when I said, "The value of Suleyman's life will not be bartered down to nothing. Someone *will* pay."

Evidently rethinking his initial decision to speak to me, the emissary frowned. He reaffixed his disingenuous smile. "His name was Suleyman? I didn't know." Straightening, he aimed no more words in my direction.

I started to rise, not certain what I intended to do, but slapping the emissary wasn't outside the realm of possibilities. Karama held my hand firmly down.

He said, "My niece is tired. It's been a trying day. Go, child."

I set my face in haughty disobedience.

"Go," he repeated, quieter but sterner.

My mother nodded. "Go, my daughter."

Jaw clenched, I rose from my chair without a word, turned, and marched rudely from the table. A few moments later, Karama caught up with me. Recognizing both the rage and the sadness that still overwhelmed me, he said nothing and put an arm around my shoulders. In silence, he escorted me back to my room.

※

On the following day, the emissary and his comrades attended the morning's court, sitting proudly among the members of the royal council. My mother endeavored to ignore them. She took audience as usual and people gathered in the pavilion to speak with her. I, on the other hand, had suffered through dinner as a show of hospitality but saw no need to continue this farce with Nupeland. They were not here out of respect or condolence. They wanted only to subjugate Zazzau. I wouldn't sit still for that, and there was no need to wait until court was over. The people of Zazzau would hear what Nupeland planned for us.

Before the citizenry could begin voicing their myriad grievances against one another, I got up. Seated on my mother's other side, Karama gave a subtle shake of his head, which I thoroughly ignored.

I gestured at the seated Nupemen. "Representatives of Nupeland bring words of condolence from the Etsu Nupe himself." In the corner of my eye, I saw Karama shaking his head more vigorously. My mother's eyes widened then hardened, and I hesitated. But only for a moment.

"They regret they cannot produce the late kaura's killers or enact justice for his death," I said. "I fear that's not the only news the emissary brings." I cocked my head, gaze fixed on the Nupeman.

Smiling that toothy smile of his, the emissary rose. He bowed at my mother and said, "Great Bakwa, ruler of these fine lands, I had not intended to bring up this matter during your morning court. However, as your daughter has already broached the subject, I humbly ask that you grant me audience."

I glanced at my mother, who glowered at me.

Focusing on the emissary, she nodded. "Approach, Sir Emissary."

"Sit down." Karama addressed me through clenched teeth.

I returned to my chair.

The emissary approached. "As you are aware, Nupeland holds the trade routes to the south."

Bakwa said nothing but leveled a contemptuous look on him.

He appeared not to notice and continued speaking as though he were talking to a friend. "Of course, Zazzagawa traders can bypass Nupeland altogether and cut themselves a route through the treacherous jungle. Or you may try the river," he added jovially. "The Great Kwara will carry you straight to the sea. But as you well know, villagers on the riverbanks and even those living upon the river itself are a violent breed. The safest routes to the south cross the heart of Nupeland."

"We are well aware of the trade routes," Bakwa said.

"Yes. And you're also aware that your traders passed through Tsoede's lands by his sufferance only."

Bakwa narrowed her eyes.

"To ensure safe passage of your traders in the Nupe demesnes, Tsoede is prepared to accept Zazzau as a protectorate."

"What?" Bakwa said. But she wasn't truly surprised. As she had told Jaruma the night before, they wanted us to submit.

Zazzau was not a large nation. Kano in the north was almost twice our size, and Bornu in the far northeast was even larger than Kano. Our southern border was about ten days' hard ride from Tsoede's northern border. His nation was already massive. If he annexed Zazzau, those independent cities between our two lands would come to heel. Seizing Zazzau would make Nupeland the largest kingdom in the region.

The emissary continued, "In return for his assurance of safe passage, the Etsu Nupe requires tribute in the amount of one hundred slaves, fifty heads of cattle, and twenty horses."

A murmur rose.

"Annually," he finished.

The murmuring increased. With a gaze as hard as steel, Bakwa cast her eyes across the pavilion. Silence fell.

Her response was gracious. "I and the people of Zazzau thank His Majesty for the generous offer of protection. But what His Majesty requests in tribute is beyond Zazzau's resources."

The emissary let out a soft chuckle. "Great Bakwa, queen of these lands, you have resources enough and more. If you do not accept Tsoede's generosity now, he will not be inclined to extend such an offer in the future."

"To hell with his generosity." I said the words that should have remained unspoken.

The emissary glanced at me and returned his gaze to the queen. "Your daughter speaks too freely. You would do well to teach her restraint."

I bristled and noticed Bakwa doing the same.

"My daughter will inherit this throne when I'm gone," she said. "It is her right to speak freely."

The emissary revealed his brilliant teeth again and turned their radiance on me. "Last night, I meant to tell you that tales of your extraordinary beauty have reached us in Nupeland, and the tales do you no justice." He wrinkled his brow and allowed his eyes to travel the length of me before returning to my face. "I'm sure the Etsu Nupe would accept your hand in lieu of, perhaps, *ten* slaves."

My nostrils flared at the insult, and I leaned forward on my seat, wanting very much to knock those gleaming teeth out of his mouth. I should have held my tongue, but anger overpowered my good sense. "Your king can rot in the deepest of hells. Perhaps I'll have the pleasure of sending him there myself."

Murmurs of shock rose once again through the pavilion. The emissary's smile faltered but did not disappear. Beside me, my mother grew rigid.

Having repositioned the smile on his face, the emissary asked, "This is your final word on the matter?" He directed the question at my mother.

I clenched my teeth to keep from uttering more insults, innuendos, or outright threats. But the weight of what I'd already said settled heavily on the court.

Bakwa coughed quietly and gave a response that would have made the old makama proud. "It is highly irregular to make an offer of marriage without the customary gift giving. Surely Tsoede would propose a bride-price before I agree to such union?"

The emissary glanced my way again and replied, "I've already made an offer of ten slaves."

Bakwa's steely demeanor further hardened. "Are you saying that my daughter, the future queen of Zazzau, is worth no more than ten slaves?" She took a steadying breath. "You and your king insult this royal house."

The emissary affected an air of indifference. "A woman who does not know when to hold her tongue is worth little in Nupeland. Irrespective of her ravishing beauty."

"Then you should return to Nupeland where the women are better behaved." Bakwa's voice was steady, though she balled her fist in muted rage.

"What shall I tell Tsoede?" His tone remained indifferent as he looked from me to Bakwa.

"What a dog speaks to his master, only the dog knows." With a curt wave of her hand, she dismissed him.

Anger glimmered in his eyes, but he quickly brought it under control. "The consequences are on your head." With a pompous huff, he turned on his heels. The rest of his party rose and followed him out of the pavilion.

In silence, we all watched the Nupemen sweep from the court.

"Everybody out," Bakwa said at length.

There was no muttering, no disappointed murmurs. Those who had traveled from afar, seeking audience with the queen, quietly left the pavilion. Soon the pavilion was clear, the last of the supplicants trickling out the palace gates, and only Bakwa, the royal council, Karama, and I remained under the palm-frond roof.

Bakwa slowly rose and turned to me.

"Mama," I began.

Her slap felt like the sting of a dozen bees.

"How dare you!" she cried. "You have declared war on Nupeland. Are you mad?"

Tears burned my eyes but didn't fall. I could not remember the last time my mother had struck me. Making a conscious effort not to touch my stinging face, I said quietly, "Tsoede wants Zazzau, and he'll have us unless we stop him. Whether we take war to him or he brings it to us, there *will* be war. The words of one woman make no difference."

"Words make all the difference, Amina."

She clenched her fist, and I feared she might hit me again. When she raised her arm, I drew back, but she merely jabbed a finger in my direction.

"*You* should not involve yourself in such matters."

My lower lip trembled, and I tried to contain the frustration bubbling inside me, but all the anger, bitterness, and pain I wanted to lock away refused to be caged.

"I will not be coddled!" I screamed and was immediately regretful.

Sighing, Karama hung his head in his hand. The council regarded me in horror.

I fell to my knees. "Mama, I'm sorry." I dropped my forehead onto her feet. "Forgive me." I hazarded a shamed look at her.

There was no anger on her face, not even disappointment. Placid features softened. "I know what it is to grieve, my daughter."

"Forgive me." My voice choked, and I buried my face in her long skirt. Anyone else might have suffered grave consequences after an outburst like mine. Groveling was very much in order.

"You are allowed your sorrow," she said.

"Forgive me. Please, Mama."

She cupped my chin and raised my head. "There's nothing to forgive, my daughter." She returned to her mahogany chair.

The heaviness that began with my words to the emissary now cloaked us like a black fog. In the stifling silence, I knelt at my mother's feet.

The waziri cleared his throat.

"What is it, Waziri?" Bakwa asked, her hand on my head.

"We do not have the military might to be victorious in a battle against Tsoede."

"But we may have time to increase our forces," Karama offered. He likely wanted to slap me too.

"How much time?" the waziri asked.

My eyes followed Karama's gaze as he looked to our newest council member.

Suleyman's successor, Fasau, was a small, physically unremarkable man. He cast a doleful glance my way before speaking. "Gimbiya Amina is not mistaken when she says Tsoede is looking for war. We cannot give in to the demands of Nupeland, but we haven't the army to defeat them. As yet, we are severely outnumbered."

"Then what do you propose?" Bakwa asked, her thumb absently stroking my cheek.

"We *must* fight," Fasau replied. "But we need to recruit. Train as many new warriors as possible."

The waziri, who preferred to seek guidance from the supernatural, said, "We must consult the Oracle before the council makes any decision."

I looked from Fasau to the waziri, then caught Siddhi's eye.

"How greatly outnumbered are we?" Siddhi asked and spared me a commiserative look.

"There is no number that cannot be overcome," Fasau replied.

"Eventually," Karama added. "Cannot be overcome *eventually*. Tsoede must already know that our army isn't even half the size of his. So talk true, Fasau. Can we overcome this disadvantage before the Nupe overcome *us*?"

"The Oracle will know," the waziri interjected. "Let me go and seek answers."

Bakwa nodded agreement. "I shall accompany you." She looked down at me. "Amina will come as well."

"And I." Siddhi got to his feet.

His expression peppered with extreme irritation, Karama said, "I'm unable to accompany you, Sister. But I will follow whatever path the council recommends." Karama was Muslim through and through. He believed in the old gods but called them devils and evil spirits. As far as he was concerned, they had no power over us in this world.

I knew better.

Bakwa gathered herself and rose from her seat. "Council is dismissed."

Everyone except for Siddhi and the waziri got up and left the pavilion. Karama was the last of the lot. With a final shake of the head, he too made his way out.

FOURTEEN

We left the pavilion together—me, my mother, Siddhi, and the waziri. Unlike Karama, I was all too aware of the power the gods had over us. Nervous tension prickled my skin at the thought of what the Oracle would say, because the wargod had already told me.

If you come crawling on your belly . . . It already is.

I should have known what those words signified. At the time Dafaru had said them, my mind had been too clouded with grief, too filled with anger at gods who had taken everything from me. Now, making my way through the city and out the gates, I saw their meaning all too clearly.

The Sacred Forest grew on a low range of rolling hills to the city's west and was forbidden to hunters. The few poachers who dared defile its sanctity paid severe penalties ranging from dismemberment to death. Two wooden posts marked the forest entry leading to the shrine of the Oracle. Our offerings to Gajere, the god of forests, came in the form of money dropped into an earthenware bowl at a priestess's feet. In contrast to my own conservative attire of kaftan and sandals, the woman wore nothing other than a wrapper and several strings of wooden, multicolored jigida waist beads. She motioned for us to pass.

I hesitated before entering. Awesome magic filled the place. It was palpable even where I stood between the two posts. Some believed it was merely the presence of Gajere that so overwhelmed those who entered. Whatever lived in these woods, Gajere or some other magic, it made me nervous.

Steeling myself with a deep breath, I passed under the arch and up a set of eight stairs cut into the hillside and hardened with use. The top of the stairs led to a heavily worn path, which marked the beginning of the true ascent into the heart of the forest. The canopy thickened overhead, our way growing darker. Bringing up the rear, Siddhi touched the small of my back. I slowed my pace and fell into step beside him.

"If it is personal vengeance you seek," he said into my ear, "war will not give it to you."

The length of my gown made it difficult to navigate the tangle of greenery. I tripped over a fallen sapling and muttered a curse. Siddhi offered me a hand.

"Our nation is in danger," I replied, accepting the assistance. "We cannot allow Tsoede to intimidate us. Personal vengeance, however, sweetens any victory."

"Vengeance is sweet, I agree. But I'm not so unfamiliar with military affairs that I cannot see the futility of war with Nupeland."

"Is that not the reason we're going to the Oracle?"

"It's men who will fight, Amina. Not the Oracle. It's men who will die."

And as predicted at my birth, the blood of thousands would be on my hands. But did I have to accept that? Did the prophecy have to be fulfilled as it was foretold? Could it be refashioned, remolded to better suit Zazzau's purpose?

We reached our destination—the stone chamber that housed the shrine of the Oracle. The chamber had been carved from a monstrous white boulder. The room beyond the low, unevenly arched doorway was shrouded in shadows.

The priest, a wizened old man with bald head and face, stood outside the chamber. To his right, a second half-clad woman pounded a mortar. The mouthwatering scent of sweet plantains reminded me that I'd eaten nothing that morning, and the sun had already passed its zenith.

"Bakwa and daughter." The priest came toward us. "May the blessings of the greatest God shine down on you."

"And on you," we answered in unison.

"Waziri. Makama." He looked at each in turn. "May you live long in Ubangiji's grace."

They replied likewise.

"We have come to consult the Oracle," said the waziri.

"Of course you have," the priest replied. "But the Oracle cannot guide you."

Confused, we all looked at one another. The Oracle always gave guidance. Sometimes it was difficult to comprehend or made no sense at all, but the Oracle *always* gave guidance.

"We do not understand," the waziri said at last.

"Amina understands," said the priest.

All heads turned toward me.

Alarmed, I looked from one face to another and shook my head. "What do I know of the motives of gods?" My heart rate rose with growing tension.

"There is one god you know well, Gimbiya Amina," said the priest.

My chest constricted.

"Ah." He nodded. "You're aware of whom I speak."

"What is this?" Bakwa's gaze jumped from me to the priest. "What god is this?"

The sting of her prior slap had not fully faded. No doubt she'd hit me again if she learned I'd kept the truth from her. Heat rising to my face, I covered both cheeks with my hands.

"The stars have proclaimed it," the priest said. "You cannot escape it."

My mother's voice grew both irritated and desperate. "Escape what?"

"Her destiny."

Clutching her throat, Bakwa shook her head frantically. "No. She can choose. She has not sought war."

"Yet, war has found her."

Siddhi remained confused, but the waziri understood. After all, the waziri been at my naming ceremony when this same priest of the

Oracle had proclaimed: "She will wade in the blood of thousands. Hers will be the face of Death." It was because of those declarations, that prophecy—and Zariya's dreams—that I feared to do what needed doing.

Siddhi and the waziri looked at me. I lowered my gaze to the ground.

"I do not accept it." My words were all but inaudible. And they were a lie. Zazzau's salvation and my vengeance lay with the gods. Did I have the courage to beseech them? To crawl on my belly and beg the god of war for his favor?

The priest, whose hearing was much sharper than his age should have allowed, said, "Turning your back will not free you. Nor will it protect your people." He faced the waziri. "The Oracle cannot guide you. Only Amina has the power to lead Zazzau from the creeping darkness." He turned and began walking toward the stone chamber. "The time for choosing has arrived." Pushing the curtain aside, he ducked his head and entered the chamber.

I stared after him, uncertain whether anger or defeat dried my tongue. Every choice I had made until now had been irrelevant. My life was half lived, my aspirations shattered before they could take root. Because of a prophecy, because of dreams, because of oracles, I was a half-trained soldier instead of the warrior my father had wanted me to be. And *now* was the time for choosing?

No one said a word. The sound of the pestle pounding the mortar matched the blood thundering in my ears.

Who was I that I could hold back the creeping darkness? Why had the gods put the fate of a nation in my hands? Why had they chosen me? What transgression had my ancestors committed for which I now bore the punishment?

Despite the steady exterior I tried to present, my insides churned with uncertainty, with bitterness and self-pity. Zazzau was in danger. I couldn't let my people fall beneath Tsoede's heel, no matter the cost to me. No matter the sacrifice. What were a few thousand lives compared to a hundred thousand?

When the priest did not return, a disappointed waziri led us back the way we had come. I was glad to get far from the crushing, dense atmosphere of the forest, from the accursed trees that seemed to watch my every move. Perhaps they *were* watching. Maybe Gajere and even the Oracle were in league with the wargod. Maybe there was never truly a choice, because no matter what, my every decision would lead to Dafaru.

I picked my way down the path, my attire again making it no easy picking. Offering me his hand for the second time that day, Siddhi assisted me in the descent.

I almost cried out my joy when we reached the entryway and the hot sun struck my face. Still out of sorts after our visit with the priest, I didn't pull my hand from Siddhi's grasp. We returned, hand in hand, to Gidan Bakwa, where he walked me to my room.

At my door, he let go of my hand and turned to me. "It's men who wage wars and men who win them. What do the gods care for the affairs of men?"

A more relevant question: *what does Dafaru care?*

I bade Siddhi enter and his mouth fell open. His hesitation didn't last. He stepped over the threshold.

He looked around the room. "The lady's chamber is far more appealing on *this* side of the door."

I walked over to the diwan and sat. "It is believed that the lesser gods may fiddle in the affairs of men. The god of war—"

"No. Certainly not the god of war." He crossed the room and sat beside me. "He cannot create conflict to further his own agenda. Else the wars of men would be endless."

"Aren't they endless?"

He thought on it. "Possibly. But ask the waziri—he is well versed in the ways of the pantheon. Ubangiji alone decrees life or death. The god of war cannot interfere with the natural pattern of things."

"Is war not a natural pattern?"

"By itself, yes. But if it's created by the god of war, it is no longer natural. The Creator doesn't allow the lesser entities to change the course of nature to suit their own agendas. That would lead to utter chaos. Men make war," he said. "The wargod can make war bigger or make it last longer or begin sooner, but he does not *make* the war." A small, pensive crease formed on his brow. "Men make war."

Men were what we needed to make war on Nupeland. More men than we had. I asked, "Do you think Daf—the wargod—can choose which side will win? Or is victory also preordained?"

"I think the god of war has some discretion there, but I don't think he has as much power as you believe."

"How's that?"

"If he could directly involve himself in war, he would do it. But no one has ever said the god of war came down from his mountain perch and led them to victory. It's unlikely he can manipulate the outcome to that extent."

"You're saying if Zazzau is meant to kneel before Nupeland, there's nothing the god of war can do to stop it?"

The crease in his brow furrowed deeper. He gave me an intense, questioning gaze. "What are you asking me, Amina?"

I gazed back with no response.

After several heartbeats, he shook his head. "What I'm saying, my dear, is that you cannot rely on the god of war to give you victory if victory was never within your grasp."

His reasoning was plausible, possibly even accurate, but it also meant Dafaru *did* have it in his power to help me, provided I had the resources—warriors and weaponry—to win.

As if he had read my mind, Siddhi slanted me an uneasy look. "The god of war is dangerous, Amina. He's chaos itself. You cannot ask his favor lightly. He'll want something in return. They *always* want something in return."

I already knew what Dafaru wanted and shuddered at the thought of giving myself over to him. But what else could I do? Without his help, Zazzau would fall to Nupeland. If we fell, those thousands dead in Zariya's dream might grow to a hundred times that number.

Siddhi took my hand. In an abrupt change of topic, he said, "You may not realize this, but I care deeply for you." He kissed my fingers, shoving all thoughts of Dafaru out of my head and pushing my heart to a quick flutter.

I stood, willing my pulse to calm. "Thank you for talking with me, Siddhi. There is an issue to which I must attend. You should go now."

He got to his feet with a sigh. "Very well." A brisk nod, and he strode out the door.

Raising my eyes heavenward, I took a steadying breath. Sometimes Siddhi inspired strong feelings in me. I sat down hard on the diwan and wiped my sweating palms on the upholstery.

FIFTEEN

After many weeks of recruiting, the army's effort yielded little result. The promise of riches and glory was not enough to sway the thoughts of so many people who believed it was folly to stand against Nupeland. The prevailing notion in Zazzau was that we should pay the tribute and have done with it. That idea was more foolhardy than outright war. If we bent to Tsoede's will, we would forever be his servants.

My mind was troubled, my way forward uncertain. I was willing to pay any man whatever cost to ensure Zazzau's continued freedom, but Dafaru was no man. How could I know whether he'd keep his promises once he had what he wanted? He wasn't subject to the rules fettering the rest of us. What contract would bind him?

And what would such a creature do to me? Would he truly require a sacrifice of men? The priest of the Oracle said that my destiny would not be denied, but was the future so rigid? Did I have no say in my own fate? Would fealty to Nupeland be so much worse than a lifetime of servitude to the god of war?

These questions clattered around in my skull. To ease the pressure of a growing headache, I made my way to the royal corral. It had been a long while since I'd last seen my horse, Galadima. The handlers took good care of him, but he liked to be pampered, and grooming him myself gave me an opportunity to clear my mind. So I went about this task with alacrity. By the time I was through, Galadima's coat gleamed in the midmorning sun.

"Isn't it the handler's job to do that?"

I spun around. At my abrupt movement, Galadima whinnied and stamped a foot. A smiling Siddhi strode into the corral and leaned against the fence post, arms crossed over his chest. Against the white of his kaftan, his inordinately fair skin appeared darker, but his fine, elegant, features still stood out from the rugged sand and wood of the corral.

I let out a long breath to settle my heart. "Don't do that, Siddhi. You startled me. You startled Galadima."

"Galadima, eh?" He raised an eyebrow. "That's a haughty name for a horse."

I said nothing and lifted one of Galadima's rear feet, examining his hoof and running my fingers along the tiny surface imperfections. Dropping the foot, I went on to examine Galadima's other hooves. "How did you know I was here?"

"That friend of yours is very protective. Or is she your bodyguard?"

"Jaruma told you?"

"Jaruma told me nothing. As I said, she's very protective."

"Then how did you find me?"

"I had to bribe someone else for the information."

"Who?" I couldn't imagine who else knew to find me in the horse corral. Except, perhaps, Fatima.

"If I tell you, I lose the ability to bribe this person again. It's best I keep the information to myself."

"As you wish. What do you want?"

"Only your company, Gimbiya."

"I already have company." I stroked Galadima's muzzle.

Siddhi sucked air through his teeth and tried another approach. "Then I wish to escort you back to the palace."

"Escort me to the palace?"

He was all teeth. "I would be honored."

I couldn't hide my own smile. I finished with Galadima and spoke some crooning words into his ear. The horse may even have understood, because he snorted as though he didn't believe me. I exited the enclosure, locked the feeble latch, and went over to where a large pot sat filled with water. I plunged my hands into it to rinse off the dirt of Galadima's hooves, then strode over to Siddhi.

"Shall we?" he asked.

Without responding, I raised the hem of my overly long mudcloth dress and began walking toward the palace. Silent, we reached Gidan Bakwa and my door. Getting to my door, it seemed, was always high on Siddhi's agenda.

"Will you let me inside?" he said.

My heart stopped for several moments before resuming at a much faster pace.

"Why?" I asked.

When last he was in my room, things between us had nearly crossed into undiscovered territory. I was still hesitant about traversing that bridge.

"Would you tread upon my heart, Gimbiya?" His voice was soft, pleading, and he clutched his chest. "You torture my soul."

I burst out laughing. He didn't laugh with me—perhaps he was serious.

He asked again, "Will you let me inside?"

The expedient answer was no. Were I a sensible woman, that's what I would have said. After all, only one man had ever touched me. And now I was contemplating spending the rest of my life in the thrall of a god.

So why not? I thought. Why not succumb and experience the sort of freedom other women enjoyed? The idea excited me, perhaps a little too much. I said nothing.

He took my hand, brought it to his lips, and frowned. "Your hand smells like manure." Dropping the hand, he leaned forward. Before I realized what he was going to do, he lightly kissed the corner of my mouth.

"Let me in," he said.

I pushed the door open.

Taking my hand again, he pulled me into the room, shut the door, and led me to the diwan. "Why have you been avoiding me?" he said as we sat.

"I haven't." I glanced at the door, debating whether to simply throw him out.

"You lie."

"Maybe I've been avoiding you a little."

"A little?" He laughed. "You see me in the street and hurry in the opposite direction." He leaned in, and I pushed him back. "Amina, it's been long enough."

"Is there a time limit for mourning?"

"You can mourn for all eternity if you like, but you cannot close your heart or it will wither to nothing. You'll die." Sometimes, the man spewed such nonsense.

I cocked my head. "Die?"

"So my grandmother says. You know how wise the old mothers are. We must always heed their warnings."

Against my better judgment, a loud chuckle erupted from my throat. "You are foolish, Makama."

"I must be."

He swept my legs up and dropped my ankles onto his lap. I almost snatched them back, but he shocked me into immobility by massaging my foot. Once the initial surprise passed, I had to admit that the man had able fingers.

"How is it that you're so adept at such a womanly skill?" I wiggled my toes.

He shrugged. "I can't say."

His fingers tickled when they ran along the length of my sole. I giggled. It felt good to laugh. I feared there would be little laughter in my future.

"Stop it, foolish man."

"You don't like it?"

"I like it entirely too much."

His fingers didn't only tickle, they enticed in the most shameful ways. I tried to draw back, to retreat from the unknown, but he didn't allow it.

He said, "I have longed for you since the moment I first saw you. I am your hopeless slave, Amina."

His effusive charm and uncommon beauty overwhelmed me. I sat very still and considered him, considered the slow heat making its way up my leg.

"You're a madman, Siddhi."

"I expect you're correct on that point."

He raised my leg. The skirt of my dress fell away. I gasped my embarrassment and clamped the hem tightly around my legs. Moving his hand from my foot, he wrapped his fingers around my ankle, sending a small tingle to my thigh. I tried to suppress a sharp intake of breath but could not hide the reaction from him. Grinning, he slid his hand upward.

"You're toying with me," I said, short of breath.

"I would never toy with you."

He lifted my leg higher and kissed the small bone on the inside of my ankle. "Honestly, your foot smells better than your hand."

I laughed, giddy with a wanton pleasure I'd not felt in ages.

"And your dress smells like horsehide," he added. "Perhaps you should remove it."

"Siddhi!" Heat rose to my neck. "Asking a woman to remove her dress is uncouth."

"Whoever told you I was couth?"

He kissed the top of my foot, my shin, then my knee, and sent a thrill darting upward. Regions of my body dormant for so many months came alive. In a highly unsophisticated manner, Siddhi ducked under my leg to nestle between my thighs. With a hand behind each knee, he rubbed the sensitized skin above my calves. His touch was a sweet sensation.

"Siddhi."

His hands moved up my legs to grasp my hips, and he raised himself higher up my body. His mouth came down on my neck.

"Siddhi." My breathing was heavy, my body tense with desire. "Siddhi."

He removed his mouth from the hollow of my neck and looked at me.

I thought I should protest, but the voice in my head was a whisper compared to the screaming need building within me. It beckoned to him, opened to him, urged him inside.

His lips met mine, disallowing me any further opportunity to think things through. At his kiss, the barricade I'd so carefully placed around my heart shattered, setting free a deluge of emotions. There was guilt—what I was doing felt like a betrayal. But mostly there was desire, strong and raw. My passion burned like hot oil. Denying or ignoring the feeling would not abolish it. Even so, I no longer wanted it gone.

I wrapped my legs and arms around him. His lips caressed my chin, stroked my neck. A soft exclamation formed in my throat, and I leaned my head back. Once again, he brought his mouth to mine, and I pressed myself into him, greedy for him. Surges of pleasure raced through me, prickling my skin. I yearned for more. Impatient, I tugged at his clothing, tried desperately to tear him free, but the cloth was sturdy.

"Where did you get this material?" The weave of his tunic, though thin, was tough like imported brocade. "It doesn't tear."

His impatience was a perfect reflection of mine. "Yukubu." He pulled the tunic off and threw it to the side.

"Of course."

I quietly cursed the cloth weaver and tugged at the drawstring of Siddhi's trousers while he fumbled with the excessive cloth of my skirt in an attempt to lift it over my hips.

"For the love of everything sacred, Amina, remove this damned dress."

I raised my hips and he made to push the dress over them, but the skirt was entangled in our limbs.

"You can't possibly love the dress too much." The uncooperative garment grew taut around my chest as he gathered up the loose fabric at the neckline. "You went riding in it."

"Wha—" I paused at the sound of tearing material. "Siddhi!"

He covered my mouth with his, ending the admonishment, and there was no more love play. Siddhi slid inside, drawing from me an extended purr of delight. With an arm underneath me, he arched my back and lowered his head until his lips touched my chest. We clung tightly to each other, moving our hips in long, slow unison.

Without withdrawing from my embrace, he raised us to a sitting position—me on top. His hands just under my waist, he held me there. "Don't move." He closed his eyes.

"Don't be silly." I ground into him and chuckled at his ragged moans of ecstasy.

He moved his hand to the back of my neck and drew my face down. Our lips touched; he ran his tongue over my lower and I nibbled his top. He groaned again, a sound that further prodded my desire.

My release took me by surprise. I cried out, crushing my chest against his face, and locked my arms about his neck. As the tremors grew to convulsions, I dropped my head and bit down on the flesh between his shoulder and neck. His body stiffened then relaxed. He got to his feet, carrying me with him.

Turning about, he laid me on my back. "You're like a caged animal finally free." And he made love to me with a fierceness I never imagined he had in him.

I was alive again, my senses so sharp that even his breath against my skin pushed me to a deeper frenzy. A torrent of warmth spread through my body. Overcome by the sheer ecstasy of it, I clawed at him. He grunted but drove on, and with a low moan, let loose a flood. Spent, he crumpled atop me.

We lay entangled as the world fell back into place around us. Then, "My dear," he said through heavy breathing, "I believe I've spilled onto your dress. Surely it's ruined now."

As if tearing it from bodice to hem had not ruined it.

I kissed his sweating brow. "You truly are mad."

SIXTEEN

The palace slept, and I dressed for war—undyed tunic and trousers, a black sash from which hung my short-sword, and thick-soled sandals of coarse leather. Because I'd never had any need for it, I did not own battle armor. Even so, armor wouldn't protect me from what was coming.

I crossed the room and pulled a cloth bundle from the alcove nearest the door. This was where Suleyman used to store his arm-knife. I could still see him pushing back his sleeve to unfasten the leather sheath.

The heavy bundle *clinked* when it dropped onto the table. I opened the cloth. Three bronze war bracelets glinted in the lamplight. The two smaller bracelets bore the sheen of newly forged weapons, while the larger showed the patina of time. I donned the smaller pair, which had been forged from one of Suleyman's. Without the requisite linen around my wrists, the near-circular implements were a loose fit. Loose enough to cause injury to me were I in actual battle.

I picked up his remaining bracelet, ran my fingers lightly along the upraised, serrated edges. It had seen many battles and wasn't as sharp as it had once been. I glanced at my own bracelets of gleaming bronze. Suleyman was gone, but a piece of him would accompany me on this journey tonight.

I raised the veil of my red and black headwrap to cover everything except my eyes. I considered strapping on an arm-knife but realized it would be of no more use to me than the other weapons adorning my body. The night was unusually still, no sounds from outside reached my ears.

"Forgive me, love." I rewrapped Suleyman's bracelet, returned the bundle to the alcove, and stepped outside.

There were no clouds in the sky, but the scent of pending rain filled the air. The night guard's wide eyes and raised eyebrows spelled his amazement, but he asked no questions, bowing, as I walked out the palace gates.

The rains had come early this year. Puddles pockmarked the dirt road. Few townsfolk were about at that hour, and those who saw me must not have recognized me; they went about their business, pausing only for perfunctory greetings. No one stopped. No one approached. I made haste to reach my destination while the weak light of the crescent moon still shone high in the sky.

"Where are you going?" A voice called from the darkness.

My heart lurched into my throat, choking off a gasp.

Jaruma emerged from a shadowed entryway wearing a black kaftan and trousers. Her takouba was strapped to a black sash, her face enveloped by a veiled, black headwrap. And she looked very much like a casual assassin.

"Why are you lurking in the darkness?" I asked, a hand over my palpitating heart. "Are you following me?"

"Where are you going?" She strode forward, appraising my battle garb.

My brow creased. "I don't answer to you. Have you forgotten your place?"

"I'm your guard, am I not? My place is where you are."

"Not tonight."

I resumed my walk, and she moved to block my path.

"Get out of my way." Every moment she delayed me, I grew more reluctant to meet my preordained fate.

"As you command." She stood aside. "But you haven't told me where you're going." Her footfalls made little sound as she fell into step behind me.

Without turning, I asked, "Why are you out at this time of night?"

"I was standing sentry."

"You? Standing sentry?"

"I'd rather gut myself than be assigned such duty, I know. But I couldn't sleep. I was in the gatehouse when you left."

"So you followed me?"

Making no reply, she continued to pace me.

I let out a sigh of resignation. "If you follow, then you must know something."

"What?" Now, she was walking beside me.

"You remember the day we went to the Oracle?"

"The day your mother slapped you in council?" She tried to stifle her laughter.

"Yes, karya, that day."

The name-calling goaded her further, and she let loose a series of chortles, titters, snorts, and giggles. When her mirth was satisfied, she said, "But you received no guidance from the Oracle." Her tone still rang with amusement.

"We received no guidance, but the priest gave a warning."

"What warning?" She turned serious, a frown settling on her face. "Why didn't you tell me?"

"Because I don't care for such warnings or for talk of destiny."

"Destiny?"

"Prophecies."

"What prophecy?"

Jaruma and I had shared many things with each other, many secrets. But I had never told her of the priest's predictions or of Zariya's oracular dreams. If she had known what my future held, she may not have kept it from her brother.

I told her now, and when the telling was through, all signs of mirth had vanished from her face. Stopping me in my tracks, she grabbed my arm, her fingers biting my flesh.

"Why have you never told me this?" Her tone was both anger and pain.

I glanced down at the hand gripping my arm. "Let go."

For several seconds, she held firm. Then, "Sorry, Gimbiya." She let go.

Resuming the walk, I massaged the ache she had left in my arm.

"But why didn't you tell me?" she asked.

"What reason was there to tell you?"

"You're telling me now. What reason is there now?"

"Because you must understand why I'm doing this."

"What are you doing?"

What I was doing was something I was afraid to admit. Something I was too ashamed to accept, even as I carried it through. My shame and regret were such that I had not told Siddhi. Like a coward, I had crept into the night and wasn't certain I could face him or anyone else in the morning.

"I've seen him," I said.

"Who?" Impatience flooded her voice, and she speared me with that piercing gaze which so resembled her brother's.

I stumbled and righted myself. "The god of war."

"*What?*" She halted.

"Quiet, Jaruma." I glanced around, looping an arm through hers to urge her forward.

"How?"

"In my dreams," I replied softly. "In my waking. He invades my days and my nights and cannot be kept away."

"Since when?"

"Ever since the Kwararafa." Spoken aloud, the revelation was shocking.

She fell silent for a time, then said, "Seven years?"

"More or less."

"For so long? And you . . . did Suleyman?"

"No one knew, Jaruma."

After another silent interval, Jaruma spoke. "Where are we going and what are you doing?" Judging from the quiet, halting manner in which she delivered the words, she had already fathomed the answer.

I stopped walking, turned to her, and stepped close. "The god of war is my only choice. There was never any other choice to make."

My eyes focused on hers, looked into the endless pools that could so easily be Suleyman's. She didn't fully understand. No one, except my mother, the priest, and perhaps Zariya truly understood.

"I will be his, Jaruma. Until I die or he releases me."

She nodded. That much she had surmised.

"And people will die." I'd finally spoken the words aloud. *People will die.* It brought back the memory of the Kuturun Mahayi who had given their lives for mine in the eastern hills almost seven years ago. It brought back all the pain, all the guilt, and I wondered how much sharper it would sting when my burden of death numbered in the thousands. *I will swim in the blood of my own people.* But I'd sacrifice those thousands to save many, many more.

Or was I sacrificing them to avenge Suleyman?

"Don't go," she said. "Don't do this. We can fight Nupeland without him."

"We can fight and we will lose. And so many more people will die. You want vengeance as much as I do, Jaruma. This is the only way. I never truly had a choice. *This* is my destiny. I see it now."

She pulled me into an embrace, her arms around my shoulders. "You can choose your life. You can choose *not* to sacrifice the lives of our people. We can avenge Suleyman without—"

"Even if we don't seek retribution, people will die. No matter the choice, people will die. Should we let them die in vain or should their deaths protect the rest?"

She had no answer

My arms slipped around her waist and held her tight. "I must choose Zazzau."

But was I truly choosing Zazzau? Could words have made the difference as my mother believed? I once led fifty Kuturun Mahayi to their deaths in the eastern mountains, was I now leading an entire nation to its downfall?

She released me and stepped back. "Then this is how it must be." With a hand on the pommel of her sword, she stood eyes forward. "But you won't do it alone."

Offering up a weak smile, I resumed the walk.

Right or wrong, my conviction couldn't waver. The path to victory wound through the spirit world, through the god of war. Regardless of whatever misery might lay ahead, Zazzau would bow to no foreign usurper.

We continued in silence, Jaruma looking pensive beside me. When we reached the city gate, she barked an order to the guards, who scrutinized me then grew hesitant. Leaving the city at night was risky for the average citizen, perhaps more so for me. However, a good bribe could overcome most reticence. I reached into my tunic for the money pouch, but Jaruma stopped me.

Giving the guards nothing more than a stern gaze, she said, "Move or I move you."

They glanced at the adjacent guardhouse. All five men within shook their heads. Whether the guards personally knew her, they certainly knew her reputation. Who didn't? And that she would kill them both before they even drew their weapons. Her face was devoid of expression, but the sharpness of her eyes, her stance, the way her fingers opened and closed on the hilt of her sword spoke the loudest warning.

The two men shared a look, came to a joint decision, and opened the gate.

✸

We got to the corral and collected our horses just as the clouds rolled in. Although the Sacred Forest was not a long walk, at this time of night, it was simply safer to ride. Far away, thunder rumbled.

"The thundergod must be angry." Jaruma looked at the sky. "He doesn't approve of this plan of yours."

"Or perhaps he doesn't approve of you accompanying me. I have an unpleasant journey ahead, my friend. It's only right for him to want to protect you. You share his name, after all."

"My name is not Dawatsu," she replied in a huff.

"Dawatsu or Dongo—the god of thunder is still the god of thunder."

The thunder boomed closer and a cool gust of wind blew across my face.

"How do you intend to find Ruhun Yak'i?" She gave me a dubious look. "His name is Dafaru you said?"

I nodded. "The Oracle."

"Supposing the priest refuses to help you?"

"He won't refuse."

We reached the forest entrance and the horses balked. I had a mind to force Galadima through the entryway but decided against it. If I was ill at ease in the place, why should I expect otherwise from the animals? We dismounted.

There was no priestess there to greet us or to keep an eye on the horses, but only the most desperate and foolish would dare steal anything from the forest entrance. We tethered the horses to one of the old, gnarled trees and entered, my heart thudding at the eerie moan of leaves on the wind. I longed to get back on my horse, to gallop away from that place.

"Are you certain about this?" Jaruma's trepidation was obvious in the way she looked about.

Steeling myself, I went up two of the stairs and looked back at her. "I know what I must do, Jaruma. But you don't have to do it with me."

"I go where you go."

Grateful for her obstinacy, her loyalty, and the strength that her presence gave me, I held a hand out for her. She took it. Together we climbed the stairs and stepped onto the well-worn path. We moved briskly through the dark forest, eyes trained on the trail before us, and we soon came to the forest clearing. As I made to announce myself, the old priest stepped out of the stone chamber.

"Greetings, Baba," Jaruma and I said in unison.

The priest peered into my face. "You've decided, eh?"

"I have." I forced conviction into my voice.

He looked at Jaruma who looked steadily back at him.

"You've brought a witness?" he asked, without looking away from her.

"She refused to leave my side."

The wind howled and the priest nodded. "This one will be a friend to you for years to come." He beckoned, turned, and entered the chamber.

The low doorway was covered by a broad wooden plank, which the priest removed so we could enter. Bent nearly double, I stepped into the chamber with Jaruma close behind. The priest came last, and returned the plank to its position across the doorway. The chamber was small and too short for us to stand upright. Faded moonlight streamed through a hole in the top, bathing us in a ghostly glow. The floor, lined with clay tiles, had at its center a stone altar decorated with talismans, beads, and petrified animal parts, including a monkey's paw.

The priest gestured toward the altar. "Sit and face the shrine."

We sat down, cross-legged, facing the pile of spiritual paraphernalia.

"You've dressed appropriately for War," he said, appraising me. "But weaponry is useless against gods."

I said, "It makes me feel safe."

"An illusion at best." He looked at Jaruma, who was also fully armed, and picked up one of the talismans.

The small amulet looked like a tiny rawhide whip except for the multicolored snail shells and bird feathers dangling from its many ends. He picked something else from the pile—a long splinter of ivory or sun-bleached bone—and held it between his teeth. He bit down, and it snapped in half with a sound that made my jaws hurt. Its pieces fell onto the shrine.

The priest began chanting, his words flowing in tune with the howling wind. He picked up another object that I couldn't quite see and shook it over the shrine. It made the sound of falling rain. Outside, Dawatsu answered with a downpour.

"The thundergod rages tonight." The priest placed two clay pots on either side of the shrine. He dropped one half of the bone into each pot, then put both on the altar. "Put your offering inside."

I removed the money pouch. "Which pot?"

"Destiny has already chosen."

I reached for the nearest pot and dropped the pouch inside. As I began to draw my hand away, it was sucked back in, my palm laid flat against the bottom. The broken piece of bone dug into me. Before I could say a word, a searing pain shot into my hand. I cried out.

"What's happening?" Jaruma leaned forward, and the priest drove her back with a single glance.

I tried to pull my hand out of the pot, but unseen magic locked my arm in place. Terrible pain raced up to my elbow. I convulsed and screamed, though no sound came from my mouth. The pot shattered, its pieces crumbling onto the floor, and only then did my arm come free. It burned like fire. I clutched it to my chest and tried to shake loose the dizziness blurring my vision.

From a distance, I heard the priest ask, "Do you still wish to follow your mistress?"

Jaruma's response was lost to me as darkness swept over my senses.

SEVENTEEN

I stared up at the light streaming through the opening in the chamber roof. The storm was ended; the clouds were gone. My arm was cold but without pain. Jaruma lay beside me, the beam of daylight slicing through the dark chamber to cast her strangely beautiful features in an eerie halo.

"Jaruma."

Her eyes fluttered.

I sat up and shook her. "Jaruma."

She groaned, lifting a hand to her face. Then her eyes opened. Coming awake, she jerked upright.

"Everything is gone." My voice echoed off the stone walls of the now empty room.

She got herself together. "It feels as though everything has changed." Ducking low, she exited the chamber. Her anxious voice floated back to me. "Amina."

The clearing outside was almost painfully bright, and after my eyes adjusted, I understood Jaruma's earlier sentiment. Things *had* changed.

The forest was possibly the same one we had entered the night before. Indeed, if I stared at one spot, it was an ordinary forest. But at first glance, from peripheral vision, or whenever my eyes were not quite focused, the trees looked . . . different. They were bigger, older. Older even than time itself. And alive. Not alive like a tree in Zazzau, but alive like a *man* in Zazzau. When viewed out of the corner of my eye, the trees seemed to move, to physically shift through the ground, trunk and all, as if they were wading through water. But when I looked directly at them, they appeared not to have moved at all.

Yet they were never *quite* still, because even as I stared at them, the leaves rustled without wind. And the sound was like the whispers of a thousand voices.

"Jangare," I concluded, my voice hushed, my heartbeat loud and unruly.

"The land of spirits? It's too quiet." She glanced quickly around. "What nightmares abound in a land of tempered voices?"

No sooner had she finished speaking when a large, red... *something* burst from the forest. Shattering the silence with a loud snarl, it launched itself at us. Pivoting away from the creature, Jaruma drew her blade but not before the monster raked its claws across her shoulder. Face twisted in pain, she dropped the weapon. I brought mine down on the beast's raised paw, but it glanced off the creature's hide as though the creature were made of stone. The thing growled and leapt at me.

Something flashed past my eyes. The creature yelped as it was tossed into the air. Then something else shot past my line of sight. The creature howled. There was a whooshing sound as something (vine, tree branch, root?) sliced at the airborne animal. With a shriek that must have woken the underworld, the creature crashed to the ground. As quickly as it had first appeared, the monster scurried away.

Jaruma frantically spun about in a full circle, her sword gripped in both hands. "What was that?"

"I don't know. A giant rat? Wild dog?" Its body was red from muzzle to tail. "Are you badly injured?"

She turned her back to me and I inspected it. Her clothes were torn where the thing had made contact, and her skin was scratched. I pulled away the cloth made filthy by the beast. Three deep, ragged, and swollen cuts glared out at me.

"Let's get out of this place." Her words strained past clenched teeth. "Which way?"

A voice responded from within the forest. "This way."

On hearing the familiar burble, my terror level dropped. I headed toward the sound. Jaruma, far less certain, followed. At the lip of the forest, she stopped and cast a wary eye into the dark interior.

"Greetings."

We each gave a start. The figure of a man—taller than most and made entirely from water—appeared before us. The rivergod crossed his arms, sending ripples through his form.

Mesmerized by the manifestation, I forgot to bow. "Greetings, Kogi-Ayu."

Jaruma, her mouth hanging open, was dumbstruck.

The water form inclined his head. "It is no easy undertaking for a mortal in corporeal form to enter the realm of spirits. You are either very determined or very special."

"We are neither, my lord. I come only to ask a boon."

"Of Dafaru?"

"Yes."

The rivergod's laughter gurgled in the still air, and somewhere, thunder roared. Kogi-Ayu glanced upward. "As Dawatsu says, our brother grants no boon. The wargod does only what it pleases him to do."

"I must ask nonetheless."

"Indeed you must. I will guide you to his abode."

He turned and walked into the forest, Jaruma and I behind him. As he moved, his water form shrank, leaving a wet trail. Eventually, the trail became a narrow streamlet, then widened into a river.

We followed the river. It seemed the trees parted for us to pass. Large jutting roots sank into the ground when we neared and low hanging branches rose higher. So it appeared, but I never actually saw them move. What I did see was that, despite the ease of our passage and the cool air of Jangare, sweat beaded on Jaruma's forehead.

"What is it?" I asked.

"Nothing," she replied, struggling to mask any sign of pain.

"Don't lie to me." I forced her to stand still. "Let me see."

"It's nothing."

I looked at the wound and hissed, sucking air through my teeth. "Nothing, my eye." The swelling was worse. The bleeding had stopped, but fluid seeped from the edges of the cuts, which were now a mottled color. It hadn't been an hour, yet the wound was festering.

"My friend is injured," I said. "The wound is severe."

The sound of the water form coming out of the river was like a dam breaking. The rivergod stepped onto the ground and walked over, leaving no wet footprints. By the time he reached us, he looked like a tall, ordinary man with smooth, brown skin. He had a handsome face, a pleasant face. I wondered if he looked as pleasant when he was drowning people.

"I do." He nodded toward Jaruma. "Show me."

Jaruma turned.

Tilting his head to one side, he examined the wound. When he touched the surrounding, uninjured skin, she flinched.

"This will be painful." He covered the cuts with a hand that turned to liquid where it made contact with her skin. His other hand moved to her chest, bracing her as the pain struck.

She grimaced and swallowed a grunt, a tear forming at the corner of her eye. But she kept still, the muscles in her neck taut with tension. After a short time, the rivergod pulled his hands away, and she cried out. She took a deep breath. Her shoulders relaxed.

"The poison is nullified," he said. "It will heal."

"Thank you," Jaruma and I said as one.

He inclined his head in a curt bow and coursed to the river, his man form reverting to water.

We continued our trek, soon coming to the edge of the tree line. A short distance farther, and we were well out of the forest. The water form rose from the river and came to rest on the surface. He pointed. Our gazes followed his finger to a big, black, misshapen tree with a tuft of black leaves at its crown. From this distance, with its tight, gnarled branches, it resembled a deformed giant. I looked past the giant and saw the structure over which it stood: an equally black, equally giant, turreted building.

"The palace of War." Kogi-Ayu gestured for me to come closer. Turning from water to man, he regarded me intently as I approached the water's edge. Unlike his brother's turbulent red mists, Kogi-Ayu's eyes were like the froth of a raging river. "Once the choice is made, the decision cannot be unmade." His eyes turned briefly dark, like choppy waters on a stormy night. "Choose carefully." Still in man form, he submerged without a splash.

❀

The wargod's palace was like nothing I had ever seen before. The mammoth structure seemed cut from a mountain of black granite. It wasn't enclosed in a compound, but stood alone, foreboding.

"I don't like the look of it," Jaruma muttered as we entered the shadow of the rectangular entry portal.

A covered lamp burned over the wrought iron door. Near the top of the door, just within reach, hung a bronze elephant head of impressive detail. It had the tusks of an old bull, its wrinkled trunk curving upward with nostrils flaring out. Jaruma touched its trunk. It moved on a hidden hinge. She pushed up, and it rose.

"Don't touch that," I said.

She let it drop.

The heavy trunk fell back into place with a loud clang that reverberated inside the building. She gave a mortified gasp and looked at me. I was about to chastise her carelessness but stopped before the words emerged. The doors were opening, and my heart began pounding in my ears. After several breaths to steady the thrashing in my chest, I stuck my head through the doorway, and silence once more folded around us.

It was too dark to see the interior, which increased my apprehension. Fear pricked every surface of my body, but there was no turning back now. Meeting Jaruma's questioning gaze, I took another steadying breath and stepped into the darkness. For a few long moments, Jaruma remained outside, her own fear unmasked. Then she stepped through the doorway to join me. The doors swung shut. Suddenly, there was light.

It came from everywhere at once. There was no single, discernible source. It seemed to radiate from the walls themselves, reflecting off the polished stone floor and the ceiling, which was at least twenty feet above us. A series of closed doors on either side of the room gave the place a tight, austere look. Like being encased in a granite tomb.

One of the doors opened and two women stepped out. They wore short wrappers that tied below their navels and terminated at midthigh. To cover their chests, each wore a band of cloth to match the one around her waist. It was exceedingly provocative to be so wrapped-up while covering nothing. Better to go without clothing than to titillate with a blatant indication of what lay beneath.

Jaruma leaned close and whispered, "Concubines?"

I frowned. "Dressed like that?"

The women reached us and bowed. Their heads were uncovered and their tightly coiled hair unplaited. They spoke simultaneously. "Welcome, Gimbiya, to the house of War. We must prepare you." Their voices were soft and airy.

"Prepare me? For what?"

"I am Salima," said one, stepping forward. "Follow us."

Hesitating, Jaruma and I looked at one another. Despite my fear, despite my distrust of these two scantily clad women, I couldn't lose sight of the reason for my coming. I started forward. Jaruma followed.

Rounding a corner, we came to a wide staircase and I let out a low whistle. Never in my life had I seen a staircase so grand, much less *inside* a house. The steps themselves were black but not granite. The smooth, uniformly patterned stone was unfamiliar. Golden spiraled rods, terminating in a handhold of the blackest ebony, made up the staircase railings. In a wondrous stupor, I followed the women up to an elaborately carved wooden door.

Salima pushed the door open, revealing a room as brightly lit as the one downstairs. Unlike the one downstairs, however, the source of illumination was immediately evident. On the opposite wall, daylight shone through a large window that rose from floor to ceiling and was almost as wide. I crossed to it and rapped my knuckles against it. Behind me, Jaruma gasped.

"Glass." I rapped again, harder. "It's glass."

She strode over and ran her palm along the unblemished surface. "I've never seen the like."

Glass was not much utilized in my native lands, and glass so smooth, so unblemished was unheard of. Even small panes from the far north weren't quite this perfect. With a daring grin, Jaruma leaned her forehead against it.

I looked out the window and quickly drew back. The view of the ground so far below made me queasy. "Such a fall would kill you," I warned, stepping away from the glass.

"Gimbiya," Salima said. "We must prepare."

The other woman stepped forward. "You as well. In the next room." She gestured toward the corridor, then added at Jaruma's doubtful look, "You'll not be far."

I reassured my friend with a nod. "Go with her."

As soon as the others were gone, Salima began undressing me. Her action was so unexpected that it left me speechless, else I would have voiced loud protest. After she stripped me of my weapons and my garments, she gestured toward a copper tub set in the middle of the room.

Out of sorts, I stepped in gingerly. Warm water rose around me, covering me to my shoulders. Salima's hands were in my hair and on my body, scrubbing in too familiar a manner. It was quickly over, though. *Thank the gods.* Handing me a cloth, she urged me out of the tub.

I dried myself off, and she rubbed fragrant oil into my skin. Afterward, she sat me, naked, on a chair and began combing out the dark mass of tangles on my head. Moving at a supernatural pace, she plaited my hair into tiny braids.

When my hair was done, she garbed me in a dress—if it could be called a dress—that barely fell to my knees. The flimsy red material draped intimately over my body, offensively revealing my every curve, the outline of my breasts. It left me so exposed that Salima's scanty outfit was no longer unsettling. Her clothing at least kept all her parts tightly contained.

"Am I to wear this and nothing else?" I asked.

The door opened and Jaruma stepped into the room. She stopped in midstride and stood gaping at my ridiculous garb.

"It's . . ." she began.

"I know."

She, too, wore a short, formfitting red tunic, but hers was of coarser material. Underneath, she still wore her black trousers. Her short hair was unbound, and she remained in possession of all her weapons.

The other body servant came into the room. Jaruma glowered at her. I smiled absently, imagining what had transpired when the other woman had tried to undress my companion.

"How is your shoulder?" I asked Jaruma as the servant skittered nervously around her.

"It's healing. As he said it would." She lowered her sleeve to show me the healing patch of skin.

"Gimbiya," Salima said, "I must finish preparing you."

"More?"

"I'm ordered to make you presentable for the god of war."

"How can I be presentable dressed as I am?"

"Forgive me, Gimbiya, but we must do as we're commanded."

As we're commanded. I cringed at the words, but squaring my shoulders, I went forward to face the additional grooming.

Salima opened a coffer and riffled through its contents. With the aid of the other servant, she adorned me in gold from head to feet. Tiny gold baubles decorated my hair. Filigreed earrings hung from my ears. My neck was layered with fine golden links, my wrists and waist with beaded gold, and a golden wire anklet wrapped several times around my left leg.

Finished at last, both women nodded their approval. Even Jaruma smiled at what she saw. "You look expensive, Gimbiya." Glancing downward, she added, "Even in bare feet."

Salima ushered us out of the room, down a long corridor, to another set of stairs, which were not as grand as the first. She took us through a second corridor and stopped at the entrance of a draughty room. Jaruma and I looked inside, but the only light came from the softly burning braziers on the near walls. Everything beyond the first ten or so feet remained in darkness. Exchanging a single look, we entered.

The floor was warm under my unshod feet, as if the devil lived beneath us. Warm floor aside, a chill blanketed the room, and the scant light did nothing to lessen the cold. We made our way forward, and one after the other, the braziers along the walls burst into billowing flames.

I shielded my eyes until they adjusted to the blaze. When they refocused, I saw that this room, like the entry hall, was of black granite. The space was elongated and large, more an indoor pavilion than a room. Like the other, it had high ceilings and a polished floor. The far end of the room, which we slowly approached, was a raised dais. A black throne stood at the center of the dais. And upon the throne, wrapped in red cloak and kilt, sat the god of war.

PART II

QUEEN OF ZAZZAU

Warrior

EIGHTEEN

The wargod raised a beckoning hand. I willed my legs forward, but they refused to obey. He rose slowly to his feet.

"Amina?" Jaruma said.

The fearful tremor in her voice prompted me into motion, and I walked toward the throne. When I reached the dais, Dafaru sat back down.

"So you have come." He glanced at Jaruma. Red eyes made his expression difficult to read, but it brought to mind a hungry man sitting to feast. "And you brought me a gift."

Alarmed, I said, "She's no gift."

"Oh?" His eyes traveled from her face to slowly course down her body. He raised an eyebrow. "Pity." He angled his head toward me. "Why have you come if not bearing gifts?"

"You know why I've come."

He tapped a finger on the chair's arm. "I want to hear it from your lips."

"I've come for your favor."

A chuckle rumbled in his throat without breaking the surface. "Have you not heard that the god of war grants no favors?"

"Zazzau is in a dire position."

"What has that to do with me?"

I opened my mouth, but he spoke again.

"You have committed yourself to a war against an enemy you cannot hope to defeat." He turned to my companion. "And you. You supported her in this grievous error?"

"My lord," I said quickly, drawing his attention back to me. "War with Nupeland is inevitable."

"Nothing is inevitable."

The beginnings of despair squeezed me to silence. Dafaru's refusal did not factor into my plans. I'd prepared no well-honed argument. He was Zazzau's best hope for surviving Nupeland. Our only alternative.

"Have you considered paying the requested tribute?" he asked.

Our only *acceptable* alternative. "Zazzau will not submit."

"Then perhaps you are correct. War is inevitable." He scratched the tuft of hair on his chin, all the while looking at Jaruma. "So it seems you are fated to fight on the losing side."

I cloaked my despair with anger. "Will you not help us?"

He shushed me as though I were a child and got to his feet. Stepping off the dais, he strode over to Jaruma and thoroughly appraised her, walking around to view her from every vantage. Gently, he pulled the tunic away from her wounded shoulder, scrutinized the three jagged lines in her flesh, and frowned.

"I see you met Dangoji." The tunic slid back into place. "And, perhaps, Kogi-Ayu along the way?" He looked inquiringly at me.

"My lord," I began.

He raised a finger to his lips, silencing me again, and moved closer to Jaruma. She stiffened. I knew she could feel his abominable heat sinking into her. His hand slipped around her waist, pulling her to him. Her chest rose and fell rapidly with her quickened breathing. I should never have brought her. Knowing the effect he had on *me*, I shouldn't have allowed her anywhere near him. What if he wanted her too?

Or wanted her more?

A cold jolt of emotion that I didn't care to define surged through me. "She's not a gift."

"As you have already said." The look on his face was just shy of amusement.

"Please." I felt sick at having brought my companion into this hyena's den.

"Please what?" He took his hand from around her waist but did not move away. "She and I are kindred spirits." He turned to me. A small wrinkle creased his brow. "Supplicants kneel in my presence, Gimbiya."

It was too easy to hate the god of war.

I set my chin, swallowed my pride, and lowered myself to my knees. His brow rose as though he'd not expected me to kneel, but the short-lived expression vanished. He stepped away from Jaruma and stood before us both, arms crossed over his naked chest.

"For my favor, Beloved, what do you offer in return?"

I spread my hands. "What can I give that will please the god of war?"

"Perhaps you have nothing I desire." He glanced again at Jaruma. "This one is a formidable warrior. She is every bit as comely as you. And perhaps more docile."

Jaruma docile?

"You disagree?" He looked her over again. "You may be right. Yet more often than most, this one has filled War's chalice with blood. Does that not make her deserving?"

My stomach clenched. The way he spoke the words and the way he looked at her, these things weighed heavy like stones in my gut. I glanced at my companion, who swayed unsteadily on her heels. She did not look at me, but I could feel her anxiety.

"My lord, I am at your command. My companion is not bound to you." I kept the desperation out of my voice, but he plucked it from my mind.

"She is bound to *you*," he said. "What would she sacrifice to spare you from me, I wonder?" He smiled in his most beguiling manner and she wrapped her arms around herself as though she stood naked.

"You cannot have her," I said, defiance now stamped upon my thoughts.

His smile dissipated. Lines crossed his forehead in a thoughtful expression. Striding up the dais, he said, "Get up, woman."

I got up.

Swinging the red cloak behind his shoulders, he dropped onto the black chair, and his demeanor hardened. "What are you willing to give for my favor?"

"Anything you ask," I replied without hesitation.

"You know what I want, Amina."

My heart jumped into my throat, but I shook it loose. There was no running from it, no turning away from this fate that had hounded me my entire life. Destiny had made my decision long before I ever laid eyes on the god of war.

I said, "I'm yours."

Dafaru was silent for a time before asking, "What you give is offered freely?"

"Willing or unwilling, you said it made no difference."

"So I did," he recalled dryly. "But a willing participant is far more satisfying."

My stomach clenched again.

"Do you offer yourself freely?" he asked.

"Yes."

"You offer your body, but what of your soul?"

I hesitated, unsure of what he was asking, but would give him anything in exchange for Zazzau's safety. Besides, the free will I thought I had was fast becoming an illusion. "Body and soul," I said. "I'm yours."

"And your heart?"

"You know I cannot."

"Why is that?"

"I do not love you."

The glow of his eyes intensified. He leaned forward, silently regarding me. At length, he said, "Tell me, Gimbiya. Have you given your heart to yet another man?"

"My heart has always belonged to another man."

"He is dead."

At that declaration, Jaruma shifted uncomfortably.

"Love doesn't always die." In a scornful tone, I added, "My lord."

His features remained passive. "Then there is no living man who might covet what is mine?"

My brow furrowed. "There is no one."

Pensive, the wargod stroked his chin. He gazed at me, tension tightening his midnight face, as he pondered whatever he saw in my mind. When he spoke again, his voice was quiet.

"You say your heart is buried in the tomb of a dead man?" His eyes narrowed. "I say you lie. And your lying tongue condemns you." He leaned forward, resting his forearms on his knees, and let out a quick breath of air. "I ask once more, Amina of Zazzau. Have you given your heart to any other man?"

It was my turn to ponder as I tried to make sense of his questions. Surely, he didn't think I was in love with Siddhi? Ours had been a mere interlude before I shackled myself to this unreasonable deity. Of course I loved Siddhi. How could I not? He'd been a rock in my time of need.

"What does any of this signify?" I asked. My body and soul were already bartered to the god of war. What difference did my heart make when, suffice it to say, I would never love *him*? Whatever damnation he planned for me would sow no warmth within my heart. So what did it matter? I looked obstinately into the boiling red of his eyes. "No, my lord. My heart belongs to no other man."

A dark expression came over his face, and he raised his eyes to the ceiling before dropping them on me. "Very well."

Down the dais he came. He grabbed my face roughly between his hands and stared down at me. The red cleared as it had once before. I saw my face in his eyes a moment before the reflection vanished to reveal another image—of me and Siddhi.

I jerked my head, but Dafaru would not let me look away. Afraid that the images in his eyes were somehow being drawn out of mine, I closed my lids tight.

"On this day, you will learn what it is to be the consort of War."

My determination faltered at the tone of his voice, the tone of his words.

"From this day forth," he said, "any man who lies with you must be dead within a day, lest your kingdom topple."

Any man who lies with me?

He released my face and I opened my eyes. Clearly, he thought me a woman of extremely lax morality. I didn't tell him to rot in the hottest hells, but the words were in my mind. He, no doubt, saw them there.

Aloud, I said, "There are no others. There will be no others."

The emotion had already drained from his expression, the turbulence in his eyes the only lingering proof of his anger. "You remain ignorant as always, Amina." Abruptly, his anger dissolved and the disarming smile returned. He clasped his hands behind his back. "But I have a gift for you, my love. A gift you may share with your delectable friend."

My hands balled into fists at my sides.

He said, "Calm yourself. I will not touch your companion. Though I might have occasion to sample the pleasures of the mortal world, yours is the only mortal flesh I crave."

A shiver darted down my spine, and I wondered what obscenities he planned for my flesh.

"Never mind that, Beloved. I have a gift. Will you accept it?"

Reluctant to blindly accept anything he had for me, I gave no response.

"I offer eternal youth. For you and your friend."

"Eternal youth?" Surely, my ears had distorted his words.

"That is what I said."

Eternal youth.

To never grow old, never suffer the infirmities of age. Never lose my vigor. It was all vanity, I knew, but to retain my youth and vitality? I looked at Jaruma, who faced forward, hands behind her back, and gave no sign of what she felt about this offer.

"My lord, may we think on it?" I asked.

"You accept now or you do not accept at all."

I looked at Jaruma again.

She answered before I asked the question. "As you command, I obey."

"Loyal indeed," Dafaru said.

"Jaruma, I cannot force this on you."

"I follow where you lead, Gimbiya."

Dafaru returned to his throne. He leaned back, tipping his head to one side, and watched us in silence.

For the past thirty years, I couldn't be the warrior I wanted to be, and in the next twenty, I'd be too old. But to remain as I was? The temptation was far too great. Nonetheless, I wouldn't accept if Jaruma didn't want it.

"Jaruma?" I gave her another opportunity to refuse.

"I go where you go."

I heard no emotion in her voice. Saw nothing in the eyes that she kept focused in front of her, nothing in her rigid posture. Nothing to tell how she truly felt about this gift from the gods.

"You must tell me something," I said.

"And you must tell *me* something, Beloved." His impatience got the best of him. "You are wasting my time."

"It's what you want, Gimbiya," Jaruma said. She knew me too well. "My life is only worth what you tell me it's worth."

Her words were like a blow to the temple. "Your life is worth everything to me." She should have known that I'd lay mine down for hers.

She faced me now, brow creased. "I am your servant, Gimbiya. My fate is in your hands."

"Decide," Dafaru said.

I glared at him.

He met my hateful expression with one raised eyebrow. "Careful, woman."

I had to be strong to lead Zazzau against the Nupe. Or the Kwararafa. Or the Songhai. Or whatever nation threatened our sovereignty. Inexhaustible youth was assurance of that strength. He offered a gift of freedom. But I needed Jaruma by my side. No matter how long my youth, no matter how victorious, it would mean so much more with her there to share it. I *needed* her to share it because I couldn't do it alone.

"We accept your gift," I said, watching Jaruma, who still gave no hint of her thoughts.

The wargod smiled anew. It was an altogether different expression from any he'd worn before. He looked pleased, but without the beguiling, perverse, or malicious manner that usually accessorized his face. He was simply pleased.

Rising to his feet, Dafaru snapped his fingers, and the room filled with people. No . . . not people.

These were gods.

I recognized Kogi-Ayu in his man form immediately. Dawatsu, the thundergod, was a shorter, more heavily muscled version of Dafaru, an iron mallet slung from the belt at his waist. Gajere's rough brown skin was as lined as tree trunks, his hair as green as the forest leaves. Nakada, the jokester god of the Crossroads, appeared as he was in carvings and sculptures—thin and angular; thick, curly hair; small, mischievous eyes. And the firegoddess, Mak'esuwa, stood in a halo of yellow flames, wearing a disquieting frown.

There were so many I recognized from artwork or descriptions, and others I didn't recognize at all. However, I knew they were all gods or minor spirits. Not the least of whom was Inna, the mother of them all and shaper of the world.

In a loud voice, Dafaru said, "This mortal woman has accepted my gift. The bride-price will be paid as agreed. Eternal youth. Victory for her kingdom."

Inna moved forward. Small in stature, she was the most beautiful being I'd ever seen. Living vines pulled brown hair away from her face and into a soft mass at the crown of her head. Her skin was the same color as her hair, and her eyes, like her children's, were a swirling mist. They shone the color of earth, of grass, and of sky. Serene greens and browns tumbling in a calming pool of blue.

She laid a palm on my cheek. Her hand smelled of sweet nectar. "You are certain of this, child?" Her voice was a whisper of wind.

"Is it wrong for me to seek his aid?"

She looked up at the wargod while fingers, smooth as silk, caressed my face. "Only you can know, Amina. Is my son's favor worth the price you will surely pay?"

"The fate of my people hangs in the balance. Without him, the scales tip to the side of our enemies."

"And your vengeance?"

I said nothing.

"Then you have already made your choice." Her eyes settled into a single, indescribable color and she said apologetically, "I shaped you too well." Her lips were warm against my forehead. "It is done and will not be undone."

She took her hands away from my face and turned to her son. "This is your wedding gift, child of my husband." Then she crossed to Jaruma and kissed her forehead as well. "And this is my debt paid. Ask no more of me."

Dafaru returned to one of his more familiar smiles, this one rabid. "You have done enough, Mother."

I stood awkwardly between mother and son, trapped in the cold emanating from both. Our legends called Dafaru the Earth Mother's favorite child. They also said that he had wronged her. Until now, I'd not believed the legends. Whatever their argument, Dafaru and Inna lost no love on one another.

He gestured for me to join him, and I climbed the dais, coming to stand directly before him. In an unexpectedly gentle motion, he took my chin in the crook of his finger and lifted my face. He bent to me, eyes quiet. His lips brushed my cheek, and he whispered in my ear, "I have loved you far longer than you know." He spun me to face the crowd.

"This woman is mine. On this day and all to come, she serves my will and mine alone. If ever she serves the will of another—be it god, spirit, man, or herself—her life and all she loves will be forfeit."

He turned me to face him again. "You desire war, Amina? To bask in the heat of victory?"

Giddy excitement bubbled inside me. "Yes."

He pulled me close, arms around my waist. "And do you desire *me?*"

His nearness was more overpowering than it had ever been, and the excitement washing over me was more than mere lust for victory. It was . . . I shivered. *Allah forbid! What had Inna done to me?*

Clenching my jaw, I tried not to say anything at all, but the word "yes" pressed against my teeth, eager to pass my lips. I did not allow it. Instead, I lied. "No."

Still wearing that rabid smile, he said, "Shall I tell you what it means to be the consort of War?" He did not wait for a response. "Inna did nothing, except halt your aging. Whatever desire you feel has always been. But now it is all-consuming and will rule above everything else." He lowered his face to mine. "Your soul and body belong to me, but your tongue is false. And you lie to yourself, Amina, because you cannot lie to me."

All but limp in his arms, my body anticipated him with fevered urgency.

He continued, "Know that I alone may satisfy the craving in your soul, the burning desire of your flesh. And your desire will control you, Beloved. Beware how you endeavor to quench the flame. It could be the death of the Zazzagawa."

Understanding dawned as he spoke the last words. Horrified, I looked at him. Whether or not I was loose-skirted before, now that our union was sealed, I was enslaved to the fierce craving growing in me even as I stood dumbstruck. He'd known it would be so. With my own two feet, I had walked into this trap.

I tried to pull away. "No. You can't—" But the trap snapped shut. He kissed me.

It was awful and it was wonderful. His lips, hot as sun-beaten pebbles, burned into me and sent a sharp flash of desire arcing through my body. I wanted to push him away but hadn't the strength of will to do it. I tried to resist but only struggled against myself as I gave my body over to him.

My life ended in that moment. And our lips parted to a roll of thunder. When Dafaru released me, his witnesses were gone. Only Jaruma remained with us in the hall.

He glanced at her. "You are the mortal witness to this."

"No." I spoke with a calm I didn't feel. "You lied to me."

"I told you no lies."

"A partial truth is a lie."

The glow of his flashing eyes illuminated his face. "No, Amina. A *lie* is a lie. And you, Beloved, have proven very good at it."

Without a word or a thought for self-preservation, I slapped him.

He grabbed me by the braided hair. "It is done. You cannot turn back now."

"Release me!"

I fought to free myself from his hold, and he let go of my hair. I staggered, lost my footing on the dais steps, and tumbled to the floor. Dafaru started down the stairs, but Jaruma was already at my side.

"I'm fine," I said as she helped me up. My mind formulated curses for my new husband, who scowled down at me from the dais. My future saw the blood of thousands on my hands. *Would they die in battle or in bed?* I wondered.

"Come here," he said in his usual chilly tones.

His eternal servant, I could no more disobey him than my servants could me. Collecting myself, I went to him.

"Take Amina's companion back to her room," he said.

"Yes, my lord." Salima had entered the hall unnoticed, and now she bowed low at her master—*our* master—then at me. "This way," she said to Jaruma.

Jaruma stayed put.

"Go," I said.

She backed away, her eyes fixed on the wargod. Part of me wished to retreat with her, but another part—a part that both frightened and disgusted me—craved his singular attention.

Halfway to the door, Jaruma paused.

"Leave us," Dafaru's tone suggested that if he had to repeat himself, it would bode well for no one.

Jaruma looked at me. I nodded. She turned and walked after Salima. And I was alone with the god of war.

NINETEEN

I stood before a set of doors made from gleaming reddish metal into which was sculpted a detailed battle scene. Men in heavy armor fought a contingent of loincloth-clad swordsmen. The faces of the swordsmen were contorted in obvious despair. The armored men bared their teeth in triumph, the severed heads of their enemies mounted upon spears. Despite the heat emanating from the body behind me, the scene drew my attention, and I peered more closely at it.

The battle came to life.

I stepped back with a gasp as the defeated men in loincloths staggered about, some with entrails dragging behind them. The armored men, merciless in victory, cut their enemies down. Then, the ground upon which the armies fought parted in the middle, and the doors swung away from me, the tiny figures frozen in their new positions.

"You may admire the relief at your pleasure, Beloved, not mine." He urged me forward with a hand at the small of my back.

A gust of air billowed over me when I crossed the threshold of the large chamber. Sheer curtains danced in the open balcony doorway. The floor-to-ceiling glass panel doors served as the only windows in the room. In sharp contrast to the dark corridors, this room gleamed white and gold, its ceiling a gold relief of men and women engaged in a multitude of lurid acts. With blood rushing to my cheeks, I looked away from the ceiling lest these figures come to life as well.

The bed, a massive gilded affair with white granite posts, was positioned at center on the far wall. Hands clasped tightly together, I crossed to it, making a vain attempt to ignore the heavy pounding in my chest. But in the ten or so paces it took me to reach the bed, my trembling knees threatened to crumple. I clutched the white bedpost with both hands and leaned my head against it to steady my tempestuous nerves.

The air around me warmed as he neared. One of his hands covered mine, the other found my shoulder, and fear tightened my spine.

He's a man, I told myself. He looked like one, at any rate. I prayed the similarity continued below the waist.

He laughed, his hand moving from my shoulder to my abdomen. "I am so much more than a man, my love. But I assure you, the packaging is compatible."

The packaging in question revealed itself when he pressed into me.

I exhaled, skin prickling, and closed my eyes. I didn't want to, but savored his touch. He pressed his lips to my neck, and his hand moved lower—to the bare skin beneath the hem of my dress.

I tried to stifle a shuddering sigh, but searing kisses traveled the length of my neck, raising my temperature. Despite all my misgivings, this was pleasure. *He* was pleasure. His burning touch charged my awareness. Lacing the fingers of his other hand through mine, he pulled me away from the post. The dress slid upward like cool liquid as he lifted it over my head.

I turned to face him, my chest rising and falling with quickened breathing. Roiling red eyes meandered over my nude body, then regarded me with an expectant expression. Anxious, I bit my lower lip. He continued to regard me as though he wanted me to make the next move.

Willing or unwilling.

Right now, I was both. Exhaling slowly, I stepped forward. A small crease formed at the corner of his upturned lips, the only wrinkle in an otherwise smooth façade. He tossed my dress aside and took my trembling hand.

"Still, you fear me." His torso was bare beneath his open cloak. "What have I done to evoke such terror?" A condescendingly arched eyebrow accompanied the last sarcasm-laden word.

"You've made me a whore," I said, snatching my hand from his. "I made you a wife. Which is more than those others did. And I have not harmed you. Well"—he removed his cloak—"not yet."

I drew back but came up against the bedpost. "You've—" I inhaled sharply as his fingers rose, and exhaled when they traced the outline of my collarbone. Frightened yet giddy, willing yet unwilling, I tried to suppress *all* of my emotions. "You've cursed me."

"You are cursed only with ignorance. You may take that up with your Creator."

When he pressed his fiery kiss to my mouth, I wanted to despise it, but my body trembled and my lips parted, the metallic flavor of him sending tendrils of flame lancing through me. A low growl rumbled in his throat. It vibrated within me, feeding the flame. As my hands moved to his chest and around his neck, I deepened the kiss, yielded to him. And when he drew back, I clung to him.

A small grin settled on his face. "Patience, my love."

Appalled by my weakness, I quickly released him, again struggling to suppress my emotions, to suppress the thoughts in my head, the knowledge that I wanted him.

"I do not need to hear your thoughts to feel your desire, Beloved."

He unfastened the kilt, and when it slipped from his waist, my treacherous knees betrayed me. I sat heavily on the bed.

"As I said." Wearing nothing but his leather bracers, he stepped close. "The packaging is compatible."

I leaned back, wary, and stared at his "packaging", its compatibility yet doubtful. He placed a knee on the bed.

"My lord, I—"

"Be silent. Unless the next words you speak are *take me now.*"

I remained silent. What could I have said? *Be gentle?* I tore my gaze away from the thing, past the blazing intensity of his eyes, and glanced at the ceiling. A shock of arousal speared through me at the thought of him doing what those images depicted.

"You have been a most elusive prize." His hand rose to my hair. He twirled my braided strands between his fingers. "Pray you are worth it."

Lips curling into an impish smirk, he cupped my chin and drew me forward. I scrambled backward. He crawled onto the bed, grasped my ankle, and jerked me forward until I was sprawled beneath him. He looked down at me, the glowing red of his eyes dissipating like smoke in the wind. Ever-changing images of us locked in sensual embraces played in his gaze. The scene unfolding in his eyes pushed my desire to a feverish high.

His mouth came down on mine. My body wanted him. *I* wanted him and could no longer deny or otherwise hide it. I draped my arms around his neck, parted my lips. My tongue delved into his mouth, and I didn't try to stop it. He slid an arm beneath me, crushed me to his hard chest. Several moans echoed in my throat. He groaned a response, lifted me off the bed and sat, lowering me onto his lap.

With a frantic gasp, I pressed a hand to his thigh to prevent my downward motion. "No. I can't. It is *not* compatible."

Laughter burst from his mouth. Even to myself, I sounded imbecilic.

Moving my hand from his thigh, he brought his mouth to mine and kissed me lightly. Fingers twined again in my hair, pulled my head backward. His lips fell to my neck. His teeth nipped my throat. I gave a stuttering sigh, a loud inhalation. I cried out.

"My lord, you're—"

He tugged my head farther back. "I have waited long enough, Beloved." His voice reverberated through me. "I will have you now if it kills you."

The offensive words stoked my fire into an inferno. I shuddered, a low croon snaking from my lips. As he marked a trail of kisses down my neck. I caressed him, my nails grazed his smooth pate. Then I all but screamed as he drove into me. Arms curled around him, I clutched him tightly, and we sat motionless for several moments. But even this pain was a pleasure that I didn't want to end.

My hips began to move.

With ragged breathing, I moved atop him. I wanted to lose myself in him, to bask in the glory of a god. I wanted all he had to offer, to be his and to give him all of me, *everything* that I was.

Humiliated by the shock of my own delirious thoughts, I stilled. He could take what he wanted from me, but I would give him *nothing*. Though he controlled my body, he would never have my love.

His shoulders stiffened, jaw hardened, and the heat of his body cooled. His hand dropped from my hair. It was all I could do not to beg forgiveness. Instead, I met his intense gaze and willed my hips to remain still, remain compliant. They didn't. And I cursed them but drew in a long, stuttering breath when his heat engulfed me once again.

"Ignorant woman," he said, stroking the length of my neck. He pressed a kiss to the hollow between my collarbones. I closed my eyes, all the while chiding my own zeal. His fingers wrapped around my neck and squeezed. Not much. But enough to drive me to the edge of rapture and increase my shameful exertions.

He squeezed tighter.

Tighter.

And I couldn't breathe.

My hand flew to his, grabbing at his fingers, trying to pry them loose. He turned us over, lying me on the bed. I writhed beneath him, in rhythm with him, the pressure in my head driving me to strange ecstasy, while I clawed at his hand, trying to undo the grip around my neck.

His spirit rose to surround me. It rode me, filled me, burning in my veins. He was me and I was him, the sensation heightened by the stars dancing behind my eyes. I cried out in a voice that wasn't mine. I screamed his name and, perhaps, my own. A tremor rocked through me. My body convulsed, shuddered wildly, and I whimpered in sensual pleasure. As he released my neck, I took in a breath of air, the inhalation waking all my senses at once, and the quake carried me into climax.

He gave a deep groan and rolled onto the bed.

The sudden emptiness tore the breath back out of me. It was like being doused in cold water. The presence that had filled me was gone. The part of him that had *been* me was gone. He exhaled and I looked at him, the yearning in my heart surely showing on my face, because I needed him now more than I'd ever needed anything. Whatever he'd done, I wanted it again.

Blazing red eyes met mine, a wicked chuckle rising in his throat. "Perhaps, my love. If you beg."

TWENTY

Despite his confession of love, what Dafaru did to me that day could not be called lovemaking by any stretch of the imagination. He inflicted pleasure and pain in equal measure. He humiliated my body and my mouth in ways I dared not describe. He used me like a whore and made me beg for more. To my utter repugnance, I enjoyed his depravities through and through.

We lay naked on the gilded bed, his fingers tracing the curve of my hip. It sent wicked thrills through me, and I hated myself for it.

"You are every bit the delicacy I thought you would be. And more." He rolled me onto my back and gazed down at me. The images in his eyes replayed our every vulgar embrace. "I would ask whether you enjoyed yourself, Beloved. But the answer was several times evident."

I turned away. That I couldn't control my body's response to his manipulations shamed me at best. That I wanted him, in spite of my shame, enraged me to no end.

"I'll be missed in Zazzau." My shoulder tensed when his fingers touched my arm.

Beyond the billowing curtains, the balcony without rails looked like a silver-white cloud against the darkening sky. I'd been gone almost a full day. If anyone noticed my absence, with Jaruma also gone, they would assume the two of us were together and would raise no alarms.

Of course, since I knew this, he did too.

With a noncommittal grunt, he removed his hand from my arm and lay back. After a few moments of silence, I turned to look at him. He was preoccupied with the ring on his smallest finger.

Lying beside me, he resembled something carved from ebony. A perfectly sculpted work of art, his body was without flaw; his proportions perfectly matched. I wondered if it was some sort of illusion. If under all that perfection was a demonic form, a monster from the deepest reaches of the farthest hell.

"I am as you see me, Beloved," he said absently and continued to fuss with the ring. Finally getting it off his finger, he held it up. The ring glinted in the light of the setting sun, the fire-red metal swirling and roiling—much like his eyes—as though it were alive.

Taking hold of my left hand, he slipped the ring onto my forefinger. It was too big. But as soon as it settled onto the base of my finger, it shrank and conformed to my shape.

"Keep it on," he said. "When you are in need, I will know. If it is in my power to aid you, I will." Scorching lips met mine and pulled away. "You are indeed Beloved of the gods."

Beloved of the gods? Then why did I feel like the accursed of the gods? Forever shackled, forever subject to his every whim. The terrible words he'd spoken in his throne room floated to the top of my mind: *Any man who lies with you must be dead within a day.*

"If I'm truly beloved," I asked, "why did you curse me?"

He groaned as though the subject already bored him but rolled onto his side and propped himself on an elbow. "I was angry and behaved like a jealous child." Strangely calm eyes looked at me.

I was more comfortable with the raging eyes.

"Why would you lie to me when you know I see your thoughts?" He rolled onto his back again, stretched, and added, "It was not a curse, merely a proclamation. Perhaps I was too harsh." But there was no remorse in his voice.

"I'm yours, my lord. I would never lie with another man."

Rolling laughter met my words.

"I don't know what sort of woman you think I am, but no other man will touch me." In the face of his continued laughter, my confidence wavered. "I don't intend to . . . what I mean is . . . if you . . ."

He drew me onto him. "If I what? If I am at your beck and call?" An impish grin spread across his face. "Luscious though you are, I will not be bound by your desire. You shall find other ways to satisfy your needs."

Needs that intensified even as his lips parted mine. He sank his hands into my hair, grasped a bundle of braids, and drew my head back to break the dizzying kiss.

"I am a jealous god. This you already know. I will not allow you to harbor fond feelings for some mortal lover. They die or your kingdom dies."

"But you needn't kill them," I pleaded. Were he not holding my hair, I would have clamped my mouth back down on his. "There will be no others. I swear—"

"There will be others, Amina. And I will not touch them. *You* must kill them."

The intense desire to kiss him faded. I pulled myself free and sat up, staring at him in abject horror. "You want me to . . . to murder? I cannot."

"You will."

"I will not."

"You have no other option, my love. I am not allowed to kill the children of men, otherwise I would . . . *daily*. Yet, your lovers must die."

"I can't. I won't. There will be no others."

But that was a lie. Even now, I craved more. And he said he would not answer to this building desire. I closed my eyes and tried to suppress it, but the more I focused on it, the stronger it grew. I struggled to put it out of my mind entirely, but it stampeded through me like a runaway horse, pushing me to search for options he claimed I didn't have.

Perhaps, if I used a woman to satisfy my needs. To do those things I could not manage on my own.

"Man or woman, your lover must die."

"No." Shaking my head in vigorous refusal, I repeated, "No."

He said nothing and his calm expression told no stories. Moisture pricked my eyes, but I wouldn't let him see me cry.

"You are vile," I said.

"So I have been told."

"Only death will free me from your madness." I turned away and buried my face in a pillow, still fighting tears. My muffled voice quavered. "Not even death. I've forfeited that as well."

"Fear not, my love," he said coolly. "You are eternally young, not immortal. You can die if you wish to take your life." He touched my shoulder and his manner grew gentle. "I told you that I love you, and it was the truth. I ask only that you love me in return."

Facing him now, I sneered, my heart fully hardened against him. "How could I ever love you when I detest the sight of you?"

Anger flashed in his eyes, fury building to a swirling red eddy, and I braced myself for his wrath. Jamming his forearm into my chest, he pinned me to the bed.

"Shall I break you like a dog, Amina? Would that make you less bellicose?"

I spat back with more bellicosity than I'd yet shown him. "You'll do what you must."

"That I will." He eased off me and got out of bed, rising to seven feet of majesty. "You would do well to remember it."

I rubbed my chest.

Adjusting the black bracers he'd not bothered to remove, he crossed the room, scooped up the discarded heap of my dress, and threw it in my face. "Get dressed. I will bring your companion to you."

❋

There wasn't much dressing to be done. All the body adornments of gold were still in place. As I'd been wearing no other garments besides the indecent dress, I was soon fully clothed. Dejected, I sat on the edge of the bed.

A short time later, the bedchamber door opened. Jaruma sidled around Dafaru to come into the room. I glanced at him, painfully aware of the stabbing desire that continued to mock my shame. He gave a sweeping bow and shut the door.

"Are you all right?" She strode forward, eyes roaming over my body. "He didn't harm you?"

"He didn't harm me."

Satisfied, she stood back. "He says we can leave whenever we like." She glanced at the closed door. "He came into my room, Amina. Without so much as announcing himself. As though *I* belong to him as well. He's disagreeable."

I chuckled but not from mirth. If only Dafaru were just disagreeable.

"Do you remember how to get back to the stone chamber?" I was both eager and reluctant to leave this place.

She shook her head. "Surely he'll provide us a guide or a map for these strange lands?"

"I think he'll let us walk in circles until our feet blister and our bones crack."

She looked at me in my flimsy dress, bare feet, and disheveled hair. "He wouldn't let your body suffer so, even if he cares nothing for the rest of you." Then she handed me a tight bundle. "I brought your things."

I unfurled the bundle of clothing and weaponry. My legs slid into the comfortable embrace of trousers, and I donned my cotton tunic over the thin dress. The feel of familiar clothing eased some of my distress but did not eliminate it.

I'd sought the god of war to control the oncoming chaos. I had wanted to reshape the future, to minimize the loss of Zazzagawa lives. I was destined to sacrifice thousands to the god of war and now knew that some, if not all, would die at *my* hands. At first, my course had seemed clear. Now, the future was far less certain. Jaruma still held my short-sword and war bracelets. Looking at the bracelets—my reminder of Suleyman—bitterness surged through me, my shame complete.

"I'll carry them," Jaruma said. "Our weapons won't touch the likes of Dangoji anyway."

Silent, I nodded. She folded the bracelets in my headwrap and strapped my sword to her sash, alongside her own weapon.

"Ready?" She tucked the headwrap under her arm.

I nodded again.

We exited the room to find Salima waiting outside and followed her to the main doors.

"Journey safely," she said as the large doors opened on their own.

Jaruma and I stepped into the dark alcove of the entryway. Without a sound, the doors shut behind us.

A mass of what appeared to be fireflies lit the ceiling of the entry alcove. Beyond it, night met our eyes.

"Might it be prudent to wait until daybreak?" I asked in a nervous whisper.

Before Jaruma could respond, a voice behind us exclaimed, "You've returned!"

We spun around to see the priest of the Oracle. We were back in the Sacred Forest and standing outside the stone chamber.

TWENTY-ONE

The cold of Dafaru's absence manifested almost immediately upon my leaving Jangare. In the days that followed, I did indeed come to understand what it was to be the consort of War. A fever rose in me, and it *was* all-consuming.

To slow the raging hunger, I conducted my business and retired to my room each night with Jaruma as my only company. It was as it had been when she first came to serve me. She slept where I slept and ate where I ate. Yet she could not be with me always, as was the case now.

She'd gone to bathe, and only a short time had passed when there came a knock at the door. Siddhi announced himself and entered without awaiting my acknowledgment, much less my invitation.

"Have I vexed you?" He folded his arms.

At seeing him framed within the early evening sunlight, my fever rose to a higher burn. I urged my heart to calm.

"No," I said.

"You've been avoiding me."

I put down the gourd of palm wine I was tipping to my cup. "I've been preoccupied, Makama." It wasn't easy to keep my voice steady, to maintain a mien of indifference.

"*Makama*, is it? And you say you're not vexed."

"I'm not vexed."

He unfolded his arms and bowed low. "My sincerest apologies, Gimbiya. Have you been so preoccupied that you no longer have time for me?" He approached.

I got to my feet, retying the wrapper that had come loose at my waist. "Please, Siddhi." His presence alone distracted me from my battle against the hunger. If he did not relent in this pursuit, the strength of my ungodly desire would likely overwhelm me.

Nonplussed, he strode forward. "What's come over you?"

I put up a hand, urging him to keep his distance. "You must go."

He took that hand, drew me forward, and enclosed me in his arms. I felt my resistance dwindling. Bit by bit, my defensive walls began to crumble, and I stood immobile against the carnal fever.

"Gimbiya?" Jaruma was in the doorway. "Amina, what are you doing?" She knew, of course, what I had become.

I broke free of Siddhi's embrace. "You must go," I said quietly, shaken by what surely would have occurred had Jaruma not interrupted.

"Amina, please." He took my hand again. "Tell me what I've done and I'll make amends."

Perhaps Dafaru was right to be jealous. If not for the proclamation he had laid upon me, I'd take Siddhi now and love him for cooling the heat that threatened to immolate me.

"You've done nothing, Siddhi." My free hand, fingers unsteady, traced the slender line of his jaw. "But I've done a terrible thing."

"There is nothing so terrible that it cannot be surmounted."

Withdrawing my hand from his face, I shook my head. "It's beyond mending."

"Amina . . ." His voice was a woeful plea.

I shook my head again.

"You cannot stay, Makama," Jaruma said.

His laughter was chilling. "Your bodyguard is throwing me out?"

I said, "Jaruma, wait outside."

She hesitated but left the room. Siddhi took a step forward and closed my hands in his. To my dismay, he dropped to his knees.

"I love you, Amina. Whatever you've done is of no importance to me." He slid his arms around my waist, holding me close, his face pressed into my bare abdomen. "No matter how terrible, it makes no difference."

The words broke my heart. I held him—wanting him, though the wanting brought death. There was no mending what was upon me now. Loosening my grip, I kissed the top of his head. "Please stand up."

He got to his feet.

"I was happy with you in the time we shared." I looked into morose eyes. "But we were never meant to be. If I'd known . . . I didn't realize how you truly felt, else I would never . . ." My brow furrowed and I lowered my gaze.

"Never what?" Anguish sharpened his words.

I turned away lest he see the torture in my soul. "You must go."

"Amina."

"Go, Siddhi." I did not turn back around until Jaruma spoke.

"He's gone."

I sank onto the diwan. "I've devastated him." I dropped my head into my hands.

"His heart will heal," she said by way of awkward consolation.

"I know." The words broke through a stuttering breath. "I think mine will not . . . Leave me, Jaruma."

"I can't leave you like this."

My face tight with misery, I looked up at her. "I want to be alone. Just tonight. Please."

"But—"

"He's gone, Jaruma. What can I possibly do?"

Though her eyes gave loud objection, she eventually acquiesced and left me to my misery. I sat motionless on the diwan until the sun fell and darkness filled the room. Until resentment replaced self-pity. Resentment at Dafaru for forcing this hunger on me, at Siddhi for loving me, and at myself for refusing to acknowledge what I'd always known was true.

Amina and War are one.

Was that not the prophecy? Although I had refused to accept it, in my heart I had known it would come to pass—as such prophecies usually did. In my pursuit of happiness, of *normalcy*, I'd been blind to the wretchedness destined to be my lot. Sighing a deep breath, I composed myself and wiped my face with my palms. Giving my body over to the god of war had been a simple matter; living with the consequences was another thing entirely. The unnatural urge had been under control for many days, but seeing Siddhi had drained me of the will to contain it. As night fell, the burning fever grew to a painful intensity, and I surrendered. Moving on legs that were not entirely my own, I left the room.

✳

"Greetings, Gimbiya."

I scarcely registered the sound before walking into him. Irritated, I glowered at the guard standing sentry in the shadowed space between the war chamber and the queen's meeting room. Unabashed, he inclined his head in a small bow.

My immediate reaction was to push him out of the way and continue on, through the administrative row, out the palace, and into the streets beyond. When my arm made contact with his body, however, my craving surged. I paused and he stared, his gaze unwavering.

In a cool tone, I said, "Your eyes crawl over me like beetles on dung."

He dropped his gaze. "Forgive me, Gimbiya. It was not my intention to stare, but your beauty . . . it blinds me to everything else." Obviously adept at flattery, the man's words flowed smooth as the richest butter.

"Yet, now you manage to see only your feet." I shoved him out of my way.

He raised his head and looked into my eyes, halting me before I stepped past. Were my eyes anything like my husband's, the guard would have fled in terror at the sight of himself being mauled by a lion in the rage of heat. He did not flee; he smiled. And the craving overrode that small sanity screaming for me to continue on my way.

"Do you know where I sleep?" I asked the question before I even realized what was stirring in my mind.

"Yes, Gimbiya. I know."

"I require a husband for the night." Though they issued from my lips, the words were crude and foreign. I tried to contain the urge, tried to fight the impulse that had grown to a fanatical need, but the words continued without pause. "Are you willing?"

His eyebrows rose so high they threatened to advance into his hairline. He made no response.

"Are you unable?" Guilt choked my heart, clawed my belly. I ignored it.

"No, Gimbiya. Uh . . . yes, Gimbiya."

"Is it yes or is it no?" The last vestiges of reason demanded that I walk away from the man, but the conflagration within ordered me to stay.

"Yes. I am able." More cautiously, he added, "I am willing."

"If you're willing, then tonight you may possess all you've dared only to look upon."

The man opened his mouth to speak.

"*Temporary* husband only," I said and turned to walk away. "For tonight."

※

Seated upon the diwan, I faced the open door with my arms stretched across the chair's back. I was uncertain he would follow but waited nonetheless. *As a spider awaits a fly.*

I was a slave to my desire, and it turned out that he was a fool to his. He arrived at my door after only a short while and slipped quietly into the room. He came forward a few paces.

"There is a door," I said, gesturing.

He quickly pushed it shut.

"Sit with me."

He came over and lowered himself onto the diwan. I reached across him to pick up the gourd of palm wine, which I pushed into his hands. After a few draughts from the gourd, he raised his brow with an inquisitive look.

Pressing close to him, I declined with a shake of my head. "I've had enough drink for one night."

Satisfied that my interests did not lie in the wine, he drank with greater enthusiasm. My breast lay against his, and our hearts raced in unison. His was likely beating a song of passion while mine beat only my guilt. Despite that guilt or because of it, I plied him with the beverage until he was fully inebriated.

Once he emptied the contents of the gourd, his impatience was perceptible. The buttery words vanished. Without so much as a kiss or soft caress, he groped for the trailing end of my wrapper, but his drunken fingers were clumsy. Brushing his fumbling hands away, I pulled the wrapper loose with a single tug and removed my blouse.

"Ah, Gimbiya . . ." He fell on me like an animal.

"Gently."

Were it not for his trousers, it would have been impossible to rein him in. Hampered by the knots in his drawstring, he slowed and leaned back on the diwan. Again, I brushed his hands away, and they migrated from his string to my body. When the ties were loose, he didn't bother to remove his trousers before pulling his shaft from its confines. It was just as well. By then I was mad with desire, my body as hungry for his as a starved man hungers for food. Climbing onto him, I guided him inside.

The guard was drunk and nearly useless, but he remained erect for as long as it took to satisfy my need. When the time came, he spilled into me with the force of a charging bull. The thrill of it forced a moan from my lips. I fell across him, spent and fully sated for the time being. We remained like that until his soft snoring came in regular waves.

Rising, I picked up my wrapper and tied it at my waist. Then I lit the lamp and watched him. Peaceful in his drink-induced sleep. The scent of wine and coupling filled the air, along with the scent of pending death. It was stifling. A lamentation rose in my throat.

Getting hold of myself before I gave way to senseless wailing, I sat down beside him and touched his face, laid my hand on his chest, saying aloud, "I needed you." As though it would free me from culpability. But nothing could erase my sin.

I continued, though my audience lay sleeping like the dead, "I needed release from this . . ." There were no words to describe a thirst that could not be slaked. "Forgive me." My hand on his chest rose and fell with his steady breathing. "But my husband is a cruel god." I gave him two brisk slaps across the face.

He looked at me through half-open lids.

"Wake," I said.

He lay still, eyes fluttering open and shut.

"Wake up." I slapped him harder.

Groaning, he pulled himself upright. "Gimbiya."

He tried to pull me to him, but I snatched myself away, stood, and drew him to his feet. He stumbled and leaned against me for balance.

"I didn't thank you for the wine," he murmured, again fussing with drawstrings as he attempted to sort out his trousers.

I took over the tying. "Do not thank me. And tell no one of this."

He swayed on his feet. "Gimbiya, I would never tell a soul. Will you allow me another night?"

"Sleep first." I shoved him toward the door. "Then we shall see."

"Have I pleased you?"

"Very much. Now go." My anxiety rose with every moment he lingered. "Go."

Bowing unsteadily, he bid me good night and made his way out of the room.

With shuddering hands, I closed the door and crossed back over to the diwan, crumpling onto it. I picked up the empty gourd, breathed a deep sigh, and recalled a lesson in plant lore.

Occasionally and irrespective of the ordinance against it, Zazzagawa archers used plant poisons on weapon tips. Although I had no pressing need of the poisons, I brewed them to keep the skill sharp. The finished products, discarded and renewed from time to time, were in my weapons bin, which lay open on the other side of the room. The concoctions worked swiftest when introduced through an open wound but were no less fatal when ingested.

The god of war had said that Zazzau would suffer if my lovers lived. The risk of testing his conviction in that matter was far too great. So, in the short time it had taken the guard to reach my door, I had poisoned the wine. He would be dead by morning. Witchcraft or some other magic would likely take the blame; no one would suspect me. But nothing would cleanse the stain of murder from my soul.

TWENTY-TWO

The hapless guard was only the first. There were more temporary husbands after that, and each death came easier, each made me colder. Over the next half year, one murder or four made little difference to my conscience. A fact that might have driven me deep into melancholy if not for the Zazzagawa change of heart toward Nupeland.

Contrary to prior sentiment, people now screamed for the head of the Nupe king, and there was no shortage of recruits. I did not stop to wonder what devices Dafaru had used to change the collective mindset of an entire people, but young men—sometimes still boys— and even women vied to become warriors. Slave-class soldiers raised from childhood and previously deemed unready were now a strong fighting force. On top of this success and, perhaps, the strangest development of all, my mother had allowed me to join the war council.

Many years had passed since the last time I'd been party to a war council, but the familiar atmosphere—the tension, strained voices, the uncertainty—had been like returning home after years of travel. Poring over the battle schematics had been reminiscent of times spent in my grandfather's war chamber. Except with Grandfather, I had never felt the anxiety that I'd felt in the chamber today. For despite the wargod's intervention, the Nupe still outnumbered us two to one. As I sat with Jaruma later that evening, not eating the dinner covering the table before us, my thoughts remained on Nupeland.

"Do you agree with the kaura?" I leaned back on the diwan, tucking my legs under me. "The most prudent course of action is to increase our cavalry?"

As opposed to my lack of appetite, Jaruma overate when stressed, and was currently stuffing meatpies into her mouth at a worrisome rate.

She swallowed. "If we put the most skilled riders on horses, within a year we could train them to give good fight from horseback. But there's no point in discussing it further. As I said in the war council, we've no means of acquiring more horses."

"And if there were?"

"Do you know of some magic that conjures horses?" She licked her fingers and reached for her cup of honey beer.

I spread my arms along the back of the diwan. "There are ways."

In an attempt to laugh, she inhaled the liquid and fell into a coughing fit. Several paroxysmal moments passed before she regained her breath. "Is your divine husband going to put it in a horse trader's mind to give you three thousand horses as a gift? Or will he send you three thousand wild horses to be broken and tamed?" A derisive sound blew past her lips. "I've never even seen a wild horse."

I raised my left hand to examine the fire ring Dafaru had given me. "He's not done much else." Dropping both hands onto my lap, I fiddled with the ring, watching its colors dance in the lamplight. "It's the least he could do."

No sooner had I uttered the words than the wargod appeared. He stood head angled to one side to keep from bumping the thatched ceiling. Spying Jaruma, he grabbed her arm, half lifted her to her feet, and kissed her soundly on the lips.

My blood boiled.

Pressing my teeth together, I urged the anger down. Dafaru took his mouth off hers and looked at me. Bitter anger rose again. He released her. Like a flower cut from its stalk, she wilted onto the diwan.

My companion turned to me, her features dark with guilt. "Amina . . ."

"Don't worry yourself," I said.

She made to stand. Dafaru took her hand and helped her to her feet. He pulled her close, whispered something in her ear. I fought the impulse to kick him but gave her a weak, commiserating smile when she looked back at me. Needless to say, I was relieved to see her step sideways to get past without touching him further. As she hurried away, I caught a glimpse of smooth ivory jutting from her belt.

"Our lovely friend has a mouth as sweet as honey." Dressed in all black, he made a show of licking his lips.

"There was honey in her food. What did you give her?"

"I gave her this."

Hoisting me off the diwan, he pulled me into an embrace that, despite my anger, melted me on the spot. The kiss all but undid me. With great fortitude of will, however, I remained unresponsive.

"You *are* angry." He smirked. "Do not fret, my love. I long for you and you alone. You called?" In response to the bewilderment in my mind and, no doubt, on my face, he took hold of the hand wearing the fire ring. "I told you. I can feel you when it is on your finger."

He had, indeed, told me that.

"And I can hear your thoughts when you hold it."

He'd told me that as well but had said it while he was doing other things with my body. The recollection threatened to break down my barrier. I struggled to quell the rising ache.

He let loose one of his devious grins. "I can do those things again if you like."

My rebellious nipples hardened against his chest.

"But first," he said, relaxing his grip around my waist. "You called?"

"Perhaps I did." I made a mental note to keep my hand off the ring. "But not to impart gifts on my friend."

He raised an eyebrow. "Such petty jealousy. I do not see why we cannot share her." He looked around the room. "How I despise this land of yours." His next words vibrated against my ear. "Come. Let me melt the anger in your heart."

And we were on the dais in his draughty throne room.

He dropped onto the black throne. "Undress."

"My lord?"

"You heard me."

"I . . . this is . . ." If he intended to melt my anger, he was doing a poor job of it. I raised my chin and crossed my arms over my chest. "I'm your wife, not a common whore."

"You are what I say you are."

I glared at him for several long breaths. The jovial countenance he had brought from the world of men vanished as he leaned back in his chair. There could be no battle of wills between us, no arguments. In this game, we were unevenly matched. Against him, I had no power. Only my dignity remained; and though I guarded it, perhaps *because* I guarded it, he intended to take that as well. His swirling eyes grew turbulent. His forefinger began tapping the armrest.

With a shudder rising up my spine, I pleaded softly, "My lord, I beg you."

"Do as I say. Or shall I do it for you?"

No weapon of mine would hurt him; but were I armed, I might have tried. He raised a warning eyebrow and I silenced my thoughts.

Slowly, I removed my blouse. The beads around my neck jangled as the garment lifted over my head. His eyes, intense and churning, watched my every move. After tugging my wrapper loose, I stood before him in nothing more than my skin and the beaded necklaces.

He cocked his head. "Infinitely better. Now what troubles you, Beloved?"

I wrapped my arms around myself. Did he expect me to discuss horses while standing here like this?

"Horses?" he said. "That *is* troubling."

A gesture beckoned me forward and I moved closer. Closer still. Until the heat radiating from his body engulfed me. Another gesture indicated for me to turn around. My shoulders tensed with subdued anger. My face flushed with humiliation at this poor treatment.

"You are mine to treat as I please." His body reciprocated the cold in his voice; the temperature dropped around me, as he said, "And you will yield to me."

I yielded and turned, loathing him all the while. But loathing was only one of many emotions. When it came to the god of war, my feelings were confused. Repulsion, attraction, hate, desire, and every other conflicting sentiment fought for preeminence in my heart. Underneath it all, excitement always hummed—even now as I stood there, naked and shivering.

The heat returned as Dafaru rose and stood behind me. He slid my plaited hair aside and kissed the back of my neck, his hand on my belly. The tangled emotions churned inside me. I tried to hate him but couldn't. Not when he touched me like that.

"Horses, eh?" He turned me to face him.

Before I could stop myself, *if ever I had the power*, I threw my arms about his neck and kissed him. My mind protested, but my body did not. His arms came around my waist. I parted my lips. The burnished-metal taste of him drove me to a state of urgency that he alone could address. Then the memories surfaced. Fractured images of dead men rose in my mind. The memories of what occurred every time this hunger took hold of me in the mortal world.

I tore my lips away.

Red mist danced in his eyes. For a fleeting moment, I wondered if he'd gone into a trance. He looked almost dazed.

The haze in his eyes settled into a clear pool of brilliant red. "You speak of horses, Amina, but your heart speaks of other matters."

Humiliated anew by my salacious behavior, I took a calming breath and drew back, my hands dropping to his chest. "I despise you."

Turbulence battered the clear, red pools into a bloody broth. "Is this how you speak to your lord and master? Perhaps we should find other ways to douse your fire."

"No!" I cursed my desperation, but if he sent me back with my needs unmet, another man would die this very night. "Forgive me."

Thus assured of my continued cooperation, he took me to his chamber. It was some time before we returned to the subject of horses.

＊

"You have slaves enough to trade for hundreds of horses." He lay sprawled across the gilded monstrosity. "Your fool of a makama has already added two hundred slaves to your count, in spite of your many rejections. As beautiful as you are, I daresay you could beguile some other fool to give you another hundred or three." He looked sidelong at me. "Or even more."

Was he suggesting I whore myself for war chargers? I felt the slice of fury and bit my tongue lest I delve into a chain of thoughts that were best kept from the likes of Dafaru. Lying on my back, I stared at the tawdry images on the ceiling until I was sufficiently calm.

I turned onto my side and faced him. "I need horses in the thousands. Several hundred won't do."

"Is that so?"

"My lord, I'm aware that you monitor my progress in this matter. You are War."

"That I am, Beloved." He folded his hands behind his head and yawned. "Give me time to think on it."

"Think on it?" I was silent for a moment before saying, "You speak the words but do not know love. If you did, you wouldn't brush me aside when I make a request of you."

He eyed me. "Between the two of us, it is you who does not know love."

"And then you spray my friend with gifts as though I'm nothing," I continued as though he'd not spoken.

His eyebrows rose. "It was a long-knife, Amina. A warrior of her skill deserves a reliable weapon of her choosing. She is terribly adept with knives. Surely, you are not jealous of that? I *would* gift you if I thought you might accept."

"I've asked you for a gift, and you want to *think on it.*"

"Horses. You think horses will win you a war?"

"Have you a more reliable solution?"

Shifting to lie atop me, he snorted. "You expect me to ponder such matters after what we just did? My mind is filled with the pleasures of you. My tactical sense is compromised."

"You cannot be compromised."

Several silent moments passed.

I deflated. "As you wish, my lord."

He chortled. "Had you succumbed this readily when I first came to you, we could have spared ourselves much grief and gnashing of teeth."

The slew of filthy words that formed in my mind bore no resemblance to the words that came out of my mouth. "Yes, my lord."

He was quiet for a time before brushing his lips against mine. "If it takes horses to prove my love to you, then you will have them."

It was my turn to be surprised. A smile began but froze on my face. Was this yet another one of his games?

"All of life is a game, Beloved, but the horses are yours. Anything else?"

I took a moment to consider. His interest in Jaruma drove me mad with jealousy, though I didn't know why. Perhaps now, while he was being agreeable, was a good time to rein him in.

I said, "Leave Jaruma alone."

His eyes, a crimson swirl moving in a hypnotic dance, were uncannily placid. They gazed at me. After a while, he groaned. "Now you ask too much, woman." His lips dropped to my neck. "Enough chatter."

I sighed—Jaruma forgotten—and ran my hands along his contoured back, taking wicked delight in the mouth slowly making its way down the column of my throat.

TWENTY-THREE

Upon my return to the mortal world, a gift awaited me. A takouba in its scabbard lay on my diwan. The scabbard was of fine brown leather, etched with delicate designs. I picked up the weapon by its leather-bound grip, and it slid smoothly from its sheath. It seemed to have been forged with blade and hilt in one piece. Longer than my own sword, it had been heated, folded, and cooled so many times that it had permanent whorls in it. In contrast to the rounded tips of most takoubas, this straight blade tapered to a sharp point. One fuller groove ran the length of the blade while two short fullers—on either side of the long groove—ran halfway from the hilt. Despite its color, which was the dark of wrought iron, the metal shone. A faceted bloodred stone glinted in its pommel.

I held the sword aloft with one hand and lowered the blade onto my other, testing its weight. The weapon was heavy but easy to maneuver. It arced through the air with a soft whoosh, almost propelling itself. It was a beautiful weapon.

And it wasn't the only gift I received.

Over the next five weeks, hundreds of the new recruits suddenly found themselves in possession of horses. The explanations were myriad:

"I won it in a wager."

"It belonged to my uncle's wife's father."

"I found it wandering, half starved."

No one pried too deeply, else we might have found that some, if not all, of the horses were stolen. If they were stolen, I wondered how Dafaru had gotten the recruits to do it. I didn't ask.

Nor did I ask how it came to be that I received six offers of marriage within a fortnight—each including sizable gifts of horses, currency, and other valuables. Many wealthy men were suddenly mad with love for me and traveled great distances to prove it. Such was my extraordinary allure that even the newly coronated king of Kano desired my hand in marriage. He sent two emissaries to make his offer. They were ushered into the pavilion after the day's court but before the council members took their leave.

"We bring greetings from the Sarki Dauda Abasama," said the lead emissary, the king's own eunuch. "His Highness is smitten by your beauty, Gimbiya. For some time, he has thought of nothing else. He sends you gifts of one hundred horses, one hundred slaves, and one hundred kola nuts." He gestured, and his porters brought forth a large clay pot filled with the bitter morsels. "Our great king hopes you will accept these gifts as acceptance of his deep and abiding affection for you."

I tried not to look at Siddhi, but the misery in his eyes was impossible to miss. The previous suitors, while wealthy, were nothing compared to a king. Perhaps, this proposal, Siddhi thought I might accept. I glanced at my mother, willing her to turn down the offer on my behalf, but she merely looked back in silent anticipation. The waziri coughed.

All eyes were on me. Pondering the best way to reject the king of Kano in such a public forum, I removed the lid of the pot and peered inside. The longer my focus remained on the kola nuts, the more awkward the silence became. Settling on the least humiliating combination of words, I sat back and gave an answer.

"Your great king is generous. I thank him and am humbled by this display of affection." I regarded each emissary in turn. "The gifts I accept with much delight, as I'm sure His Highness well predicted. As for marriage." I sighed. "Though I'm truly honored by His Majesty's desire, I do not share it. I am content to remain as I am. A woman bound by no master and subject to no will but my own."

The emissaries exchanged looks of dismay. The lead said, "Exalted Princess of Zazzau, His Majesty does not seek your submission. He requests only your hand and your love. You've stolen the heart of a great man."

The smile affixed to my face spread even wider. "His Majesty need not request submission. But by accepting his offer of marriage, I am accepting him as master. As his wife, my position would be clear."

"Your Highness, as his wife, you would rule both Kano and Zazzau."

"If I become his wife, he rules Zazzau."

At a loss, the emissaries looked at each other again. "How can we carry this rejection to our king?" the lead asked.

Although Dauda Abasama had been in office less than a month, he was said to be a reasonable man. Such a man would not be harsh on his emissaries. If he only knew my entire truth, he would thank them for keeping him far away from me. The emissaries' furrowed brows indicated their apprehension. I could only hope they had no cause for it.

I said, "Surely a king so generous as yours would not treat his emissaries poorly because of the rejection of a lowly woman? Perhaps you may tell him Amina is no longer young and comely."

"All the world knows that to be untrue," the emissary argued.

"Then tell him Amina is past the age of bearing children." I was, after all, thirty. "Because of this, Amina cannot accept His Majesty's request for marriage. I would not want to shame your great king in a union without offspring. Surely, he would understand when it is put thus?"

The emissaries shared another look before the lead said, "Surely he would." However, he sounded doubtful. He bowed, his partner following suit. "May you and your kingdom remain blessed." Rising, they made their way out of the pavilion.

❊

Once I started attending the war council, it seemed natural that I should attend drills as well. Karama was abroad, soliciting the aid of our friends in the north. With no formal contract of alliance already in place, I doubted my uncle would be successful in his endeavor. I took advantage of his absence, however, falling into rank with his unit of cavalry soldiers, which Jaruma temporarily commanded. I trained with them, often ate with them, and occasionally caroused with them. In half a year, my previously neglected abilities became natural to me once more. After months of sword training, I could again face the likes of Jaruma, though I wondered if this rapid reacquisition of skill was the wargod's doing.

"No," Jaruma said when I expressed my concern. "If he could give you skills you never had, why hasn't your spear improved?"

We had spent the afternoon on the plains. Moving target practice with bow and arrows, then fixed target with spear.

"You can throw as far as anyone. But then, you've always had the distance." She tossed the bamboo javelin. "Your issue is aim."

I caught it in one hand. When it came to the spear, there was no previous ability to reacquire. The slightest flick of the wrist made the weapon fall short, so I aimed long. And missed my mark every time.

"Forget spear," I said. "And forget archery. I'm a child of Zazzau, after all. We're born with bows in our hands."

"So what remains?" She leveled one of her piercing gazes at me. "Your swordsmanship? It isn't as though you've been idle these past seven years."

I'd not been entirely active either. Those occasional jaunts onto the plains with her brother had ended in lovemaking under the stars just as often as they had ended in sparring. And he had usually allowed me to win. Both in love and sparring.

She said, "Your swordsmanship was good before. And you've been relentless with training. I think, if not for you, the recruits wouldn't work as hard as they do."

The corner of my mouth quirked. The conviction with which these new recruits had joined the army was more than enough to carry them through the rigors of training.

"That young boy. I forget his name. The one from Rizga." A wrinkle creased her brow and she looked at me to jog her memory. "The one who wanted to fight the Kwararafa."

"Zuma?"

I had sparred with the boy—now a man—once or twice and frequently saw him on the training fields.

"He makes every effort to please you. They all do," she added.

"They don't do it for me; it's for Zazzau."

Still, her words of validation erased some of my self-doubt. I raised the javelin to throw it again and noticed Jaruma looking at me with a queer, ponderous expression.

"Why are you doing this?" she asked.

"What?"

"Training. Why are you training so hard? Are you going to fight?"

I said nothing, merely drew my arm back, lining up the javelin for another throw.

"Forget throwing." She snatched the stick from me. "Restrict yourself to short jabs. In and out." She took a single step forward, thrusting the javelin, then straightened. "You intend to fight." Regarding me intently, she held the stick like a staff at her side.

My husband was War. Was it not fitting that I should lead the army into Nupeland? I had contemplated it over the past months but had not been certain until this moment.

"Yes." I nodded. "Yes, I plan to fight."

"And your mother?"

I shrugged.

"If you're going to fight, we have to improve your hand-to-hand."

"The scar on your head says otherwise." I gave her an arrogant smile.

"The scar on my head was given me by a drunken brawler."

She had said as much after her head had landed on that rock so many years ago. She'd won the fight fairly then, lain me flat on my back. In anger, I had yanked her leg from under her. I'd grown quickly sober when the blood began pooling on that stone slab.

She said, "Your blind style of fighting may give you the upper hand against *one* opponent. But against two or three? You must fight always as though you have a sword in your hand—fully aware of everything around you. If you lose your head in battle, you *lose* your head."

My brow rose.

She shrugged. "It's something my brother used to say."

"That's the sort of thing he would say."

"Yes." She tossed the javelin aside and assumed a fighting stance. "Now fight."

❀

The rainy season came to an end. I went to my mother, announcing myself at the doorway to her private chamber.

"Enter," she said.

I pushed the door open and stepped into the cool interior to find her sitting on her oversized diwan. An import from Fezzan in the north, the entire thing was carved from a single colossal tree. It was so large that her room had been erected around it.

I bowed. "Greetings, Mama. May the blessings of the highest God rain down upon you."

"I'm already blessed, my daughter." She nodded in acknowledgment of my deep genuflection. "Or do you seek to soften me with sweet words?"

"I've yet to see Bakwa Turunku softened by words."

She tittered. "You've not come here merely to flatter your mother, have you?"

"No, Mama. There is something we must discuss."

She held a carved figurine of Inna in her hand and scrutinized it as she spoke. "The Mother Goddess had many sons. The one she loved most was the one who caused her the deepest pain." Setting the figurine on her lap, she looked at me. "You are so much like your father." She gestured at the empty space beside her.

Removing my sandals on the tiled section, I stepped onto the raffia-covered floor and sat on the blue-upholstered diwan.

We were silent for a time before I said, "I require your blessing, Mama."

"For what?" Her eyes shone in anticipation. "Have you accepted a suitor?"

"No, Mama. But the dry season is upon us."

Her face fell. "And?"

"And the army will make its way to Nupeland."

"Yes." She nodded. "When Karama returns from the north."

"Uncle will be away for several weeks yet. Kaura Fasau is sending messengers to him; the army will leave without Uncle. The kaura plans to inform you at the council meeting this evening."

Bakwa frowned.

Steeling myself, I prayed she wouldn't make things difficult. "I intend to ride with the army."

She knitted her brow and lowered her eyes to her lap. Many moments passed before she returned her gaze to me, her face expressionless.

Softly, I said, "I believe I shall go even without your consent, Mama."

If she truly wanted, she could use force to keep me from going. For now, however, she remained silent.

I added, "If we await his return, Uncle will not stop me." At least, I hoped he wouldn't.

More silence.

At length, she sighed. "So like your father. You no longer need my consent to live your life; you are a woman fully grown. I can only give advice and pray that you heed." Disappointment dulled her voice. "You may live as you choose. But Amina, you break my heart."

Her shoulders slumped as she spoke—as though her heart were truly breaking. Her stricken demeanor weighed on me like a heavy stone. But the heft of that yoke wasn't enough to sway me from my course. Victory loomed, vengeance was mine to take, and I planned to see this thing through to its conclusion.

"You've pledged yourself to the god of war, haven't you?" she asked abruptly.

My mouth fell open and I sat frozen. How long had she known? *Did* she know? I stammered a sound that even I couldn't comprehend.

"Save me the indignity of lies. I know what you've done. Your success with building that army is proof of it." She took my hand in both of hers, eyes searching mine. "But why?"

A garbled sound wedged in my throat. I pressed my mouth shut, catching my lower lip between my teeth. After a time, and in a small voice, I spoke. "It was the only way to secure Zazzau."

She shook her head. "You didn't do this for Zazzau." A lengthy pause followed, and she spoke again. "There are always other ways, Amina."

My voice came in a cracked whisper. "None that guarantee success."

"Nothing is guaranteed."

"Dafaru has guaranteed victory over Tsoede."

"Dafaru? Ruhun Yak'i?" Her voice rose, but she maintained her outward composure. "What of the next nation that threatens? Victory over Tsoede does not guarantee victory over Muhammadu Kanta of Kebbi or Usman Nawa of Katsina. What if they decide that you, Amina, are standing between them and the territory they desire? What then? What will you give to guarantee the next victory? What can you give the god of war that you've not already surrendered to his pleasure?"

With a hiss of frustration, she released my hands and got to her feet. The wooden figurine fell out of her lap. It wobbled across the floor, coming to a stop just before reaching the far wall. The sounds of life within the palace compound—the piercing wail of an infant, bleating goats, courtiers' loud voices—were all so very far away.

My mother, pacing, halted in midstride and turned to me. "You put Zazzau in this position. And now you've sold yourself for a single victory. At what cost? How many will suffer for your decision?"

How many indeed?

"You're slated to bring war and death. A destiny that you, yourself, have now embraced," she said.

"But, Mama . . ." I choked on my words.

Her gaze tore into me, accusing me, and she sat back down with a heavy sigh. For the first time, I saw my mother's age written on her face, saw the creases at the corners of her eyes, the deep lines on either side of her mouth. She sighed again, and the sound carried all her disappointment, her anger, her despair.

She lowered her lids, long lashes pressed tightly together, and let her head drop as though she'd lost the strength to hold it up. After a while, she straightened her spine and raised her chin to me, arms spread. "Come."

I knelt on the floor before her.

She put her arms around me, squeezing tightly. Resignation marked her tone. "The choice is made. We must persevere, no?" She kissed my brow.

Releasing me, she went to one of the alcoves and removed a tiny, heavily bound sachet through which a strong and pungent odor leached. She returned to the diwan and sat down slowly, her back rigid, face blank. Her hand was smaller than mine, her fingers delicate. Like Zariya's, my mother's fingers had never held a weapon. They took hold of my wrist now and turned my hand palm up.

She dropped the sachet into my hand and closed my fingers around it. "In the event that your new patron has difficulty keeping his promise."

Nodding, I took the protective amulet and attached it to my belt. "Thank you, Mama."

"Go and ride with your army, my daughter."

The scent of earth rose past the raffia mat to meet me as I bowed my head to the ground. "We will be victorious."

Her depression fell about me like a heavy cloak, and she put a hand on my head. "Yes. This time it is guaranteed."

TWENTY-FOUR

The Southern Kingdoms, circa 1565 CE

My army rode south to Nupeland, our progress hampered not only by our numbers but by hostilities from certain "independent" kingdoms along the way. Those minor kingdoms, who could never hope to defeat us in open battle, had taken to frustrating our progress with small but frequent attacks. Fortunately, most nations claimed no allegiance to either side and let us pass through their lands uncontested.

To avoid aggression, we routinely made camp a fair distance from any occupied territory. Thus, we bivouacked on open savanna about ten kilometers outside the city of Niyabo. The location wasn't ideal for seven thousand soldiers. It offered only elephant grass for cover. Granted, elephant grass grew upward of six feet, but its coarse edges made for uncomfortable sleeping. Using machetes and swords, we hacked away a clearing.

Once perimeter guards were in place, the rest of us went about preparing our respective dinners. We ate standard-issue military fare—roasted bushmeat and more roasted bushmeat—all cooked by campfire. It was a fine repast after a day of endless riding. Or, for some of us, walking.

We ate, then bedded down for the night. The air was still, the sky clear. I lay on my sleeping mat beside Jaruma, the stars shining down on us like the sparkling eyes of a thousand civet cats. Excitement stirred in me but could easily have been trepidation. Since the first two attacks, my nerves had been perpetually on edge.

I heard a noise in the darkness. "What was that?"

As one, Jaruma and I sat up. All was silent. The slow swish of movement through the grass might have been the perimeter guards walking their designated routes, but I couldn't see them.

"Perhaps my ears are playing me false," I suggested. Perhaps my twitching nerves had finally gotten the best of me.

"I heard it too," Jaruma replied. "My ears never play me false. When in hostile territory, yours shouldn't either. Gather your weapons."

I did as she said, donning my war bracelets and getting to my feet. The sheathed takouba was already hanging from my sword belt. I drew the weapon and listened for further noise, my eyes probing the night for the perimeter guards. There was a muffled cry, silenced even as it began. All around me, Zazzagawa jumped to their feet, weapons drawn.

"Intruders!" came the shouts.

Screams erupted in the night as marauders burst from the grass to course over us like mist. They began striking us down. The Zazzagawa scrambled away from the enemy, and Jaruma shouted at us to stand our ground. But my heart beat wild panic.

These were creatures of nightmare. Several hundred wild, hellish animals walking on two legs. They were horned with matted fur covering them from head to waist.

"They are men!" Jaruma charged into their ranks.

Danladi and Gambo were fast on her heels. The enemy moved so quickly that, before I reacted, Jaruma and the other two were overwhelmed. I ran into the fray, heedless of what manner of beast awaited.

One of the enemy ranks caught me around the waist and flung me to the side. If these warriors were men, they were possessed of great strength. I stumbled onto my feet and the demon warrior loped toward me. My takouba was in my hand, starlight reflecting off the faceted jewel in the pommel. Moments later, the sword was in his belly. It slid effortlessly through.

Until that moment, I'd not known the thrill of combat, the power of looking into the enemy's eyes when he drew his last breath. My muscles tightened with morbid excitement. Howling in triumph, I yanked the weapon from his body, slicing upward, and split his abdomen like a bloated lamb. His guts spilled onto my sandals. The man toppled.

The sight of his entrails, the slick feel of them, and the dissipating warmth of life draining at my feet drove me into a battle rage. I hacked at the dead warrior's neck. His head came away from his body. A hideous mask fell from his face. The horned mask, enveloped in long strands of thick grass, had covered the entire top half of him. Thus masked, the man had been frightful.

Another warrior screamed his battle cry. I turned, swung my takouba, and met his blade with a loud clang. The impact jolted me, but I adjusted quickly as yet another demon appeared beside me. His sword arced downward. Jumping to the side, I disengaged from my first opponent. With resistance gone, the first warrior stumbled into my emptied space and almost found death on his comrade's sword.

The comrade gave a roar and stepped around his friend, who righted himself and came for me. Unsure which man to dispatch first, I gripped my sword with two hands and swung it wide. The blade sliced across one warrior's chest, cropping short the grass of his mask. The sharp point cut a trough in his flesh but didn't slow him. My other opponent jerked backward, away from my frenzied swing. Both men rushed forward again, swords raised.

Our swords met. The impact of the two blades against mine drove me to the ground. Flat on my back, I kicked. My foot rammed into one opponent's knee. He staggered backward. Rolling onto my side, I untangled myself from the other warrior. His sword struck the ground where I had lain moments before. I scrambled to one knee and thrust my weapon before he could right himself. The blade sunk into his thigh. I withdrew it and thrust again, this time into the man's abdomen. There was no time to savor this kill; the other man was upon me. I rose, blade slashing, and sliced through his forearm, lopping off arm and sword as one. The warrior bellowed his pain, but I cut it short, driving my weapon into the man's chest.

I met the next demon warrior head-on, parrying each of his spear thrusts. His chosen weapon gave him tremendous reach. I couldn't get close enough to finish him.

He made a quick jab to my left. Taken by the feint, I stepped to the right. His left side was open. I moved in, too close for him to make effective use of the spear, but he swung it anyway. The wooden shaft slammed into my ribs. The pain almost doubled me over, but I pushed it from my mind and continued the advance. He leapt backward and swung. I blocked it with my war bracelet. He made another backward leap.

Grabbing the neck of the spear, I brought my takouba down on the shaft. To my satisfaction, it cleaved the wood neatly in two. He swung what was left of his weapon; I parried with my own, ever advancing. In a blind spurt of stupidity, the warrior charged forward. My braceleted wrist met his temple. The serrated ridges tore into his skull, and he crumpled in a heap of convulsions.

I left him there and faced the next demon, whom I felled with relish, my rage increasing as the blood grew thicker on my sword.

The vicious battle was short-lived. Despite their masks, their uncanny silence, and their initial advantage, we defeated the demon warriors. Those that remained standing—at least fifty—were rounded up, bound, and brought to kneel before me. Unmasked, they still looked like wild animals, their eyes ablaze with hatred.

"Where's Fasau?" I asked as Danladi came to stand with me. My voice, thank the gods, was not as shaky as my hands, which trembled from the rush of battle. A vague ache prodded my side. Come morning, the blow to my ribs would be bruised and painful. For now, however, victory veiled my injuries.

"The kaura didn't survive," Danladi answered.

The nearest of the kneeling marauders raised his head and gave a signal, inciting his defeated troop to take up a cry in praise of

Nupeland. Then, in a further show of arrogance, they chanted, "Death to Zazzau! Niyabo rises! We rise from the ashes of Zazzau!"

"We should have gagged them." Wiping the blade of her knife, Jaruma also joined me.

"They're fools," I said.

Fasau had been a great warrior but a cautious general. He had constrained the army. In our previous two skirmishes, he had made certain we kept our fighting as far from the towns and their civilians as possible. He didn't want the deaths of innocents on his head. Now Fasau was gone, and the rhythmic chanting of the demon warriors strengthened the battle rage burning within me.

When they quieted down, I said to the most vocal of them, the one who had begun the chant, "Niyabo, eh?"

He didn't deign to acknowledge me, evidently thinking me unworthy of his attention. Certainly, I wasn't worthy of his fear. *We would see about that.* With Fasau gone, I meant to exercise the full extent of my power.

"Keep these alive." I pointed to the nine demon warriors at the fore then gestured toward the back. "Eliminate the rest."

"As you command, Gimbiya," Danladi said and began doling out orders.

At the mention of my title, the loudmouthed leader of the forsaken lot glowered at me. Then spat on my foot.

Jaruma took a step toward him, but I caught her elbow and she settled back. Frowning, I looked down at my filthy feet. Considering the drying blood and guts from the battlefield, spittle should not have bothered me. However, the sentiment behind it—the warrior's derision, his lack of concern for his current position—needed adjusting.

I kicked him in the face. He toppled to the ground but got quickly back up, looking no less arrogant than before. His stoicism did nothing to assuage my anger, but I was granted a small consolation when he spat out a tooth.

Jaruma raised a disapproving brow. "You are royalty, Gimbiya."

I wiped my foot on the man's naked chest.

She observed this action with a slight grimace. "Clearly your stomach for bloodletting is stronger than I supposed."

"It would seem so." My stomach was, perhaps, too strong. Even now, with the battle over, I felt nothing for the fallen—mine or theirs. Perhaps my association with the god of war had made me callous.

She indicated the nine warriors. "What do you want to do with them?"

I looked the men over. Prisoners of war certainly deserved death more than the random men I used in Zazzau. If I kept one until tomorrow, no one would dare question me or lament his death afterward. But my belly recoiled at the idea of lying with these demon warriors, and it occurred to me that my fleshly craving was gone. I couldn't feel the small ache that usually hummed in my core at Dafaru's absence. I was as sated as though I'd lain with the wargod himself.

I turned to Jaruma, a giddiness spreading across my face. "Bind them to horses. They are coming with us."

"To Nupeland?" Her narrowed eyes asked a deeper question, a query about my all-too-happy mood.

I'd have to explain later. Right now, I intended to teach these persistent night raiders a lesson in hospitality. "No. To Niyabo."

At the mention of their city, the warriors' eyes grew wide, and the lead noisemaker began hurling curses at me. My soldiers gagged him and hauled the trussed-up prisoners onto horses. Twined stalks of elephant grass made sturdy ropes that cut into the flesh of the prisoners' wrists and feet when we tied them to the saddles. They didn't react to their collective pain, nor did they look away when, one by one, my executioners slit their comrades' throats.

✱

We marched on Niyabo that night. From a distance that kept me out of the general melee while allowing me to bear witness to it, I sat astride. Jaruma, my prisoners, and nearly all of the Kuturun Mahayi remained with me. We watched the city go up in flames.

Fasau wouldn't have condoned the destruction, but I was less inclined to care and wondered whether Dafaru had made me this way or if I'd always been devoid of compassion. Maybe the murders I had already committed had hardened me to the horrors of warfare. Whatever the case, no emotions surfaced in me, no pity for the people of Niyabo or for the demon warriors who had, admittedly, fought well. My battle rage continued to feed on the devastation.

By the time Niyabo was reduced to ashes, my prisoners were reduced to tears, shuddering in grief-stricken fury. Their arrogance had died along with their city.

"As Niyabo rises, it is quick to fall," I said to the loud one.

All pride, all life had drained out of him when his city had burned. He didn't respond. Or spit, for that matter. As flames shot into the sky, Gambo and Danladi came out of the city. Jaruma and I rode to meet them.

"The city was unguarded," Danladi said when we drew close. "It's done."

The people of Niyabo had sent their warriors to cut us down in the night and had left the city vulnerable. Foolish.

"Survivors?" I asked.

"The streets are full of them," Danladi replied. "But some perished in the flames. Should we round them up?"

"We have no use for them. Let them go."

Jaruma gave me a sidelong look. "I thought you might like to execute them as well," she said in a dry tone.

I wasn't sure whether she was serious, but I saw no jest in the statement. "Do you take issue with my leadership?"

"No issue, Gimbiya."

The flippant remark still nettled me. "Would you rather I execute them? The children as well?"

Jaruma glanced at the other two and motioned toward the city. They rode back to deliver my orders. She said, "It was no criticism, Amina."

"What then?"

Other than the exasperation that briefly shadowed her features, she ignored my rancorous tone. "You surprise me, that's all. You've never been a war leader, yet you do it now with certainty. As though you were born for this purpose."

Her response dulled my anger. Indeed, I felt somewhat churlish for snapping at her in the first place.

"Is it not my destiny?" I looked up at the black smoke blotting out the stars. "Amina and War are one. For as long as it pleases him."

We returned to the group. Part of me considered offering the prisoners some solace in their last moments and telling them their families yet lived. But that part of me was relegated to the background. The demon warriors of Niyabo would get no peace of mind before they looked into the eyes of Death. A petty triumph, I knew, but a triumph nonetheless.

"Execute the prisoners," I said.

TWENTY-FIVE

Nupeland, the Southern Kingdoms, circa 1565 CE

From then on, we camped only in small, isolated villages. At every stop, we enlisted the locals to help us erect an earthen wall. The walls did little to protect the army during the ten or so days it took to complete one, but the collective task strengthened the solidarity of the soldiers. And the occupants of those isolated villages were more than willing to assist in fortifying their meager towns. Building Amina's walls—Ganuwar Amina—sparked a sense of loyalty among the locals. Who knew if their loyalty would ever be tested? Still, each walled town was one less potential thorn in my side.

From Niyabo to Nupeland, we erected four walls, which further delayed our progress toward the enemy. But the enemy was in no hurry. The Nupe could afford to wait. In the year since they had blocked the southern trade routes, Zazzau's economy had suffered tremendously. Irrespective of my personal reasons for bringing the battle to Tsoede, we needed to restore the southern flow of goods. Tsoede had dealt us a crippling blow when he had closed the roads to us. We would reopen those roads and, if need be, pave them with the bones of every Nupe man, woman, and child.

❋

A day's ride from the royal seat of Nupeland, Atagara, we made camp near the Kaduna River. The village of choice was scarcely a village at all; its townsfolk were all members of one extended family. Still, they were eager to have a wall around their land and welcomed the building effort.

For eight days, we toiled. In that time, we heard nothing from the Nupe, saw no activity whatsoever. The lack of Nupe response made me uneasy, and my overactive nerves knotted the muscles of my neck and shoulders. Every night, I went to my tiny adobe hut with a massive headache.

On this night, I only managed to lie down after chewing a piece of bitter kola nut to ease the throbbing in my head. As I drifted into uncomfortable sleep, a pulsing band of heat pressed around my forefinger. At the risk of Dafaru's displeasure, I considered tearing the accursed ring from my hand but was not so bold. Sluggish, I sat up and found myself on the floor in the wargod's bedchamber. The master of the house stood above me, holding out a hand that I grudgingly took.

"Welcome, Beloved." He drew me to my feet.

Exhausted, I leaned against him. The heat from his body permeated my forehead and soothed the ache better than any kola. I turned my face and rested my temple on his chest. His skin was so hot that I wondered whether blood or fire surged through the heart beating in my ear.

"First things first, my love." He lifted me into his arms, carried me to an adjoining room, and dumped me in a tub of water. "You reek."

Shocked out of my musing, I screamed, cursed, sputtered, and choked.

"Salima is on her way," he said with a devilish smirk. Suppressing laughter, he backed out of the room.

❀

A short while later, my headache was a thing of the past, and I lay on my side, naked in his bed. Dafaru had entered into the first order of business—the ravishing of his wife—without preamble and concluded it with his usual aplomb.

By now, I was half asleep and failing every effort to keep my eyes open. "I must return to my world." I let my eyes close for a moment. "There is a war to win."

"A war against whom? There is no Nupe force awaiting you."

I raised my brow but could not pull my lids apart. "That has not escaped my attention. Tsoede was always good at keeping his plans from us, but we're too near his capital for such persistent silence."

"Undoubtedly."

"We should smell his plans. Yet there's nothing. No Nupe scouts, no guards to greet us, no fortifications. Not even assassins. *Nothing.* Is there magic afoot?"

"Fear not, Beloved. There is no conspiracy or magic being worked against you."

I rolled onto my back and scooped the covers to my chest. "Why isn't the Nupe war band gathered?"

He yanked the sheet out of my hands. "Because you have beaten Tsoede before even stepping foot on his land."

"How?"

I reached again for the cover, but he tore it away, pulling it off me entirely. The shock of cool air sweeping over my body beat back the invading sleep. I shivered and opened my eyes, then gave a start when he caught me by the waist and lifted me onto him.

"Tsoede is occupied with Oyo on the other side of the river," he said.

I scowled. "What did you do to make this happen?"

"I did nothing." He affected a look of innocence, which must have been a strain for him. "Although, I did manage to cultivate a seed of thought in Onigbogie's mind."

"In *whose* mind?"

"The king of Oyo."

"A king whose name is unknown beyond his borders is nothing to fear. Surely this . . . er . . . what's his name?"

"Onigbogie."

"Surely this Onigbogie can be no threat to Tsoede?"

"You have no idea what strength lies south of that river, my love. Oyo is powerful; its monarch is a great conqueror. His borders are constantly expanding. Now he believes that Nupeland is ripe for the plucking."

"Why would he believe such a thing?"

"Nupeland *is* ripe. Is it not?"

"I wouldn't know."

"Because you are preoccupied with destruction rather than acquisition."

Knitting my brow, I regarded him.

He said, "Tsoede is like a man trying to keep a pack of hyenas from entering through the front gate when a herd of elephants is stampeding from the back. He should stand aside and let the elephants through. They will keep the hyenas at bay."

"Zazzau is the elephant? Tsoede is aware of this?"

"Beloved, without your help, Tsoede would likely defeat Oyo. At worst, our two kings are evenly matched, although Onigbogie now thinks he has the upper hand." He gestured at my furrowed brow, narrowed eyes, and downturned lips. "What is this?"

"Why would Tsoede pledge allegiance to Zazzau if he can defeat Oyo on his own?" I asked. "Or better, why not form an alliance with Oyo and defeat Zazzau outright?"

"Because I have also nudged Tsoede. He well knew that if he allied with Oyo, together they would crush you. But now he believes that, in the end, Oyo will betray him and again be at his neck. He also believes he does not have the military strength to defeat Oyo on his own, and for this he needs you. As far as Tsoede is concerned, it is safer to ally with Zazzau. Your army is smaller than his, much weaker. He can turn on you at a later date and claim both Oyo and Zazzau."

The wargod's lips pressed against my throat. "Besides . . ." The words vibrated down my neck. "I have eradicated all thoughts of peace from each king to the other. There will be no cooperation between them."

"My lord, you've cultivated seeds of war in the minds of kings?" I didn't know whether to be angry or impressed.

"What have I already said?"

His terse response made me settle on anger, but it was tempered by fatigue. "Had you cultivated these seeds sooner we could have spared many lives on our journey across the savanna. We could have—"

"Your rampaging war band has little to do with me, Amina. Even so, it is not as simple as that. The foundation for war must be present before I can build on it. The seed of conflict must be in the ground before the tree of chaos can sprout. Onigbogie already believed his kingdom was not large enough to suit him. I suggested only that Nupeland was *desirable*. Had he not already been primed for expansion, he would have dismissed any suggestion I put in his head as a passing fancy."

His hand eased down my back. A long shudder followed in its wake. Despite an attempt to keep it intact, my anger dissipated.

"So you see, Beloved, your army can do without you for a time."

His crimson eyes cleared, and I stared at my reflection for just a moment before he showed me an image too scandalous to ignore. "I doubt my body will bend in that manner," I said before he tried to indulge in the suggested activity.

"You never know what your body can do. Shall we find out?"

My interest was hardly piqued. "May I not rest awhile?"

"You are spent? Already?" Nevertheless, he obliged and took his arms from around me.

Grateful for the prospect of undisturbed rest, I rolled off him, closed my eyes, and welcomed oblivion.

His voice cut through the miasma of blessed sleep. "Perhaps I should visit your friend. Surely her stamina exceeds yours."

"She's not so pliant, my lord," I said through a yawn. "You would break her."

His rolling laughter was the last thing I heard before sleep finally voided my senses.

❁

The morning brought news from Zazzau. Outside my hut, soldiers shouted, heralding the arrival of . . . *the makama?*

"Siddhi," I said under my breath and rose quickly from the floor, where I was mending my battle tunic. Only the gravest news would have brought the makama himself to the battlefield. I pushed back the cloth curtain in the doorway and stepped outside.

As I emerged from the hut, a number of soldiers cast surreptitious glances in my direction. My dress, a gift from Dafaru, was what I had on when he returned me from the spirit world. It was longer than my usual Jangare attire—it reached my ankles. But it suited the wargod's tastes in other ways. It had a deeply cut neckline and high slits along the sides. The dress was as indecent as everything else he made me wear. Frankly, I should have covered it with a wrapper before coming outside. There was nothing for it now.

Upon seeing Siddhi, I waved maniacally, my heart growing light. At the same time, the sight of him flanked by at least two dozen guards filled me with dread. What news could be so dire? Before his horse came to a complete stop, Siddhi vaulted from the animal's back and came to stand before me.

He bowed. "Greetings, Gimbiya." His face was drawn.

"What news from home?" Anxiety undermined all courtesy.

"We must be alone."

The feeling of dread increased. I led him into the hut, pulling the curtain closed behind us.

He took my hands. "Amina." He was travel-worn and weary, tunic and trousers filthy, his hair—free of any headdress—was unkempt. Even his meager beard was disheveled. He looked as though he'd not eaten in days. His cheeks were sunken, and the light that usually shone in his eyes was not there.

My fingers closed around his. "What news have you brought?"

"Amina, it's the queen. Your mother."

My chest tightened. "What of my mother?"

"She . . ." He paused.

Was she ill? Had there been an accident and she was injured? What could have happened in the mere two months that I had been away? Siddhi's mouth opened and closed several times, but no sound came out. What was so bad that he could not speak?

I jerked my hands from his grip, the dread now shrill in my voice. "What news, Siddhi?"

At last, he said, "Great Bakwa Turunku has . . ." He wrung his empty hands.

"Has what?"

"She has gone into the next life, Amina."

"What?" Surely, I'd not heard correctly. A cold tremor trickled across my skin and sunk into my soul. It ran alongside my veins, like some terrible creature, to strangle my heart. Tendrils of cold engulfed me. My knees gave way and I sank to the ground.

My mother was healthy when I last saw her. Scarcely two months. Too stunned to speak, I looked up at Siddhi, who closed his eyes in misery.

"Amina." He dropped to his knees. "I'm pained to be the bearer of such news." He took my hands again.

Numb, I stared at the fingers twined about mine. "Dead?" My voice cracked. "How can this be?"

"Waziri says it was an affliction of the heart."

A bitter jolt sliced through me and I recalled my mother's words: *But, Amina, you break my heart.*

Sharply, I said, "What does Waziri know?"

"The medicine men agree. And the priests. Everyone we consulted says the same."

Affliction of the heart?

The noise of the soldiers bustling about seemed my only anchor to reality. Inside the hut, Siddhi said, "There is more, Gimbiya. I'm sorry."

"More?" My soul was already sundered. What more grievous news could he bring? My eyes rose to his face, but I did not see him. I saw nothing beyond my terrible veil of grief.

Haltingly, he told me the rest. "Your uncle is her successor."

The outside noises faded away entirely. All my awareness focused on Siddhi. My brow dropped and I stared at him.

Again, I drew my hands out of his. "You did this?"

"I had no choice, Amina," he said in feeble explanation.

"No choice? But you're one of the kingmakers."

"It was decreed."

His face blurred over as my eyes resumed staring at nothing.

"You're a kingmaker," I said to the emptiness around him. "You decide who is fit to rule."

He grimaced as though he were in physical pain and reached for my hands.

"Don't touch me." I got to my feet.

"Amina, please." He rose with me.

At that moment, Jaruma ran into the hut. "What's happened?" Her eyes shifted from me to Siddhi. "Siddhi?"

He disregarded Jaruma, again reaching for my hand. "I'm sorry, Amina. I had no choice."

I snatched my hands away. "Don't touch me."

The vote of the Sarakunan Karaga *had* to be unanimous; they made their decision as one. Siddhi had cast his vote in Karama's favor.

"Amina?" Jaruma said.

That single word, laden with a thousand questions, hung in the air until it was dislodged by a heart-wrenching cry of anguish. The sound, in all its agony, issued from my mouth. Another scream rose inside me. I pushed it back and tried to hold off the flood of tears already wetting my eyes.

"Leave me," I said, barely able to breathe.

Tentative, Siddhi took a step back.

"Leave me," I repeated with added force.

He left, but Jaruma did not. I fell to my knees.

"Amina, what's the matter?"

"Leave me, Jaruma."

"No."

I looked at her through a mist of tears. "Mama is dead and Uncle is king." Like the sharp tip of a sword, the words drove deep.

"Oh, Amina." She dropped down beside me and put her arms around my shoulders, pulling me close. "I'm sorry."

I was grateful for her love, but she wasn't the one I needed.

"Please, let me be, Jaruma."

She didn't say anything, though I knew she wanted to. What could anyone say? No words would bring my mother back. So she did as I asked. Releasing me, she made her way out of the hut.

Before my fingers touched the fire ring, Dafaru was there.

He asked, "What has distressed you?"

"Take me home."

Silence.

Then he said, "I cannot take you home."

"My mother has gone from this world, and Karama usurps my throne." Sobs broke my voice; tears streamed down my face. "I must return home."

"Is it sadness at the loss of your mother or at the loss of her throne that distresses you more?"

My heart knotted. "How can you ask that? Don't you know I'm shattered?" I looked at him, silently begging. "I caused my mother much grief, and grief has brought her death. I pray only to look upon her face before she is forever entombed."

"What of her throne?" His cool, deliberate tone flayed me like a whip upon my back.

I wept into my hands. My mother was gone from this world. I had lost her and could not bear to lose her legacy. "She bequeathed it to me." The words thrummed hollow against my heart.

"The Sarakunan Karaga have chosen. It is they who bequeath a throne."

"Then I'm left with nothing." I looked up at him, misery tensing my face.

Dafaru's brow furrowed as well. He lowered himself to the ground before me. Sobbing, I dropped my head back into my hands. He removed my hands, lifted my head, and looked into my tear-filled eyes. His were calm yet intense.

"You will reign when it is your time to reign," he said. "If such a time ever comes. Are you not content to be Amina, Beloved of the gods? Are you not content to have the heart of War?"

"Amina does not have the heart of War," I said bitterly.

"Does she not?"

"If you'll not take me, then I must go on my own." My body grew warm as he pulled me close. In my suffering, I clung to him.

He held me until the weeping ceased. "I cannot take you, my love. I can bring you to Jangare, but when I return you to the world of men, you will return to the place from which I took you. My heart—"

"You have no heart."

He sighed but did not take his arms from around me. "I do not know what pain you suffer, for my mother abandoned me centuries ago. And she will never die." The last he said with resentment. "You will not reach Zazzau before your mother is entombed. For this, the heart you claim I do not have aches for you."

And he was gone, leaving me clutching air. Cold, empty, and lost.

TWENTY-SIX

The sound of trumpets blaring in the distance jarred me from despondency. I stood and shambled to the doorway, worn from crying. Jaruma was waiting outside.

"The Nupe are coming." She looked at me. "Your face, Amina."

"Why didn't your scouts send warning?" I snapped as she stepped into the hut to retrieve my water gourd.

"I apologize. I didn't know whether to disturb you." She poured water into my upturned hands. "It's only the emissary. Siddhi can speak on your behalf."

My lip curled. "Siddhi? He does not speak for me." I washed my face and neck, splashing the liquid into my eyes to clear away the burn of weeping.

"Your attire." She gestured at my exposed body parts.

I entered the hut, wiping my face with my dress before tugging the garment over my head. After donning trousers and tunic, I tucked my hair into a headwrap and stepped back outside. My horse was ready for me.

The trumpets blasted closer. I climbed into the saddle, making off toward the herald. Hoofbeats sounded behind me. A backward glance showed Jaruma and Siddhi following, along with his two dozen guards, and a few armed soldiers.

Jaruma pulled up beside me. "Gimbiya, you shouldn't ride ahead. You don't know what trickery Nupeland has in store for us."

She would have been right, if I didn't already know better.

Coming within a hundred paces of the Nupe convoy, we slowed to a walk. A procession of people marched toward us. Aside from the guards flanking the emissary, who rode at the head of the march, none looked in any way battle ready.

"Greetings, Fair One. The Creator keeps you ever youthful," the emissary said when we were within arm's reach of one another. "We have come to offer gifts of peace, friendship, and allegiance to your queen, Bakwa of Zazzau."

As my mother's name came out of the emissary's worthless mouth, I said, "Bakwa Turunku, queen of Zazzau, is no more."

A quick reassessment. "Then I offer gifts of condolence to the new queen." He bowed his head. "Your Majesty, Amina of Zazzau."

I didn't respond.

The emissary looked over his shoulder as the rest of his convoy drew to a halt—thirty or forty men dressed in short robes and short trousers, each with a pack slung over his shoulder. He turned back to me, flashing a brilliant smile that gave him an expression akin to that of a wild boar.

He gestured at the men. "Forty eunuchs who are well trained in government administration and bookkeeping. As we're aware of the late queen's liking for kola nuts—we hope kola nuts suit your taste also—we've brought you ten thousand."

"Ten thousand kola nuts?" What was I to do with ten thousand kola nuts?

"We hope you will accept these gifts to honor your mighty kingdom."

"The kingmakers decide who rules Zazzau," I said. "As you impart gifts, have you also brought the men responsible for the death of my betrothed?"

The emissary remained silent, and several moments went by while birds and monkeys shrieked in the nearby trees. At length, I gave a small wave of the hand. Token acceptance of his pittance of a tribute.

"Why has Tsoede experienced so dramatic a change of heart?" I asked. "Not even two years ago, you were spewing threats."

The emissary let out an insincere cackle. "Threats? No disrespect, but perhaps Your Majesty misunderstood my words." He cackled again. "It was so long ago. Who can remember clearly?"

"*I* remember clearly, Sir Emissary."

For a moment, he seemed perturbed. His lips opened and closed as he stammered incoherent words. Then he made a token bow. "I apologize if I misspoke so many months ago."

As though in tune with the bulging tension between me and the Nupe emissary, the treetop chatter of animals faded, though a single, persistent bird cawed incessantly.

The emissary cleared his throat. "We hope you will join us in celebration of our new friendship. We've followed your battle path closely and find you to be quite formidable. Surely as a foe, but even more so as an ally. We have no desire for an altercation between our two kingdoms."

I eyed him coolly. "If Tsoede would call me friend, he can prove his allegiance by coming to me."

"Tsoede come to you?" His chin rose in outrage.

"Has he not sworn fealty to me? Or do you surrender without the sanction of your king?"

The emissary puffed out his chest like a peacock on display. "I'm fully authorized to speak for Etsu Nupe Tsoede. But we offer allegiance to Zazzau, not to you."

"As far as you are concerned, I am Zazzau. Tsoede will meet us here by sundown, else when we take your city, I will make him watch as I carve his children's heads from their shoulders."

To my right, Jaruma didn't react, but on my left, Siddhi slowly angled his gaze toward me. Without sparing anyone a second glance, I turned and rode away, my heart cold in my chest.

When we reached the camp, Siddhi said, "That wasn't the sort of threat one would expect from a woman of your breeding."

"I didn't ask your opinion," I replied, without looking at him.

Jaruma cut in. "If Tsoede comes, you'll have to stay and negotiate Nupeland's surrender. What of your mother?"

My mother's body would not hold, and I would never reach Zazzau in time to see her on her journey to the Crossroads. As for the throne, if Siddhi had not fought for my right to sit on it, why would anyone else? On my own, I could do nothing in Zazzau, and my presence was required in Nupeland.

I said, "I have business to settle here."

※

Tsoede's trumpets sounded at sundown. By the time his banner came into view, I stood at the edge of our encampment, outside the wall, with Jaruma and Siddhi. Danladi and Gambo sat astride horses, along with Zuma, the boy from Rizga.

I smacked Zuma's horse on the rump. "Move aside."

The horse swished its tail and shifted to the side, its rider looking sheepish. "Sorry, Gimbiya."

Atop a black stallion and with brightly colored robes flapping in the breeze, Tsoede rode toward us. His emissary rode on his right. A young woman as regally dressed as Tsoede himself rode on the left. The party drew near, and I realized for the first time that Tsoede was an old man. *Ancient.* From the look of him, he might have been well over a hundred years. It was hard to believe he could *lift* a sword, let alone fight with one.

My gaze fell to the woman at his side. It was possible, despite his age, that the woman was a wife. She was no beauty, but she was very young; young enough to be interesting to an oldster like Tsoede.

Tsoede's physical appearance aside, when he reached us, he jumped from the saddle like a spry man half his age—whatever that age was. He hefted a large gourd from where it had been secured to the horse and laid it before me with a flourishing bow. When he spoke, his voice didn't carry the crackle of old age. It was strong and steady.

"My deepest condolences at the loss of your mother. I present wine, that we may pour a libation to her spirit."

The potent scent of wine drifted from the vessel, and I accepted it with a small bow of my own. Zuma dismounted to take the gourd.

"We are pleased that Zazzau and Nupeland will no longer be in discord," I said.

"As are we," Tsoede replied. "Let us dine to good friendship and in memory of a great sovereign."

Tsoede graciously provided the food, otherwise, we would have dined on smoked guinea fowl and kola nuts. As it was, we feasted on roasted plantains, rice, goat meat, an assortment of fruits, and a soup laden with enough hot spices to fell an elephant.

"My emissary's description did your beauty no justice," Tsoede said as we ate. "You are lovely beyond words."

"I'm surprised," I replied. "Your emissary has an impressive command of words."

He smirked and took a long draught of his wine. "You would certainly make a fine wife."

"For you?"

"Or whomever."

"Or whomever." I took a sip from my cup and glanced at the woman he had brought with him.

He gestured at her. "The exalted priestess of the Oracle."

I ignored the introduction. "You've not told me why you are declaring friendship. Surely the great Tsoede is not afraid of a mere woman and her band of emasculated warriors?"

Looking around at the rowdy men, Tsoede laughed. "Emasculated? I think not. And you are no mere woman, Amina of Zazzau. It should be obvious to you why I need your friendship." He studied my face.

I looked back at him just as closely. "Oyo."

He nodded.

"And once Oyo's jaws have been pried from your throat?"

"I shall be in your debt." He put a hand on mine and squeezed.

"That you shall." I looked down at his hand and slid mine from under it. "We're not on equal footing here. I have the high ground." I also had little patience for the unsubtle arrogance of men.

Tsoede frowned. For an instant, he looked at me with the same contempt that his emissary had shown. He exhaled. "You truly are no mere woman."

"I asked your emissary to produce the assassins who took the life of my betrothed. He has yet to comply."

Tsoede sighed, a small frown creasing his brow. "He cannot comply because the assassins were never found. No one has taken responsibility."

"Because murderers usually come forward on their own?"

The crease in his forehead deepened. "There are factions within my government who favor more decisive action. Were they involved, they would have made it known. I do regret what happened in my territory and wish to express my deepest condolence at your loss. He must have been a remarkable man to have captured your heart. We will, of course, continue the search and bring the assassins to justice."

I watched him in silence. He looked sincere when he spoke; his eyes never wavered from mine. Yet the words lacked emotion. As though he'd rehearsed them to perfection before coming to me. It was clear the assassins would never pay for what they had done to Suleyman, what they had done to *me*. Conquering their nation would have to suffice.

"Do you swear fealty?" I asked.

"I give you my allegiance in this matter."

"What I require from you is obedience and loyalty at *all* times. Do you swear fealty?"

"One has to admire a woman with the will of a leopard." The forced tone of voice, however, didn't sound as though he admired me. His jaw clenched and unclenched. He was not a stupid man and was well aware the price he'd have to pay for my help against Oyo. Finally, he gave a harsh sigh. "You have our fealty."

Thanks to Dafaru, there had been little doubt in my mind.

"Very well." I downed the rest of my wine. "How may Zazzau assist you?"

✻

The Nupe capital was a plush land near the confluence of two rivers. The soil, perhaps being so close to the Kaduna River, was dark silt—unstable and prone to sinking beneath one's feet. Some of the homes along the shores were built on tall posts, keeping them elevated for such times that the river rose past its banks. A few homes were on posts within the river itself, their inhabitants shuttling back and forth by boat.

Many of the biting vermin of the region had died out with the onset of the dry season, otherwise, our extended stay in Nupeland would have been a nightmare. Still, when the time for battle finally arrived, my warriors breathed a collective sigh of relief. We'd been here nearly two months, and they were anxious to return home before the harmattan took hold. The sooner we rid Nupeland of its antagonist, the sooner we would be on our way.

The designated battleground was on the other side of the Kwara River, into which the Kaduna flowed. I took two thousand mounted bowmen—horses and all—across on wide rafts. Tsoede was not sanguine about leaving the remaining four thousand soldiers in his city unattended, but I assured him that my men would behave themselves on pain of death. Besides, Siddhi had also remained to finalize the negotiations with Tsoede's emissary. Irrespective of my anger toward the makama, I would not leave him in Nupeland without ample protection.

"The Oyo are marching north to meet us," Tsoede said after we made camp. He had chosen a site several kilometers south of the river where the land was fairly level. "The battlefield is beyond that rise, a kilometer away, in a shallow valley."

"And trees?" I asked.

"The land is fallow, few trees grow there." He eyed me. "Are the ferocious Zazzagawa afraid of trees?"

"Arrows do not bend around trees."

"Mm-hmm." Tsoede nodded thoughtfully. He ordered his people to set out the food they had ferried across the water and shared his dinner with us. Given all the good cheer and festivity, one might have thought we were celebrating a wedding rather than preparing for war.

"Victory is at hand, Amina," he said between gulps of water. He claimed to never imbibe spirits when battle loomed. "I can feel it." He stole a look at his priestess, a woman whom he never let out of his sight. She looked back at him and chewed slowly on a slice of roasted cassava.

"Yes," I replied. "As soon as that victory is in your hands, I can leave these sweltering lands." Even without rain, the air was thick with moisture.

"I'll be happy to see your backs," he said, still looking at his priestess.

"We'll be happy to show them to you." I got to my feet and bowed. "Your Majesty." Taking my leave, I went off to a makeshift bamboo and palm-frond hut to await the coming day.

❀

With the cockcrow came the sounds of the first battle drums. The Oyo army was coming. Donning our gear, we made haste to our battle positions atop the rise. It was the most advantageous position for midrange archers. Our task was simple: ensure Oyo never gained the upper hand. From our vantage point, we could see the entire battlefield. Targeting Oyo's warriors would make for short work.

The Oyo host came into view with their battle drums beating. Theirs was a large contingent. About ten thousand. Mostly infantry but far more mounted men than expected given the intelligence from Nupe spies. They wore little by way of clothing or armor. Simple loincloths, crocodile skin breastplates, and shields.

Onigbogie, distinguishable from his warriors by his copper headdress adorned with coral beads, rode at the front of his battle line. The old man, Tsoede, also rode at the front. His headdress was a woven circlet of leather and long feathers, which fanned out like a multicolored wreath. I looked down at the Nupe king in anticipation of his upcoming performance. Irrespective of his astonishing displays of virility, Tsoede was old.

But he was impressive. He rode into the fray, machete aloft, aiming for his Oyo counterpart. Two men intercepted him before he reached their king. Tsoede was a blur as he sliced into the first man's neck, then the second in quick succession. A battle-axe hurtled toward him. I took in a sharp gasp of air. The old man pressed his torso to his horse's back, narrowly dodging the axe. As he came out of the tuck, he jabbed his machete into the other man's side. The Oyoman tumbled off his horse and I exhaled.

Tsoede was deft. He felled another man and another, then faltered when he took a lance to the arm. I grimaced at the blow and paused. Might Tsoede not serve me better dead? My bargain with him spoke only of assisting Nupeland to defeat the Oyo nation. What reason was there to preserve Tsoede's life? From where I stood, I could dispatch him with little difficulty.

Recovering from the strike, Tsoede regained his momentum and swung the machete. The weapon pierced his opponent's armor, catching the crocodile skin breastplate on its tip. Tsoede yanked. He tore the breastplate away from the Oyoman and swung the machete again. The useless piece of armor flew off the iron blade. Another pass at the Oyoman and Tsoede furrowed a gorge into his enemy's bare chest.

Despite his effort to reach the Oyo king, Tsoede made no progress. The gap between him and his quarry spread ever wider, as warriors from both sides crashed into one another. Dafaru was correct; these armies were evenly matched.

Each side had arrived with two thousand horsemen, though most of the combat was on foot. Both armies—mounted warriors included—used heavy weaponry and weren't hindered by it. Large battle-axes, jagged clubs, thick machetes, and even chains hurtled swiftly at their opponents, a single blow sufficing to eliminate the foe or his mount. Riding his horsemen at the fore, Tsoede lost many mounted warriors in the first charge.

The much lighter takoubas used by the Zazzagawa were better for quick slicing and good for killing men, but the blow had to be well aimed to drop a horse in one swing. In a fight against either of these two nations, I surmised it would be better to stay out of the close-range fracas for as long as possible.

"Hold, Galadima." I coaxed my fidgeting horse. "You won't step foot on the battlefield today." Nor would any of my warriors. I wouldn't sacrifice a single Zazzagawa life to save Nupeland.

An Oyo soldier, swinging a chain over his head, ran toward Tsoede. The chain lashed out, wrapped around Tsoede's neck, and yanked him off his horse. I swore under my breath. As much as I wanted to eliminate the old man, this battle wasn't yet won. If he died right now, it might put his army in disarray. Whatever happened, I could not let Oyo take Nupeland. A nation that large at my southern border would pose a greater threat than the Nupe alone ever had.

I pulled an arrow from my quiver, my eyes skimming the field for the fallen Tsoede, and shouted, "Flanks."

Jaruma gave the signal. Our drums sounded and bowmen nocked their arrows. Another signal modified the drum sounds, and we let loose volley after volley in rhythm with the steady beat. Mounted Oyo soldiers at flanks began to fall. Oyo's rear guard of bowmen oriented on us.

"At the rear," I shouted, still searching for Tsoede.

Enemy archers sent a volley our way but didn't have the range. My whinnying horse stomped an impatient foot. I squeezed my thighs against him. Heeding my unspoken command, the horse went still, and I took aim at Oyo's rear guard. Like the Oyo archers, I was better at shorter ranges, but the elevation made up for the distance I lacked. My arrows found their marks.

Our battle drums beat on. Oyo soldiers at flanks and rear continued to fall. Then Nupeland altered its strategy. No more blind press into enemy lines. The remaining Nupe horsemen broke formation and edged toward Oyo's flanks. Once the Nupe breached the flanks, with or without Tsoede, the enemy's army would be crippled.

Down to my last arrow, I positioned it in the bow and gave another cursory scan of the battlefield. Now that he wasn't needed, I hoped the old man was finally out of commission. My hope was for naught. He had lost his crown of feathers, but Tsoede was still on his feet and swinging his machete as though he were channeling the spirit of the wargod himself. My brow fell, a scowl tightening my face. This was my last arrow, and I would use it well.

I took aim at the old man, silently tracking his erratic movements on the battlefield. His feet remained planted, but his upper body moved with a fluidity that truly belied his age. I inhaled slowly as I drew my arm back, the arrow snug between my fingers. Tsoede raised his machete for a killing blow, his back straight, head high.

And I felt her eyes on me.

Eyes that so resembled her brother's burned into the side of my face. Jaruma didn't speak, but Suleyman's words from so long ago came back to me. *Only a true warrior can stand and face the enemy.* Was I a warrior or an assassin on the wind?

"Damn you," I muttered at any and everyone. With my last arrow, I instead took aim at an Oyo bowman and felt no satisfaction when the arrow burrowed through his breastplate.

Holding my bow at my side, I watched the Nupe horsemen charge through Oyo's flanks. Oyo foot soldiers scattered. Victory was Tsoede's, but there was no victory for Suleyman. I had failed to avenge him, failed to avenge our child, and my failure tasted like dust in my mouth. I wanted to go home.

On the battlefield, all semblance of order fell by the wayside. As evening descended, the Nupe pushed the enemy back, deeper into Oyoland. I turned and rode away.

TWENTY-SEVEN

Once word spread of Nupeland's surrender, those independent kingdoms between fell in line. We left the southern lands with new vassals and returned to Zazzau amidst great fanfare.

The sound of drums met my ears as I entered the city gates at the rear of our military procession. We rode down the main street in the company of singing voices. People danced in the streets. Children ran alongside our horses. From every compound, it seemed, came cries of joy, as families found their loved ones among my soldiers and joined them in the procession.

While it was good to be home, I dreaded the meeting with my uncle. It had been many months since I had last seen him, and things were drastically changed. He was king, *Sarkin Zazzau*, and I was what? Still heir apparent? Or would his firstborn, a boy of four years, take on that title?

We arrived at the palace sooner than I would have liked. With unsteady nerves, I dismounted and handed my horse's reins to the guard. I didn't wait for Jaruma or Siddhi, who had divested himself of his hired guards, before entering the palace compound. The pavilion was less than thirty paces away, and the people gathered there had been watching me even before I came through the wide-open gate. There was no hope of darting past them unnoticed. Particularly when those who had been seated, got to their feet. Resigned, I made my way through the masses.

The crowd, bowing in tribute, parted to reveal my sister seated on Karama's right. The broad grin on her face widened, and she angled her head in greeting. I returned her bow with a quick nod and looked at my uncle, whose gaze rested squarely on mine.

Sitting on what used to be my mother's throne, my uncle wore a flowing white *babariga* over equally white tunic and trousers. "White" did not mean that the cloth was undyed; it was, in fact, *white*. The dazzling, voluminous gown, stark against the mahogany of the throne, shouted my uncle's station to anyone listening. Judging from the number of people crowded onto the pavilion, everyone was listening. My mother had looked at me and found me lacking. She had chosen him, given him everything that should have been mine. Karama had once been my protector, my refuge. But now, with each step I took toward him, the chasm between us grew.

When I reached the throne, Karama stood. Until this moment, I had expected him to be altered along with his position. I thought he'd be bigger, have a sager appearance, a certain deification of countenance. But he was the same man, albeit more brilliantly dressed.

"Greetings." A ghost of a smile wavered on his lips. "You bring good tidings?"

There was a time when I would have flung myself into his arms and kissed his face like a zealous fanatic, but that time was so very long ago. Now, all I wanted was to escape his unwavering gaze. Just being in his presence filled me with a cold, dark fury. But my feelings were inconsequential. This was the man my mother had chosen. If anyone had hoped to see me tarnish the day of our homecoming with a violent display of objection to Karama's new title, they would be disappointed.

Blanking my features, I lowered myself to both knees and pressed my forehead to the ground. I raised my head, straightened, but remained on my knees.

"Your Majesty, Sarkin Zazzau. I bring the best tidings." My voice sounded harsh in my ears, the words empty.

He held out a hand. I slipped mine into it, and he drew me to my feet.

"We will feast this night, and tomorrow you meet with the council," he said.

Stepping close, he pulled me into an embrace. Each of us stood rigid against the other. I glanced at my sister, who looked back at me, brow furrowed in consternation. Surely she saw how difficult it was for me to embrace the man who had taken my throne. Never mind my mother's decree. That Karama had not fought for me made him complicit in my punishment. And it was a harsh punishment for doing the one thing I could to protect Zazzau and exact justice from those who had sought to subjugate us.

He whispered into my ear, "I'll come and see you. We can talk."

"I'd rather not, Uncle," I said, stiffly, for there was nothing to discuss. "May I go?"

Without another word, he released me. His face remained devoid of expression, but fractious eyes regarded me. After several breaths, he dipped his head in a small bow. I turned and left the pavilion, certain that my uncle and I would never embrace again.

❋

Zariya made her presence known outside my door on the following afternoon. "Open, Sister," she shouted as she banged on the door.

Jaruma, sleeping off a drunken night, raised one groggy eyelid. "Are you going to open it?"

I half lay on the diwan, my legs folded on the seat, head resting against the back of the chair. I'd not drunk as much as her, but she was closer to the door. And in the heat, I'd doffed my blouse; her full-length kaftan lent more modesty. An arched eyebrow gave her my response.

Groaning, she collected her carcass from the floor and let my sister in. "Good morning, Gimbiya," she said, greeting Zariya with an unenthusiastic bow.

"Morning?" Zariya laughed. "The sun has already reached its peak." She entered the room, looking very much like our mother in a long, yellow, loose-sleeved dress. A matching headwrap draped her head, cascading down either side of her face and over her shoulders.

"Good afternoon, then." Jaruma stepped outside.

"You may stay," Zariya said.

My companion followed Zariya back into the room and pushed the door closed.

Zariya made for the diwan, pulling the wrap off her head as she approached. I sat up and drew my folded legs closer to my body. She sat beside me, and Jaruma sprawled back onto the floor, propping herself on several cushions.

"Mama's burial ceremony was beautifully done." Zariya flung the headwrap about her shoulders.

Her words brought a painful lump to my throat. I swallowed. "I tried to return. I wanted to."

"How? You couldn't reach here in time."

I said nothing.

After a prolonged silence, my sister spoke again. "The council will be meeting soon. The morning's audience is concluded."

I nodded. Jaruma and Siddhi could handle the debriefing on their own, but the council members would expect me to be there. It was me, after all, who had led the army after Fasau's death. Besides, they needed to vote on a new kaura. While I had no voting power, I did have some newfound insight on the potential candidates.

"Uncle would like to speak with you," Zariya said.

"I don't want to see him."

"He is heartbroken."

"Then he knows how I feel."

She sighed. "It wasn't his choice."

"Of course, it was. He could have refused."

"Refuse Mama? When has he ever refused her?"

She posed the question as though Karama had always bent to my mother's will. Bakwa Turunku was stubborn, but Karama's bones were made of the same Tuareg steel. Queen or no, my mother could not have forced him into anything he'd not wanted. Although my mother had decreed it, no one but Karama had put Karama upon the throne.

"She was afraid, Sister," Zariya said on our mother's behalf.

"Afraid of what? Me?"

My sister shook her head slowly. "Of realizing the prophecy. Because of what you've done."

My face tightened.

"I'm not rebuking you," she said quickly. "I might have done the same, if I had your courage." Zariya could spin her words with the same diplomacy as our mother once did, but I knew she meant what she had just said.

"What else could I have done?" I said. "I ran from this prophecy my entire life, but there was only one way forward. There was *always* only one way forward."

"I agree," Zariya admitted.

Jaruma's eyebrows rose as mine converged.

"I'm sorry," Zariya said. "I should have told you long ago, but what did I ever truly know? And what good would it have done to tell you or to tell Mama that you can't write your own future?"

Silence.

"Perhaps, had I told her," she said then sighed. "I don't know if it would have changed the outcome. Your patron isn't one to whom Mama would have wanted Zazzau beholden."

And yet, Zazzau *was* beholden to him. Every time I took a "temporary husband", my people were forfeit. It didn't matter if I was queen, they would always be at ransom.

I remained silent. Zariya looked from me to Jaruma, who stared back at her, eyebrows still raised.

My sister sighed again. "I just want you to understand Mama's position. And Uncle's." She scratched her head vigorously, evidently perturbed by my continued silence. "You did what you thought best, for the good of the realm. Mama did the same. And Uncle . . . well, you know how he feels about the old gods." She turned to Jaruma, arms spread. "Help me. She cannot harbor enmity against Uncle; he's all we have left."

He was hardly all Zariya had left. She had a husband and four children. Jaruma opened her mouth. I raised a hand to silence her. She spoke anyway.

"He's your blood, Amina."

"Quiet, woman," I said.

"Amina," she continued.

"Silence."

"Amina," Zariya said, her eyes beseeching my friend.

"Gimbiya," Jaruma now addressed my sister. "You know Amina is as stubborn as a horse's—"

"Silence!"

Jaruma's voice took on a sharper edge. "Your uncle is alive and well. You still have him. Do not throw that away because you're angry."

"*Angry?*" At this point, I was all but frothing at the mouth.

Zariya said, "He's all we have, Sister."

"Karama isn't all *I* have," I said. "I have you and I have"—I waved a dismissive hand toward Jaruma—"that one."

"You loved him once," Zariya said. "And he loves you even now. You cannot hate him for this thing." She shook her head. "You cannot."

Sweet, sweet Zariya. Always trying to make peace. She was so quick to forgive, quick to love. We were not cut from the same cloth, she and I. Forgiveness was not foreign to me, but I didn't hand it out so freely as did my sister.

I would not forgive Karama.

"Damn both of you," I said.

Zariya leaned toward me and pressed a palm to my cheek. "Please, Sister. You cannot hate him."

"It's irrelevant whether I hate him," I muttered. "All that matters is whether I can serve him."

My sister and my companion shared an annoying look of joint understanding, and Zariya said, "Can you?"

I did not know.

TWENTY-EIGHT

City of Gora, Kingdom of Gora, Western Hausaland, circa 1574 CE

More than eight years had passed since Karama took the throne. I remained the heir apparent, though, clearly, there was no benefit to the title.

Much of the army that had marched on Nupeland was still intact and remained fiercely loyal to me, splintering off—in spirit if not in actuality—from the core military of Zazzau. Because of this, and likely to ensure that I spent most of my time far away from the capital city, Karama charged me with keeping our vassals in line.

On some occasions, we transported prisoners sentenced to servitude by their vassal leaders. It was a menial task of my own choosing because, depending on the nature of their crimes, I could execute them. I felt no guilt in using condemned men to satisfy my carnal cravings.

My current assignment was in the western kingdom of Gora. Like the Nupe had once done in the south, the western kingdoms of Hausaland were frustrating Zazzau's trade. Unlike the Nupe, however, the West had not preempted diplomacy by murdering a state official. Nor had they demanded tribute or extra tariffs. They simply waylaid our traders and stole their goods. Such ambushes occasionally resulted in the death of the trader or members of his cavalcade, but the bandits' primary goal was to prevent our people from reaching the lucrative desert outposts.

Because Gora covered a great deal of territory, it wasn't feasible to route our traders around those lands. It behooved us to seek some accord between Zazzau and Gora. Hence, after a nine-day journey, I reached the gates of the capital city, also called Gora.

Two days later, I was still outside.

❀

We were on our third day of camping outside the gates when the Sarkin Gora, Hambaro Rana, sent his royal guard—thirty men on horseback—to meet us. I approached the gates on foot with Jaruma, Danladi, Gambo, and two other soldiers. Siddhi trailed behind them, looking thoroughly put upon. My uncle had sent the makama to make our trade negotiations with Gora more diplomatic. We were, after all, proposing an equal partnership.

When we reached the gatehouse, one of the red-and-black-clad royal guardsmen said, "His Excellency, Hambaro Rana, has asked that you leave your weapons outside."

I glanced at my warriors.

The guard clarified. "He has asked that *you*, Gimbiya Amina, leave your weapons outside. Your guards are allowed a single weapon each."

Hambaro Rana thought he could assert his dominance by disarming me. It was an interesting tactic. Chuckling softly, I made my way back to the waiting bulk of my excessively large contingent and undid my sword belt. Unlike the others, I rarely fought with a knife, so the black takouba was the only weapon I carried on my person.

I handed the sheathed sword to Zuma of Rizga. "Send runners back to Zazzau. Tell them that Hambaro Rana has refused."

My uncle had instructed that we send word back if our negotiations reached an impasse. He intended to join us here, to give his personal assurances in return for Hambaro Rana's consideration. I could already see where our concessions would lead us.

Zuma bowed his head. "As you command, Gimbiya."

I turned back toward the gates.

The others stripped themselves of arm-knives, leg-knives, and every other not-quite-hidden weapon they carried, leaving only their swords. All except Jaruma. She decided on the ivory-hilted long-knife—her gift from Dafaru. No matter how far she threw it, the dagger always returned to her. Siddhi, who was never armed, watched us with knitted brow.

With our collective weight significantly reduced, and the royal guard ushered us through a small wooden door set into the earthen wall.

We met Hambaro Rana in his audience chamber. Clusters of people milled about the adobe great room. Although the thatched roof was elevated half a handbreadth from the tops of the walls to allow adequate ventilation, the sheer number of people overwhelmed the structure. A dank odor hung in the air.

When the first of the guardsmen entered the room, those inside shuffled to the sides, pressing themselves against the walls to let us through. Scuff marks on the earthen floor bore testament to heavy traffic and light sweeping. We strode toward the king, our signature marks mingling on the ground with hundreds who had come before us.

Hambaro Rana sat upon a hideous throne woven from thick ligaments of knotty, greying wood. When his subjects parted, he looked up, a smile hovering on his pudgy face. The smile thinned into a straight line, and he observed our approach with wrinkled brow. The white headwrap, which veiled him from chin to chest, looked incongruous against his fair skin and the gold brocade of his babariga. But compared to my demure full, green dress and headwrap, his gold and white reeked of splendor.

I lowered myself nearly to my knees in deep genuflection. My soldiers bowed. The smile that had previously faded from his face returned with less enthusiasm. It did not extend to his wide-set eyes.

"Many blessings upon you, Benevolent King," I said.

"Rise all," Hambaro Rana replied, gesturing his words with one hand. "Peace unto you, Gimbiya. Had I known sooner that it was Amina at the gates, I would have sent a more suitable greeting party." The smile broadened but still did not reach his eyes.

"Your royal guard was more than suitable, Your Excellency."

"Were they? I'm pleased." He cleared his throat. "What is your reason for coming to my city with a war party in tow?"

I shook my head in innocent denial. "Mine isn't a war party. Merely an escort. Have you not heard that the roads are unsafe for the Zazzagawa?"

He cleared his throat again, more softly. "I had not heard that, Gimbiya." His eyes fell on each of my guards in turn. "By our count, there are three thousand mounted warriors at my gate. Surely you don't need three thousand warriors for safe passage through these lands?"

I presented him with a flamboyant smile of my own. "It is better to be safe than dead."

"To be sure." He nodded, paused, and followed with a sudden round of ribald laughter. His court laughed with him.

The noise coming from his mouth grated me to the bone, but I did my best not to look annoyed and waited for him and his people to finish.

His laughter ebbed. "There are some who say that a dead man is always safe."

The double meaning in his words did not escape me. We each took measure of the other for several breaths before he spoke again. "State your reason for coming here."

"I traveled safely past Dai'i and Telwas," I said. "But only because there were none who dared attack three thousand soldiers. Agents of those two nations have wrought countless disaster on Zazzagawa merchants. Telwas and Dai'i are under your jurisprudence, and so I've come to you."

Hambaro Rana narrowed his eyes. "You come in vain. Their land is their own and many times Zazzau has plundered it. I have no say in the affairs of free men."

"They may be free men, Your Majesty, but they are vassals to Gora. Your recommendation would go far."

"Why should I involve myself in your quarrel with Telwas and Dai'i?"

"Because it would be a reasonable thing to do. Trade between our nations is beneficial to all involved."

"You have nothing we cannot get from someone else."

The statement was mostly true, but we probably had more of whatever his nation needed and could get it to him at a better price. Still, he knew as well as I that trade with Gora was not my reason for coming. Zazzau didn't need his nation; we simply needed to pass through it.

Trade was our bread and butter. As long as Gora barred us from the most profitable trading posts of Gao and Timbuktu, Hambaro Rana and I would remain at odds.

"If you want to be reasonable," he said. "Perhaps your people should content themselves with trade inside your own borders, which lie a fair distance south of your capital."

"You are refusing my proposal?" *The prideful, pompous buffoon.*

"You've made no proposal," he said. "Only threats."

"I've not yet begun to threaten you."

"What do you call three thousand warriors at my door, if not a threat?"

I felt Siddhi's tension behind me. He cleared his throat.

Hambaro Rana said, "You wish to speak?"

Siddhi came forward.

"Then speak," Hambaro Rana said. "If your lady will allow it."

I eyed the Sarkin Gora in exasperation. To his credit, Siddhi didn't look to me for permission before speaking.

He bowed low. "Greetings Your Excellency."

"Greetings," Hambaro Rana replied.

"Our apologies for arriving as we did, without advanced notice. We were wary of making our plans too widely known. Particularly as we travel with our sarki's niece. And the soldiers—three thousand, as you've correctly counted—were for the sarki's peace of mind. The spate of tragic accidents befalling our merchants in these regions have put him in the utmost distress. He wanted only to ensure the safety of a niece that is most precious to him."

Amusement glittered in Hambaro Rana's eyes, but he listened patiently as Siddhi attempted the diplomacy that I was certain he knew was for naught.

"We have no quarrel with either Telwas or Dai'i. Nor are we accusing them of any foul deeds. We are here merely to ask that they assist us in defending our caravans."

"Then why are you not at Telwas or Dai'i? Why have you come here?"

"Because we would not presume to broker any agreements with your vassals until we have reached an agreement with you. We are, of course, willing to compensate them."

"Is that so?" His eyes lit on me. "Perhaps you and I should be discussing compensation."

Siddhi interrupted, "I have Sarki Karama's authority to negotiate on his behalf."

"I would much rather negotiate with Amina."

I crossed my arms. "I have no intention of continuing this wordplay. If you refuse to cooperate—"

"Gora has never denied the Zazzagawa safe passage, though we are well equipped to do so," he said.

Siddhi bristled. Tossing innuendos back and forth wasn't his idea of trade brokering. "Your Excellency, if I may—"

"You may not," Hambaro Rana said. "Gora has nothing to do with your trade caravans. My vassals govern themselves; I won't dictate to them which nations to do business with."

I said. "You speak with a forked tongue. This attempt to hobble Zazzau will be met in kind. Know that we will defend our right to do business with whom *we* please."

I would gladly burn a path through these lands in advance of our trade caravans. Never mind my uncle's desire to settle this dispute in a more amicable manner.

"Is *that* a threat?" he said.

"It's merely a statement of fact, Your Excellency. When I threaten you, you'll know."

With a sigh of resignation, Siddhi hung his head.

Hambaro Rana stood and stepped forward. While seated, his rotund physique gave the appearance of a short man, but he was taller than average. Eye to eye with Jaruma. He advanced until he stood close enough for me to see the tiny, red veins in the whites of his narrowed eyes.

Rather than voice his simmering outrage, he chuckled. "You and your guards will enjoy my hospitality this evening, and you will be on your way by first light. Not even a tongue as sharp as yours will tax my good humor today."

TWENTY-NINE

We sat in the palace courtyard, seated on pouf chairs at a long a row of tables. Dinner was an uninspired dish of ground millet, steamed into balls of *tuwo*, with groundnut soup and roasted goat. The goat was roasted hard, and the tuwo was too heavy; it sat in my stomach like sand. By the time dinner was through and the servants had cleared away the water bowls, I wanted nothing more than sleep.

Unfortunately, mine was not the only party being hosted by Hambaro Rana this evening. A delegation of statesmen from one of the small northern kingdoms was also in attendance. For them, Hambaro Rana had planned entertainment.

After the servants removed the water bowls and tables, the figure of a man peeled itself away from the shadows between the king's audience chamber and the gatehouse. The elderly man shuffled into the light with a lopsided gait supported by a thin walking stick. He bowed as best he could, his entire frame trembling with the effort. I heard his bones creak.

Hambaro Rana leaned close. "The *mai tasuniya*."

Sitting on his left, I folded my arms and prepared to fight the sleep that was sure to descend once the storyteller began.

Hambaro Rana leaned in again. "This man has impressive talent, Gimbiya. Don't close your eyes."

"Pfft."

"*Ga ta ga ta nan,*" the mai tasuniya shouted in a voice much smoother than his gait.

In response, the audience yelled back, "*Ku ʐo, mu ji ta.*"

A drum began to beat, and the story issued forth in song.

"Spider is hungry," sang the mai tasuniya. "Crows destroyed the harvest of his farm, and he needs food." The drum beat the sound of Spider's despair at discovering his hard-sown harvest gone.

Sleep did not descend for me. It left entirely once the drums began. A vision appeared. A man with six arms. *Spider?* My mind remained cloudy. No doubt an effect of the sour palm wine.

I blinked rapidly, but the vision did not fade. Surely, it was an actor playing out the scene of the distraught spider. Except, I could see through him—to the mai tasuniya and the drummer beyond.

I was evidently quite drunk but, intrigued, I watched the spider flail his many limbs and beat upon his chest. Even more intriguing, a farm sprang up around him, complete with damaged field and large blackbirds jeering mercilessly.

"Soon, Hyena passed by Spider's way," the mai tasuniya sang as another man entered the vision.

The spotted fur of a hyena covered the man from head to toe. He approached the spider and asked what caused such anguish. The spotted man's lips moved, but the question itself came from the mai tasuniya's song.

Spider wailed, "My crops are finished!"

Hyena said, "I have plenty to share. Come to my abode, and I will give you what you need."

Spider accepted Hyena's offer. Little did he know it was Hyena who had sent the birds to eat Spider's crops in the first place. Hyena was jealous of Spider because Spider's crops always did well, while Hyena was forced to plant twice as many seeds and toil twice as hard to yield enough.

"There is one thing you must know," said Hyena to Spider. "At the turn in the road lives a large snake. The snake is blind and feeds on travelers. To pass by unharmed, you must say these words, 'I am food for many.' Do not forget. If you say, 'I am food for one,' the snake will eat you right off, but if you say, 'I am food for many,' he will let you pass."

"And if I say that I am not food at all?" asked the spider.

"No, no, no!" said Hyena. "If you say that, he will kill you and throw your body to the crows."

Spider shuddered at the thought of such a fate.

"And night fell," the mai tasuniya sang.

The sun in my vision dipped low to be replaced by a bright moon, which was immediately replaced by the sun. The start of the next day.

The multi-limbed man left his compound and went in the direction the hyena had gone the day before. At a bend in the road, another man lay. Dark scales created a variegated pattern over his body. This man was obviously the snake, for he had no eyes in his head.

The spider tried to creep around the blind, sleeping snake, but the snake woke before Spider could get past.

"Who goes there?" hissed the snake.

In his fear, Spider forgot the words he was to speak and blurted out, "I am food for one!"

The snake rose up, stuck out his long tongue, and said, "Then pass. *One* will eat well today."

Uneasy in his belly, Spider went on until he reached another bend in the road.

The song of the mai tasuniya rang in my ears as though he sang from within my skull. I could see him and the drummer beyond, but my eyes focused only on the new man in the scene—the man with a lion's mane.

Spider knew nothing of the lion at the second turn because Hyena, expecting Spider to be eaten by the snake, had not mentioned it. In that moment, Spider understood the trick Hyena had played on him. He turned back and went home.

Enthralled, I sat bolt upright in my seat and watched Hyena return to Spider's house that evening.

Confused at seeing Spider alive and well, Hyena asked, "Did you go to my farm today?"

To which Spider replied, "I did not. I came to the turn in the road. However, before the snake knew I was there, I overheard him say that he was too hungry for morsels and that he would eat you when next you passed his way."

Hyena's fur stood on end, and he began to shake. A quiver full of arrows was slung across his back. With bow in hand, he ran quickly to the bend in the road and killed the snake. He then brought the carcass back to show Spider how he had taken revenge on the traitorous snake.

The hyena again invited Spider to his house, telling him that there was a lion at the second bend. "To pass the lion, say, 'I am food for one.'"

Spider did not ask why Hyena had failed to mention the lion before. Rather, he thanked Hyena and urged him to leave the snake's carcass so that Spider could throw it out for the crows. Hyena left the carcass. Spider took it and cooked the meat for himself.

My stomach turned at the sight of the large man-spider eating the large man-snake, but the scene quickly faded. As the sun went down in my vision for a second time, it was replaced by the moon and rose again on the third day.

The mai tasuniya sang these words, "Spider waited for evening to come. When the sun fell, so came Hyena to Spider's abode."

Once again, Hyena found Spider alive and well. Baffled, Hyena asked, "Did you go to my farm today?"

To which Spider replied, "I did not. When I reached the second turn in the road, I heard Lion cursing his memory. He said he could not remember the words that allow a traveler to pass. So I hid in the bushes and whispered, as if from the gods, 'I am food for one.'"

"Food for one?"

"Yes," Spider replied. "Is that not what you told me?"

Hyena nodded. "Food for one. Of course." He was thankful because he had lied to Spider and would surely have used the true words—which were now wrong—had Spider not told him otherwise. Before Hyena went on his way, Spider invited him to have a drink of wine. Hyena accepted.

But Hyena had not seen what I'd seen.

With one of his many hands, Spider had poured something into the gourd of wine. Undoubtedly, the wine was poisoned—a trick I knew well. Oblivious to what Spider had done, Hyena drank and went on his way.

When he reached the lion, he called out, "I am food for one!" At that, Lion pounced on Hyena and ate him.

Feeling half-drugged myself, I saw the lion sway as the poison worked its way into his system. Soon the lion lay dead on the ground, and his body faded away to nothing.

"So it was," concluded the mai tasuniya, "that Hyena, who plotted to destroy the spider, lost his life to Spider's cunning and Spider took ownership of all that was Hyena's. Thus was Spider revenged against his enemy."

The drums beat out their last few notes; the storyteller ended his performance with the words *kungurus kan bera,* and everyone sat silent.

It was some time before I emerged from my stupor. Looking around, I saw that the vision had not been mine alone, for everyone sat still, silent, stunned. The mai tasuniya had woven a remarkable spell.

Hambaro Rana nodded approval at his storyteller and grinned in satisfaction at the rest of us. With a sidelong look at me, he proclaimed, "No Zazzagawa storyteller can tell a tale like that, eh?"

I had to agree with him. "Your mai tasuniya is a treasure, Your Excellency." My eyes remained glued to the spot where the vision had manifested. "Take care he doesn't fly away."

The king fell into one of his annoying guffaws, and I made an attempt not to roll my eyes. In the flickering torchlight, no one noticed my failure.

"You've had your entertainment, Gimbiya," he said, still chuckling. "And you have yet to enjoy the full measure of my hospitality. But come morning, it is *you* who shall fly away."

"As you say, Your Excellency."

Still eyeing me intently, he leaned close and whispered into my ear, "If you enjoyed the mai tasuniya's magic, perhaps tonight you might know the pleasure of *my* magic." If he leaned any closer, we'd be sharing the same seat.

Obviously, he was drunk. He could not truly have meant what I thought he meant. My heaving stomach did several somersaults.

Turning to face him, I drew back and leveled a contemptuous gaze upon him. "My pleasure would come in the morning when my patron feeds on your heart."

Unperturbed, he moved his eyes from my face to my chest and, again, to my face. "You're like the mantis that kills her husband after a single moment's ecstasy."

My brow rose a fraction.

"You didn't think your exploits went unnoticed by *all*, did you?" He bared his teeth in something a little less than a smile and cocked his head to one side. "But, you *did* think just that." His raucous laughter began again.

He fell silent. "They say Ruhun Yak'i. is your patron god. Is this why Amina has gone without defeat?" He eyed me now with a contemplative look. "If I send for you tonight, will you truly attempt to kill me in the morning?"

Once again, my stomach recoiled. "I would not come. Not even for the pleasure of killing you in the morning."

"Then it's true!" He slapped the table, causing some of the nearby guests to look in our direction. He lowered his voice. "You take a husband for the night and murder him before he wakes?"

I had heard the rumors about me. Whispers that had spawned from one vassal slave I'd taken to my room before we'd left his kingdom's territory. Palace guards were a verbose lot. Since then, I made sure to take the prisoners only after we put their cities behind us. *My* warriors always kept their mouths shut.

It was discomfiting to learn the rumor had traveled so far.

"What type of king puts stock in such filthy gossip?" I asked.

"Ah, but you and I know it isn't mere gossip." He touched my cheek with one finger, and I resisted the urge to snap it off. "It is difficult to keep secret one's"—his eyes traveled my body again—

"aberrations. Yet, you manage to silence your partners." He took his hand away. "There is only one explanation. You must *truly* silence them."

"*This* is your explanation?" I asked. "Has it not occurred to you that, perhaps, I'm not as wanton as the rumors claim? Has it also not occurred to you that men remain silent because they have no secrets to tell?"

He appraised me further, eyes narrowed as though he were trying to glean the secrets directly from my mind. "It's been said that you do not age." He continued to peer at me. "Truly, your appearance does not betray you. I know you are much older than you seem."

I could hide the men but could not hide my youth. Not for much longer. I would soon be in my forties, then fifties, then sixties. And I'd still have the face of a young woman. Once Zariya, who was two years younger than me, started to show her age, people would take closer notice of mine. I would deal with it when the time came.

I asked, "How old do I seem?"

"Barely into womanhood."

"You cannot judge my age because you do not know me. Perhaps if I had a husband to encumber me at every turn—"

"Dead men can be no encumbrance."

"Or children to grey my hair before its time, I might look as old as my years. But even *I* wouldn't be so vain as to say my appearance is that of a girl barely into womanhood."

"The moon shining brightly in the midnight sky cannot look upon its own radiance." He spoke with such sincerity that I was too taken aback to respond. The broad smile returned to his face but was not punctuated with meaningless laughter. After a slight nod, he turned away and began a conversation with the man on his right.

THIRTY

We left Gora early the next morning. Karama had instructed me to await his arrival, but I refused to spend another eight nights sleeping outside like a vagabond. If Karama meant to debase himself to that oaf, Hambaro Rana, he could do it alone.

On our journey into Gora, we had circumvented the chiefdom of Dai'i by several kilometers and had planned to retrace that route on the ride home. However, two days into our travels, a sudden urge pushed its way to the front of my mind: I had to meet with the ruling chief of Dai'i.

I could not say why the idea had come to me, but upon consideration, it seemed idiotic. A personal audience with me *might* impress upon the ruling nobility the wisdom of keeping their mercenaries in check. But it was unlikely, given that their patron king, Hambaro Rana, did not see fit to rein them in. Delaying my return home merely to suffer rejection from a minor chiefdom was a foolish notion. A notion that had sprung from nowhere and would lead me nowhere.

Why, I wondered, was I arguing so vehemently *against* going, when there was no reason to go in the first place? But detouring into Dai'i felt like a sensible course of action. As if I'd lost something there and could only find it if I traveled into the heart of the chiefdom. The more I resisted the idea, the more pressing the need to go. The more I debated with myself, the more certain I was that we *must* pass through that city.

Without fully understanding the compulsion, I gave in to it and issued the command.

We altered our course.

Jaruma was soon riding at my side. "Why are we going to Dai'i?"

I shrugged

"You don't know?" She raised an inquisitive brow.

I frowned. "Why do you always question me?" My annoyance was not at her, but at myself, because there was no point in going to that godforsaken city. Yet something gnawed at me, prodded me, *insisted* we go to Dai'i.

Jaruma scowled at my surly response but gave no argument. Not that any argument would have mattered. We were going to the chiefdom of Dai'i

❋

Silence rippled down the ranks when we came within sight of Dai'i and eye to eye with two of the runners I had sent to Karama three days before. I stared at their faces because there was nothing else to look at. Their heads sat atop tall wooden stakes driven into the ground. The center stake, not as tall as the other two, held a wooden placard with Arabic wording etched into it.

I subdued the shudder trembling through me. "Who here reads Arabic?"

The question passed from soldier to soldier until Zuma came forward. I should have known the boy could read. He dismounted, strode to the placard, and scrutinized it.

"What does it say?" I asked.

His eyes flicked over the words for a moment longer before focusing on me. "It says, 'There is only one fate for the enemies of Dai'i.'"

Bitter heat rose in my belly and up my neck. "Is that everything?" My voice quavered with the fury I was trying to mask.

"Yes, Gimbiya."

I angled toward Jaruma without moving my gaze from the disembodied heads. I had dispatched three runners to Karama. There were only two here. Either one had escaped, or his head was in no condition for display.

"We wouldn't have seen this had we gone around," Jaruma said solemnly. "Is it supposed to be a warning?"

"A threat more likely," Danladi replied.

"We should make haste to inform your uncle. There's no hope for cooperation between us and the West." A thoughtful frown pinched Jaruma's brow. "How did you know to come here?"

How had I known? I'd not given this town a second thought after we had left Zazzau, scarcely considered its ruler, much less the need to speak with him. Yet the urgency to pay this chiefdom a visit had overridden all my good sense. Silent, I pondered.

"The god of war," I said at length. "It was his urging that brought us here."

"His urging?"

"I'll explain another time."

She nodded and glanced at the heads. "What are your orders?"

"Take them down."

I turned away while the nearest soldiers did my bidding. Those farther off fidgeted on their horses. Only three thousand warriors had accompanied me to Gora, and we'd been riding now for almost two full days. Having had little opportunity to spy heavily within the walls of Dai'i, we knew neither how strong their fortifications nor how well defended their city.

I looked into the distance, scanning the top of the wall, then faced Danladi. "What do you know of this city?"

"Only that what they've done here is an affront to Zazzau." He, too, cast his eyes toward the wall.

That decided me. "Leave only the chieftain's house untouched."

As evening fell, our war drums began to beat.

❋

The sacking of Dai'i was brutal barbarism at best. If they had ever expected their enemies to come through the front gates, they certainly weren't prepared. If they had an army, it was a pathetic one because the city might as well have been unguarded when my three thousand warriors poured into it.

The city went up in flames. The Zazzagawa were outnumbered, but the Daiawa were outmatched. Before the night was out, Dai'i was reduced to a smoldering battlefield.

I had regrouped with my senior officers outside the gates and was about to head back into the city when I saw two Zazzagawa scouts riding toward me. A man, bound at the wrists, staggered behind each horse. One of the men fell before they reached me, but the rider didn't slow. The horse dragged its burden across the tall grass.

"What is this?" I asked as the scouts drew to a halt.

"Spies," the two replied simultaneously.

"Tracking us from Gora," one added as his prisoner fell to his knees.

"Cut them loose," I said.

The two scouts dismounted and freed the spies. The one who had been dragged did not move. I went to him. He was still breathing, though barely. I dropped to my haunches for closer examination. A hole in his tunic revealed the caked blood marking the boundaries of a deep gash in his side. The fact that it no longer bled gave good indication of the amount of blood the man had already lost. It was a wonder he was still alive.

"I think this one's going to die." I rose. "Take him into the city. If there's a medicine man, let him deal with the wound."

"And the other?" the scout asked.

"Leave him. He can find his way back to his master in Gora." With that, I returned to my horse, climbed on, and rode into the city.

Most of the city's denizens were alive—many uninjured. They ran helter-skelter through the streets while my men looted jewelry, currency, whatever valuables they could carry. Bloodletting was never our goal when we raided a city, and in this case, the point was only to show that Zazzau would not be intimidated by the likes of these western nations. What better way to make a point than by leveling a city?

Zuma rode out of the sooty shadows, his saddlebag just as flat as before the raid. Although he fought well, he was a reluctant warrior, seldom joining in the looting but occasionally absconding with an article of scholarly value. He harbored no dreams of wealth, seemingly content to live a humble life on his soldier's wage. More than likely, he had joined the military in the hope of one day fighting against the Kwararafa, of avenging the family he'd lost so long ago, in that faraway place, when I had been a different woman.

"No treasures?" I gave a sardonic smile as he joined my party.

Sarcasm was lost on him. "None, Gimbiya."

I shook my head in wry amusement. "The chieftain's abode?"

"This way."

As ordered, the abode was intact. Now the city's nobility could look upon their land and remember what arrogance had wrought. I rode past the compound's high walls, watching the frightened citizens scurry into its refuge. Many, however, did not make it to safety. With people being the most valuable loot, we took our pick of slaves— mostly young men and women—and loaded them onto horses liberated from the chieftain's corral. By first light, the devastated city was far behind us.

❀

About a third of the way into our journey home, I caught sight of something in the distance and let out a long breath. Evidently, the third messenger had escaped capture.

Jaruma said, "Is that . . ."

"Karama," I finished and muttered a curse.

My uncle had been explicit in saying I couldn't use force on Gora, but he had said nothing of the other cities. The murders of our messengers could not go unanswered. Failure to punish Dai'i would serve only to weaken us in our enemies' eyes. Certainly, Karama understood that. Regardless, I would have preferred to make the report after we returned home. For him to come upon me like this— toting a load of slaves? My shoulders tensed in anticipation of the upcoming confrontation.

Karama and his troop of soldiers drew near. His eyes darted across the captives. Riding two to a mount, my warriors leading their horses, the prisoners were bound to one another, back-to-back. Hunched shoulders, tear-streaked eyes, a general aura of misery marked them as nothing other than human bounty. Karama rode past me, circled the captives, and rode back to where I sat stiffly on my horse.

"What is this?" Muted anger simmered in his eyes. Before I could answer, he said, "Ride with me."

He turned his horse down the long row of warriors, and I followed. When we had ridden beyond the hearing of the soldiers, Karama stopped. I rode up alongside him. His breathing was heavy and sweat glistened on his forehead.

"Why did you deviate from our agreed course of action?"

I opened my mouth to respond, but he continued, "You were to send word and await me. Where did you get these people?"

"They're from Dai'i."

"Dai'i? Why did you go to Dai'i?" A brisk wind blew, but the sweat continued collecting on his brow. "Answer me!"

The sudden outburst startled my horse. Galadima shook his head and stepped sideways several paces.

"Uncle—"

"You rush headlong into conflict, Amina. Without consideration of cost or consequence. Are you deliberately trying to usurp my authority?"

I jerked the reins to keep Galadima still. My chin rose with indignation. "I've done no such thing."

"No? What you've done is declare war against every state between Zazzau and the desert. What you've done is go against the orders of your king."

"Forgive me, Uncle." I tried to keep my voice level. "But Zazzau was threatened."

"Threatened by Dai'i?" His voice was incredulous.

"Yes, Uncle. Threatened by Dai'i. Is it not Dai'i that made the trade routes impassable? Was it not because of this you sent me to Gora?"

"Because of Dai'i? Dai'i is nothing, Amina. Dai'i couldn't even defend itself against you."

"Uncle—"

"Silence!"

Like a child being chastised, I straightened in the saddle and pressed my lips together. Karama judging me for what I'd done in Dai'i was like being put on trial for killing a man who had attempted to murder my family.

He said, "Dai'i is but one stone atop a mountain of boulders. And Gora . . . Gora is a single boulder within that mountain." He rubbed his face with both hands then held them in a prayer position in front of him. Palms still flat against each other, he turned his fingers to point at me. "You are so very, very stupid!"

I bristled, brow raised in anger. My brow dropped, and I inhaled in slow realization of what he was saying. At last, I understood the true nature of the threat. The western nations had formed an alliance. Perhaps the northern nations as well. Against us. But why hadn't Karama told me this from the beginning? Why had he sent me blind into Gora?

"I . . . Uncle, you should have told me."

"Why? Why did I have to tell you? I needed only to give you an order. And you needed only follow it." He regarded me for an interminable time. Finally, he gave a loud sigh. Lowering his head, he rubbed his temples with the heels of his palms. After several vigorous revolutions, he raised his head, eyes blazing into mine. "We are no longer in any position to negotiate peace; we've attacked one of their own. They killed two men and, in response, you destroyed an entire city. The message you've sent is louder than anything we can possibly say in our defense. We could have avoided all this"—he gestured at the slaves—"had you not failed with Hambaro Rana."

I shook my head, dropping my eyes to Galadima's mane. "There was no reasoning with that pompous buffoon," I murmured. "Conquest of Amina was uppermost in his mind."

"So because of your foolish pride, you've brought war upon us?" His hands were again on his horse's reins, gripping them so tightly that the skin stretching over his knuckles shone. "Do you think no one knows what you do with men?"

I let out a sharp gasp before I could stifle it.

"Though no man dares speak of his encounters with you, it's common knowledge that you're more than willing to entertain them." With disgust thick in his voice, he added, "What is one more man to a woman like you?"

His words stabbed me in the heart. I raised a hand to my constricted throat.

Oblivious to my distress, he continued, "If we come under attack from an allied force, Nupeland will not long be ours."

I said nothing, unable to speak around the mass that had formed in my throat.

"Nor will Zazzau." Again, he gestured toward the captives. "This is *your* mess. Be sure to clean it up." With a quick flick of the reins, he urged his horse into a gallop and rode back to the waiting troops.

THIRTY-ONE

City of Turunku, Kingdom of Zazzau, Central Hausaland, circa 1575 CE

The rainy season came upon us like a lion. Torrential storms, the likes of which were rarely seen, poured from furious skies. It was as though the gods had decided to wash us away before we could kill each other. And killing was undoubtedly on the horizon.

The Hausawa between Zazzau and the western desert outposts had joined forces and were preparing to do battle against us. Week after week, at war council, we received dire news in one form or another. My uncle's worry showed on his face, aging him beyond his fifty-three years, and his anger where I was concerned had not waned. For three full months, the man had spoken no more than a handful of words to me.

As for my soldiers, hardly a day went by, wet or dry, that I didn't drill them until they were near collapse. For the past few days, however, the heavy rain had not let off. The training fields had turned to marsh, and spirits were low all around. It seemed an ideal time for a short leave from training. The soldiers were glad for the respite. In all honesty, so was I. Lulled by the steady rain pattering on my thatched roof, I slept late.

And I dreamed.

I climbed a mountain that rose far into the heavens. With toes firmly gripping into nooks, fingers tugging on outcroppings, upward I climbed. Without tearing or soiling my long white dress, without scratching my palms or my bare feet. Upward, beyond the clouds, to where the way grew less steep. Until I could climb with legs alone, until the ground became level, and I stood atop a plateau.

Yellowish grass covered the mountaintop. It swayed in a mild breeze. All was quiet. No birds sang, no insects buzzed. Not a sound. Only the gentle breeze and dancing grass.

An old man walked silently toward me, his overgrown white beard reaching his chest. When he was a few paces away, he halted and held out his arms. His eyes had the opaque, misty look of the ancient. The hands that beckoned were twisted with age. He stepped closer, closer, and I recognized the face beneath the beard.

"Siddhi?" My voice carried across the vast field.

Aged by eighty years or more, he was like a walking corpse, his very appearance repulsive. His lips moved as though he spoke, but he made no sound. He took another step forward and another. Until his crooked fingers brushed my arm.

I drew back.

The old man howled. A sound so full of anguish that I clapped my hands over my ears. Before my eyes, his skin cracked and flaked, sloughing off in large sheets until nothing remained but the bleeding flesh underneath. Shutting my eyes, I backed away in revulsion.

Abruptly, the howling ceased. I opened my eyes. Dafaru stood in the old man's place.

"That was unpleasant," he said.

"Why do you bring me such nightmares?" I tried to keep the tremor from my voice, the sight of Siddhi's sloughing flesh now seared into my mind.

"This is *your* mind, Beloved." He gestured wide. "I am merely visiting."

I opened my mouth to give a bitter retort but stopped and looked past him. There was someone else on that mountaintop. I squinted, focusing on the newcomer. The god of war turned to look as well. He looked back at me, the violent color in his eyes registering anger. I felt my own eyes widen as I too recognized the man. My heart crashed against my ribs, and I brought a palm to my chest. Sparing no consideration for my rightful husband, I gathered my skirt in my hands and ran off.

"Suleyman." My breathing quickened as the whisper floated away on the breeze. "Suleyman!"

Running was like wading through a swamp. The tall grass slashed at my legs. It wrapped around my ankles, hindering my every step. My legs couldn't move fast enough, but I reached him and flung myself into his arms. He held me only a moment before a set of long fingers wrapped around his neck, dragging him out of my embrace.

I screamed in half mad frustration.

As if Suleyman were a bundle of rags, Dafaru threw him across the plateau. I screamed again and began running toward the crumpled mass, but Dafaru seized my arm. He yanked me back.

Spouting a stream of rude epithets, I kicked and pushed and scratched to no avail. Then I balled my hand into a tight fist and rammed it into his jaw with an unnerving crack. My fingers throbbed from the blow that would have knocked an ordinary man off balance. The god of war didn't even flinch.

Fear held me rigid as red eyes, blazing with the fires of countless hells, stared back at me. With the back of his hand, he touched his jaw where I had struck him. Then that hand swung out to smack me across the face. The blow reverberated through my body. I cried out, flailing, as I fell to the ground.

I woke, my hand flying to my face. And I stared into the wargod's burning eyes.

"Your heart still yearns for the touch of a dead man," he said in a low tone.

"Even in dreams you spy on me." The sting of his blow lingered. I rubbed my face and rolled over to escape those angry red eyes.

He clutched my shoulder with a grip of stone and flipped me onto my back. "Why do you long for a man whose marrow has since been consumed by maggots?"

It was difficult to tell whether he was being deliberately cruel. Still, fury rose like bile from my gut. I loved Suleyman; death had not changed that. But those feelings, the cherished memories, were all locked away. I missed him but did not *yearn* for him.

Flexing my still throbbing fingers, I swallowed the venomous words filling my mouth. Instead, I said, "Look into my mind and find your answer."

Dafaru narrowed his eyes and gave me a wry smile. "You have become adept at guarding your thoughts, Beloved. But when you dream, your soul is open to me."

There was a time when such words would have caused great me anxiety, but that time was long gone. I fixed him with an unperturbed glare. "Then tell me what you've seen in my soul."

Baring his teeth, he growled some words at me. Or perhaps he simply growled.

I yielded.

"May we avoid a clash of wills, my lord?"

Easing his grip on my shoulder, he broke into soft chortles. Gradually at first, then wholehearted laughter. Were I not accustomed to his abrupt mood changes, this dark laughter might have terrified me.

"You do not learn quickly, but you learn well. Come with me and I will show you love."

He knew nothing of the word. He possessed me as a man possessed livestock, and only because it suited him to do so. Once he grew tired of my favors, he would cease caring. Even knowing this, my body responded to him as it always did. I sighed, sliding my arms around his neck as desire tempered my anger.

"Perhaps you could remain here?" I suggested.

The frown on his face gave a good indication of how he felt about the idea. His eyes scanned the room. "You could never comprehend how distasteful I find this world of yours."

"Husband, please."

He cocked an eyebrow. "Husband? In a decade, it has been nothing but 'my lord' and 'Dafaru.' I believe you have even referred to me as 'Ruhun Yak'i' once or twice. But never have you called me 'husband.'"

"Sometimes I forget," I replied indifferently. "You don't treat me like a wife."

"Do not provoke me, woman."

"I intend only to please, my lord." My fingertips brushed the side of his face. "You're most agreeable when pleased."

"My brother has turned your world into a muddy cesspool. It is your desire to remain *here*?"

"Is there no rain in Jangare?" I asked, realizing that I'd never actually seen rain in the spirit world.

"No."

"There's much to be said for a good storm." With a soft yawn, I arched my back in a languid stretch.

He glanced downward. "You are very tempting."

"Enough to keep you here?" I held the stretch longer than necessary.

"Perhaps. Though you irritate me to no end."

He undid my wrapper and slid an arm around my waist. The supple leather of his bracer glided softly against my skin. His arm came to rest, and the metal fastenings jabbed into my back. Our legends told that the bracers were his source of power. He never took the damned things off. I'd not yet dared to ask if the legends were true.

"Then we've put aside our argument?" I shifted my back in discomfort. "For a short while at least?"

He laughed. It was a disarming sort of laugh. A sound that did not often issue from his lips. He said, "Can we both be satisfied in a short while?"

"I am but a mortal woman. Can *you* be satisfied?"

"That, my love, depends entirely on you."

※

After the wargod left, I slept again. Until midday, when Jaruma woke me with a round of ignoble shaking.

"Leave off, karya," I muttered into the bed.

"Your uncle summons you."

I groaned and lay limp on my belly. Only after Jaruma had shaken me several more times did I drag myself to my hands and knees, cursing her all the while.

My uncle conducted most governmental affairs from my mother's palace, Gidan Bakwa, but he did not live there. I, however, did. Karama's private dwelling lay two kilometers south, and he had an irksome habit of summoning me there whenever he wanted to discuss matters of state

"Trust him to send for me on the wettest day of the year." I fumbled for my clothing.

"A good soaking cleanses the soul," she said.

I paused to scowl at her. "Get out and send for my horse."

She made a sweeping bow. "As you command, my ill-tempered mistress."

※

Hands clasped behind his back, Karama paced back and forth in his private chamber. He stopped and looked up as I burst through the open doorway, clothing plastered to my body.

"You're soaked," he said.

It was all I could do not to curse at him. Teeth tightly clenched, I bowed in greeting. "You sent for me, Uncle?"

"Yes." Frowning, he looked down at the puddle forming at my muddy feet. "You've heard the news of the Western Alliance?"

To avoid glaring at him, I looked everywhere else. The bright colors splashed in nonsensical patterns from the clay-tiled floor to the palm-thatched ceiling gave the walls a cheerfulness that contradicted both my mood and the dark clouds outside.

"Yes, Uncle. I've heard the news. I'm present at every war council."

He disregarded my tart response. "They will be on the move once these clouds dry up."

I nodded. Of course they were coming. The western kingdoms had created a formidable alliance—Gora, Telwas, Maji, Kuzu, and what was left of Dai'i. From the information our spies had gathered, the western army was more than ten thousand strong.

"We are prepared for the strike," I said.

Karama shook his head. "You must strike first, Amina. Because you will only have seven thousand warriors."

"Seven thousand against more than ten thousand?"

"If I gave you ten thousand, the risk that the Western Alliance would repel your attack is still too great. Five thousand warriors must remain behind to defend the city."

"But three thousand warriors can hold Turunku indefinitely. Give me nine thousand and it will ensure victory."

"Will it? Have you that much faith in your god?"

"Uncle . . ."

"Your patron guaranteed you Nupeland alone. Has he also guaranteed the Western Alliance?"

"Give me nine thousand warriors. The only guarantee you need is mine."

"Seven thousand."

"Uncle, you yourself say the battle will be risky even with ten thousand. Or is it your intention that I should perish?" The accusation was out of my mouth before I could halt my tongue.

Silence ensued.

"You are mad, Amina." He evinced no strong emotion at my indictment of him. "You've become an abomination to nature. Your very lifestyle goes against all the teachings of the Great Prophet, Muhammad. But you are still my sister's daughter and I wish you no harm." He eyed me. "Besides, there's talk that you cannot die, that you are *yan tauri*."

"Yan tauri?"

"One who is impervious to metal."

"I know what it is."

We all grew up hearing of those special people who could withstand assault by any metallic object. Sometimes, traveling bands of yan tauri put on performances, slashing themselves with blades then revealing their skin to show that no mark was made.

But I was not yan tauri.

I crossed the room and snatched his sword from where it hung on the wall. Karama tensed, his eyes tracking me warily, but he made no move to stop me. Holding the sword before me, I wrapped my hand around the blade and slid it a short way along the sharp edge.

"I'm not yan tauri." I raised my palm for inspection. "I bleed. And I die."

He stared at my open palm.

Infuriated, I almost threw the weapon down at his feet. Instead, I replaced it on its hooks without wiping the blood.

"I can give you victory, Uncle. But only if you give me the means to take it. I need nine thousand warriors. You must trust me." The wound stung. I had not meant to cut so deep and could feel the blood collecting in my closed fist.

"How can I trust you, Amina? You defy me at every turn."

"I took necessary action at Dai'i. It was not defiance."

"And you put your faith in demonic spirits."

So that was it. Karama was a modernist. One man for every woman; many women for one man. And the gods of old? To Karama they were nothing more than devils, ancient spawns of evil.

He rubbed his face and looked at me with tired eyes. "You *will* have nine thousand but not all from Zazzau. Bugwam has agreed to join us in this fight. I have a strategy. If it is properly executed, you could be victorious with even six thousand men against the western ten thousand. If defeat is imminent, you have room to retreat."

"Retreat?"

He heard the outrage in my voice.

"You will retreat, Amina. And we'll take our final stand here. You do what you can to keep them from our gates; but if they overwhelm you, it is my order that you retreat."

I said nothing. My hand was beginning to throb.

"Obey me."

I bowed. "As you command, Uncle."

He nodded. "Stay until tomorrow. We'll discuss strategy in the morning. Retreat is not so bad as you think and is often the wisest plan of action."

"Yes, Uncle."

He dismissed me, and I dashed back into the rain, wondering just how much he hated me. Enough to send me to my death? But perhaps this strategy of his was sound. He was, after all, brilliant in the art of warfare. For now, I would reserve judgment.

※

Wearing a borrowed wrapper and blouse, I spent the rest of the day in the company of Karama's wives and children. When night fell, I retired to the guest room that his junior wife had prepared for me. The god of war was waiting in the shadows.

"You startled me," I said, attributing the flutter in my heart to the shock of his abrupt appearance.

Without a word, he pulled me to him.

"Twice in one day?" I chuckled. "Surely, I don't deserve it, my lord."

"Careful, woman. Or I might agree with you."

He took my hand, scrutinizing it in its linen bandage. In his, my hand was small, fragile. With the slightest squeeze, he could break my fingers like twigs.

"Playing with swords?" His lips touched my bandaged palm.

He looked at me with serene red eyes, a smile playing about his perfect mouth. At times, his flawlessness was overwhelming. I raised myself onto my toes and pressed my mouth to his. He arched a suspicious brow, but I had no ulterior motive.

As the heat poured from his lips to mine, I squeezed my body against him. The flutter in my heart doubled its pace. I closed my eyes, and my senses woke. Those parts of me that twined with his spirit reached out to him. His hands slid around my waist. I let out a sigh.

"I detest the world of men," he murmured through scorching lips.

"I know."

He took me back to Jangare, to his bed, removing my blouse, plastering kisses on my neck and down my chest. I shivered with desire. Not the irrational lust that was my curse when he stayed away too long, but something more powerful. Perhaps it was the morning's love play that had left me primed, but this longing went beyond physical, beyond the mere need of an acolyte—by now, I was undoubtedly an acolyte—to bask in the glory of a god. This emotion, which had come upon me so insipidly, went deeper than all of that. It was reminiscent of love. Too much so. I didn't like it.

Damn you, Husband. The words hung only in my thoughts, but he heard.

"What have I done to warrant your wrath this time, Beloved?" From his tone of voice, he wasn't the least bit interested in my response.

"Nothing."

I could never love him. This emotion that was pounding in my heart . . . whatever it was could not be love. I tried to shift from under him.

"What is the matter with you?" He pressed a hand to my chest, pinning me to the bed, his disinterest a thing of the past.

I tried to shift again. "I don't love you."

"Is that all?" The blazing red of his eyes cooled to a somber glow, and he regarded me in silence for a while. "Since when has love been necessary for what I plan to do with you?" He lowered his face to mine.

I turned my head away. "I will *never* love you."

Perhaps I wanted to incite his wrath, push him to the sort of rage that sparked my own anger. But I didn't know. I knew only that the emotion spreading within me was stifling, and I had to get away from him.

"My lord, I need air."

He let me go, and I rushed to the open window.

The air in Jangare was sweeter than the air in the mortal world. It was clearer, purer. I inhaled deeply, exhaled slowly.

I had grown accustomed to Dafaru. Fond even. But it wasn't love. To love someone who forced me to murder time and time again would be a travesty. To love someone who loved me only at his pleasure, *used* me at his pleasure, would make me the abomination my uncle said I was. The god of war had made me his slave when he'd made me his wife. That was our only bond.

Fondness I could live with, but not love.

Another inhalation and the panic dissipated. I rubbed my temples and turned to find him standing before me. As our eyes met, the anger faded from his.

He took my face in his hands and kissed my brow. His hands fell to my waist. They lingered there, fingers stroking the bare skin before untying my wrapper and lifting me off the ground. I snaked my arms about his neck, kissing him as he carried me back to the bed and set me down on the silken coverings.

The bed was cool against my back. His skin was hot against my belly, against my thighs, against my breasts. He wrapped himself around me, enveloped me in his arms, in his spirit. My mouth parted, invited him inside as I, in turn, wrapped myself around him. Our bodies twined into a single breathing mass, a single heartbeat, a single soul.

For the first time in our marriage, he was not just a god, not even a man, but everything that made me who I was. He entered slowly, his hands exploring my body, each touch a brand new sensation. Light kisses scorched a trail down my neck, and it was as though he had never touched me before. I let out a long breath.

"Dafaru—"

"Say nothing you may later regret, Beloved

His lips covered mine, smothering the words I didn't say. I slid my tongue along the roof of his mouth and tasted the burnished-metal flavor of him. I kissed his face, his chin, his shoulder, his chest. His body was such a contradiction to the senses. So hard and so soft. Skin so supple, yet tough.

"Perhaps I have never truly shown you what I feel in my heart," he said. "For you have always doubted my love."

His heat spread through me, and I clung to him, unable to speak past the rhapsody I found in his arms.

"Perhaps you are correct in saying I do not treat you like a wife, but it is my nature." He took hold of my wrists, held them above my head and pressed them to the bed.

Splaying my fingers, I submitted to his control, to the spirit riding me. My hips rose in time with his. My body was part of his, and I swallowed the cries straining against my throat.

"Amina." His voice was the most sensual caress. "Release."

My legs tightened around him, pulled him closer. And as our coupling spirits merged completely, a low moan escaped me.

"My love for you is torture." His words came from within me and all around. "It claws at my guts. It shreds me from the inside. And I am . . ." His fingers intertwined with mine. "Helpless."

With a soft groan, his body tensed. Mine began to quiver. I saw with his eyes, heard with his ears, and felt with his heart. A savage hunger took over, heat engulfing me as our lips met. Another groan—from him or me—and I trembled. I quaked. I could not contain the flood, the pressure building within. But it was him—not me—shuddering, grunting his efforts, his arms crushing me to him, as I cried out in the most exquisite ecstasy.

Then he relaxed.

And shutting my eyes, I exhaled.

THIRTY-TWO

120 Kilometers from Turunku, Western Hausaland, circa 1576 CE

The rains ended and the dry season began. It was our plan to head north and meet the enemy head-on. We set out from Zazzau, intending to reach the designated battleground at the border of Telwas in three or four days. Two days' ride from Telwas, we joined forces with Bugwam.

A major chiefdom, Bugwam was a vassal to Zazzau and bolstered our seven thousand warriors with two thousand of its own. The Bugwamawa swordsmen were to have marched as a separate contingent on my army's left. Their war leader, however, insisted that his soldiers, accustomed to long rows and shallow columns, would be hampered by the formation that wedged them into the left flank. He wanted them either in the vanguard or at the rear.

I'd no time to argue with the man. As long as his warriors could fight, I'd take them in any formation they chose. Except for the vanguard. Bugwamawa fighters in the vanguard would diminish the effectiveness of my mounted lancers, so I sent them to the back with my infantry.

That decision, made in haste, turned out to be a mistake. As we neared the battlefield, Bugwam showed its serpent's head. For that chiefdom had joined the Western Alliance, and its two thousand warriors now turned their swords on us.

We had no time even to sound the alarm before the first of the ground runners began to fall. There were more of us than them, but the Bugwamawa had the advantage of surprise. They attacked with startling precision, sending my soldiers into a state of confusion. I drew my sword and raced down the ranks, shouting orders to regroup my men.

Battle drums sounded and they were not mine. Nor did they belong to the treacherous bastards cutting down my rear guard. My heart dropped. The Western Alliance was here.

They charged down on us, screaming their battle cries. Kuturun Mahayi riding the flanks loosed their arrows at the oncoming war band. My ground runners were scattered, trying to gain some balance, while the Bugwamawa cut their way toward the center.

"Defensive positions!" I rode down the row of mounted lancers in the vanguard. "You." I pointed my sword at the chest of a befuddled soldier. "And you." I touched another. "Go back to Karama."

The two soldiers rode through the mass of men. I prayed to all the gods of Jangare that at least one of them would make it to Turunku.

"Defensive positions!" I shouted again at the surrounding men and rode toward the rear to take on the enemies in our midst.

Something crashed against my temple with a brilliant flash of light. I didn't realize I'd fallen from the saddle until my body hit the ground. Lying on my back, I groped for my dropped takouba and tried to focus my eyes in the chaos unfolding around me. I blinked to disperse the black spots, but my mind was hazy when I climbed, swordless, to my feet.

Metal glinted, sharpening my thoughts. I stepped back. Too slowly to avoid the curved blade. It grazed my midsection, cutting a shallow trough. The swirling dizziness rose again and sent me reeling to my knees. The enemy raised his blade. I flung out an arm, hitting his shin with the serrated ridges of my war bracelet. Howling, the warrior fell.

My head throbbed. I got to my feet, eyes scanning for my sword. My attacker, weapon in hand, rose as well. For an instant, he looked at me and paused. Perhaps he recognized me. Or perhaps he merely hesitated at striking down a woman. I swung my arm again, hitting him in the face with the war bracelet. His body twisted in response, and I hit him with my other wrist. Blood flew out of his mouth, and he fell to the ground, deep gouges parting his flesh.

My blade was at my feet, though it hadn't been there before. I scooped it up, grabbed Galadima's reins, and climbed onto his back. Slicing my way through the havoc, I tried to reach what had been my rear guard. I shouted orders but couldn't be heard over the noise of slaughter. The straightforward, organized attack Karama had planned had disintegrated into insanity.

Two swords attacked at once. I sidestepped one, parried the second, bashed the first one's face with my war bracelet, and opened the other's throat with my takouba. Another warrior attacked, but his weapon slanted sideways as though he'd lost his grip. With a silent prayer for continued good fortune, I jabbed my blade between his ribs.

Gambo and Zuma battled a little way off, soldiers of the Western Alliance closing in on them. I didn't see Jaruma, but knew she was all right. She could handle herself in battle. A flurry of blades refocused me. I fought my way through enemy soldiers, sword slicing through leather armor as though it were slicing banana leaves.

A fighter sprang from the throng to seize Galadima's reins. The horse spun round, swinging the westerner through the air. I clubbed the man's hand with my braceleted wrist. The warrior fell onto his back. Galadima reared and dropped, his hooves coming down squarely on the enemy's chest. Blood spurted from the man's mouth and nostrils as his ribcage collapsed under the horse's weight.

Wrapping Galadima's reins around the horn of the saddle, I closed two hands on the takouba's grip. Despite the blade's uncanny qualities, I needed the strength of two arms to slice clean through a man's neck. Pressing into the mass of fighters, I forged a trail of severed heads.

Enemy soldiers poured in from all sides. Galadima reared and bucked, kicking a skull here and shattering a knee there. Warriors fell, but many more took their places. *Too many*, I thought as Galadima whirled. My sword sliced through air to strike an enemy warrior. I missed. Or, rather, I *thought* I'd missed, but the man keeled over, his body split from breastbone to pelvis. Another man shrieked then gurgled, his head rolling back to expose his bleeding throat.

I stared, perplexed, at the bodies falling around me. When I looked up, an arrow was a heartbeat away. My breath froze in my lungs. The throbbing in my skull rushed back in full force, and I saw my death. But my time hadn't come. The arrow fell short and dropped to the ground.

Maybe I *was* yan tauri.

Now the fear showed in my enemies' eyes, and they fell away from me. In the lull, I scanned for Jaruma but instead found Gambo and Zuma again. They were down to one opponent. A big one. Swinging a straight-sword that was twice the length of mine, he struck at Zuma's horse. Both horse and rider fell. While Zuma lay trapped beneath the horse, the big warrior ran his sword through Gambo's body. As Gambo slumped to the ground, the warrior placed his foot on Gambo's chest and yanked the long-sword free. Then he turned to Zuma.

The ever-quiet Gambo would speak no more, and Zuma would be the next thing skewered on that sword. I sliced off the business end of a spear wielded by one brazen fighter who had regained his courage. The man's forward motion did not slow. His face met my heel and he fell backward. Urging Galadima to a gallop, I charged ahead as Zuma struggled to free himself from his horse's bulk.

The big warrior raised his sword, prepared to bring it down on Zuma, and went stiff. The sword dropped from his hands, and he fell to his knees, an ivory hilt sprouting from his neck.

Relief flooded me. I couldn't see her, but Jaruma still stood. *Thank the gods!*

Westerners converged on me, a swordsman gashing my arm before my takouba took his fingers. Another got hold of my ankle. I kicked out, but his grip was strong. He tugged and I tumbled from the saddle.

As I rose to face the enemy, a piercing pain shot through my leg. I cried out. The enemy advanced and I opened his skull. My knee buckled, but I stayed on my feet, looking down to find the shaft of an arrow protruding from my thigh. Without thinking, I yanked the arrow out of my leg and screamed as pain seared through me like fire. The arrowhead was unbarbed, but it could have been poisoned. I prayed my good fortune held.

Rallying the effort to remain upright, I felt, rather than saw, the western warrior at my back. I spun around, jabbing the arrow at his head. It sunk into his eye. The soldier staggered backward, clawing at his face. I loped toward him and ran my blade through his belly.

Blood poured from my leg and my head swam. Galadima whinnied, reared, kicked a westerner in the chest. More men assailed us. I raised my blade. The impact knocked me off balance. I stumbled over a prone body. Galadima whinnied again. He kicked out, spinning in one direction then the other, bucking, bellowing frantically. Frothy spittle flew from his mouth as enemy soldiers thrust spears, swords, and even knives at his flanks.

Then he began to teeter.

I climbed to my knees, sick in my gut, and could only watch as my horse toppled.

"Galadima!"

My soul splintered. And his hulking frame crashed upon the blood-soaked earth.

No.

From the ground, I fought like a fiend, bludgeoning my attackers with war bracelets, splitting the flesh of their ankles, their calves, their knees. Slowed by the pain in my thigh, my movements were clumsy as I scrambled to my feet, gripping my sword in one hand.

A dagger sailed toward me. I used the takouba to bat it away. A hot flash of pain carved a chunk of flesh from my side. Mad with agony, I reeled around in time to see the enemy thrust the spear again.

My heart slowed to a stop. I tried to parry the attack, tried raising my sword, but couldn't dodge the forward thrust of that spear. My breath caught.

But the deathblow did not come.

Between me and the man that should have been my demise, stood a creature I had seen only once before. This same creature had attacked Jaruma in the spirit world. A rat or dog or demon. It possessed a long snout, dagger teeth, and was just over three feet in height. Tufts of hair sprouted from beneath the dark red scales that covered its body. It looked at me over its shoulder with bright yellow eyes. There were holes where its ears should have been.

The demon Dangoji curled its fingers around the blade of the spear and wrenched it from the man's grip. My assailants fell back. The spearman let out a terrified scream—I almost screamed with him—and the creature swiped upward with scythe-like talons, opening the man's belly. As the warrior's guts spilled onto the ground, Dangoji spun. His hairless tail swished, and another enemy soldier cried out behind me. I turned to see the man's neck twist and snap. Then the creature was gone.

The westerners ran screaming.

Ignoring the pain stabbing my thigh, I went to my horse and knelt beside him. At the touch of my hand upon his heaving chest, he thrashed about, trying to rise. Blood poured from a deep slash in his rear fetlock, another in his stifle. Terrified eyes looked back at me. I rubbed his muzzle, tried to soothe him.

"I'm here." I stroked the neck craning toward me. "Brave horse, I'm here."

The horse had served me long and well. He was one of the most constant things in my life, that thing upon which I could always rely. And he was in pain, *so much pain*. I could not let him suffer. Though I wiped at them with my bloodied hands, the tears continued pouring from my eyes. Grimacing from my own pain, I got to my feet and nearly dropped the sword as I tremulously placed the blade in the space between Galadima's ribs. He tried to raise his head again but could not.

"No more pain," I muttered. With all my strength, I drove the blade into his chest.

Almost blinded by tears, I pulled the sword out of my horse. Dangoji was either gone or invisible and a few of the westerners were closing in. I faced them, Galadima's blood dripping from the point of my blade. My feral howl filled the air. No harpy's shriek was more horrifying. It was frightening even to me, and the warriors paused their advance. Like a woman possessed, I threw myself upon them.

The pain in my thigh was so sharp that I tasted it on my tongue. Still, I fought on. As though each foe were my last.

Karama's plan had called for a systematic retreat if we were overrun. First to Bugwam, then back to Turunku. Retreat to Bugwam was not an option, and we couldn't go all the way home with the enemy on our heels. We'd already lost too many fighters; there weren't enough of us to hold the westerners back. Either we stood our ground here or we fell. Following my lead, my warriors pushed forward. Somehow, we broke through their right flank.

We pushed forward still.

Zazzagawa soldiers fell around me. The battlefield was so strewn with bodies that those of us left fighting clambered over our dead to reach the enemy. I caught no glimpse of Jaruma, but told myself over and over, with each westerner I felled, that she was alive.

The sun dropped and war drums sounded. Not mine, for I had nothing more to lose. The Western Alliance had whittled away at my numbers; more than three-quarters of my force was lost. Yet, these drums were theirs. *They* were in retreat. They had the advantage but, for whatever reason, were backing down.

I didn't stop to ponder, merely praised the gods for their mercy.

THIRTY-THREE

My wounds were clean and bound, but I'd taken nothing for the pain that I tried to ignore as I sifted through bodies in search of my companions. Gambo was gone, but there was still Danladi and, of course, Jaruma.

She is alive, I repeated to myself, sometimes aloud. But as evening dragged into night and the soldiers lit fires about the camp, my chest grew cold. There was no sign of my companion. Everywhere I looked, dejected warriors dragged bodies from the field, piling the dead in a heap or carrying the living to the medicine men at the edge of camp. The odor of death pressed upon me, and I fought the urge to vomit, to fall to my knees and cry, to lose my mind.

My hope was fading. We had lost too many. No amount of speechmaking would lift the spirits of those who remained. And I couldn't find Jaruma. But I held myself together. When the soldiers found her, they would notify me. *Surely, they would notify me.*

My body ached. With each step, pain jolted my wounded leg. The gash in my side tore anew every time I moved. Myriad other injuries throbbed all over my body, but none compared to the agony building in my heart. Hands clenched tightly at my sides, I pushed back the despair threatening to engulf me and waded through the blood of my people.

"Amina."

I turned around, further aggravating my injuries, but relief numbed me to any more pain. The tears inched forward. They wetted my eyes. Brow wrinkled from the effort of holding back a deluge, I brought my hands together, lifted my face to the night sky, and gave thanks.

310 | J.S. EMUAKPOR

Blood caked her brow, a small trail trickling into her eye. She wiped it with the back of her left palm. Her right arm hung limp at her side.

"It's dislocated," she said.

"It looks painful." I flashed a weak grin.

"Your entire body looks painful." She flinched, sucking in a sharp breath of air.

"Mine are mere nicks."

We stood silent for a moment longer, then she stepped forward and brought her good arm around my neck, drawing me in. Our foreheads came together.

"I feared I'd never see you again," I said, an arm around her waist.

She gave a small grunt of pain. "But we live to fight another day."

We disengaged, stood looking at each other for several grateful moments, and I pointed at her arm. "Shall we repair you?"

❋

We sat beside a fire eating dried meat. Jaruma's arm was in a sling. My wounds were tightly wrapped. The medicine man had given us some pain-easing roots. We chewed on them as we conversed.

"This isn't how I expected to end," Jaruma said.

"Nor I."

"Danladi . . ." Her face lost all expression.

We'd not found Danladi. It was most probable that he was among the dead, yet Jaruma showed little emotion. He and she had shared a long relationship—longer than she and I. Comrades-in-arms certainly, friends perhaps, lovers occasionally. Yet she took his presumed death as a matter of circumstance. I wouldn't be so calm were she still missing.

"What of Zuma of Rizga?" she asked.

"I saw him with the medicine men when I collected these foul roots. He is injured but mending."

Her head bobbed in an absentminded nod. "That's good. He's lucky."

We each drank from our shared water. The cry of a hyena sounded nearby.

"*Chi mutani,*" she said.

I nodded. "Eating people. Yes. The scent of death will draw them far and wide this night."

We said no more as the cacophonous yips of predators sliced through the night.

After a while, Jaruma straightened and peered into the darkness. "Something is out there."

"Where?" I followed her eyes but saw only the night. "I see nothing."

"Moving. Through the shadows." She stood.

"Hyenas?" The fires usually kept them away.

"No. A man."

Every muscle protested as I climbed to my feet and scrutinized our surroundings. A few men were busy erecting bamboo huts while others stood guard at the fringes of light from our scattering of small fires. All in all, there was little activity.

"Jaruma, you're tired," I began but stopped short.

Something flitted from one shadow to another. It passed almost unnoticed through the meager light as though it were a specter.

"Behind me, Gimbiya." She stepped in front. With her left hand, she pulled the ivory long-knife from her belt. The knife zipped across open space, into the darkness beyond. A hand emerged from the shadows, plucked the knife from the air, and faded back into the night. Jaruma gasped.

I sighed, my burden suddenly lighter. "Shall we retrieve your knife?" Hampered by my sore body, I moved toward the shadows, but Jaruma hung back. "It belongs to you. I don't think he'll release it to me."

Still, she hesitated. "I . . . he's . . . I can't . . ." She exhaled. "Will he be angry?"

"Because you threw a knife?"

"Because I . . . I meant to kill him. Because he'd be dead if—"

"He's immortal."

Dafaru's voice came from behind us. "And fortunate for it. You are not the first to make an attempt on my life."

We turned to see him dressed entirely in black—shoes, trousers, tunic, and cloak. Where the firelight reflected off the cloak, it shimmered like a heat haze. And where the shadows touched it, the cloak vanished entirely. He looked insubstantial where he stood. I touched his arm. It was solid as ever.

He held out the knife to her. "Left-handed?"

"I—I learned to use both," she stammered, taking the knife.

"Impressive."

He looked toward the battlefield where soldiers still sorted through the dead. "For all your pungent human odor, your blood smells so rich. So invigorating. So metallic." He inhaled deeply and frowned, looking pointedly at me. "You, my love, are in need of a bath." He sat down on the ground, pulling me with him. My body screamed in objection. "Stay or go, Warrior." He spoke the words without looking up at Jaruma.

"Gimbiya?" Her tone begged me to dismiss her.

I nodded.

She hurried away.

"I do so like her." Dafaru took my hand and splayed my fingers across his open palm. "You have blood under your nails, Beloved."

I drew my hand away, self-conscious because his nails were impeccably clean. "Things did not go well for us today."

"How so? Your enemy has retreated."

"Only after they killed six thousand of my men."

"Ah, but you almost had them. In the end, they turned tail and fled with scarcely two thousand warriors themselves. But," he added, "they do have five thousand in reserve.

"And they'll reach here in another day."

"Your uncle has some to spare."

"What if he doesn't send them?" I said. "What if he's left me here to die? What if the messengers don't make it back to him? What if—"

"You have too many 'what ifs.' What if you and your officers devise a battle plan that will give one thousand warriors an advantage over seven thousand?"

"They have pressed us to the wall. No matter which move, no matter the strategy, I see only defeat." My frustration brought me near to tears. "Husband, can you not—"

"You know I cannot."

My heart grew heavy again, then I remembered the red monster. "But you sent that demon."

He laughed. "Dangoji is no demon, but you need not bother yourself with details. Suffice it to say that the creature exists only to protect you and your friend. I am allowed to protect my charges, Beloved. But there are limits to my liberties in the mortal world. Of course"—he glanced at the wound in my thigh and raised my tunic to inspect the wound in my side—"the creature is more effective if the two of you are not so far apart during battle."

"It's difficult to keep track of my companion's location when people are trying to kill me."

He responded with a dry chuckle. "I will bring something to help you heal. As for Dangoji, this is its penance for attacking your friend. I would have destroyed it, but it serves me—you—better this way."

"Dafaru, I need guidance. If all is not lost, I cannot see it. What should we do?"

"I think you rely too heavily on the god of war." He stood and inhaled the air, his cloak billowing in a nonexistent breeze. "Remember that one Hausa warrior is much like another. You are fighting your equals." His eyes closed; his features became serene, as though he were savoring the aroma of carnage. "You mortals are a vicious, murderous lot. And you, my love, are one of the most ferocious. Plan wisely." He crept back into the shadows and was gone.

❉

Early the next morning, we assembled a strategy session in one of the bamboo huts.

"The Western Alliance has five thousand soldiers in reserve," I said. "They will be here in two days. I sent word back to Turunku, but who is to say that Karama has received it? There are one thousand of us. How do we defeat them?"

"If we could mount a surprise attack?" said an older officer.

"But we cannot," said another. "If we advance, we enter Telwas territory proper. If we retreat, we enter Bugwam. We're surrounded by our enemies."

"I agree," I said. "We stay here."

"The sarki's assistance would make all the difference," said a third.

"We need no assistance from the king," said Bashiru, one of the youngest officers. Despite his lackadaisical countenance, he was a hothead and truly believed himself yan tauri. More of a brawler than a soldier, he was one of Jaruma's men. Regardless of what I thought he might be, she wouldn't have advanced him so quickly if she doubted his aptitude.

"No disrespect, Gimbiya, but we are more skilled than they." His slow manner of speaking lacked any urgency. He shrugged. "They managed to surprise us in the beginning when we took the heaviest losses, but we pulled together and drove them off, no? We suffered no defeat but sent them running like frightened jackals."

"We cannot rely on brute strength to win the day, Bashiru." My impatience mounted. "We are not fighting barbarians."

"Exactly," said the older officer. "We should consider fighting in the manner that a lesser opponent would."

"How's that?" Jaruma asked.

I knew what he was going to say before he said it.

"Magic abounds. We should harness it for our own use."

Had I not been standing between them, Bashiru might have lunged at the older man. "You dishonor Zazzau!" Bashiru shouted. "You dare suggest we take a coward's route?"

"Control your mongrel," the older officer said to Jaruma.

"Control him yourself," she replied. "If you dare."

The older man took it as a challenge. His hand went to his sword. Bashiru followed suit.

I drew mine and slanted Jaruma a withering look. "The first to draw his weapon will face Amina's blade."

Both soldiers dropped their hands to their sides, and the bickering quieted to silence.

"We may fare better if we reserve our anger for the enemy." I sheathed my sword. "Does anyone have a suggestion on how we might leave this battle victorious?"

The silence drew taut.

"The use of magic is not an option," I said. "Who knows what demons we might summon? I will not allow it. If you need magic, go and pray. Neither will I allow any disrespect between my officers. Bashiru, apologize."

"But," Bashiru began. He caught my warning look. "Apologies, sir."

The older man responded with a stiff nod.

"Now that we've squashed this issue, let us decide on a battle plan." I glanced at each of my officers in turn. "And no one leaves until our strategy is in place."

❀

That night Dafaru came to me again. I was sitting cross-legged on the floor of my impromptu war chamber when he appeared in the doorway. He bent low to enter, then dropped to his haunches.

"You smell like rotten bushmeat," he said. "Do you people never bathe?"

Personal hygiene was not, at the moment, a high priority, but the comment made me sniff my clothing.

Maintaining his distance, he handed me something. "Courtesy of my brother, the rivergod. It will heal your wounds. So tell me," he said as I took the tiny clay pot from him. "What is your battle strategy?"

Inside the pot was a clear, odorless ointment that turned to liquid on the tip of my finger. I laid it aside and returned my attention to the wargod. His stare was hypnotic. The swirling mists beckoned me to lose myself within them. To forget the madness, all the chaos. To forget that, out there, hyenas lay in wait. But the screech of reality was far too loud for me to ignore.

"There are no elevations in this place," I said. "No advantage for us. We lost most of our horses but have enough to put the best bowmen on horseback. When the Western Alliance reaches the outer limit of our aim, we'll attack."

Dafaru raised an eyebrow. "That may slow the inevitable advance."

"It *will* slow the advance. From what we can gather, they haven't the range to mount a meaningful defense. Once they're near enough, of course, they won't hold back. I pray that my longbowmen live up to their legend." I sighed.

"Your longbowmen are indeed more skilled than others, but your enemy will quickly come within a range they can manage. Then what?"

"If yesterday was any indication, we can assume the West aims for maximum penetration. Kuturun Mahayi at vanguard and flanks can hold them off better than spearmen, mounted or otherwise. Without the archers in the rear guard, my backside is weakened, I think. But our options are limited."

He gave me a critical look, and I returned an inquisitive one. His silence fueled the apprehension blooming in my chest.

"I think, Husband, they will attempt to scatter my center and throw my entire defense into disarray. That was their focus yesterday, and they succeeded, but they won't take us from behind a second time."

I visualized our defense formation in my head. Only a thousand of us. Less than three hundred mounted bowmen holding the vanguard and flanks. We wouldn't last long.

The swirl of red in his eyes seemed to converge into a single intense point, which bored into me as he studied my thoughts.

"And where will you be?" His brow dropped when he pulled the answer from my mind.

"I have no horse, my lord. Only the best archers will be mounted. I'm more effective on the ground."

The wargod did not comment.

Hesitant, I continued, "Of course, the success of our strategy relies on the enemy's assumption that we're utilizing our usual battle formations—with the lancers at the vanguard. They'll expect us to advance closer before engaging."

After a significant pause, he said, "It is an obvious strategy. They will anticipate it. After all, they are just like you."

"Then we're as good as dead." My words carried no emotion, only finality.

"Ah, my love, do not be so quick to accept death."

In his eyes, a battle scene played, a field piled high with bodies. I stood atop the pile, felling warriors as they charged at me from all directions.

"Fear not," he said. "Your enemy has not finalized its strategy. Perhaps they will disregard the obvious and settle on a plan that makes exactly the assumption you need."

"They will?" My voice was thick with hope.

"Perhaps. It is not easy to nudge a mind that is already embroiled in battle. Certainly not an entire alliance of minds."

"After I've washed, Lord Husband, I will show you my deepest gratitude."

"I doubt you will ever be clean again," he murmured. "But before you rush into the river to scour yourself, I said *perhaps*."

Silence.

"One thousand of you. Seven thousand of them." Dafaru stroked the tuft of hair on his chin. "It will be a hard-fought battle. Stay alive until your uncle arrives. Dangoji is not infallible."

My many injuries told me as much.

"So Karama is coming?" I asked.

"Despite your differences, he has not abandoned you." He touched a finger to his lips then pressed it to my mouth. "Nor will I."

THIRTY-FOUR

"Gimbiya. Gimbiya, wake." Jaruma shook me. "They're nearing the site of attack."

My eyes shot open and I jerked upright. "How long did I sleep?"

"Not long. Three hours. The sun is only just rising."

"How long before they arrive?"

"An hour at most."

Nodding, I jumped to my feet and strapped on my weapons. In more than ten years, I'd not fought without a horse, but I was a ground runner for the day, along with many other cavalrymen.

Because the most accurate bowmen had the front lines, Jaruma and I were again separated. I couldn't see her. But we'd run our drills dozens of times over the past two days. The vanguard knew to retreat to flanks before the enemy overpowered them. We needed our archers alive.

In silence, we waited—the only sound our collective breathing. A blanket of anxiety settled over us. The silence grew thick, the rush of blood in my ears deafening.

The signal came. I heard the drums, heard the arrows flying free. Another signal and another volley of arrows. I waited, sword in one hand, nerves strained to breaking. Arrows continued to fly until the drums played another beat. The archers at flanks went into action, loosing their arrows at will.

The enemy answered in kind.

We raised slapdash bamboo shields over our heads. Arrows penetrated the stalks, a few flying through. I heard the pained cries of the warriors around me. My mounted bowmen continued their assault while the enemy pulled nearer.

The ground runners fidgeted. *I* fidgeted, eager to jump into the fray, but the war drums hadn't given the signal. Our archers were doing what they were assigned to do: keep the Western Alliance at bay.

"Hold your positions," I said to the antsy infantry around me. "Wait for the signal." I tightened my grip on the sword, loosened it, tightened it again, and shifted my weight from one foot to the other.

Not knowing exactly what was going on in front of me was almost painful. I understood the battalion's restlessness. I too ached to break formation, to attack something, if for no other reason than to end the torturous waiting.

The ground runners' signal sounded, and the Kuturun Mahayi in the vanguard moved to flanks, parting down the middle for the infantry to advance. I couldn't assess their numbers, but I hoped the bowmen had retreated before taking many losses. It may not have been wise to put them in the vanguard, but there was no point in doubting myself now.

We advanced, shields raised. The bowmen had done well. The first lines of the Western Alliance were carrion. Still, there were so many of them and so few of us. Were we at our usual strength, the westerners' current state of disorder would have provided the perfect opportunity for us to cut into their center. They'd swarm us if we tried it now. So we maintained our positions as best we could while marching forward to the beat of war drums.

The Western Alliance attacked.

Using the same maneuver *we* might have used, they surged toward us, screaming their battle cries. Zazzagawa archers were not idle; westerners crumpled, arrows protruding from their breasts.

"Wait," I said, mostly to myself, quelling the urge to spring into the enemies' midst. "Wait for them to come to us."

Western archers fired back. Arrows flew above us, past us, through us. Still, we stood our ground in tight formation, nearly shoulder to shoulder. Until at last, the alliance crashed into us.

No more waiting.

I jabbed forward, drew my blade from my opponent's body, and pivoted to jab at another westerner. My blade sliced the air as I spun to face forward. The enemy jumped back, the tip of my takouba barely nicking his tunic. His comrade stepped into my opponent's place, gripping a long-sword in both hands. He slashed downward. I slashed upward. Our weapons met. The force of his strength sent a jolt through me, pushed me back, but he lacked the skill to finish me. I withdrew my weapon. He stumbled forward, and I thrust my blade into his belly before he could make another move.

We had waited for them to come to us. Now we cut them down.

❀

By midday, the archers had lost all effectiveness. Most of the fighting was close combat, where the skill of the Western Alliance matched ours man for man. The West had gained the upper hand. Their host was inexhaustible and I couldn't tell how many of my warriors still stood.

I was fighting not only enemy soldiers but weariness as well. The Zazzagawa couldn't last much longer, but we wouldn't go down easily. There were so few of us that every so often I caught sight of Jaruma. Zariya had once said that Jaruma's fate was linked to mine. We would die here together. And before we did, we would kill as many of these western Hausawa as we could.

The sound of distant battle drums penetrated the morass of noise rushing about me. *More?* There were more of them? Our intelligence had told us the Western Alliance forces totaled just over ten thousand. Bugwam's treachery brought them to twelve thousand. We'd slaughtered nothing less than eight thousand. So four thousand remained on the battlefield. How could they have more? How could we have miscalculated?

Whether they were four thousand or forty thousand, we were going to die. A sense of calm washed over me. Karama had insisted on keeping five thousand warriors in Turunku. That had been a brilliant strategy. When the West reached him, the city would be protected. Euphoria swept in behind the calm. The takouba that had grown heavy in my hands now lifted without burden. My people were safe. Knowing that, the prospect of death wasn't so grim.

The battle drums neared. I fought on. Redoubling my efforts, I opened an enemy's throat with his own knife, sunk it to the hilt, and grinned in morbid satisfaction when he keeled over. My men were shouting. The same words over and over, but I couldn't hear. One of them tugged my arm. I yanked it free and clubbed an enemy soldier who had stepped too close.

Hands closed around my arm. I tried to shake myself loose, but the hands tightened their grip. Words in my ear. Shouting. Battle cries. A mob of Zazzagawa soldiers swept past. I stopped struggling and stared in confusion at these men who fought with more vigor than the day's battle should have allowed.

"Gimbiya!" a voice shouted into my ear. "The sarki has arrived!"

A loud breath whooshed out of me. *He came.* He had not abandoned me. Karama was here. I searched for my uncle among the warriors. Hundreds of them. Thousands. He had brought them all! And they were slicing down the enemy host with inhuman zeal. My heart soared, *truly* soared, as though it had wings and could take flight.

I retreated from the battlefield with the warriors who had fought since daybreak. My heart soared higher when I saw Jaruma riding in my periphery.

Karama, upon his horse, trotted up and down the rows of exhausted soldiers. He saw me and swung his horse around. "Amina!" He rode swiftly to where I stood.

My brow furrowed when I saw his tight features, the straight set of his mouth, the way his eyes darkened as he took in my appearance.

"I feared I wouldn't make it in time." He continued to appraise me, his eyes rapidly traveling over my body. "Are you badly injured?"

Kogi-Ayu's ointment had healed most of the injuries from the first battle, but I'd since received many more. Two gashes—one at my temple, another at my shoulder—dribbled blood. My battle dress was coated in the stuff—both mine and the enemy's. I limped from a fresh leg wound; my knuckles and wrists were raw from hand-to-hand.

"I'll heal."

His lips twitched; the dark look in his eyes lightened. He wanted to say something but did not. As his features smoothed over, he said, "My medicine men have joined yours in the camp. Go."

"I can't. Not until the others make it to safety." I glanced back at the fighting men.

"I ordered your drummers to sound your retreat. Your men are safe. You were the last."

I looked again at the battlefield and noticed for the first time that the men fighting beside me in that last burst of frenzied energy were yet unbloodied, showing no signs of fatigue.

Karama dismounted, eyes surveying my various injuries. He came forward, cupped my face in his hands. "Gods or demons, you are blessed." He pulled me into an embrace.

A dam burst in my heart. I looked up at him, one hand still clutching my sword, the other knotted into a fist at my side. "I thought you'd abandoned me."

"I would never abandon you." He kissed the top of my uncovered head.

A bevy of emotions cascaded through me. They rushed by so quickly that I couldn't make them all out. What I knew for certain was that the animosity I'd harbored against him for the past nine years was washing away in the torrent. I lay my cheek flat against my uncle's chest.

A commotion rose behind me. I felt my uncle's body stiffen. He drew back and flung me aside. My wounds screamed out as I hit the ground. Karama staggered backward.

Hambaro Rana advanced on me, black fury in his eyes. His personal guards, fighting my uncle's men, were a red and green blur at his back. Karama drew his takouba, and it clanged against the curved long-sword descending toward me. Growling like an animal whose prey had been ripped from its jaws, Hambaro Rana swung on my uncle. Their swords met again. Karama pushed Rana back and feinted left. Rana wasn't fooled; he lunged to the right, jabbing his sword. Karama grimaced as the other man made contact.

I fought the exhaustion battering my will and got to my feet. Sword raised, I stepped forward. My eyes were trained on the two men, but I couldn't fix on Hambaro Rana. Karama moved quickly. A pivot, a thrust, a slice, he edged in close, war bracelet poised to crash against Rana's skull. The pudgy king of Gora was no less agile than my uncle. He parried the sword, ducked under Karama's upraised arm, and slashed across his midsection. My chest clenched.

Karama spun away from his adversary, a deep red patch blossoming on his tunic. I searched for an opening, any way to come between my uncle and the king of Gora. But my uncle wasn't finished. The sharp tip of his takouba jabbed again and again until his enemy was awash in blood. Rana responded, no less a warrior than his opponent. I took another step forward but could do nothing. Not while he and my uncle were so tightly locked in their violent dance.

Hambaro Rana's wrist slammed against Karama's temple.

"Uncle." The word whined from my throat.

My uncle wobbled on his feet, but his headdress had taken much of the war bracelet's impact. He righted himself then doubled over as Hambaro Rana's sword plunged into him.

This time, the scream tore from my lips. "Uncle!"

Clutching his abdomen, Karama staggered. Hambaro Rana raised his weapon for the kill. Karama straightened. His sword, swinging an upward arc, took Rana's arm off at the elbow. Hambaro Rana let out a screech, and Karama drove his blade into the other man's chest.

Both men fell backward.

Three steps brought me to my uncle. I dropped to my knees and flung myself over his still figure. "Uncle?"

"I'm fine." His voice was strained.

I looked down at his belly. His right hand covered the wound. My hand went to his.

"I'm fine," he said, grunting the words.

I moved his hand. Blood and fluid oozed from his belly. It smelled like bile.

My eyes rose to meet his, and he said nothing.

"Amina?" Jaruma was there. She tugged me away from him, and two soldiers gathered him up.

❀

Karama lay in my bamboo hut, his wound cleaned and bound. The medicine men could do nothing else for him. I had offered Kogi-Ayu's healing salve, but he had refused. He believed his life was in the hands of Allah alone. Perhaps he was correct. While he slept, I had slathered the ointment onto the gaping hole in his abdomen. Hours later, it had not even begun to heal.

Kneeling on the ground at his side, I prayed for Dafaru to come, to bring the rivergod with him, but he did not answer my plea. I touched the fire ring, held it in my hand and called to the god of war. He made no appearance. And my uncle slept.

Nine years lost.

In nine years, my uncle had given me great leeway to govern the vassals as I pleased. In that time, I'd shown him only the thinnest respect. My mother had chosen him for the crown. She had believed him ready when I was not. And I'd held that against him, blamed him. For nine years, my anger had shaped our every interaction. *My* anger. Not his. I couldn't see it then but saw so clearly now. He had loved me through it all, had wanted to love me, and I had met his love with resentment.

I hung my head.

Nine years lost. I could never get them back.

"Amina," he whispered.

I raised my head, and he gave me a feeble smile.

"Save your strength, Uncle." I took his hand, lifted it to my lips, and flattened his cold palm against my cheek.

"I should have given you nine thousand soldiers." A rattling sound in his chest was his attempt at laughter.

"Don't say that." I kissed his palm. "The first attack would still have annihilated us. Had you sent those men with me, today Zazzau would have fallen."

He tried to shift but was unable to raise himself. Clenching his teeth, he grimaced. "That pompous buffoon bested me, eh?"

I leaned forward. "It was a lucky strike." The weight of nine years pressed heavily upon me as I touched my lips to his. "You sent him to his ancestors for it."

"I shall soon meet mine." He attempted another weak chuckle then took several ragged breaths. "Amina, I've been unfair to you."

"Please, Uncle. Rest."

"Let me speak, child."

I wrapped my other hand around his, clutching it to my chest.

"Whatever you've done, if it was for the sake of Zazzau, it was the right thing."

My eyes filled with tears. I pressed my lips together to stop them from quivering. It seemed to take all his effort to reach up and touch his fingers to my face. He wiped the tears away.

"My time has come." He took another rasping breath. "May Allah be easy on my soul."

Karama was my uncle, my brother, my father. And I loved him. Though I'd been too full of rage to see it, I had never ceased loving him. To lose him now? The barbs of irony sank deep into my soul. With my stomach twisted in knots, I squeezed his hand in both of mine.

"Uncle." Nine years of tears fell freely down my face. "You've not been unfair. Your concern, like Mama's, was out of love. I know that now."

His hand in mine twitched. Through tears, I saw him close his eyes.

"Uncle?" Panic rose in me.

"Be at ease, my daughter."

The endearment, which he had not used in the last nine years, tore at my heart.

"Uncle, don't leave me," I whispered.

His hand twitched again.

"Uncle."

His shallow breathing slowed.

"Uncle?"

His chest rose in one, long, rasping breath that went on and on.

"Uncle?"

He exhaled, his chest falling, and Karama breathed no more.

Through my curtain of tears, my uncle's face was tranquil in final slumber. Bending over him, I kissed his frozen lips. "The load is lifted from your shoulders, Uncle. Allah welcomes you home."

I lowered my head onto his motionless chest and wept.

PART III

QUEEN OF ZAZZAU

Queen

THIRTY-FIVE

City of Turunku, Kingdom of Zazzau, Central Hausaland, circa 1577 CE

I sat on the rock, savoring the cool breeze that blew about me. Tandama, little more than a large hillock of slate, had become my watchtower. From this vantage, I could see for many kilometers around. I kept watch over my city, my kingdom, *my* Zazzau.

It had been a year since my coronation. The Sarakunan Karaga had made their decision quickly and had found me fit to rule. During the ceremony, the priest of the Oracle—that same priest of the Oracle—had stated to the world that I would forever be a spider growing strong from the life force of her mate. The mate in reference was obvious to me. For those who knew nothing of the wargod, however, the proclamation sounded like a warning and greatly diminished my prospects for "temporary husbands."

I could have wrung the priest's neck for that. Except my voracious appetite had lessened and my husband's need for me had increased. He visited often. I could sometimes wait for him to make an appearance before sating my hunger. Thus, it was only a little hardship when the men who had once vied for my attention began avoiding my pleasures.

I drew my knees to my chest, wrapping my dress around my ankles to keep the wind from buffeting it into my face, and contemplated the empire.

With the Western Alliance defeated, Zazzau had annexed those western kingdoms, and my border now stretched to the edge of Kebbi territory. In the south, vast Nupeland, bordered by the Kwara River, was mine. Slave territory lay in the east, along with the mountain regions. The Kwararafa dwelled beyond, and we'd heard little from them in twenty years. The Songhai still held much of the north, and what they couldn't secure had gone to Kano, which expanded its borders almost as steadily as I expanded mine.

Kano was a large trading hub sitting conveniently on the northern desert route. It had the most direct access to the Arabian ports and did much of its business with the nations north of Fezzan. Zazzau and Kano were not formal allies, but age-old treaties—unwritten, yet never forgotten—kept us on friendly terms. Only a fool knowingly trod upon a hornets' nest.

My dark grey horse grazed in the distance. He had a steady temperament but seemed somehow slow-witted. Perhaps I was comparing him too closely to Galadima, who had stood a caliber above most horses. Regardless, I needed a reliable mount, and no common horse could replace Galadima.

There were, however, horses of another breed that would suit my purposes well. Sleek and powerful implements of war, which their owner guarded as jealously as he did everything else. With the proper persuasion, I could prevail upon him to give me a battle charger. It would be no imposition. I was his wife, after all.

I curled a finger around the fire ring, calling out to him with my thoughts. Before long, a shadow fell over me, and the wargod's towering figure stood dark against the sunlight. I took his outstretched hand, rose, and strode into his arms.

"Welcome, Lord Husband."

He lowered his face to mine and kissed me. Lips still pressed to my mouth, he straightened to his full height, lifting me off the ground. "You stir a need in me that grows stronger even as I tarry here with you."

"Do not tarry long before you satisfy that need."

He looked around, turning a full circle and carrying me with him. "You see much from atop this boulder, my love. I wonder what sees you." His bloodred eyes displayed an image of the two of us.

As I watched the lascivious picture, the heat of my own desire rose several burning notches. He lowered me to my feet and continued to drop until I was on my back.

I raised my shoulder off his bracered forearm. "Must you wear them all the time?"

He slid his arm from under me and sat up.

Sitting up with him, I took hold of his wrist. "The fastenings always leave their marks."

The lewd image in his eyes dissolved, the fire cooling to a swirling fog. "Either you have become exceedingly soft in your sovereignty or you wish to render me powerless."

"How can a god be powerless?"

The red mist thickened in eyes that pondered something distant. It made me wary of his response.

I altered my tactic. "Could it be that you don't trust me?"

"I trust that, if you could, you would murder me in my sleep."

Such ideas had once crossed my mind frequently, but I had not contemplated killing gods for several years, and he knew it. Despite my ability to cloak my thoughts, he often managed to hear them.

"I could not murder you in your sleep if I wanted to," I said. "Your argument has no merit, and we return to the matter of trust."

"Trust is not an issue either, as you cannot touch the bracers without my leave. On promise of painful death."

I snatched my hands away from his wrist.

He smirked. "Only when I am not wearing them."

"Is that why you keep them on?" I gave the bracers a dubious glance. "To spare me a painful death?"

He shook his head. "No, Beloved. The truth is that I do not remove them in the presence of others."

"Never? No one? Not even your mother?"

"Especially my mother."

I briefly considered him and, not for the first time, wondered whether he had ever been a child-god. Or if he had been created fully grown, bracers and all.

"Well, I am your wife. Destiny has made us one." Hitching up my skirt to my thighs, I sat cross-legged beside him. "If you cannot remove your bracers, even for me—"

"You are mortal; I am not. We can never truly be one."

I tried to ignore the unpleasant weight settling in the pit of my stomach.

"Why this sudden interest in the bracers?" he asked. "And why do you continue to speak when there are more effective ways to use your mouth?"

The heat spreading through me gave lie to my indignation. Still, I raised my chin. "I am a queen."

He leaned close. "And what magic in that royal tongue of yours, so perfectly constructed and sublimely agile." Chuckling softly at my mortification, he laid me back on the rock.

I wriggled in exaggerated discomfort, silencing his chortles. He frowned down at me, and I responded with a demure smile. Neither the frown nor his turbulent eyes were caution enough to keep me from wriggling again, this time with a painful groan. He opened his mouth to speak, closed it. A low growl rumbled in his throat. With a thoughtful crease wrinkling his brow, he unfastened the bracers.

＊

The hard rock beneath me had been no less a discomfort than the bracers, and my back now protested its ill-treatment. Lounging beside me on the rock, his forearm resting in my lap, Dafaru looked out to the plains.

I turned the bracer over in my hands. "It smells like leather but doesn't feel like it."

"The cows of Jangare are suppler than those of the mortal world," he replied without looking away from the plains.

"There are cows in Jangare?" I had never so much as heard the low of a cow or even the cluck of a chicken. In point of fact, the only animals I had ever seen—save for the demon Dangoji—were the horses in Dafaru's herd.

When he began to laugh, I realized he was teasing me. I glowered at him and subdued the urge to smack him across the face. Still laughing, he raised his arm, and I slid the bracer onto it.

As I fastened it, he said, "You pleasured me like a woman with a purpose, Beloved. What is it that you want?"

I secured the final clasp and adjusted my dress, smoothing it around me. "Your pleasure is my pleasure, my lord."

"My pleasure is your duty, my queen." He stood. "What do you want?"

I craned my neck to follow him. No need to be circumspect. "I hoped to ask a favor of you."

"Ask." He offered me a hand and pulled me to my feet.

"I'm in need of a strong war charger. And—" The rest of the sentence was lost as my world fizzled to leave me standing in a copse of monstrous baobab trees.

"There are times, Queen of Zazzau, that even without dreams your heart is open to me." He pointed beyond the trees. "Yonder is the beast you seek. But take heed, Beloved. The horse will not come willingly." He raised a hand. In it appeared a saddlecloth of spun gold.

I looked at it, at him, and back at the saddlecloth he had plucked from nothing. There were too many things about my husband that I didn't know.

"If you want to win the creature, place the cloth on its back." He handed it to me. "It is a brute of a horse that can never be tamed. Catch it, however, and it is yours."

"Catch it? Is it wild?"

"It is, indeed."

"But how do I catch it? You have many trained horses, my lord. Give me one of those instead."

"The victory of a hard-fought battle is always the sweetest. The hard-earned prize most treasured." He caressed my chin as he said the last. "May you be worthy of the demon horse, my love. Though, I daresay, you will be hard-pressed to remain on the scoundrel's back once you have it caught." Chuckling, he strode away.

The god of war had a way with laughter that inspired severe anxiety. Nevertheless, I walked between the large baobabs, each one wide enough to host a group of ten, and emerged onto a flat plain.

A horse, bigger and stockier than the horses of my region, grazed in the distance. It looked too big to control but was fitted with a bridle, thus likely not as wild as Dafaru implied. The horse—male—was black all over, save for a white sock on his left rear limb. Laughably long hair covered his eyes like the locks of a shaggy desert man, and his tail nearly brushed the ground. Unkempt locks aside, his coat shone from good grooming, which indicated that *someone* managed him.

I walked casually toward the horse, arms at my sides. The horse watched me warily with eyes as red as the wargod's.

Calling up my meager natural and learned abilities, I spoke gently to the horse. It seemed the creature would allow me to touch him, so I stroked his flank. He didn't react more than to blink an eye at me. With soothing words, I moved my hand to the creature's withers. He twitched his skin but did nothing else. The horse's lack of response emboldened me.

"Not too difficult," I crooned, making to settle the cloth on the animal's back.

The horse whinnied and bolted. I swore aloud as he dashed away a short distance before coming to a halt. He spun and bolted in the opposite direction, running only as far as the trees lining the perimeter of the clearing. He was a beautiful creature, well-proportioned with a perfect gait and clearly sound of body. What went on in his mind, however, was anyone's supposition.

His behavior well fit the moniker Dafaru had given him.

Cursing whoever had bridled the horse without reins, I kept my eyes on him and backed into the center of the clearing. "Stay calm, demon horse."

When the beast was sufficiently composed, I ventured near. Again, he let me rub my hand along his flank, but when I flung the saddlecloth, he darted and began galloping along the clearing's perimeter. By the time he slowed, foamy sweat flecked his skin. Shaking his ridiculous mane, he drew to a halt and resumed grazing.

Four times I tried to catch the horse, and four times he bolted. On the fifth attempt, my perseverance prevailed. Perhaps weary of the game, the animal allowed me to place the cloth on his back.

Mentally applauding my triumph, I dug my fingers into the long mane and heaved myself up. As I swung a leg over, he bolted yet again. I lost my grip and fell flat on my back.

The horse didn't reach the perimeter before stopping and turning to me, his head bobbing. I could have sworn the monster was laughing. Scowling, I got to my feet, and he trotted over to nuzzle my face.

I grimaced, wiping slimy spittle from my chin. "Are you apologizing?"

The horse shook his mane vigorously.

Curious.

Perhaps he understood. Who knew what intelligence the animals of the spirit world possessed? The creature nudged me roughly with his head.

"Stop it."

He stopped.

I rubbed his muzzle and walked around to his side. The beast remained motionless. I grabbed a handful of mane, and he did not stir. I tugged. The horse ignored me. With a steadying breath, I pushed off the ground and tried again to swing a leg over his back. If not for my cumbersome dress, I might have succeeded. As it was, the animal darted off with me still clinging to him. A few jerky head nods, however, forced me to let go.

I slammed to the ground. "Oomph!"

The horse cantered over and nudged me.

I raised my head. "Amused, are you?"

He nudged again.

Still reeling, I dropped my head to the ground and lay motionless to gather my wits before climbing to my feet. I surveyed my grimy hands and torn dress. I should have taken it off entirely and had an easier time of it, but going naked in the forest of Jangare didn't appeal to me.

With what looked vaguely like a mocking sneer, the beast stood still long enough for me to clamber onto his back. Even without him deliberately making things difficult, I'd not energy enough to mount in one attempt. Before my head could swell with satisfaction, he reared and threw me off.

I lay staring at the passing clouds and pretended not to feel the throbbing in my backside. Nearby, the creature made an assortment of gleeful noises.

"Catch it and it is yours," I scoffed. "Indeed."

Perhaps the maniacal demon horse felt sorry for me. Or perhaps it was true that merely placing the cloth on his back made me his master because he clomped over and nudged me again.

"Leave me alone."

He continued nudging until I reluctantly got on my feet.

Ask.

Ask? The sudden idea was as foreign as the strange land in which I stood. My eyebrows drew together, and I stared into the horse's eyes.

"This is absurd." Bruised in various places, I approached the damnable beast and said, in the most irritated tone, "Please, horse. Will you let me ride?"

His head might have dipped, just a little, but I wasn't sure. Regardless, he stood as still as the baobabs while I mounted with much grunting, pulling, heaving, and cursing. Holding tight to his mane, I sat rigid, knees locked, in case he tried to throw me off again. He did not. A slight squeeze of my thighs and the horse moved forward.

We trotted along the perimeter of the clearing several times. "Now that I've tamed the savage beast, are we trapped here?"

The horse whinnied and began bucking. I clutched his mane, but he wasn't trying to throw me off. He dashed forward, halted at the edge of the clearing, and began bucking again. Nothing tangible kept us enclosed, but the horse could evidently see or feel what I could not. Another idea came to me, as abruptly as if someone had dropped it into my mind.

I gave a direct command. "Take us out of here."

The horse broke into a gallop and made for the far side of the clearing. Whatever he planned to do would likely kill me if I fell. Bracing myself with hands, knees, and thighs, I ducked low. We reached the far edge and the horse soared into the air with the grace of a cat. We landed beyond the perimeter of his barrier.

"Ha!" I swam in the sheer power of the beast, giggling like a mad person.

Weaving between the trees, he flew over streams and plunged into dense thickets without a care, shooting back out unhindered.

"*This* is a charger!"

The horse whinnied his agreement.

When the demon steed grew tired of racing through the forest, he slowed and returned us to the clearing. I reached down to pat his foamy withers.

"You are quite a stallion. What shall I call you?"

The horse neighed.

"The god of war didn't lie about your disposition. The flames of hell burn in you. Perhaps I should call you *Demon Horse* since that is what you are."

The horse snorted.

"You don't like it? Just *Demon*, then. I think it fitting."

He didn't react.

"If the arrival of Amina caused consternation before, men will quake when I ride forth on the demon steed." I laughed at the fire-breathing horse image conjured in my mind.

The sun was setting. Being alone in the spirit world after nightfall sobered me. I touched the fire ring and Dafaru appeared.

His eyebrows rose. "You have tamed the impish beast?"

"You thought I would not?"

"Clearly, I underestimated your tenacity."

"Clearly."

"Come down from there." Hands around my waist, he lifted me off the horse and set me on the ground before grabbing the saddlecloth, which vanished as it had appeared. "The creature led you on a grueling chase, I see."

He looked over my body, going so far as to lift my dress to see my legs. The most painful bruise began at midthigh and terminated at my hipbone. He pulled the dress higher to scrutinize.

"He is"—I snatched the cloth out of his grasp—"spirited, my lord."

"Spirited indeed. The foul beast would as soon trample you as carry you into battle. But you have claimed it, take it where you will. All roads are open to you now." The fast-approaching darkness made him into a silhouette, red eyes blazing fiercely in the fading light.

Words tumbled from my mouth of their own accord. "If you desire it, I will take Demon to the palace of War." I bit my lower lip, but the words were already out.

The god of war was inherently cruel. He despised all mortals and would likely exterminate us if he could. He still required the deaths of my lovers, no matter the fact that I only used other men when *he* refused to address my raging need. No matter that I debased myself every time I lay down with a common criminal. No matter that I wanted only him.

My feelings for the wargod, ever tumultuous, were painfully intense. And why not? He was powerful in all respects. He was pleasing, *very* pleasing. And—for now, at least—he was mine.

"In every way imaginable," he added.

I looked elsewhere, internally throttling myself for the careless manner in which I had projected my thoughts.

Hooking a finger under my chin, he turned my head toward him. "Is my pleasure truly your pleasure, Amina?"

"Will you have me or not?"

"Should I have you when you are in such a disagreeable mood?"

"If I'm disagreeable, it's because you make me so."

A wry smile spread across his face. "Tell me what I have done to make it so."

I jerked my head from his grasp but gave no response that might further fuel his amusement. Regardless, he laughed softly at my silent fuming. Demon, who had been standing still as stone behind me, shifted.

"Perhaps it would be my pleasure to keep you here, my queen, but you are battered and doubtless in need of recovery from the thrashing this . . . *Demon* inflicted on you. Would you not prefer the comfort of your own demesnes?"

My eyes narrowed. "Are you sending me home?"

After a long stretch of silence, he asked, "Why do you wish to remain here?"

There were many reasons to stay with Dafaru that evening, not the least of which was the rapidly encroaching darkness. Black shadows menaced like sinister giants closing in on me.

"You want me to travel alone through Jangare? In the dark?"

"Surely you are not frightened?" Amusement continued to dance in the muted red of his eyes, but there was nothing humorous about the spirit world—in dark or light.

I scowled.

He pointed at Demon. "Believe me when I say you are well guarded in that horse's care."

"I don't need the horse's care," I said tartly.

"Mind yourself, woman."

After a moment's hesitation, I slid my arms around his neck. God or no god, he could be swayed like a man. Standing on the balls of my feet, I looked into eyes that had taken on a severe glow. "I need *you.*"

The horse snorted.

The wargod stared at me for a time before stepping back and disengaging from my embrace. "You smell like horse sweat."

My heart dropped into my gut, but he would not see me beg tonight. Turning, I made to hoist myself onto the horse. Dafaru's fingers closed around my arm.

"You should fight harder for what you desire, Beloved."

"Fight for you?" I asked over my shoulder.

"I fight for you daily. For the heart you refuse to give."

Although the baobabs were silent, the other trees of Jangare continued their whispering chatter. The unearthly noise flooded my ears.

I faced him. "I want to stay with you tonight, tomorrow, longer if you wish. Does that not indicate my . . . my . . ." Unable to say the word, I dropped my gaze and suppressed my thoughts.

"Your what?" His grip on my arm tightened.

"You're hurting me."

"Your what?"

I raised my eyes to his and fumbled for a benign word. "My affection."

"Affection?" Annoyance manifested in his eyes as swelling clouds of red in a brewing storm. He released his grip as though my arm were some diseased thing.

I took his hand in both of mine and pressed his palm to my chest. "Dafaru, I . . . I've been . . ." *Faithful* was what I wanted to say. Inasmuch as I could be. "Only what you turned me into. But know, Lord Husband, that my heart beats for no mortal man."

As I held tight the hand against my breast, indecipherable emotions churned in his eyes. At length, he drew his hand out of mine to leave me clutching my own fingers.

My empty hands fell to my sides.

"Demon, eh?" He glanced askance at my new steed. "Appropriate."

He regarded me for several long breaths, and I dropped my gaze to the ground. He cupped my chin and raised my head, lowering his face to mine. "The horse will come when you call."

THIRTY-SIX

I could not say what road Demon traveled to reach Zazzau, but when I returned home two mornings later, I returned to a frantic Fatima. She was my lady of the house, my uwar soro. At thirty years old, she had three freeborn children—the result of an ongoing liaison with an elderly courtier. Although she still had the face of a child, motherhood had made her the most worrisome thing alive.

Before I could chastise her for bursting into my room, she crossed her arms over her chest and put on her haughtiest of palace airs. "Two days, Sarauniya." She had transitioned easily from calling me "gimbiya" to "sarauniya," yet she never managed to behave as though she were in the presence of a queen.

"Really, Fatima, this isn't the first time I've been away for two days."

She gave a barely audible huff. "Two days *without word.* Yesterday, the council sent for me. I didn't know what to tell them." Frowning in a way that almost made me apologetic, she added, "Waziri wasn't pleased."

"What pleases and displeases Waziri is not my concern." Still, two nights in the spirit world without making suitable arrangements in Zazzau had been irresponsible.

I finished dressing and gestured at the headwrap piled on the bed. Fatima retrieved it, while I lowered myself onto my diwan.

As she wrapped my hair, she asked, "Would you like something to eat?"

"So you're finished reprimanding me?"

She huffed louder. "Will you tell me next time before you travel overnight?"

"Do I answer to you?"

"Sarauniya, please."

"Calm yourself. I will take more care in the future."

"Thank you." She finished with my headwrap. "Should I bring food?"

"I've eaten." I stood. "And I will now face the council."

✻

I sat on a wooden chair across from the members of my royal council. The council chamber door and both windows were open, allowing a blessed breeze to swirl through the room.

"What do you have for me?" I asked without preamble.

Siddhi flashed a dazzling smile at which the waziri frowned. This was the same waziri who had served both my mother and Karama. He was in every way my elder, and as he turned that frown in my direction, guilt threatened to shame me.

"Where have you been?" he asked.

No amount of shame could smother my irritation. First Fatima, now the waziri. I wasn't a child to be rebuked. "That is *my* business," I said.

"You are wrong there." His narrowed eyes censured me. "You're state property."

My mouth opened, but before I could hurl any verbal abuse, Siddhi said, "What he means, Sarauniya"—he threw the waziri a look—"is that your welfare is important to the people of Zazzau. As our sovereign, you have a responsibility to us. We were concerned when you didn't arrive for council yesterday. And justly so."

Siddhi, of course, made sense, but the words didn't mollify me. State property? As though I were a slave. In truth, our slaves had a good deal more freedom than me. But that didn't excuse the waziri's lack of tact. I hoped he would give up his post soon. Then his son could take his place. The son was much better tempered and appropriately deferent.

The waziri, unmoved, asked again, "Where have you been?" This time, he added, "My queen."

"Hunting." I raised both eyebrows, daring him to contradict or inquire further, but he did neither. My eyes swept across the council. "So what do you have for me?"

The galadima said, "The irrigation ditches are dug, and we've obtained the saplings you requested."

The news lightened my dark mood.

Siddhi said, "We can only hope the plant will grow outside the sweltering heat of southern lands."

"No," I retorted. "*You'd* better hope those farmers you gathered know what they're about. Those saplings were expensive."

"They said they could grow it, but it's never been done," he replied. "This is new territory for them and for you. But if they're successful, we'll be the only state in the savanna that has them."

"Our northern neighbors would pay well for the product," the galadima added.

"Isn't that what Sarauniya Amina has been telling us?" Bashiru said.

Bashiru, my latest kaura and Jaruma's latest lover, had no head for the business of governance. He rarely took anything seriously and often appeared bored at our council meetings. Jaruma and Siddhi had banded together and convinced me to install him as our war leader; in that respect, he excelled. He was an outstanding horseman, had great skill with weapons, and kept the troops—what troops we had left—in fighting form. It was also possible that he was the genuine yan tauri he fancied himself to be, for not once had he been injured in battle. Despite my early misgivings, Bashiru had proven to be a good choice for the position. He left it for the rest of us to fill the kingdom's coffers.

"Yes." I nodded. "That's what I've been telling you."

"You are very wise, my queen," Siddhi said reverently. "Though I can't understand why anyone likes it. The stuff is disgustingly bitter."

"That bitter stuff calms headaches," Bashiru said. "And I hear it's an aphrodisiac." The last bit earned him a sharp look from me.

"Back to the subject of hunting," the waziri said, lighting a new flame under my ire. "As I recall, you do your hunting with your companion, yet she's not here."

I gave no response.

He continued, "Which brings us to another pressing question. Why is she serving as your representative in Nupeland? She has no official title, no authority to speak on your behalf."

"She has *my* authority." The words scraped past my clenched jaw.

"There's no official declaration to that effect."

"Is that what you want? A declaration?"

"What I want is unimportant, but there are laws regarding this very matter. Your companion has no official role in this government and cannot serve as your ambassador or emissary or whatever role she's currently filling."

I caught my lower lip between my teeth, inhaled a calming breath, and exhaled loudly. "Fagaci is my emissary."

"In name alone."

The galadima interjected, "The law allows the queen to designate any citizen as an emissary."

"An emissary nominated by the council," the waziri said. "You of all people know that, and I do not recall nominating Jaruma Dongo."

"Perhaps I should title her then." I gestured at the group of men. "As the law allows any of you to serve as my emissary without nomination, I should replace one of you with her. Waziri, perhaps?"

Bashiru burst into laughter but silenced himself when my scorching glare fell on him.

Unperturbed, the waziri said, "You've sent her to Nupeland to address delicate issues, Gim—Sarauniya. She isn't qualified."

"The issue isn't as delicate as you say," I argued. "Our agreement with Tsoede prohibits him from having an army of more than three thousand soldiers, including the old soldiers he keeps in reserve. His standing army is currently at three thousand and Jaruma is there to remind him of our contract. She doesn't have to be delicate."

"In that case, why not send the kaura? He's as well versed with military matters as she."

"The kaura is needed for recruiting."

"Surely an absence of several weeks won't make much difference to our recruiting efforts here."

Bashiru made a rude noise. "You'd think differently if the Kwararafa were rattling our gates."

"Enough," I said. "All this talk is academic. Waziri, your concern is noted, but Jaruma is already in Nupeland. It's done."

The waziri did not respond, merely scratched his thick beard and regarded me as one might regard a willful child.

"Fagaci will advise her if he thinks she needs it," Siddhi said.

I rose. "Are we through?"

The galadima cleared his throat, eyes downcast.

The waziri spoke. "There's one more thing."

"What?" I asked sharply.

"You're barred from leaving the palace grounds without an armed escort."

"*What?*"

"The council decreed it in your absence. As no one knew your whereabouts, it was a prudent course of action. Now, at least, we know you're protected."

This was the price I paid for two itinerant days?

In the subsequent silence, my gaze sliced across each man, coming to rest at the kaura. "Bashiru, you agreed to this?"

He shrugged. "They outvoted me."

"And you?" I faced Siddhi.

"I could do no less." A sly grin spread on his face.

My jaw clenched in repressed aggravation. "Anything else?"

"No, Sarauniya." The waziri got to his feet; the others followed suit. "I believe we're through."

In unison, they bowed. Leveling one last querulous look on my royal council, I strode out the door.

❧

It was four months before I could persuade the council to loosen their hold. While they didn't do away with my guards entirely, they no longer posted one outside the queen's chamber at night. Come evening, I could escape the palace compound and summon the horse without worrying that my escorts' watchful eyes would recognize him for what he was.

Demon's exceptional size set him apart, though it did not exclude him from being an ordinary horse. In the mortal world, his eyes did not glow the fiery red of the spirit world. But upon close inspection one could see the netherhells blazing in his gaze.

As he had refused the standard saddle, I'd commissioned one especially for him—a lightweight seat cradled atop a ram's fleece saddlecloth. Never tethered or penned, he always came when I called, and he tolerated the bridle but hated the reins. Not that he needed them. It seemed he took his cues directly from my mind.

Having sent my guards away for the evening, I dressed myself in an indigo kaftan and trousers. With a headwrap veiling my face, I casually joined a cluster of courtiers strolling toward the gate. Head bowed, I slipped outside. The return, of course, would not be so easy.

When I was a sufficient distance from the palace, I rounded the corner and said, "Demon, come."

Within moments, I heard his whinny. Hoofbeats sounded behind me. As he trotted past, I grabbed a tuft of mane and swung myself into the saddle.

I didn't know where I wanted to go, only that I wanted to *go*. I urged him to the left. He resisted. Moving my hands from the saddle horn to the reins, I tugged. He resisted more emphatically, violently shaking his head to yank the reins out of my hands.

Despite special treatment, the horse had a mind of his own. He sometimes took perverse pleasure in testing the limits of my patience. Today, I had much to spare. If he didn't want to be led, he could go wherever he pleased.

He turned northward, gaining speed as he galloped across the terrain. He moved so fast, so smoothly that it seemed he remained in one place while the earth shifted under his hooves. The savanna turned to bleached desert then lush grass so quickly that I grew dizzy from watching the ground. By the time the whispering trees of Jangare came into view, I'd already surmised our destination. The horse halted at the black palace.

❋

"When I said all roads were open to you, I did not mean for you to arrive on my doorstep unbidden or unannounced." The god of war stood in the bedchamber doorway wearing trousers, his irritation, and nothing else.

I rose from the gilded monstrosity, clad in one of the flimsy dresses that were my Jangare attire. His vexation raised my own ire and I couldn't keep the sharp edge from my voice.

"I didn't ask him to bring me here."

"Did you not?"

I scowled.

"He will take you only where you wish to be taken," he said.

Damned horse. Evidently, he could read me with more ease than I read myself. I sat sulkily on the bed.

"For your pleasure, my lord, I've already scrubbed from head to foot."

A flicker of emotion passed over his face and vanished too quickly. Crossing the room, he said, "I will exact a hefty price for your boldness in coming here like this."

"Will I enjoy paying it?"

"I imagine so." The red cleared from his eyes and he showed me the price he had in mind. "But not yet."

"Why wait?"

"I was otherwise engaged."

I took in his near nakedness. Until this moment, I'd given little thought to what *or whom* he did when he wasn't with me. A knot tightened in my chest.

Tamping down the anxiety, I said, "Engaged in what?"

He cupped my chin. "That is not your concern." His lips briefly met mine. "Your arrival, though inconvenient, will prove a pleasant distraction. Stay." He turned to leave.

"Stay? I'm not a—"

He turned back to face me.

Dog, I finished in my thoughts. Aloud, I said, "Yes, my lord."

THIRTY-SEVEN

Ngazargamu, Bornu Empire, Land of the Kanuri, circa 1585 CE

Many peaceful years had passed. I'd had to manage a few small uprisings in the vassal states, but nothing approaching full-scale war. In the west, Kebbi still had no interest in upsetting the balance. Kano, though it encroached upon other kingdoms, remained on good terms with Zazzau, honor bound by ancient obligations.

To the east, beyond the vast mountains, Kwararafa was as yet a quiet rumble. Thanks to Bashiru's recruiting efforts, my army had swelled to more than eleven thousand and continued to grow. Despite the Kwararafa's impressive talent for navigating the mountain passes, making the crossing with enough warriors to defeat mine would not be an easy undertaking.

Then there was Bornu.

Rumor had turned that swiftly expanding nation into a gleaming empire layered in gold. Its king, Idris Aloma, was said to have the power of thunder and lightning at his fingertips. With the Kwararafa groaning like a belly to be sated, it was imperative to know where Bornu stood.

On the council's advice, I had sent runners to the northeast. They'd delivered my message to the king of Bornu himself and had brought back his response: Idris Aloma was willing to accept the hand of friendship, provided Amina extended that hand in person.

Thus, I'd undertaken the journey to Bornu with a retinue of courtiers, some of my highest officials, Jaruma, a host of Kuturun Mahayi, and several dozen slaves.

Upon reaching the city gates, we met a mass of armed horsemen, many hundreds strong, standing shoulder to shoulder in a line that extended far to the left and the right.

"It's good to see that we were expected," Bashiru said in a sardonic tone.

Blinded by the metallic sheen glinting off each soldier and horse, I raised a hand to shade my eyes and leaned forward to get a better view. The men wore tunics made from small links of metal, loosely draped over their battle garb. The same material was draped over the horses.

The loud report of a trumpet rent the air, and the soldiers parted. From inside the city came a procession led by a man on a white horse. The horse, whose lustrous coat contrasted with the dark coats of its cohorts, stood out so boldly that I found myself staring at it.

"Look at that horse." Jaruma's tone was almost wistful.

Demon whinnied.

"No horse is as magnificent as you, Demon, you conceited brute." I stroked him between the ears but never took my eyes off the white steed.

As the king of Bornu—for it was he on the white horse—rode past his soldiers, a small contingent broke off, flanking him with at least twenty on each side. He reached us and made a gesture with his hand. His flanking soldiers fell back. He looked from me to Jaruma and back again before speaking.

"The warriors of Zazzau are exceedingly more beautiful than those of Bornu." He had an air about him, a power that could not easily be dismissed or forgotten, even were he not a king. "But the queen of Zazzau"—he looked pointedly at me—"is most entrancing of all."

I spoke the greeting that Muslims generally knew, but I rarely used. "*As-salamu alaikum,* Mai Aloma."

"*Wa alaikum as-salaam.*" He nodded.

"I am pleased that you find me entrancing, but could it not be my companion who is queen of Zazzau?"

"Your beauty is much touted, and there are just as many tales of the dark-skinned warrior at your side. There could be no mistaking which of you is which."

His face, though not mean, was not friendly. Except when he smiled, at which time it lit up with a warm radiance. He didn't wear the metal tunic of his cavalry. Instead, he was dressed much as the nobility of my own land in flowing babariga of soft green brocade and a white turban. Garbed as he was, Aloma was indistinguishable from any other rich man, but his countenance portrayed a conqueror of nations.

I swept a hand behind me. "Zazzau brings gifts."

One slave brought a gourd filled with kola nuts, and four more brought gourds of wine. They placed them at the feet of Aloma's horse and prostrated before him. Three more slaves came forth, leading horses laden with additional gifts, while the remaining slaves came behind. They all knelt.

I said, "The servants and horses are yours as well, Your Excellency."

His smile broadened. "You and your people are welcome in these lands. Come, lay down your weapons and be my guest, Great Queen."

"You do me an honor, Mighty King. Gladly do I lay down arms."

With that figurative setting aside of weapons, Aloma turned toward the city, and his guard closed the space behind him, blocking our forward advance. After their king was sufficiently ahead, the soldiers led us through the city gates.

❋

One could not fully appreciate the splendor of the city until one was within its gates. Ngazargamu, the Bornu capital, virtually sparkled. The mud walls of the domed houses were polished smooth, their windows precisely cut. Wood or heavy mats covered all doorways. No abode was in disrepair. The closer we came to the palace, the more wealth each home reflected. Tall minarets rose skyward. Buildings featured high balconies or rooftop pavilions. Many of the smaller houses were thatched, but the taller structures had solid adobe roofs.

We rode past the palace to the royal guest compound. It seemed Aloma's custom was to keep unmarried men and women separate because there were interior walls dividing the compound into sections. The women went to one side while the men went to another. Those who arrived with official consorts slept elsewhere.

My guesthouse, though larger than the others, was a simple structure with a wooden door but no window covering. The bed at the far end of the room was chiseled from stone with thickly stuffed padding atop. I crossed the room and prodded it. Sheep's wool filling, perhaps.

"The polish of the walls gives these huts the look of stone," Jaruma said from outside. She entered my chamber. "Did you see their armor?"

"Who didn't?" I replied.

The contemplative expression in her eyes reflected my own feeling about the chain tunics.

"I should like to take a sample home," I said.

"Would Aloma give you a sample?"

"Doubtful."

She let out a regretful moan.

I said, "We can deal with that after we've addressed the state of our personal affairs." I gestured at her person, which, like mine, bore testament to hard travel. We needed baths and clean clothing before we set out to find what this city offered.

✻

A short time later, we were clean but not rested. We weren't supposed to roam the city without Idris Aloma's guards escorting us, but we didn't want our quiet outing to become an exhibition. To ensure our anonymity, we each dressed in the undyed, traditional short blouse and wrapper. Heavy kohl lined our eyes and lips, while red and yellow ochre made up the rest of our skin embellishments. With headwraps draped about our faces, we casually strode out of the guest compound. The guards in the gatehouse did not so much as raise an eyebrow, which was almost disappointing.

Ngazargamu's central market was a one kilometer walk. Unlike most markets, this one wasn't on the outskirts of town; it was indeed at the city's center. The expansive open-air bazaar had stalls set up in neat lanes. People from Ngazargamu and beyond bustled about, haggling over wares.

Here were the much renowned Bornu oxen. A trader selling pink slabs of potash spread parchment on the ground for a fisherman to arrange his two basketfuls of fish. Even Arab merchants from the far north peddled their expensive goods here.

Spying a vendor with a multicolored display of glass beads, I strode up to her and pointed at a small pile of light blues. "How much?"

The market woman grinned, showing a mouth nearly devoid of teeth. "They come from Egypt."

"Egypt?"

"Beyond Fezzan."

I had once purchased a small mirror from an Arab trader who had claimed it had come from Egypt. Such imports brought good money. Clearly, this woman intended to ask some outrageous price.

"Many goods come from beyond Fezzan," I said, as though the tiny glass beads were a common sight. "So, how much?"

A horizontal line appeared in her chin as she puckered her lips in thought. "Eighteen cowries."

"Eighteen cowries?" Jaruma exclaimed. "Are they made of gold?"

"Nine cowries," I said.

"Fifteen," the old woman said.

"These and those"—I pointed at a pile of pale yellow beads— "for twenty."

The woman pulled a roll of coarse cotton thread from under a heap of cloth. "Plus thread for twenty-five."

"Five cowries for thread?" Jaruma said indignantly.

I didn't want to go back and forth with the woman; my impatience wouldn't stand it. "Plus thread," I said, reaching into the folds of my wrapper to produce a money bag.

Jaruma rolled her eyes.

The woman's toothless smile appeared again, and she produced two frayed cloth pouches while simultaneously calling, "*Dylala. Dylala!*"

A smallish fellow with big eyes strolled our way. The market woman addressed him.

"Dylala," she said. "We have come to an agreement. Blue and yellow beads." She gestured at each pile in turn. "Plus thread. Twenty-five cowries."

The man nodded and scribbled something onto his scroll as the woman wrapped my goods into a compact parcel. When she finished, she handed him the parcel, and he put his mark on it—his personal guarantee of the goods—before giving it back to her. If I later had an issue with my purchase, I could return to the market, and the dylala would have a record of the transaction.

Fishing into the money bag, I counted out twenty-five cowrie shells. The woman took the money and held out the goods. I cocked my head in Jaruma's direction and the woman handed the package to my companion, while I refolded the money bag.

We moved on. Past the stalls of jewelry and other adornments, past the weavers and the cobblers, beyond the livestock, the hyena men, and the lion-handlers. Until we came to a row of blacksmiths.

I stopped to watch one work, while Jaruma continued to the next stall where she engaged a husky old man of the profession. My smith, a man of middling build, wore only a filthy cloth tied at his waist. Sweat glistened on his neck and ran in rivulets down his chest. His hands and face were dirty with soot. He pounded away at a length of glowing metal.

Seemingly unaware that he had an audience, the blacksmith plunged the red-hot metal into a container of water. With a loud sizzle, the water boiled and steam rose to his face. The warmth of it reached me where I stood. With the back of his soot-covered arm, he wiped the moisture from his forehead, leaving his already darkened face covered with even darker smears. He looked up.

"Greetings, friend," I said.

He glanced around, possibly searching out my man. While there were many unaccompanied females in the place, the women tended to do their shopping through the "market matron," who was similar to the dylala with an added duty of ensuring that the traders did not take unfair advantage of female patrons.

I ran my eyes along a row of stalls until my gaze fell on two men in casual conversation. One of the men looked up. I blinked slowly and offered him a shy smile. Smiling back, the man gave a deep nod of acknowledgment. I turned to the blacksmith, hoping he didn't know the fellow chattering away in the other stall. The metalworker looked from the other man to me, then tilted his head.

Apparently satisfied that I was properly attended, the blacksmith said, "Greetings. Have you come to buy or to stare?" He pulled another strip of metal from the fire.

His stall held elaborately wrought pieces of jewelry. He also carried the types of metallic goods that might be found in the home of a rich man—large tubs, kettles, cups, trays. What had truly caught my attention, though, was the weaponry. Beautifully forged swords and knives, some with fine designs emblazoned on their blades.

"Perhaps I shall buy," I replied. "But I wonder do you not sell armor?"

"What armor?" He grunted, slamming his mallet onto the strip of hot metal.

"The chain tunics worn by soldiers and horses." I shouted to be heard past the sound of the mallet banging on metal.

"What sort of woman is interested in chain mail?" He shouted back.

"What sort of woman is not?"

He stopped beating on the metal and appraised me before giving a loud huff. "Chain mail is reserved for the royal army. I would not be permitted to sell it."

"But you can make it?"

He dropped the metal into the water, which let out a steaming hiss. "I'm busy, woman. You pester me with questions. Are you going to buy something?"

I scowled but nonetheless purchased a brass bowl. After the dylala signed his mark to the purchase, I took my leave of the surly blacksmith. Jaruma, who'd had no better luck, came away from hers with a silver arm band. I'd have to broach the subject of chain mail with Aloma himself. I couldn't begin to imagine how that discussion would progress.

THIRTY-EIGHT

Aloma didn't summon us to the palace until the following evening, and dinner was served in a courtyard scattered with fruiting cashew trees. We bowed to Aloma when we came into his presence. He nodded in return.

"As-salamu alaikum." He rose as he spoke the greeting.

"Wa alaikum as-salaam," I replied. "May you live long, Your Excellency."

"You as well." He spread his arms. "Welcome, friends!"

We took our places at the king's table, Aloma surrounded by his officials and I surrounded by mine. Servants brought water bowls for us to wash our hands before the food arrived.

The fare was both familiar and unfamiliar. Of the familiar, there was pounded yam and soup with goat meat and chicken. Of the unfamiliar, there was a victual made from ground beans; it was steamed in plantain leaves, served hot, and had the consistency of a heavy cake. Some of the other foods did not look particularly appetizing, as Jaruma's suspicious gaze across the table attested. She leaned toward me and whispered something in my ear. A chant that I had often heard the palace children recite during play.

"*Kunru nama ka de wari.*"

I whispered back, "Don't eat it if it makes you sing of rotten turtle meat, you insufferable peasant."

She tittered and put a little of everything on her plate.

During dinner, our host regaled us with historical accounts of the Bornu Empire and of his own impressive conquests. The present dynasty—to which Aloma belonged—had, within my mother's lifetime, defeated an ancient foe and conquered Kanem, which lay on the east of the wide lake. Lake Chad, they called it.

Over the course of the evening, I learned that Aloma's military prowess and administrative savvy were second only to his devoutness. He was a Muslim who ruled his country under strict Muslim law— Shari'ah. Karama had been leaning toward such law when he ruled Zazzau, and many of Aloma's personal ideologies were identical to his. I had my own opinions about Shari'ah, but it was not for me to debate religion with Aloma. In this world ruled by men, it was wise to keep one's own counsel.

✳

That night, gorged like a fattened ox, I lay on the bed of stone but did not sleep. My mind had been occupied since dinner. Aloma's feats of conquest and his state reforms were nothing less than revolutionary. Except for his religious system, which precluded women in any position of power, I found his ideas intriguing. I found the man himself intriguing, and I saw the majesty of Ngazargamu as though the image were branded across my eyes. If a city bore testament to the might of its ruler, Aloma was a mighty monarch indeed.

The fire ring pulsed around my finger.

A wave of warmth radiated from my center, my face stretching into a grin. It had been too long since Dafaru had last visited. Though I'd called, he'd not responded in many weeks. I had considered riding Demon into Jangare, but if my husband couldn't even be bothered to respond, I wouldn't chase him.

His voice rose from the darkness. "I am, as you know, not at your beck and call."

His ill humor was undaunting.

"Greetings, Husband." I sat up.

He stood, arms folded, leaning against the open door frame and blanketed in faint silver starlight that accentuated the god within.

"Even with your idiot makama at your side," he said, "you still lust after the king of Bornu?"

"Pfft." I stood, tightening the wrapper at my waist. "I look at his city and choke in envy. Besides, you've not seen fit to call on me. If I have any lustful cravings, they're your doing."

"That they are."

"And now you are jealous?"

"Always." His eyes roved over me, but he did not leave the doorway.

I went to him. "Come inside." I took his hand, drawing him forward. The wooden door shut behind him.

He allowed me to lead him into the room, a furrow deepening on his brow. His eyes lost focus. Though he appeared to be looking at me, his attention was not entirely mine. Nine weeks of absence and his mind was still elsewhere?

"What troubles you, Lord Husband?"

Although their red glow intensified, the churning eyes that met mine remained cold. He was here yet not here, his gaze upon me yet so distant.

"Are you angry with me?" I stepped away, attempting to release his hand.

He held fast. "Not with you."

"Then who?"

He came forward, the fingers of one hand rising to his temple. "There is an entire pantheon inside my head," he hissed through gritted teeth.

Eyes closed, he kneaded his temple. "They reach across worlds to voice arguments with no resolution." When his eyes opened, they were calm. His fingers dropped from his forehead to stroke my face. "You are an island of tranquility in a sea of chaos."

I drew him into an embrace. He held me, his body heat rising.

Abruptly, he disengaged. "What possession of Aloma's could you possibly envy?"

My breath caught and resumed at a quickened pace. I drew back, stumbling into the bed, and sat heavily.

"He has an empire; you have an empire." He bent close. "He has an army; *you* have an army."

Closer still and now one knee on the bed. I inched away from the heat that excited me entirely too much. An arm at my waist kept me from moving very far.

"He has horses; you have horses. He has slaves; you have slaves. What more do you need, my love?"

A soft kiss to my throat robbed me of all common sense. "I—I don't have a bed of stone." I clapped a hand over my imbecilic mouth.

He drew back, amusement lighting his eyes. "A stone bed?" He laughed and looked at the fleece filled mattress. "This?" More laughter.

I closed my teeth on my babbling tongue.

The backs of his fingers skirted my collarbone and drew a small shudder from me. For nine long weeks, he'd ignored me—an exercise in self-restraint that I never wanted to repeat. Fumbling with his trousers, I got them loose and slipped an impatient hand inside.

"You have waited long enough." Laughter still laced his voice. Moving my hand aside, he situated himself properly. "You desire a stone bed? Amina, Beloved, I will build you a stone palace."

❈

I lay on my belly, head propped on my husband's chest, my fingers running up and down the ridges of his abdomen. "Why did you stay away so long?"

Red eyes looked down at me, studying my face, though what he sought I couldn't say. "I have obligations here, in Jangare, that preempt even the queen of Zazzau."

"But nine weeks? It was unbearable."

"I have been gone much longer in the past. You bore it well then. As I recall, it was even your preference that I stay away as long as possible."

"You were my adversary then," I said tartly. "And as *I* recall, you never failed to come when I needed you."

Without responding, he gently pushed me aside and sat up, swinging his legs over the edge of the gilded bed. In the lengthening silence, I sat up with him and snaked my arms around his waist.

"What troubles you, my lord?" I kissed his shoulder.

"Do not worry overmuch about the troubles of gods."

"I care nothing for the troubles of gods, only for the troubles of my husband."

"Yet you are not equal to the task of addressing them."

His bracers appeared on the bed beside me. I tucked my legs underneath me and picked up the leather implements. I'd hoped our interlude would be longer, but he was evidently of another mind. Holding out one arm, he turned to face me.

"You've underestimated me in the past." I slid the bracer onto his arm.

"So I have. You are no mere mortal, Amina. Yet you *are* mortal. I cannot forget that."

I frowned at the enigmatic words but said nothing, merely fastened the gold clasps and proceeded with the other bracer. When both were secure, he caught my face between his hands and tilted my head to kiss my chin.

"The sun sets on the past, Beloved. We of the pantheon *are* the past."

"What are you saying?"

"Dawn is approaching."

"What does that mean?"

This time, he kissed my forehead. "We stand upon ever-shifting sands, and the Creator, alone, endures." His words, if not his tone, were ominous.

I couldn't keep the anxiety from my voice. "Are you . . . are you . . ."

"Never." His mouth touched mine. "You are my sanity, and I am not ready to part with it." He embraced me. "But dawn *is* approaching."

At his raised hand, the curtains parted and purple daybreak streamed through the window. I glanced outside, my frustration manifest in a loud exhalation. Those devout Muslims of Bornu were early to rise. Regardless, I didn't want to leave.

"And I would have you stay," he said. "But if you are not in Aloma's palace after the dawn prayer . . ."

"I know. Very well, then. Send me back." I kissed him. Decisively. Possessively. "But don't stay away so long next time."

He raised a brow. "You forget which of us is master, my queen."

❉

I broke fast with Aloma in his private quarters—a spacious chamber whose walls displayed a shining array of weapons: a finely carved bow and its lion-hide quiver of arrows, two battle-scythes, a long-sword, a short-sword, and several throwing-knives. Two female attendants stood quietly in one corner while a group of men and women that I took to be his relatives sat in the adjoining antechamber.

Aloma bade me sit.

As I lowered myself onto a large wooden chair, he laughed. "You were born to rule, for only a true sovereign would have chosen the king's own chair."

I jumped to my feet. "My apologies."

Because there was no door separating Aloma's room from the antechamber, we spoke with raised voices over the hum of the relatives' chatter.

He waved a negligent hand and took the seat opposite me. "It suits you."

Without the pomp and ceremony of our previous meetings, Aloma looked like any other man. He was slender, almost thin. Against the slim frame, his broad shoulders and chest stood out more distinctly. He had a warrior's body. For a moment, I glimpsed Suleyman in my mind's eye and smiled.

"The chair pleases you?" he asked. "Or is it the room?"

I took in the weapons hung about the walls. "It reminds me of my younger days. My fighting days."

"You are still young," he said as one of the attendants placed a tray of food onto the wooden table between us. "And I'm sure you have plenty of fight in you."

"I'm not as young as you might think."

He nodded. "I've heard tales. Impossible tales." After the attendant stood back, Aloma said a quick prayer over the meal. "Let us eat."

The morning's repast was even less familiar than dinner had been. I recognized few of the foods laid before me. But there was milk, so I poured it into a cup and took a sip. It had a dry, empty taste.

"What is this?" I took another sip of the flat white liquid.

"Milk."

"I gathered as much, Your Excellency. But from what animal? Surely not goat?"

"Goat's milk is somewhat pungent, don't you think?"

"Compared to what? This?" I held up the cup. "This is somewhat bland."

He laughed. "You must travel more, young one."

Young one? He and I were probably the same age.

"You must travel out of Hausaland," he added. "You're all the same, you Hausawa. You eat the same foods, drink the same wines. You even worship the same gods."

"The same Allah that you worship." There was only one Creator. No matter what one chose to call Him. I reached for a roll of what appeared to be bread but was darker than bread made from sorghum.

"Nonsense. You worship whatever god suits your fancy."

I couldn't tell whether he was judging my entire nation, judging only me, or merely stating a point.

Evenly, I said, "We are Muslim, Your Excellency."

He shrugged. "When it pleases you to be."

My neck grew warm. I exhaled in silent exasperation. Aloma's notions were true where I was concerned, but many of my people revered only the Supreme God—Allah or, as He was named in Hausa, Ubangiji. It was presumptuous for the man to say otherwise. I kept quiet, lest my words betray my irritation.

After several long moments, he said, "But the argument is of little consequence." His eyes lit on mine and did not waver. "I suppose that as long as you observe the appropriate rites and obey the teachings of Muhammad, despite your natural inclinations—"

"Forgive me, Your Excellency, for interrupting you." I swallowed a bland piece of *something* I had put in my mouth. "Can we speak of religion and the inclinations of men at another time? Perhaps, when my makama is with us? He can speak for hours—*years*—on such philosophical matters. I fear my expertise runs along the lines of state administration and battle strategy."

Interrupting a king of Aloma's stature was beyond general rudeness. For a moment, he looked put upon. Lips pressed tightly together, he regarded me, the knuckle of his forefinger gliding back and forth along his chin.

After a few tense breaths, he nodded. "As you wish, Great Queen. I heard you were an able strategist." He reached for his cup. "As to your original question . . ."

Simultaneously, we put our cups to our mouths.

"It's cow's milk."

I forced myself not to spit out the mouthful and tried to keep my face from twisting into a grimace as I swallowed. Lowering the cup, I resolved not to ask for any other details of the strange foods on his table.

Abruptly, I transitioned to discussion of body armor. "I noticed that most, if not all, of your soldiers wear chain mail."

Aloma's hand halted with a piece of bread poised above his cup. He looked at me, brow raised.

I continued, "Is it made here in Ngazargamu, or do you import it along with your Turks?"

Upon arriving in Bornu, we'd heard much but seen little of his foreign mercenaries and their impressive firearms. Those we *had* seen, though they did not dress like Arabs, looked very much like them in skin tone and countenance.

He dipped the bread into the milk and chewed slowly before swallowing. "The Turkish musketeers are a great asset, but I wasn't aware that Zazzau was familiar with chain mail."

"It is uncommon." I spoke as though I'd known such armor existed before coming to Bornu.

"Not so uncommon here. I have talented metalsmiths."

"I've had no opportunity to closely inspect their handiwork."

"That's unfortunate. But I assure you, the armor is of the best craftsmanship."

"I do not doubt it."

"So what of Kano?" He, too, could change subjects with ease.

"What of Kano?"

"Its people raid the edges of my kingdom and hide behind their walled cities. Such activities could be taken as an open threat, don't you agree?"

"Kano may be aggressive, but those border skirmishes are localized disputes. Kano has not ventured past the borders of Zazzau in several generations."

"Might this then be the time for it?"

"For Kano to march against Zazzau? Ha!"

He glanced sidelong at me. "What do you think of their defenses?"

"If you plan to invade Kano, it won't be easy. Dala, the royal seat, is well placed with strong fortifications. Besieged, Kano could hold out indefinitely." I shrugged. "Or until you tire."

"Mmm." Aloma nodded.

I finished eating my breakfast, praying all the while that my belly would not disagree with it, and sat back.

He downed the last of his milk. "Still, we must keep an eye on Kano."

"We?"

"Indeed."

We was a step in a favorable direction. Although, my purpose in coming to this place was to solidify a friendship, not to join forces in an attack on my neighbor. If Bornu made any moves against Kano, I'd ensure that *we* reverted back to *he*.

❁

The day of our departure from Bornu arrived quickly. Shortly after sunrise, Aloma met us at the city gates. He had with him his standard guard and two camels laden with leather skins and earthen pots.

"As-salamu alaikum, Amina of Zazzau." He inclined his head.

"Wa alaikum as-salaam," I replied.

"Let it not be said that Idris Aloma sent the queen of Zazzau home without parting gifts." He gestured to a servant to bring the camels forward.

"Camels." I smiled, feigning interest. I had never found much use for the stubborn, vicious creatures. "Thank you."

"The camels are nothing and may have some difficulty traversing the mountain pass. I apologize in advance if this is the case. It's what the camels carry that I'm gifting you." He nodded toward the single-humped creatures. "The pots and skins contain cheese, honey, and wine. Also wheat, rice, and other grains."

"Wheat?"

"We make our bread from wheat. At first, the crop was imported from the north, but it grows readily enough here." He gestured to another servant, who brought a length of brightly colored cloth folded into a thick bundle. "The cloth comes from Fezzan, and the other is Bornu made."

I glanced askance at him and took the bundle from the servant; it was heavier than a piece of cloth should have been. Balancing the bundle on Demon's withers, I unfolded it. Links of metal gleamed beneath. Bashiru leaned in to see what Aloma had given me, but I refolded it quickly and grinned at the monarch.

"I accept these gifts with honor and humility, Your Excellency."

"I hope it is a testament to our friendship." He brought his horse closer, put a hand on mine, which was gripping the cloth as though the bundle might sprout legs and run. "Wear it well, Warrior Queen."

THIRTY-NINE

City of Turunku, Kingdom of Zazzau, Central Hausaland, circa 1585 CE

We were a few kilometers outside Turunku when we beheld the massive peak. With the top of its plateau blocking the lower curve of the slowly dipping sun, the mountain loomed dark against the sky. I pulled on the reins and stared, slack-jawed, at the anomalous structure. It was not the biggest mountain I had ever seen, nor had it any distinctive features. It was not remarkable in any way, save one: it had not been there when we left.

Perhaps the long journey from Bornu had taken a toll on my sanity. Perhaps there was, in fact, nothing there. "Do you see it?" I asked no one and everyone.

No one answered. I looked at my comrades, each of whom sat motionless on their steeds, expressions ranging from terrified to flabbergasted. Of course they saw it. I was not mad. But if my faculties were intact, then yonder behemoth was as real as the demon horse pawing the ground beneath me. All things considered, madness was the least alarming explanation.

"Allah preserve us," the fagaci said, the first of my fellow travelers to regain his tongue.

"Allah has much to do with the shaping of worlds." I nodded, forcing myself into calm. The situation called for panic, but I couldn't afford that luxury.

The fagaci shook his head slowly. "No. This is not the work of the highest God. He would not cause such a disturbance in the order of things."

"A lesser god, then?" Siddhi suggested in a subdued voice.

"Or an evil spirit," Jaruma added. "Affecting our minds."

"Whatever it is," I said, "we should find out." I started forward.

An aura of quiet blanketed the area. I wondered what had become of the people residing in the capital city, and why we had received no word prior to coming upon the sight ourselves. Surely, the sudden appearance of a mountain within the city walls was enough to send the denizens of Turunku racing for shelter from the wrath of God? Surely, those who visited the city left with stories of a great miracle? We should have been intercepted by someone—messengers, refugees, travelers—informing us of this new *development*.

Bashiru thought the same. He muttered, "We should have come across the people fleeing for their lives. Where are they?"

The city gates were open, as was usual in the daytime, but there was no steady, familiar trickle of citizens, travelers, or traders. No noisy banter, no rowdy laughter. Were it not for the handful of people milling about, conducting their daily business with quiet voices, the city may well have been deserted. As it was, nobody paid any attention to the arrival of my sizable convoy of bewildered, bedraggled travelers and our lumpy camels.

A woman with a basketful of fruits balanced on her head sauntered across our path. Bashiru stopped her.

"Madam." His tone reflected the city's atmosphere.

She looked up at him, her expression all but vacant. "Sir?"

"What is happening here?"

"Sir?"

He leaned down and snatched her arm, giving it a rough shake. "What magic is this?"

The woman gasped, her basket tipping. She reached up to steady it. From her wrist dangled no less than a dozen amulets.

"What is that?" He released her arm to point at the mountain in the background.

Shaken out of her stupor, she replied, "It's Tandama, sir."

"Are you mad, woman?" Bashiru voiced my thoughts. "Tandama was an anthill when we left here. Only three full moons have passed."

The woman looked around Bashiru, her eyes again empty, and glanced back at the mountain. "Some say it's the beginning of the end of days. Others say it's a gift from the greatest God."

"What do *you* say?" Jaruma asked.

"I await the queen. We all await the queen."

The others looked at me.

"Why have you not left the city?" I asked.

The woman seemed to notice me for the first time. She scrutinized me, vague recognition crossing her face. It was quickly gone.

"We await the queen," she said again and moved on.

"This is madness," Bashiru said, turning to call the woman back.

"Leave her," I commanded.

We continued to Gidan Bakwa.

As with the rest of the city, the palace was without the normal buzz of daily activity. People were about, but they moved quietly. Like spirits walking the earth. Even the animals we left tethered outside the gatehouse became caught in the strange mood of Turunku. They stood silently without so much as a swish of the tail.

Zariya broke the stillness. "Amina!" She ran toward us.

I was so relieved to see her, to see one lively human being, to hear her shout, that I too began running. We reached each other in several strides and embraced tightly for a moment.

My voice dropped to a whisper. "What's happening here?"

"We don't know when it began," she said. "No one noticed until its shadow first fell over the palace." She took my hand. "Come, Waziri and Galadima await you in the council chamber."

I hurried behind her. "Why have you remained in the city?"

She looked back at me with a puzzled expression. "Because there is nothing to fear, Sister. Don't you know?"

"I know only that there's a mountain where there should be none, and I feel as though I'm the only one who realizes it. Why has no one left here, taken refuge in Kufena?" The tension in my nerves manifested as an increasing shrillness of my voice.

Zariya replied in a tone that was meant to pacify those nerves. "Some have gone but most didn't. As I said, the hill had already grown massive before we noticed it, and those farther out never noticed at all."

"What kind of magic is this?" My racing mind sought answers but could formulate none.

The waziri and the galadima rose to their feet as I entered the council chamber.

"Long life to you, My Queen." The waziri bowed. This was the son of the previous waziri. Like his father, who had passed away last year, he spoke with a lilting, almost hypnotic voice.

The galadima bowed as well. "Welcome back, Your Majesty."

Neither of them behaved as though anything out of the ordinary had happened.

"Is that *thing* Tandama?" I asked, my nerves teetering on edge.

"It is," the waziri replied calmly. Also like his father, he was a scholar of the occult.

In a blustery tone, I said, "And why is the city not abandoned? Why is the town behaving as though it's under a spell?"

"I shall answer presently." The waziri gathered his robes about himself. "But your journey was long, you must eat."

"Eat?" My voice grew shriller still. "This is hardly the time for it."

"But the food has already arrived." He gestured at the servants, who entered with pots of the sweetest smelling food I had encountered in weeks.

My stomach responded to the scent with a soft rumble, and my mouth watered at the heavenly aroma of a genuine Hausa meal. A voice at the back of my mind screamed sorcery, compelled me to remain vigilant. It insisted upon answers. It wanted to rebuke the waziri, slap Zariya. Sanity dictated that I do something. But there was no denying my intense hunger. Maybe that was why I could no longer think.

Quietly, I sat down feeling oppressed yet oddly accepting of it. The waziri nodded in an irritatingly patronizing manner. Again, I accepted it and listened calmly when he described what had occurred in my absence.

Under a citywide shroud of madness, no one had noticed the birth of the mountain until the rocky hill had more than doubled in size. Granted, there had been no earthquake, no loud rumbles, not even the slightest tremor. Unless one was looking in its direction, one would not have seen Tandama sprouting skyward like a growing termite mound. When my proxies had realized what was happening, rather than evacuate the city, they'd consulted the Oracle.

"So you stayed?" I asked. "Because the Oracle predicted no danger?" More and more, it sounded like insanity.

"That was not the only reason," the waziri said.

Zariya spoke. "There was—has been—something hanging in the air as you say. A lethargy of body and mind. It makes even the idea of fleeing too onerous to bear and gives one the impression that nothing is amiss."

"Except, where before there was only a pile of slate, there is now a mountain rising a hundred meters into the sky," I said.

"Even so," the waziri replied. "It's that same lethargy that has kept the town from panic."

"Though some have not been fooled," the galadima added.

"Those fled the city," Zariya finished.

"Yet the story of Tandama hasn't spread. Not even a hint of it." Siddhi said, staring out the window at the enigma that peaked in the distance.

"Why is that?" I asked. "Why was there no news of this anomaly?"

The galadima provided an answer. "It would appear that the cloud covering Turunku also confers some forgetfulness."

My laughter began as a series of small snorts, which escalated into something verging on hysteria. "Forgetfulness?" The laughter increased in pitch. "You are mad." I swept a finger around the room. "You are all mad." I stood and strode to the door, my laughter ceasing. "And that thing." I pointed at the mountain. "That thing is an illusion conjured by our deranged minds. Whatever this haze"—I waved my arms about frantically—"that has stricken an entire city with madness, a mountain does not one day rise from the earth!"

No one said a word. The usually glib Bashiru was as subdued as the city. The fagaci, who was visibly terrified, sat in wide-eyed stillness on a leather-covered chair. Siddhi cogitated by my side. The others simply watched me.

"That mountain is a gift, Amina," Zariya said after a time, and my hysterical laughter began anew. "A gift for the Beloved of the gods."

The laughter came to a halt. "This is what the Oracle said?"

"It's not the Oracle that visits dreams upon me, Sister."

No wonder her dreams of foretelling were sometimes vague or questionable in their accuracy. But that was neither here nor there while the monstrous Tandama stared down at me.

"You must climb to the summit," she said.

"I must do what?"

"Climb to the summit and receive your blessing. Then the fog will be lifted."

Coming away from the door, I regarded her. "Who tells you this? If not the Oracle, then who? And why should I heed?"

"Mafarki. The dreamgoddess."

"Dreamgoddess?" I appraised my sister from head to toe. *The goddess of dreams.* I'd not known there was such a deity. "What is this dreamgoddess to me?"

"Climb to the top, Amina," Zariya pleaded. "Otherwise the city remains in this half conscious state."

I stared at the mountain as though it might get up and walk. Given its sudden appearance, it might have done just that. Or, if providence were with us, it would crumble into nothing and return to whence it came. If not, we were all mad. I scratched my head, contemplating this dream from which I hoped to soon wake.

"Perhaps we should leave the city and this mountain behind." I stopped to consider what I had said. *Perhaps.* Barely two hours since we had entered the aura of madness, and my will to flee had already dwindled. I squeezed my eyes shut. Opened them. The thing was still there. Dream or insanity, answers were at the summit.

Curse the day the gods took an interest in me.

※

Tandama had been solid rock when last I stood upon it. This mountain, however, was covered in lush forest. Lush enough to rival the dense foliage of the southern climes. There was a path, overgrown with vegetation and crisscrossed with brambles, that led to its plateau. It wound along the side of the mountain in an unnatural and precise manner, as though it had been deliberately carved and then forgotten, allowing the greenery to encroach. With Jaruma a few paces behind, I reached the summit and a cooling breeze. Unlike the mountainside, the flat ground of the summit was without vegetation. Dark patches of earth, however, were visible amidst the layers of slate.

As impossible as it was for a mountain to materialize in a crowded city without inciting panic, what I saw atop that hill was no less shocking. A few feet from where the path ended, a tall gatehouse was built into a slightly shorter wall. The gatehouse was turreted, but there wasn't an actual gate. Instead, the gatehouse itself spanned the only visible opening into the compound—a single door that would fit a single person on foot.

The color of the wall and gatehouse matched that of the ground. Both looked as though they were hewn from the mountain itself. They may have been constructed from a light-colored clay, but I was beginning to suspect that wasn't the case.

I will build you a stone palace. He'd said the words, but it never occurred to me that they had meant anything to him.

"It's stone," Jaruma said, confirming my suspicion. She ran a hand across the smooth front of the gatehouse.

I let out a sharp breath. "He did it."

"Who?" Jaruma asked. "Who did what?"

My hand rose to my mouth, and I stared at the structure in awe. "He did it," I said from behind my hand. Snatching hers, I ran through the open gateway and into the compound beyond.

Several box-shaped houses were arranged in conjoined clusters in a layout similar to that of Gidan Bakwa. There was a cluster of guesthouses and an administrative row. Each house, though not cut from rock, had smooth, seamless walls. The roofs of the smaller individual boxes were of grass thatch, so tightly packed that they would last nothing short of a year without repair. The larger conjoined boxes had adobe roofs. Wooden doors covered each doorway, none was left bare. A mature traveler's palm grew in the center of the compound.

Jaruma pried her hand out of mine and bounded toward the guesthouses. I heard her exclamation but was, myself, hurrying past the administrative row and didn't pause to listen further.

Beyond the administrative row grew a small orchard of fruiting trees, which surrounded a cluster of houses that I took to be the master chambers.

I will build you a stone palace.

Excited, I hurried through the orchard, past the master chambers, and to the far wall, in which a heavy wooden door was set. A slight push and the metal latch gave. The door swung away from me. Anticipation rose like pressure in my chest as I walked through to the other side.

A raised and level section of the mountaintop, covered with a domed roof, made a small pavilion. At the pavilion's center sat a great stone chair. My dark and brooding lord, looking immensely satisfied, reclined in the chair and absently tore a leaf from a homely kola tree.

"Are you pleased, my queen?"

I lowered myself in obeisance. "I am well pleased."

He looked expectantly at me and I came forward. When I reached him, he rose from the chair to give me a curt bow. I stood silent, because no words came to me, because no words were adequate. I threw my arms around his waist then drew back to look into eyes as tranquil as the setting sun.

Tossing his cloak over his shoulders, he returned to the chair, pulling me down with him. His swirling eyes regained their usual intensity and focused on me.

"You've set us astir in the thick of madness, Lord Husband."

"You are a simpleminded people. It does not take much to set you astir."

"We are like the walking dead."

"Unlike the walking dead, you will eventually wake from your stupor."

"What have you done to them?"

"Mine is the power of chaos. The serenity that lies over your people is not my doing."

"Inna?"

It hardly seemed likely that the Earth Mother would have done *anything* for her son. At last recollection, they were barely civil to one another.

His response, however, didn't carry the bitterness that usually manifested when he spoke of her. In fact, he sounded proud. "My mother is talented, is she not?"

I gestured at the stone compound. "All of this? But why?"

"To elevate you to the clouds, Beloved."

The answer was in no way enlightening, but I asked no more questions and lay my head against his shoulder. His heat snaked into me, to my very soul. I exhaled slowly in response to the sensation.

He stroked my hair. "Your body trembles, my love."

"As it often trembles when you're near."

The creak of a door echoed in the air as Jaruma exited the compound. Scarcely registering her presence, I looped an arm through his. Both Jaruma and the sleepy Turunku far below us were another world because in my world there was only him. More creaking signaled her retreat.

"Amina." He spoke over the top of my head. When I looked up, he said, "I am pleased that you are pleased."

Again, no words came to me. None except the awkwardly spoken, "Thank you, my lord. For the palace."

Behind him, the sun splashed the last of its crimson paint over the horizon.

FORTY

City of Zaria, Kingdom of Zazzau, Central Hausaland, circa 1599 CE

Nearly fifteen years had passed since Tandama Mountain had risen through that sleepy haze. The nation was stable, most of the vassals sated. My people wanted for nothing. The streets were safe at night, even for lone women. The state took care of the poor, the widowed and orphaned. The kingdom was fat, its wealth rivaled only by Bornu and Kano. And because the greatness of an empire was reflected in the glory of its capital, I built a new one.

The new capital was thirty kilometers north of Turunku. Before it became a city, that expanse of savanna had lain in the path of our major trade routes. The city's natural fortifications, limited to several rocky hills, offered a meager line of defense against foreign attack, but what the hills could not hold, my army could repel. Any who made it past the army would then have to deal with the city wall.

Sixteen kilometers around, the earthen wall was over nine meters tall with seven narrow wrought iron gates for foot traffic and two larger gates to accommodate supply-laden beasts of burden. Ramparts built into the wall made it easy for us to rain fire upon any attacking horde. The gates were its only weak points, and these were continuously manned.

The actual task of designing our new capital had fallen to Zariya, who had a talent for such things, and she'd done it well. The city was her legacy as well as mine. So, even before it was built, I'd decided—and the council had agreed—that it would be named after her. Thus was the city of Zaria was born.

The stone palace remained my private abode—Demon ferried me quickly between cities—but official matters of state were conducted in Zaria. Following this morning's audience, she after whom the city was named waited for the pavilion to clear.

Zariya's husband had died six years ago. She lived in the new palace compound but did not frequently attend morning court. When she did grace the populace with her presence, it was usually because she had a pressing need to speak with me. I rarely remained in the Zaria palace after the daily business ended.

Seated on my right, she now turned to face me. "I had a dream last night."

I looked into warm brown eyes so like my mother's that, for a moment, I saw the mighty Bakwa gazing back at me. "What did you dream?"

"War."

"I see."

"Death."

"To be expected with war."

"Misery."

"Likewise."

The beginning of a frown puckered her lips. "You aren't surprised."

I inhaled deeply and let out the breath before speaking. "The Kwararafa rumble louder each day, and Nupeland is too quiet for comfort. War is brewing; though from which side, I cannot tell." The information gathered from spies suggested that Kwararafa was the more likely of the two. But that damned Tsoede, who refused to die, was wily and hid his secrets well.

A knitted brow joined Zariya's puckered lips. "How long have you known?"

"I know nothing really."

"I have a bad feeling."

I met her comment with a dry chuckle. "When has war ever inspired good feelings?"

"I will leave you to answer that next time you meet your patron god." Several breaths later she said, "Kwararafa was only a matter of time, I think. But Nupeland? What will you do?"

"I'd like to help Tsoede to Death's door, but none of my operatives can get close enough to ensure subtlety. We don't want to incite rebellion."

"You contemplate weighty matters, Sister." Zariya paused. "Whether Kwararafa or Nupeland, I fear what's coming."

"War is not certain." I took her hand. "As Mama once told me, words make all the difference. We'll attempt diplomacy, no?"

"Against Kwararafa? They don't respect diplomacy."

Nor did they respect weakness, indecisiveness, or any lack of conviction. When it came to Kwararafa, one either triumphed or died.

❀

A storm blew into Turunku before I reached the stone palace. By the time I entered my private chamber, my clothing was soaked through. I lit the oil lamp that sat on a tall wooden stool near the door and doffed my sodden garments, cursing all the while.

"Such foul words should never fly from so beautiful a mouth."

The very sound of his voice made my body stir. I raised my head to see him standing in the shadows.

"My queen." He stepped into the light.

"Wargod. It's been more than a fortnight."

"Has it? I lose track."

I shivered as a soft breeze blew over my damp skin. "I've thought of you often these past days."

"I have no doubt, for your enemies have risen."

I pulled a wrapper from my trunk and tied at my chest. "Both Kwararafa and Nupeland are up to something."

"But the Kwararafa are the more immediate threat."

"I hear they're assembling war parties."

"They are."

"And this is why you've come? To warn me of the Kwararafa?"

"You are already well-informed, my love. You need no warning from me."

"Then why have you come?" I inched my arms around his waist, but his tense, unyielding body did not respond. "You don't seem inclined toward other affairs."

The red in his eyes burned brightly. "It has only been a fortnight, Beloved. Surely you can contain yourself."

I rose onto my toes to kiss his chin.

"I came to give counsel, but we can do pleasure before business." His arm slid around me. "To Jangare?"

✳

I lay atop my husband, my head rising and falling to the steady rhythm of his breath.

Kwararafa be damned.

"If only it were that simple," he replied to my thought. "You know, they are Kogi's brood."

"The rivergod?"

"Yes. Like prodigal children, they have forgotten their origin. It causes my brother no end of distress. Which causes me no end of glee."

"You bicker like mortals."

"We bicker for much higher stakes."

"Speaking of higher stakes."

"How do you fight the Kwararafa?" he asked before I could raise the question.

"They're like no other enemy we've engaged. They wield both metal and magic. I . . . My lord, stop distracting me."

"You are too easily distracted." Still, he withdrew his roaming hand from my thigh.

"If only I knew how they would strike. Whether to be more wary of their swords or of their sorcery."

"Perhaps you should consider fearing both."

"Why? Do you know something?"

"I cannot see so deeply into men's minds. Until their thoughts are well focused on the brewing conflict, your enemy's strategies are as unknown to me as they are to you." He looked perturbed by this uncertainty.

"Then how do you intend to counsel me?"

"You know from your own past dealings that the Kwararafa should not be taken lightly. They can destroy you. Your people may be above magic, but others are not."

"Are you saying that magic will defeat us?"

"I am saying that magic *can* defeat you. I am saying that you should prepare to fight against it. And do not underestimate their warriors. The Kwararafa fighters can match yours skill for skill. Except for . . ."

"Archers," we said simultaneously.

"If yours are disabled," he said.

"Disabled how?"

"Magic works in many ways. Perhaps your archers will be struck blind."

"Allah forbid!"

"War has little to do with your Creator, Beloved. Magic aside, perhaps the enemy will attack by night. You cannot shoot what you cannot see."

"Then what's your advice?"

"Do not underestimate your enemy." He rolled me onto my back. "There are some who may yet guide you, though their magic may not be sufficient."

The gaze that met mine burned hot. "If Kwararafa magic is strong enough I may not be able to penetrate it without alerting He who might sanction you because of my interference."

"He who . . . *Who?*"

"My father. And I may never see into your enemies' minds."

Once again, Zazzau would meet the Kwararafa, and this time, we had to finish them. If we didn't, they would finish us.

"If I cannot, you must find out what your enemy is about. You may have to fight magic with magic, Beloved."

A frown formed on my face before I could stop it.

He frowned back at me and sat up. "They are coming."

The passion I'd brought to Jangare drained, leaving me cold. With a small shiver, I said, "We always knew they'd come to claim what they once could not. But how soon?"

"That I do not know. Neither how soon nor how strong." Frustration made his eyes turbulent. It cooled his body and, by extension, mine. "My innermost nature tells me you should expect war in the upcoming season, but if they were so prepared, I should have picked it from their minds by now. Yet I hear nothing."

Discomfited, I too sat up. "Could it be that the magic has already begun?"

He looked uncharacteristically uncertain. "If that is the case, then they are more powerful than I thought. Are you ready for them?"

"We are."

"Make sure of it."

"Dafaru, you frighten me."

"It is not my intention." He stroked my arm. "Father has risen from slumber and is not pleased. I will protect you, but I hesitate to provoke the Creator's wrath." His fingers rose to my neck and curled gently around my throat as he drew me close. Lips brushing my cheek, he spoke absently, as though speaking only to himself. "I do not know if I could endure His anger a second time."

A second time? I drew back, took his face in my hands, and looked into roiling eyes. "Have I—"

"It was a time long before you, my love." He pulled my hands away from his face. "Father's vengeance is swift but rarely clean. I cannot wash away the stink of a millennium of suffering."

He was showing a side of himself that he'd never shown before. His vulnerability, while unnerving, touched something deep inside me and conjured up a host of strong emotions. I put my arms around his neck, but he quickly collected himself. Unhooking my arms, he looked away.

When he looked back, he said, "I have a matter to attend."

"Now?"

He rose from the bed and pulled on his trousers. "Stay here."

❖

The skies above Jangare had turned the deep red of late dusk. I surmised that I had slept for at least two hours. Dafaru's burnished-metal taste still lingered on me, but he was not in the room. I slid out of bed and donned his discarded tunic before going in search of him.

There was no one in the corridor, so I made my way toward the throne room. Despite its chilling draught, that room above all others appealed to him most. Perhaps it was the dismal gloom of the place that he loved. It was the sort of room that lent itself well to brooding thoughts.

There were two entrances into the throne room. The larger entrance, the one used by visitors, was off the main corridor. Usually, the double doors—huge granite slabs—were open. When I reached them, however, they were shut. Pressing my shoulder to one door, I pushed. The granite did not budge. I'd not expected it to. Suppressing a groan of irritation, I turned away.

"Gods of Jangare!" I pressed a hand to my chest as though it could calm my racing heart.

"My apologies, Your Majesty." Salima bowed. "I did not mean to startle you."

Not for the first time, it crossed my mind that Salima and the other servants were the spirits of those long dead. They always appeared so suddenly and so silently, as if in response to mere thought. And sometimes, like now, they made the skin at the back of my neck prickle.

I shrugged off the eerie feeling. "I'd like to go inside."

"We do not enter when the doors are closed."

"Yes, Salima, I know. But can you open them?"

She shook her head. "I cannot."

I glanced at the top of the doorway and back at the servant. "Then take me to the other entrance. The entrance the master uses." Several times, Dafaru and I had exited the throne room from a door behind the dais, but the passageway beyond was so convoluted that I could never find my way back. And I had tried many times.

She hesitated before responding. "Our master would not like to be disturbed. But if it is your desire," she continued, just as I was about to protest, "I will show you to the other door."

"Thank you."

With a gracious nod, she spun on her heels and led me through passages that felt like an ever-shifting maze. When we reached the throne room door, Salima gestured. I acknowledged her assistance with a quick nod, and she retreated down the darkened corridor.

The door made no noise when I shoved it open and sidled into the room. I entered to the sound of Dafaru's voice.

"If, in the end, this will be the outcome?"

"You should not have gone to her," a woman's voice replied. The voice was sultry and sweet, a sound that represented everything female.

My face grew hot when I realized whose conversation I was intruding upon.

Inna continued, "My sister should never have told you. She should have known what you would do."

"She did know, Mother." It wasn't Dafaru's voice. This one was deeper and rumbled like thunder. *Dawatsu?* "She wanted to give him a choice the rest of us do not require."

I entered farther into the room and, lest I be accused of eavesdropping, climbed the dais stairs to pause beside the throne. Inna stood with her back to me while the thickly muscled thundergod—also with his back to me—sat on the dais steps tossing his iron mallet from one hand to the other. Dafaru faced them both, his eyes fixed on his mother.

"Please, my son." To my shock, she fell to her knees. "If you do this, you may as well tear the heart from my breast."

Dafaru glanced up, saw me, and scowled. *Oh greatest God!* His scowl deepened. *Husband, forgive me.* My heart beat tremulously in my ears. The wargod's eyes lit momentarily on his brother, who turned to look at me. Dawatsu tilted his head in acknowledgment, which further raised my frantic pulse. *Forgive me.* But I didn't know whether the thundergod was listening my thoughts.

Dafaru took his mother by the shoulders and drew her to her feet. Decades past, their animosity was almost palpable. Now, he gently pulled her into an embrace.

"I have caused you much heartache, Mother, and do not wish to cause further pain. But this . . ." He raised his scowl to me once more. "She is . . ."

"She is my doing," Inna said. "I molded her for you. But, my son, *she is mortal.*"

They were talking about me? My silent apologies ceased, and I stood in rigid discomfort. Inna's head turned as she finally noticed me. Gaining some common sense, I scurried from my position near the throne. "Forgive me, Mother." I dropped to hands and knees, head lowered. "I didn't mean to—"

"Hush, child." Inna said.

I lifted my eyes and looked from her to Dafaru then to Dawatsu, who now got to his feet. Inna came toward me, her body gliding across the floor like a soft breeze. She climbed the stairs, bent, and took my chin in her hand.

She tilted my face. Eyes of earth and sea and sky looked deeply into mine. "Rise."

I obeyed.

She regarded me. "Indeed, I shaped you too well. He loves you more than you know." She pressed a kiss to my lips. When she pulled away, her sweet nectar scent hung about me. "Come, Dawatsu." The layers of her dress rustled as she turned. "Let your brother attend his wife."

The god of thunder bowed at me again. This time, from the waist. I returned with a deep genuflection.

He offered Inna his arm. "Choose well, little brother."

Together, the two deities strode down the long hall. The double doors swung open at their approach and remained so after they had passed through. Dafaru came up the stairs and sat heavily on the black throne. I moved to stand before him. His quiet, vacant eyes looked far away, and I lowered myself to the ground, my hands on his knees.

"What is it, my lord? What is this thing that pains your mother so?"

"Do not concern yourself." Slow mists danced in his eyes when he looked at me. "I told you to stay put. Do you wish to return to the world of men?"

"No."

"Then why did you come for me?"

"I . . . I don't know. I woke and you'd not returned, and so much time had passed, and . . . and . . . I don't know." It was difficult to think when he was gazing so intensely at me. I glowered at him. "You're troubled, my lord. I can see that much. But send me home if it's your pleasure."

"It would be my pleasure to have you back in my bed."

I cursed the ripple spreading through me. The way my body reacted, one would have thought me a young girl at first flush of passion.

"Will you tell me your troubles?" I asked.

"No."

I sighed.

"Stay with me tonight," he said. "In the morning, you return to Zazzau and your duties. You must prepare for battle."

The uneasiness apparent in his voice and in his eyes filled me with dread.

"Fear not, Beloved."

But I *was* afraid. Zazzau was like a lone jackal hunted by a pack of hyenas.

"That is why you must prepare." He appraised me carefully, as though his appraisal was not of me, but of Zazzau itself. "I do not think you are cautious enough."

"Dafaru—"

"Prepare, my love. I may not be able to assist you this time."

"We are prepared. We *will* prepare. When the hyenas strike, my lord, the jackal will show that she, too, has sharp teeth."

FORTY-ONE

Western Bank of the Jamaa're River, Northeast of Zazzau, circa 1600 CE

The Kwararafa had reached the Komadugu River. Forsaking their previous mountain route, they had traveled across the flatlands. It was a much easier path than the mountains, but it kept their twelve thousand warriors within full view of my trackers.

My forces bivouacked a kilometer off the bank of the Jamaa're, just outside Kano territory and about two days from the Komadugu. I sat on a grass mat alone in my bamboo hut. Jaruma was with Bashiru tonight.

I had consulted with the witches, those so-called priestesses of the old magicks, but they were useless against the Kwararafa. They fathomed nothing of my enemy's plans. To the waziri's distress, the Oracle was also unhelpful. And the god of war was reluctant to use his full power to penetrate Kwararafa minds. It was just as well. Better not to draw the Creator's attention.

I yawned. In my mind's eye, I conjured up a picture of our battle schematic, but my thoughts did not progress much further. Suddenly too tired to keep my eyes open, I lay down on the mat. Sleep caught me unawares. It swept over me like a savanna wind.

I woke in a copse of baobab trees.

All traces of fatigue vanished as I climbed to my feet to face the god of war, who sat atop a copper-brown horse. Beside him, in rippling water form, stood the rivergod. I bowed low.

Kogi-Ayu inclined his head.

Dafaru dismounted, gathered me into his arms, and kissed my forehead. "I fear my brother's offspring have more powerful magic than I realized." He glanced at Kogi-Ayu. "Tell her."

The water form turned into a man, and Kogi-Ayu came forward, scalding his brother with a look. His eyes were like a black river after heavy rains. "Even now, the Kwararafa are upon you, and your camp sleeps the sleep of the dead."

I stared blankly at him, not comprehending his words.

"My children were born of the rivers. Now they are more like him." He gestured at Dafaru. "Creatures of chaos."

The sleep of the dead? Was that the powerful fatigue that had overcome me so swiftly?

Trying to control my rising impatience, I stepped out of the wargod's embrace. "What are you saying?" I looked from one god to the other.

"I am saying that you cannot wake your warriors," the rivergod replied.

Dafaru turned to his brother and said in a voice as sharp as a finely honed blade, "I made you a promise long ago, and so I will not force it from you. But I know what you are keeping from me."

Kogi-Ayu said nothing, his black eyes churning to a frothy grey.

"You must tell her what she needs to know," Dafaru said.

"I have already told her too much. The covenants forbid—"

"I care nothing for the covenants!" He exhaled and his voice softened. "Tell her, Brother. Please."

"This is beyond my authority. Beyond yours. We have risked much for her already."

"Then risk nothing more for me. Only . . ." I faced my husband. "If my people must die, send me back that I may die with them."

"Silence, woman," Dafaru said. "Queen you are, but you do not have the power to command gods. We do what it pleases us to do. And my brother will do as I have asked."

I fell silent, closed my eyes, and willed Jaruma to wake, willed the entire army to wake and face the threat advancing on them that very night. For the second time in as many encounters, the scouts had been wrong about the Kwararafa. The enemy had waited for us. We had marched into their trap.

Kogi-Ayu spoke. "Cross the Jamaa're twenty-six kilometers south of where you are camped. Your horse will only take you part of the way; you must manage the rest on your own. Cross at twenty-six kilometers. Not before. Or else you will not succeed."

I nodded.

"Once you cross the river, you will come to a hut. The source of your enemy's magic is within. Destroy it."

So simple?

"Will I know the source when I see it?" I asked.

"I have told you all I can." He stole a glance at Dafaru. "Destroy the magic at the source, and you may yet achieve your victory. Your army will wake."

"You must make haste, my love," Dafaru said. "Your horse awaits you."

I turned to see two red eyes glowing from the shadows of the forest like candles in the night. When I looked back, the gods and the brown horse were gone—vanished in silence—and I stood at the doorway of my hut.

I rushed inside to collect my weapons, then back outside to climb aboard my steed. Without command, Demon started forward.

❋

Whatever magical wards had been placed by our foes, Demon couldn't breach them. Not quite eighteen kilometers into the journey, the horse balked. I urged him on with harsh words and hard kicks, but it was all useless. After several attempts to spur the horse into motion, I gave up and dismounted.

I left my takouba where it was, affixed to his saddle. Whether or not I presented myself as a common village woman, a sword like that was nothing other than a warrior's weapon. My war bracelets were also trademark weapons of combat, so I removed them and slid them onto the sword's grip. As for the bow and arrows, any hunter might carry those. If I were caught, an explanation would be simple enough.

There were still eight kilometers to traverse and the going wouldn't be easy. Demon had stopped at the gravelly base of a mountain, which once I started up, proved to be a difficult ascent.

After an hour of climbing, I had only managed about three kilometers. I tried to increase my pace, but my progress didn't improve until the mountain leveled.

I continued onward, moving briskly now. Even at half, the moon let off so much light that it shone green through the canopy. The higher I climbed, the steadier my pace and the easier my path through the thickening mountain forest.

Another three kilometers into the trek, the first Kwararafa guard came into view. He sat on the far side of the river, which was at that point only about four meters across. His face was lit by a lantern hanging from a post driven into the ground. His weapon, a thin machete, jutted from the ground beside him. Had he been more alert, he might have seen me under the eerily bright moon. His head nodded, jerked upright, and nodded again as he battled sleep at his post. I passed by unseen.

The next guard was on my side of the river, about another kilometer up, sitting in a tree and very much awake. To his misfortune, he was inordinately light skinned and stood out from his dark surroundings. I saw him before he saw me. Taking careful aim, I loosed an arrow.

The man toppled from his seat, the loud thud of his body sounding his demise. I nocked another arrow and approached the body to prod it with my foot. The arrow had pierced the man's ribcage. He didn't move.

Satisfied that he was dead, I began to turn away, but something caught my eye. A flash of filtered moonlight reflected from the man's hand. I dropped to my knees to examine the thing further, then wrenched it from his death grip, nicking my palm in the process. Muttering a string of foul words, I raised the object to the light.

It was a thin piece of flint, no longer than my middle finger. Polished to a brilliant shine, it was sharpened to a fine edge. I turned it over in my hand and studied it. It might have been an arrowhead, but its tip was too rounded for good penetration, its base too wide to attach properly to a shaft. The weapon was, in fact, shaped in such a way that it nestled comfortably between two fingers, its tip jutting out past my knuckles.

The crafty little weapon was the sort utilized by men who fought when fighting was least expected. A weapon that could be easily hidden, easily palmed, and easily used to kill without the opponent ever laying eyes on it. It was the sort of weapon that a lone woman would do well to carry. Securing the flint blade tightly in the knots of my belt, I moved away from the dead man's body.

I passed two more guards on the other side of the river before reaching the point that I estimated as twenty-six kilometers. The incline had grown steep once again, turning the river into a tumultuous mass of water. I cringed at the thought of entering but, bracing myself, dove in.

The water was cold. *Freezing.* I struggled against its pull, kicking, pushing, and pulling against the current. Several times I was dragged under and came back up sputtering. The rivergod had said I'd be seen if I crossed before twenty-six kilometers, but he had said nothing of drowning. My strength, already compromised by the upward climb, waned further as I was dragged under again and again. I feared it might be the end of me. And Zazzau.

Before panic took root, an arm wrapped around my neck, heaving me to the water's surface. Gasping for air, I struggled against the restraint around my throat.

"Stop it! Stop it! You'll drown us both, stupid woman!"

More from fatigue than from presence of mind, I went limp. The man hauled me across the river, dragged me onto the riverbank, and deposited me on the grass with a look that could have scorched metal. His glare did not soften when I started coughing up water.

"What in the darkest hells are you doing here?" he asked in a growl.

I spat water from my mouth and lay on the ground, trying to catch my breath. At some point during my crossing, the river had carried away my bow and arrows. Without weapons, I felt naked under the Kwararafa soldier's gaze.

"What are you doing here?" he asked again.

"Catching snails," I replied between gasps.

"Catching snails?" The skepticism in his voice wasn't lost on me, but snails were the only excuse my frazzled mind could conjure. He eyed me suspiciously. "Alone? At this time of night? In those clothes?"

I didn't know what was odd about trousers and tunic, but, hopefully, he attributed my inappropriate garb to foreign eccentricity, but the suspicion didn't leave his eyes.

After several breaths, he asked, "Are you mad?"

"Yes, sir . . . no, sir." The reply likely confirmed his notion.

He got to his feet and jerked me to mine. "Can you walk?"

I nodded.

"Good. Where is your village?"

I looked around then pointed upriver. "On the other side."

"You came all this way in the river?"

My blank expression seemed to be answer enough for him.

He skewered me with another scorching look. "As much as I would like to, I cannot leave you here. Follow me."

We traveled deeper into the forest until we came to an earthen hut with a number of amulets draped over the cloth-curtained entrance. He stopped at the doorway and called to the hut's occupants.

"What is it?" asked a gruff voice from within.

"I've found something."

There came the sound of shuffling feet. Firelight spilled under the curtain then blasted outward as a large man appeared at the entrance. He raised both eyebrows when he saw me shivering.

"Is *this* what you've found?" He raised a lamp to peer into my face.

"Yes."

"Well, throw it in the river."

My rescuer made an irritated sound. "It's in the river that I found her."

The big one took in my sodden appearance. "What was she doing in the river?" He looked expectantly at me.

"Catching snails," I said under my breath, refusing to meet his gaze.

"Catching snails?"

"So she says," said the other.

"In all that clothing?" The big one laughed. "Ah, well this is the best time for it."

Was it? Having never gone snail catching, I wasn't aware of that. The gods still smiled on me.

My rescuer grunted but remained doubtful. "She says her village is upstream."

"You should have let her drown."

"I wasn't thinking." Sarcasm layered his every word.

"Oh, you *were* thinking. She's a fine thing."

"Besides that," my rescuer said curtly, "the girl needs care."

The big one gave me a hard look. "She could be useful. *I* certainly won't touch the brat, and she's beginning to smell. Catching snails, eh?" He grabbed my arm. "You must be a sorry snail catcher to be sucked into the river." Casting another glance at my rescuer, he dragged me into the hut.

FORTY-TWO

The first thing to stand out was indeed the smell. Not so much the smell of fire or even the smell of men, it was the smell of magic. It shimmered in the air and hung on the senses, setting my nerves on edge. It left a foul taste in my mouth.

Another, smaller soldier sat on the floor just inside the doorway. Toward the back of the room, and partially blocking my view of a bundle on the ground, was a third man. The man was small, thin and frail looking, likely not a warrior. His skin was so black that even in the firelight it had a blue tinge to it. Sweat dripped down the back of his closely shorn head as he chanted words and rattled talismans over his bundle.

There was the source of magic. Were my weapons not lost in the river, I might have killed the magic man before the other two could stop me. I ran my fingers along my belt and almost exhaled my relief. The sharpened piece of flint was still there. The small soldier was looking at me now, so I dropped my hand to my side.

"What is the name of your village?" The small one rose from his position on the floor. He walked over to me while the big one took his place. We were the same height, the small one and I, but he looked down his nose at me, a snide expression on his pinched face. When I didn't answer, he said, "Have you forgotten?"

"No, sir." The first name that entered my head was what I told him. "Gyangi." It was the name of a fantasy kingdom in a fable once told to me by my grandfather.

"It must be tiny indeed." The small one wrinkled his nose and glanced back at the magic man. "Have you finished with the child?"

I peered over the soldier's shoulder.

"Sit there." The small one nodded toward an area near the magic man.

I took my seat and noticed that the smell of both magic and unwashed people grew stronger. I also noticed that the bundle on the ground was not an inanimate thing but a girl. She was no more than twelve or thirteen years old and painfully thin. From where I sat, it was evident that the odor of human filth came from her. How long had she been like this? What had they done to her?

Anger pushed my heart to an unruly beat. I turned to the magic man. "Is she ill?"

"Is that your business?" the big one asked.

The magic man didn't say a word even though he had ceased chanting. I too said no more but watched him sway over the girl, waving the talismans that he held in both hands.

The child was emaciated. The plaits in her hair looked as though they'd not been tended in months. Her skin was tight against her flesh, like dried fruit. Every so often, her body jerked, but otherwise she remained in her state of deep slumber. A state that, I now realized, the magic man had put her into.

When he finished his swaying and talisman rattling, he knelt perfectly still, head bowed as though in prayer. Concluding his sorcery, he got slowly to his feet and left the hut.

"You have some time to get the stinkpot clean," the big one said of the little girl. He pointed at a second bundle lying in shadow. "Clean cloth."

The smaller soldier gestured at his comrade. "Let's leave the woman to it. Once she moves the urchin, the smell will be unbearable."

The big one considered for a moment then agreed. They strode out of the hut.

The smell was indeed harsh when I opened the child's wrapper. Strong fumes burned my nose and eyes as I lifted her off the mat. Other than being filthy and extremely thin, her little body was unharmed, her breathing even. Pressing my lips together in disgust at the state of the child, I laid her on the earthen floor and went to the door.

"I need water to clean her," I said to the soldiers.

One of them grunted an acknowledgment. A short time later, a gourd of water was pushed into the hut.

Several layers of cloth covered the mat upon which the girl lay. Each layer was soaked through with what I could only hope was urine. I peeled the soiled cloth off the mat, wiped it clean and laid three dry cloths over it. Since she was so thin, maneuvering the girl took no effort. I sat her up and wiped her as well. She looked clean when I finished, but the stale smell of waste still lingered. *This poor child.* They would pay for what they'd done to her.

Scooping up the soiled cloth, I made my way out of the hut and toward the river. The guards shrank back at the odor. Here the river was much calmer than it was downstream. I immersed the cloth in it, scrubbing until each piece was reasonably unsoiled. From where they stood, the two soldiers watched me spread the cloth on the riverbank. After a while, and still watching me, they entered into a heated discussion.

I returned to the ramshackle abode. The big soldier followed me inside.

From outside, the small one said, "Be quick about it." He did not enter.

Apart from the sleeping girl, the big one and I were alone. Without a sound, he dropped a heavy hand on the back of my neck. I stiffened. He spun me to face him, and I resisted the urge to spit in his face.

"Even though you dress like a man, you are a sight for weary eyes," he said. "Do you have a husband?"

His jaw tightened at my lack of response. Seizing my chin with one hand, he released my neck to draw from his belt a small knife, which he pressed to my cheek. "You are not so beautiful that I wouldn't split you from ear to ear."

My nerves were already on edge. His grating voice frayed them further. Obviously, the man was of the ilk that took what he wanted whenever he wanted. A man like that held a lone, snail catching woman in no more esteem than the snails themselves. Gritting my teeth, I tried not to ram my head into his mouth.

"Do you have a husband?" he repeated.

I nodded.

He shrugged. "His loss is my gain, no?" Still holding the knife to my face, he released my chin and reached down to untie my belt.

"No!" The flint blade was hiding in the knot. I clutched his hand, then gasped as he pressed the knife into my skin.

"Easy, woman."

"Please." I attempted to hide the tremor of rage in my voice. "Please. Let me do it." A slow drop of blood trickled from the cut in my face.

"You're well trained," he said with an ugly grin and moved his hand from my waist. The other hand kept the knife against my cheek.

I lowered my head and said slowly through gritted teeth, "But the others." The forced words lent some authenticity to my feigned fear as I untied the belt, palming the blade.

"What of them?" He stood back as the belt dropped to the ground, closely followed by the tunic. Satisfied that he had done away with whatever resistance I possessed, he returned his knife to the sheath at his waist and ogled me with hungry eyes. He stepped close.

Biting my lower lip, I glanced at the doorway and prayed the other two would stay away long enough for me to finish the task at hand.

"They're occupied," he said, recognizing but misinterpreting my trepidation. His fingers found the ties of my trousers. "You're mine for now."

"How unfortunate for you."

He stared down at me, at first in confusion then pain, as I drew the piece of flint across his neck. He dropped to his knees, one hand clutching his throat and the other reaching for his knife. But it was in my hand.

When it fully registered what I had done, his painful expression turned to fury. He grabbed at me, but I stepped out of range and he fell onto his face. For several seconds, he struggled to move, fingers scratching at the ground. Then all movements ceased, and he lay still in a puddle of blood.

"Bastard," I said aloud.

I dressed quickly and dragged the man's still body into the shadows. There I waited. The source of magic—the magic man—was outside, courteously allowing me to be raped.

After a long time crouching in shadows, I heard noises. The other men had returned. Although there were two of them, the magic man didn't have the appearance of a fighter so could be discounted. Then again, nothing was ever as it seemed with the Kwararafa. The magic man, with all his slight build, might well have been a doughty warrior. I stood and took several steps deeper into shadow.

"You've had your tumble." The small soldier entered the hut, oblivious to the smell of death and the absence of his comrade's gruff response. "Save some of the woman for the marketplace."

The bastards planned to sell me. I had only a moment to gauge my target before the knife left my hand. It lodged in the soldier's chest. He looked at me, made a gurgling noise, and crumpled.

The magic man entered the hut, his sharp exclamation falling short when I grabbed his arm and threw him to the ground. He opened his mouth to scream, but I capped the noise with a fist to his face. I struck him repeatedly then jumped to my feet and kicked him in the ribs. As he lay curled on the floor, trying to reclaim his breath, I snatched the knife out of the other man's body, returned to the magic man, and shoved him onto his back.

I held the knife for him to see. "Wake the child or die."

He took a breath, and I pushed the point of the weapon into the hollow under his chin.

"Shout and you die sooner."

He made a whining sound. I rammed a knee onto his chest, pinning him down.

"Wake her."

"I cannot." He looked fearfully from me to the girl. "The magic is within her. It will cease after running its course."

The child was the source of magic? Had the gods known this? Did they expect me to kill a child? I looked down at my captive. He had to be lying. My journey into the mountains was not for the purpose of killing a child. Surely this man beneath me, paralyzed by fear, was the source of magic? He had to be. But there was no bluff in his eyes.

I pressed my knee deeper into his chest. "Then I should kill you now."

"If I die, she dies," he said quickly.

My throat constricted. I glanced at the sleeping girl, at the magic man, and backhanded him across the face. "Wake her. Dispel the magic from her body. Or else I *will* kill you."

"The magic is hers," he said in a whimper. "It will fade of its own accord. She'll wake in time. Unharmed. The child is helping us fight our enemies. Nothing more."

A groan passed my lips. I looked again at the girl.

"The magic will end at sunrise." The man's body shook so furiously that mine vibrated with it.

Sunrise was in four or five short hours. If the magic was slated to finish at that time, my army would also be finished. Perhaps they already were. My head was beginning to hurt. I squeezed my eyes shut, opened them, and saw the man's mouth moving. He was muttering something under his breath. Without another thought, I sliced into his bottom lip. He howled in pain, but I cut off the sound with another fist to his face. Something crunched under the blow. His nose, pouring blood, began to swell.

Sobbing, gasping, desperate, the man said, "What do you care? What do you care for those foul savanna rats who decimate everything in their paths?" He choked, turned his head, and spat. It was a weak effort. Blood-filled spittle ran down the side of his face. "You say you come from yonder hills?" His words slurred around the gash in his lip. "You and your people remain free but not for long. That bride of demons, Amina, will have your freedom. She'll take your land and your livelihood, and she'll kill your men. She and her kind are vermin to be stamped underfoot." He tried to spit again with the same result. "What is Zazzau but a kingdom of eunuchs led by a whore? Who are you that you concern yourself with the fate of those mongrels?"

I had suffered many slights in my life; the magic man's tirade was nothing new. Still, hearing the words straight from his ruined mouth gave them far more substance than they deserved. Like the point of an arrow, his insults struck deep.

Shifting more weight to the knee on his chest, I pressed the knife into his chin until it drew blood. "*I* am the bride of demons."

His already panicking eyes widened.

"I am the queen of Zazzau."

The blade was through his chin so quickly that his face froze in its mask of horror. Beneath me, he went into convulsions, warm blood flowing over my hand as I twisted the blade deeper into his throat. Deeper still, until his convulsions turned to feeble jerking and air bubbled out around the knife.

The cur was still alive when I got off him and went to the child, praying to all the gods that the magic would cease once the man's last breath bubbled from his gaping neck. The girl let out a loud gasp and began thrashing on her mat. Gathering her into my arms, I cradled her.

"Mama!" the child screamed.

"Hush, child." I rocked her back and forth.

Sobbing, the child opened her eyes. "Mama." She clutched my arms.

I stroked her head and kissed her face. She clung to me and continued to call for her mother.

"I'm hungry, Mama."

"I will bring food," I said softly.

She let out a long, moaning, breath. "I'm tired."

Behind me, the gurgling noises ceased. A quick glance told me the body had quit jerking. The magic man was dead, and the child was dying. Holding her in my arms, I felt her grow weaker, felt her life draining. Whether or not she was the source of magic, she was certainly the sacrifice for it.

"Sleep." Tears stung my eyes and pain filled my heart. *I might as well have killed her myself.* Drawing the child closer, I squeezed her to my breast.

The girl looked at me with unfocused eyes. "Mama, is that you?"

"Yes, my child."

"You were lost. But I've found you."

"Yes. You've found me."

"Papa will be pleased." Her whisper was almost inaudible. "He's hunting." She yawned. "Tired, Mama."

"Sleep, my daughter." Tears rolled from my eyes. I was responsible for so many deaths. This child was a casualty of war from whom I should have walked away, but I looked at her and saw every innocent life lost because of me. I couldn't let her die alone.

She lowered her lids and her breathing slowed. Wrapping myself around her, I held her tightly, my tears wetting her shoulder and back. Her chest hardly moved, each breath coming slower and fainter. She took one long, shuddering breath that trembled through her entire body. I held her as she let out a slow exhalation and passed from life into death.

Head bowed, I too exhaled. Part of me wanted to follow the child into the afterlife, but I could not linger. Dawn was approaching, and the survival of my empire remained uncertain. I fed the fire, using the grass mat upon which the child lay and the pile of dry cloth. They served well as kindling, catching quickly and spreading the flames to the roof even before I was out of the hut. By the time I reached the river, tendrils of fire were shooting into the night sky.

Warning cries rose through the darkness. I made my way northward along the riverbank. Distracted by the fire, the soldiers didn't notice me scrambling downhill, and I avoided detection until—

"You, stop!" A soldier ran toward me.

There was nothing for it. Shivering at the mere thought, I plunged into the cold, choppy river. A gasp formed in my throat but was drowned by water filling my mouth. Immediately, the current swept me away while I tried desperately to keep my head above the surface. Again, the water tugged me under. Moments might have been days as I struggled against the frigid river. My chest grew tight, my muscles screamed, and I tussled with the river, which dragged me farther down.

Caught in the belly of the current, I tried to fight my way upward. The distorted shape of the moon shone like a beacon above me. But even as I tried to reach it, the surface retreated. The river was stronger than me. It refused to let me go. My chest burned for breath; my body demanded air. I was drowning.

Suddenly, the angry water pressed me on all sides, buoying me in its swell. As my head broke the surface, I inhaled a mouthful of air. Then I was racing downstream. The ride was swift, cold, and terrifying. I knew it wasn't my own power keeping me afloat. It certainly wasn't my own power that pushed me toward the western bank and weaker currents. I was not a child of the waters.

"Thank you, Kogi-Ayu," I whispered, half swimming and half crawling to the water's edge. After the rage of the river, I was happy to fall facedown onto the hard, unmoving earth.

I lay still, thankful to breathe even the dirt under my face. It wasn't until Demon began tugging at my tunic that I climbed to my feet and pulled my exhausted bones into the saddle. Secure on Demon's back, I looked to where the river meandered down the slope. The trip up the mountain had taken three hours, but the river had returned me in minutes.

I slumped in the saddle. "I'm tired, warhorse."

Silent as a breeze, Demon took off toward the battlefield.

FORTY-THREE

The camp was on fire, the night aglow with flames. The sight of burning huts and charred carcasses chilled my heart, bringing a bitter and familiar taste to my mouth. Despair. Just like the battle against the Western Alliance. This time, Karama would not arrive to save the day.

Twelve thousand Kwararafa fought what remained of my army, which was—thank the gods—much of it. They'd woken in time but had not rallied fast enough to prevent the horses being slaughtered. The Kuturun Mahayi were on foot, fighting hard. Longbowmen without bows fought with swords or even the enemy's own weapons.

Tonight, it was not difficult to tell friend from foe. Those of my warriors in full armor stood out from the rest, firelight reflected off chain mail vests. Even without armor, my warriors were easy to spot among the swarm of Kwararafa soldiers. Our bare-chested enemies fought without battle gear, some with little more than a loincloth. And they fought like creatures from hell. With their bodies aflicker in the flames, they *looked* like creatures from hell.

The rush of battle pushed fatigue from my bones. I donned my war bracelets, unhooked my takouba from the horse's saddle, and rode into combat, screaming my own war cry.

A spear bounced off Demon's hide. I turned to hack at the nearest Kwararafa, all but severing his head from his neck. They came at me in a wave. I cut down one warrior and another. A third man, face distorted with rage, tried to yank me from my seat but fell to a blow from my war bracelet. The night's exertions had drained me. My movements were slow, almost clumsy. And there were so many of them. As one soldier fell, two more rushed to fill the space.

Demon reared, coming down on a Kwararafa neck. I kicked at a spear, then at the spearman's face. The man went down, but others swooped in behind him. Battle-axes swung at Demon from all directions. He ignored the fruitless blows as he stampeded over a cluster of half-nude warriors.

A man lunged for me. He caught Demon's mane. I swung my blade, and the weapon arced through emptiness. The man's hand still clung to the horse's hair, but the rest of him was gone, lost to the invisible Dangoji. I let out a shuddering breath, overwhelmed by relief at the imp's presence. My reflection ended abruptly when a machete hurtled toward me. Demon veered to the side. Despite the shouts of warriors, the whinnying of horses, the clang of metal, and shrieks of death, the sound of that machete swooshing past my head was deafening.

A warrior's roar reached my ears. He swung a battle-axe and I raised my sword to block it. His weapon met mine with such force that it jolted my arm. I dropped the blade. Pivoting in the saddle, I leapt to the ground. The battle-axe swung again and missed, as I fell to my knees at the warrior's feet. His weapon came down for another pass. I snatched my sword off the ground and held it over my head, one hand on the blade, the other on the grip. I cried out at the impact, the blade cutting into the flesh of my palm. The battle-axe rose again. I had to move, get out of the way, because I didn't think I could block the next strike. But my legs were like boulders. Angry, impatient snorts sounded behind me. I tucked into a crouch.

Demon sailed overhead, shattering my opponent's body under his hooves. I climbed to my feet. Around me, Dangoji tore the Kwararafa apart. Warriors fell in pools of glistening guts.

A sharp pain in my side forced my attention away from Dangoji's work. I was vulnerable without armor, but the spear tip had glanced off my lowest rib, leaving a deep gash. The spearman jabbed again. I pivoted backward, grimacing as I snatched the spear's shaft. The man came forward with the weapon, and I ran my blade through his belly.

The Kwararafa plowed through us in an endless stream of warriors. I spun this way and that, trying to face my attackers. Three, five, twenty of them, I couldn't tell in the dizzying flurry of bodies. Demon was at my rear, unearthly sounds bellowing from his throat. Spontaneous eviscerations marked Dangoji's presence, and it occurred to me that he'd been near since my arrival on the field. Not bolting between me and Jaruma. Did that mean . . . No. It didn't mean anything. Where in hell *was* Jaruma?

Metal glinted in my periphery, and I sliced to the right. A warrior fell. Another warrior raised a battle-axe. He swung and I jumped out of reach as a short-sword bore down on me. Parrying the sword, I ducked another pass of the axe and stumbled into a broad back. The Zazzagawa soldier spun around. Recognition lit his eyes before he pushed me out of the way. I regained my balance in time to watch him fall to his knees, a spear lodged in his chest.

He had taken that spear for me, sacrificed his life for mine. They were *all* sacrificing their lives for mine. Since the first time I had set eyes on the Kwararafa, men had died. Because of me. How many more? How many more of my people would die before this night was through?

The spearman, five or six paces from me, yanked his weapon from my warrior's chest. With a shriek tearing from my lips, I advanced on him. One of his comrades stepped into my path. I hollowed his face with my bracelet before he could raise his weapon. Another ran at me, and I slashed his legs from under him. Still shrieking, I continued the advance. The spearman lunged. His metal burrowed into my shoulder, but I felt no pain as I jabbed at him. He staggered back, blood streaking his belly. To my left, a thick machete sliced down. My arm flew up to block the attack.

The blow of the machete against my war bracelet sent a shock of hot pain shooting up my arm. I clenched my teeth against the jolt, my fingers going numb. Blood flowed freely where the enemy's curved blade had cut through linen and into flesh.

This time, I couldn't ignore the pain; every movement drove my war bracelet into the wound. Half-naked enemy soldiers surrounded me. I swung my blade, grunting my agony. Demon circled around me and kicked at a Kwararafa skull.

My left arm was useless. The war bracelet entrenched in my wrist sent continuous coils of pain through me, but that didn't slow the enemy. A loincloth-clad warrior faced me. I tried to counter his short-sword but was too slow. I cried out as his weapon sliced into my thigh. He drew back, pressed forward, and struck low. The sword met the bone of my shin. I fell to one knee.

My life would end here. Mine and those of my people. The Kwararafa took no prisoners. They would raid the city and kill everyone in it. All because of me. Because I failed to stop them. *Gods above, please don't let it end this way.* But what could they do? Kogi-Ayu had given me the means to triumph, and I'd failed. With both hands sinking into bloodied mud, I tried to rise, tried pushing to my feet. I raised my head—death would look me in the eye when it took me— and the tip of an arrow appeared in my opponent's shoulder.

The warrior stumbled, righted himself, and glanced at his shoulder. He took a step forward, and another. A second arrowhead appeared below his collarbone. He continued forward. Sword raised, he let out a roar. His body jerked. The sword slipped from his grip and landed in the mud at my fingertips. The man fell.

Jaruma stood behind him, blood-drenched knife in hand. Her eyes darted to my bleeding arm. I saw her mouth move, saw her step toward me, but heard only a loud crack.

I toppled onto my side, jarring the already injured arm. A scream streaked from my throat but exited my mouth as a wet gurgle. My chest was tight. Too tight to breathe. Though I struggled to inhale, my ribs would not expand. The bare feet of Kwararafa warriors scuffled with the sandaled feet of the Zazzagawa. Black hooves stomped and kicked, circling me. I rolled onto my back. My chest clicked with inhalation, bitter pain shooting through me. It clicked again as I slowly let out the breath.

Disoriented by pain, I closed my fingers over the grip of my takouba and rose to my knees. A barefoot warrior burst through Demon's circle. I slashed wildly at the man's legs, managing only to gouge his calf before falling back into the dirt. Hoisting his spear in both hands, he made to ram the thing through me. Dangoji struck. Blood spurted from the man's mouth and nose.

Jaruma was at my side. She grabbed my arm and dragged me to my feet. "Get on the horse!"

I wanted to protest, but no words came from my mouth—the pain in my chest so intense that I couldn't even scream.

"Amina!" She shoved me into Demon's flank. "You've lost too much blood!"

It was only then that I noticed the red soaking my tunic. I raised my arm. Rivulets of blood flowed from the wound in my wrist. She snatched the takouba out of my hand and climbed into the saddle. Someone on the ground hefted me onto the horse with one shove, and I sprawled behind her. Again, the breath stuck in my frozen chest.

Demon started moving. First a walk, then a canter. The spirit horse was like fluid beneath me, cushioning my clicking ribcage.

"No, I must stay." I tried to rise, but could not summon the energy. I lay there, eyes half-closed until yellow daylight forced them open.

The sun was rising.

The roar of the Jamaa're River reached my ears over the noise of fighting. We were still in the thick of it. Demon quickened to a trot, then a full gallop. And he charged forward, trampling the enemy in his path. I heard Jaruma's war cries, heard her clash of swords, and saw that my own weapon was harnessed to the saddle.

An enemy soldier seized my leg. I'd not the strength to shake him off, so I let go of the saddle's harness. Jaruma twisted backward, as I slid off Demon's back.

She jumped from the saddle.

My war bracelets were my only weapons, and my left arm was out of action. With a last, desperate influx of energy, I swung my right arm maniacally, splitting the forehead of one enemy who ventured too close. The tip of a spear came into view, and my gaze followed the weapon to the warrior's face. His eyes, at first gleaming with hatred, went dull as my takouba sprang out from between his ribs.

Jaruma pulled the sword free and tossed it to me. The man's blood trailed from the blade as it sailed through the air. I caught the weapon. Not too deftly, but in time to hack savagely at another spearman.

"Get back on the damned horse!" Jaruma shouted, dispatching my opponent.

If she continued coming after me like this, I'd be even more of a hindrance. So I obeyed and, with her assistance, climbed into the saddle. Demon shot forward, barreling through enemy soldiers. When the river came into view, he drew to a stop.

"*Wallahi*," I said under my breath.

Three wide raft bridges, anchored in place with poles and ropes, spanned the river. The Kwararafa had built them as we slept. Thousands of enemy soldiers crowded onto the bridges, with thousands more waiting on the other side.

While we'd had our sights trained on the twelve thousand soldiers coming across the plains, we had missed thousands that had climbed through the mountains. *Like invisible flies.* Theirs was a clever ploy. As we had fought to exhaustion, these reserves had maneuvered the bridges into place.

On this side of the bridge, bowmen and a brush fire held the enemy at bay. My bowmen shot flaming arrows across the river. The Kwararafa shot back, taking a few of us down. Another volley of flaming arrows left my warriors' bows, but without enough fodder to keep it alive, the brush fire was dwindling rapidly. Our arrows would not hold the enemy off for much longer. There were simply too few of us.

I wanted to scream in frustration but couldn't gather enough air. After all, *after all*, we would still die here. Everything was for nothing. It might have been better to die in our sleep. Better to die without knowing that everything we loved, everything for which we'd striven, would all be wiped out by these near-naked warriors who fought without fear, without mercy.

No. That could never be better. Though Death hounded the Zazzagawa, we'd drag these bastards to the netherhells with us.

The first group of Kwararafa spilled off the bridges. My bowmen shot into the throng, renocked, and shot again. The enemy fell, but many made it across. They attacked us with a vengeance. I rode into the fray, acutely aware that mortality hid beneath my youthful facade. My uncle had once thought me yan tauri, but I'd already proven that blades could pierce my skin easily and often. Several hundred blades awaited me at that river. And it was an honorable way to die.

A creaking sound nudged the fringes of my awareness. The steady *creak-creak, creak-creak, creak-creak* didn't sound like the noise of battle. It was like the groan of a beating heart.

The bridges.

They bobbed up and down in choppy water that had been calm only a moment ago. A thunderous rumble filled the air, followed by loud shouts from the soldiers on the bridges. The warriors fighting on the riverbank paused, and we all—friend and foe—turned to look upriver.

The Jamaa're had swollen to a bulge. It heaved, pushing a monstrous wave ahead of it, rocking the bridges. The wave crashed into the water and heaved again to form an even bigger wave. Explosive in its fury and growing larger by the second, it plummeted downstream.

"Run," I tried to shout but didn't have the lungs.

Warriors scrambled and Demon carried me away from the growing wall of liquid. Terrified shouts came from behind. Then came the water. It hurtled down on the bridges, shattering the wooden rafts like kindling under a giant's foot. A jagged chunk of wood flew past my head.

"Amina!"

I didn't know how I heard Jaruma's voice through the din, but I rode toward it. Demon slowed just enough for her to hoist herself precariously onto him. When the river was well behind us, we stopped to survey the damage.

Splintered pieces of floating debris were all that was left of the bridges. The river had poured over its eastern bank, sweeping the Kwararafa into its wet embrace. What enemies still lingered didn't dare swim across the wrathful water. Instead, they scrambled away from the water's edge.

The rivergod had evened the field.

No longer outnumbered, we rallied for another stand—possibly our last—against our most infamous foe. Unable to raise my arms, I mostly clung to Demon and let him and Dangoji and Jaruma fight for me.

If we lost this battle, we lost everything. So the Zazzagawa fought like tomorrow didn't matter. In their berserker madness, they cut the Kwararafa down. The battlefield was drenched in blood. Bodies of soldiers sprawled where they fell atop one another. The sun, long risen, cowered behind a thick cloud.

Having spent myself simply by staying in the saddle, I had no strength left. I fell off Demon's back. The last thing I saw was Jaruma's face as she bent toward me.

FORTY-FOUR

I was drowning.

Coughing, gasping, struggling for air, I tried to open my eyes but could not.

"Amina. Amina, wake."

My eyes opened a sliver. Jaruma knelt beside me. She put down the small bowl of water she was tipping to my mouth, grasped my shoulders, and shook me gently. My brow rose as I forced my lids apart.

"Jaruma." My throat was parched. Scratchy and painful.

"Yes. I'm here."

Memories of the battle returned but only in bits and pieces. "What's happened?" I was having trouble keeping my eyes open. "The Kwararafa?"

"Are defeated."

There was a sharp pain in my chest. I winced.

"Easy, Amina. Your ribs were broken."

The day's events began to come clear. A bludgeon to the chest and the war bracelet digging into my flesh. I raised my left arm. The linen dressing wrapped around my wrist and forearm had a small dark patch where blood had leaked through. The pain, however, was considerably dulled.

"The cut was deep. It will be slow to heal," Jaruma said. "Last night, in delirium, you opened the wound. I'll give you new dressing after you eat." She put the bowl to my lips. "Drink now."

The water was cold but did not soothe my aching throat. I pushed her hand away and attempted to sit but balked at the pain in my ribs. "Help me."

She took my hand. Supporting me with an arm under my back, she raised me until I was sitting erect. The bandages around my chest restricted my breathing, so I took one shallow breath after another and leaned against her.

It was over. Finally over. The Kwararafa were truly defeated. They wouldn't be back. Not in this generation. Not when so many of their warriors lay dead on either side of the Jamaa're.

I looked down at myself and noticed that I was naked. "Where are my clothes?" My hand rose to my chest and absently rubbed the coarse linen bandaging my ribs.

"They were ruined. Too far gone for washing and mending. Besides, you've had a fever for three days. I've been bathing you with cool water."

"Three days?" The hoarse exclamation was a strain on my throat. Regaining some coordination, I straightened until I was sitting on my own. Small aches and pains came to life throughout my body.

"Three days," she said.

The melancholy in her response made me fear asking the next question: how had my warriors fared? From what I could remember of the battle, Zazzagawa numbers had steadily dwindled. For every one of *them* we dispatched, one of us fell.

"How—" I began. *How many dead?* I wanted to ask but couldn't bear to hear the answer.

Before I could steel myself to broach the subject again, Jaruma spoke. "We moved the camp farther south. Medicine men are tending the wounded, and I've been tending you."

Cloth covered the doorway of the grass hut in which we sat. Outside, the sky was bright and the sun beat down on the little domicile, keeping the temperature within from cooling effectively.

"It's no wonder I was fevered," I muttered under my breath.

She sat back and hugged her knees to her chest, regarding me with a blank expression. After a time, she spoke again. Quietly. "I thought you might not come through the fever. You lost so much blood and you were so ill. I prayed to your patron even though he's not in the business of sparing lives."

I put a hand on her knee. "Perhaps someone heard you."

She covered my hand with hers.

"I was ready to die, Jaruma. I thought I was going to die, that we would *all* die. That makes being alive so much sweeter." *And so much harder.* Why had I survived when so many of my warriors had not?

She inhaled deeply, knitted brow and quivering lips speaking her sadness. "Our victory is bittersweet. You didn't see it, but we were like animals in the end. No mercy at all."

I'd seen most of it. The Kwararafa would have massacred us had we given them the opportunity. And *they* wouldn't have shown mercy.

I said, "Remember who we were fighting."

"We lost so many." Her shoulders sagged under an invisible weight.

This woman had witnessed so many battles, fought in so many battles. Like her brother before her, she had lived for the fight. Seeing her so affected put a sharp pain in my heart. Again, I wondered how badly we'd fared. This time, I couldn't ignore the question.

"How many Zazzagawa remain?" I asked. We'd gone to war with fourteen thousand soldiers. By the time Kogi-Ayu had made his appearance at the river, there had been, perhaps, four thousand of us left. How many more had died?

"Three thousand."

My heart stopped. "Three thousand more dead?"

"Survived. You asked how many remained."

I exhaled. "Yes. Yes, that's right." My spirits rose, though they didn't soar. Three thousand still alive was considerably better than only one thousand. "Aside from you, what officers remain?"

"Only Zuma."

So Zuma had lived to see justice meted out to those who had massacred his family. That was a good thing.

I nodded. "His vengeance is served. He must be glad."

"Glad to be alive," she agreed. "He says it's his last battle. *Was* his last battle." Absently, her hand rose to her head. She rubbed it across the top of her cropped hair and down the back of her neck. "I don't blame him. Too many lost their lives."

I squeezed her knee. I didn't blame Zuma either. Watching friends, comrades, good men and women die was more than sobering. It showed one the fragility of life.

"They won't be forgotten, Jaruma. You know that." I suddenly realized she had said *only Zuma*. I asked, "What of Bashiru?"

This time, she didn't answer. Instead, she broke down in tears.

For several painful breaths, I stared as she sobbed into her hands. Surely the man wasn't dead? He was too flippant, too self-assured. And he was yan tauri. He'd been in the army nearly thirty years and had never so much as suffered a scratch. It was impossible that he had died on the battlefield.

Except Jaruma's tears, which flowed but rarely, told me otherwise.

A hard lump rose in my already sore throat. "Jaruma, I'm sorry." But words carried no weight against such grief.

"For what?" She attempted a smile.

"For bringing us here. For war."

I wanted to apologize for everyone who had died under my leadership. From those fifty men in the mountain to the little girl in the hut to Bashiru. Even Bashiru. I'd not much liked him, but *she* had. If I could have done it, I would have rewritten the past to ease her sorrow.

She attempted the smile again but did not succeed. "You did nothing wrong, Amina. And he died a good death."

Was there really such a thing as a good death? Dafaru had once said the dead had no use for honor. What then remained? The living and their grief? There was nothing good in that.

I squeezed her knee again. "I'm sorry you're suffering. I'm so very sorry he wasn't yan tauri."

Straightening her back, she drew her eyebrows together and raised her chin. "But he was, Amina. He was yan tauri."

My mouth fell open. I closed it.

She had never believed in yan tauri. To her, those who claimed imperviousness to metal were lying braggarts. Bashiru was no exception. As far as she was concerned, his uncanny ability to walk away unscathed from battle was nothing more than luck. In death, he'd proven her right. He was not impervious to metal. Her change of heart was not only surprising, it was irrational. My own brow furrowed in silent query.

Dropping her knees into a cross-legged position, she fussed with something at her waist. When she faced me again, she held the thing out to me. I took it from her and scrutinized it.

At first, I thought it was made from ivory, but closer inspection revealed it was made from bone. From the tip of its slightly curved blade to its leather-wrapped hilt, the dagger had been carved from an animal's bone. Or perhaps from a man's. Both edges of the blade were sharpened to precision, and the tip was a fine point. Foreign symbols were etched into the blade. Runes? Words of power? The owner's name?

"No metal touched him." She took the weapon from me.

Incredulous, I stared at the knife in her hand. Then I chuckled, ceased abruptly with a paroxysm of coughing, and rubbed my throat. "Leave it to that man to hold true to his bragging."

She put the knife back in its holster and brought the water back to my mouth. "Yes. Leave it to Bashiru . . . Drink. And I will bring you something to eat."

Perhaps the dead were beyond caring for such things as honor. But the legacies they left behind bore testament to the characters they had possessed in life. Bashiru's morals had been questionable, and mine were worse. It was up to the living to find honor in the dead.

I took the bowl from her, set it aside, and caught both of her hands in mine. "He died an honorable death, Jaruma. A good death."

"He did." She nodded. "He died a good death.

FORTY-FIVE

City of Zaria, Kingdom of Zazzau, Central Hausaland, circa 1606 CE

Defeating the Kwararafa had taken the thorn from my side once and for all. Over the next six years, Zazzau's reach spread to all the territory around the mountain kingdoms and we entered our golden era. However, as my contemporaries marched into the setting sun alongside their empires, time did not shine its beacon on me. I remained unchanged. Jaruma was unchanged. And those around us grew white with age.

Fatima, a child when she had come to serve me, was now fifty years old. Her sons by the old nobleman had inherited considerable wealth from their father. With it, they had purchased her freedom. Freedom notwithstanding, she remained in the palace as the head of my household servants, managing palace affairs with extraordinary aplomb.

"The makama has sent for you." She bent down to load my used earthenware onto a wooden tray. Her maturity had brought with it a stateliness and grace that were evident in her movements, in her speech. Or perhaps it was simply the palace airs at work in her demeanor.

I made a point of looking irritated with knitted brow and downturned lips. "The makama is too familiar with me. He sends for me often and for no reason."

"Yet you always go to him."

"You are also too familiar."

She countered with an insolent shrug.

Siddhi was seventy-five years old and senility had set in. On some days, he was a doddering fool who spent a fair portion of his time reminiscing on youth and all his regrets. On other days, on those days when I couldn't bear to be with him, he didn't remember his own name.

It tormented me to see him reduced to such a pathetic creature. Siddhi's mind was gnarled, his eyes almost always dull. More often than not, our conversations were pointless. Yet when he called, I went to him.

"Should I send word that you're coming?" Fatima's voice shook me out of my sullen reverie.

I sighed. "Tell him I'll be there after the council meeting."

❦

It was already past midday when court and council ended in the capital city of Zaria. Riding Demon, I made my way to Turunku and to Siddhi's abode. His guards greeted me at the gate. Demon they ignored, having learned many years ago that it was best to leave the horse to his own devices.

Siddhi sat slumped on his diwan, dozing, when I entered the chamber. I touched his shoulder. He woke with bright eyes, alert and full of life. He was whole of mind. Our visit would be a good one. I sat in a chair opposite him.

The faint lines of a smile appeared at the corners of his mouth. "Where's Jaruma?"

I raised a brow. "Am I her keeper?"

His sharp look of disapproval made me laugh.

He said, "You should be. She always knows where *you* are."

"She's my bodyguard."

He snorted. "When was the last time she guarded your body?" His eyes moved over the length of me.

"Even in old age, you are a foolish man, Siddhi."

"I've been foolish all my life. Why should I change now?"

I shook my head in mock chastisement. "You look well. Why were you not in council?"

"My dear." He rubbed the back of his neck as he heaved himself to a sitting position. "You are very much aware that I'm *not* well."

"Not well, indeed. You're using old age as an excuse to laze about. Your predecessor, your uncle, died in the council chambers. He was no layabout oaf."

Hearty laughter filled the room, warming me from the inside. It was good to hear Siddhi's jollity. Too many times I'd visited and a sad stranger had stared through his eyes.

His laughter ended with a quick cough. "You're a terrible liar."

"You know nothing of my silver tongue. I've convinced the new kaura."

"That my uncle died in council?"

"Indeed."

"Then your new kaura must be an idiot. Are you certain you want him leading your troops?"

I smirked. "He's adequate, *my dear*."

"Ah, to hear such endearments slide from your silver tongue. You are truly the queen of my heart. Speaking of my heart," he said before I could give a retort. "Mine isn't as strong as it used to be."

"What are you saying?" I leaned forward and put a hand on his chest. The heartbeat against my palm was irregular and not at all strong. Disguising my consternation, I said, "You have many years before this heart ceases to function. Look at Tsoede. He was old when we first met him. Surely he'll die before you."

"That man's life is extended by witchcraft." His bitterness made it evident that he would not have minded a little witchcraft for himself. Out of his funk as quickly as he had entered, he asked, "Where did you say your friend has gone?"

"Would you rather be with Jaruma? I'm sure we can locate her."

"Come now, love." He placed his hand on top of mine and twined our fingers. "There is no one I'd rather be with." Eyes sparkling, he winked at me.

"The exertion may kill you, Siddhi."

"And what a way to die." His other hand joined our two entwined.

"You *are* a foolish man." With my free hand, I stroked the white beard covering his chin. "You know I hate this thing."

"Other women tell me it's becoming."

"Other women lie."

He began to laugh, and I squeezed his hand.

"You never told me." His eyes were still vibrant.

"Told you what?"

"Why you refused me for so long and with such vehemence against my dogged determination." He inclined his head. "You once loved me, did you not? Surely it wasn't only in my dreams."

I groaned and pulled my hand from his beard to drop it back onto my lap. "Why do you worry me with such questions? How long has it been since you loved me?"

"When did I stop loving you, my queen? Knowing that you breathe the same air as me makes every breath sweeter."

"Eloquent words, Makama."

He once had nothing but eloquent words for me.

Freeing our fingers, he caressed my arm. His touch, always gentle, sent a wave of nostalgia through me.

"Such discussions are not productive," I said.

"Not for you, perhaps. But for me? It would lighten some of the load on my heart."

"It would do nothing but increase your burden." I drew my arm away from him.

"Not so, my dear."

I sighed. "Can we not discuss more mundane matters?"

"Such as?"

I regarded him in silent consideration, then said with a nod, "Exports. All of our transactions went well this season."

"Yes." Clasping his hands over his belly, he slouched in his chair. "Quite mundane."

I relented with another sigh. "I cared too deeply for you, Siddhi. Such feelings were dangerous then. You know the fate of my . . . my . . ."

"Temporary husbands?"

I detested that term.

"The last requests of already condemned men," Siddhi said. "That has been an interesting strategy. How many did you grant over the years? Fifteen? Twenty? Could any of them fill the empty spaces of your heart?"

"Eighteen." The last had been more than a year ago. Flashing him a sly look, I added, "It wasn't my heart that needed filling."

More laughter from Siddhi and another round of coughing. It took a while for him to catch his breath. "So, your feelings for me were dangerous then. And now?"

"And now what, old man?" Amused, I gazed at him.

"And now I'm so near death that your love will hardly bring me any closer to it."

Old, weak, tired, and that abominable beard. Yet he was as pretty as he had ever been. And he wanted to seduce me.

A rush of affection welled in me. "You're talking nonsense, Siddhi."

"Though you love another, my heart still belongs to you." He leveled a contemplative look upon me. "But I've not asked you here to discuss your inclination for war . . ."

He was more clearheaded than I'd supposed.

"Or even to discuss my feelings for you." He sat up straighter, his levity returning.

"Then what is it?"

"I wish to propose a new makama."

I cleared my throat. "Siddhi, I need no other if you would simply come to council."

"You jest, Amina." His voice evinced no mirth. "Whether you like it or not, my queen, I'm dying."

"Siddhi . . ."

"You have an administrator in Zaria. Gowon. The man you moved from Turunku."

"What of him?"

"He's very organized."

"And?"

"Is he a free man?"

An unclear picture of the man in question rose to my mind, but I'd moved three administrators into Zaria and couldn't remember which one had come from Turunku. Nor was I certain which one of them was freeborn. Or which was called Gowon.

"If he's a slave, free him," Siddhi said. "He's best suited to serve in my position. You should announce it at the next council meeting."

My eyes narrowed. He stared back, unblinking.

I said, "This is your desire?"

"It is my request, Amina. In all the years I've served you, I've requested very little, if anything at all."

There was no refuting that.

"He's more than capable, my dear. He'll serve you well."

I took a deep breath and let it out slowly through my mouth, reflecting on a request that sounded more like an order. At length, I said, "You've always given excellent advice. Of course, I'll take it now."

"You are such an obedient woman." He leaned back to slouch in his seat once again.

"Don't make me change my mind, old man."

He laughed.

There were several questions that needed answers before I approached the council with the declaration of a new makama. I made a quick mental list and began prattling it off, one item after the other.

"The man, obviously, can read and write," I said. "And you know he doesn't have to be free to hold the position. Don't worry, Siddhi, if he isn't already, he'll be a free man. I'll free them all. Has he any wealth? Property? Does it need to be provided him? Siddhi?"

I looked at him. His head was tilted to the side—almost limp—with eyes half-closed. *Still so pretty.* I leaned in to kiss his cheek. He opened his eyes and grasped the back of my neck, drawing me forward. As I fell against him, our lips pressed together in a crushing lock. His heartbeat, still irregular, pounded against his breast to reverberate in mine. The grip on my neck loosened.

"You're a madman, Siddhi," I said with a chuckle.

He didn't respond.

I sat back. "Too much activity for one day, eh?"

Still, no response.

I stared at him. The light in his eyes began to dim. It went dark. His eyebrows squeezed together, his mouth opened and shut several times as he sought the word he already knew but couldn't speak. My face fell.

"Amina," I reminded him in a whisper.

"Amina?"

The way he spoke my name, familiar yet unfamiliar, was painful to hear.

"I know you." He looked so confused. "Yes. Yes. But why are you so young?"

I clenched my eyes shut, struggling to keep the moisture from escaping. My tears would not be staunched. As they trickled down my cheeks, I raised a hand to my face. My belly strained from tension, and I rocked back and forth, trying to regain control. After a few quiet sniffles, I took a deep breath, exhaled, wiped away the tears, and stood.

Bending low, I took his face in my hands and kissed him, holding my lips to his mouth for several long moments. Then I touched my forehead to his. "I am not young, Siddhi."

FORTY-SIX

The god of war sat in the pavilion of the stone palace. There was something odd about him that I couldn't place. I strode forward, rolling my neck to ease the tension from my visit with Siddhi. Taking my hand, Dafaru drew me onto his lap.

"What troubles you, Beloved?"

Whenever my husband was near, it seemed nothing on earth could hurt me, but the pain of Siddhi's deterioration was beyond the wargod's touch. I rested my head on his shoulder. "Life presses onward. Without me."

"Your thoughts are on that fool of a makama." His overly controlled tone belied his irritation.

I straightened to pierce him with an appropriately searing look. "He is dying."

The revelation did not stifle the wargod's annoyance. He looked back at me with churning eyes.

"All around me . . ." My voice faltered. "Those who are closest to me grow old and die. Siddhi is dying. Then it will be Zariya. And Fatima."

But it would never be me. Never Jaruma. Six years out, her misery at losing Bashiru was still tangible. It weighed her down. I rarely saw her now except in official capacity. Most of the time, she locked herself away in her private quarters. I couldn't help but think the heaviness in her heart was my fault.

Dafaru said, "She made the choice of her own free will."

"I made it for her."

"I follow where you lead, Gimbiya," he said, repeating the words Jaruma had spoken so many years ago.

"And where have I led her? She's alone, my lord."

"She has you." The furrow in his brow deepened. "Does she *want* to grow old?"

I shook my head. "I don't know. But it's difficult to watch others die, knowing you may never taste the sweetness of oblivion."

He looked almost apologetic. "You cannot age, my love, but Death creeps nearer nonetheless. It may yet catch you unawares."

"Morbid words, Husband. Perhaps I should ask what's troubling *you.*"

His turbulent gaze was especially agitated as he fixed it on a distant point. "In your grief, you leave your heart and mind open. Tell me why you still have such feelings for him."

"For who? Siddhi?"

His eyes berated me, though no words came from his mouth.

"We are friends, he and I. Companions. Nothing more. You would know if there was anything more."

"Is it merely companionship that puts you in this deep melancholy?"

"Have I given you reason to doubt my affection for you?"

"Affection. Is that what it is?"

"It is whatever you say it is. I'm yours to command."

"Yet it is I who serve *you.*"

It was tempting, but I wasn't fool enough to laugh. "I wouldn't presume to call you my servant. I am mortal . . . and a woman. As you never fail to remind me, it is not in my power to command gods."

"Your presumptions do not matter to my father, Beloved. He says it is so, thus it is so."

"Your father?"

He uttered a blasphemous string of words and said, "Your Creator took notice of the affair at the Jamaa're."

"Affair?" I struggled to keep my voice neutral. "Twenty thousand warriors lost their lives at that *affair.*"

"Kogi broke certain covenants by coming to your rescue."

"He shouldn't have done it."

"Had he not done it, you would have perished that day. You, your people, your empire."

"If it was our destiny to perish—"

"Quiet, woman."

"My lord, I don't want to be the cause of discord among gods."

His laughter echoed across the mountaintop. "There has always been discord among the gods. You are hardly the cause of it, my arrogant queen." He smirked at my indignation. "Though I do suspect—purely suspicion, of course—that my brother may be a little in love with you."

The words gave me a start. A flush of embarrassment rose up my neck to my ears, and I averted my gaze from eyes that saw too freely what was in my soul.

"Do not worry yourself about my brother," he said with a chuckle. "He is the spirit of rivers, is he not? His essence is fluid. It touches, tastes, and loves everything. Easily and often."

"Except when it doesn't," I said dryly, recalling stories of Ayu, the wicked aspect of the rivergod.

"Undoubtedly. As you have seen, Kogi can be as ruthless as the rest of us."

With his fingers, he traced the outline of my chin, the column of my neck. Heat rose between us and around us.

He said, "He has stripped me of some power."

"Who's done what?" I asked, pulling away from him.

He tried to draw me back into an embrace and sighed when I resisted.

"I no longer have the power to protect you. Barely a blink from my father and Dangoji ceased to exist."

Before the war against Kwararafa, Dafaru had mentioned the Creator waking. The revelation hadn't provoked any thought in me then, and it hadn't occurred to me that He could take Dafaru's power. But Ubangiji was the God of gods. All powerful. He could do anything. I glanced down at the ebony arm resting across my thighs and realized that the arm was bare. *That* was the difference I'd noticed upon seeing him. He was without his bracers.

I took hold of his forearm with both hands. "I'm sorry."

"For what, Beloved? The sin was mine. I would change nothing, for I am still not ready to let you go."

Sadness cut through me like a knife. I pressed a kiss to his temple.

"I must tell you," he said. "I do not have the power to influence a man's mind. If any wish to do you harm, I can no longer dissuade them."

"No *longer?*" I blinked several times, as the implication of what he'd said came clear. "Assassins? *Assassins?*" I jumped to my feet.

"Beloved—"

"How many times?" I began pacing.

"Amina—"

"How often have men risen against me?" I halted just long enough to see the darkening color in his eyes.

He quelled the brewing storm and rose to his feet. "Not often, my love. Not to the point that their intentions were clear to me."

"Why didn't you tell me?"

"Why would I?"

I gave him a blistering look and stomped over to the mountain's edge.

Joining me there, he said, "I am telling you now only because I cannot protect you. The Creator has taken away my power over conflict. If conflict comes, you will be on your own."

"And the rivergod?" I feared that Kogi-Ayu, who had always been kind to me, might also be punished for my sake. The guilt over thousands of mortal lives and one immortal were already on my head. I didn't know if I could carry the weight of yet another. And after his display at the Jamaa're, gods forbid that I find myself on the receiving end of Kogi-Ayu's wrath.

"We have our differences, Kogi and I. He owed me a debt and so gave me your life. I could not allow him to shoulder Father's fury for that. He is my brother, after all. I bear his punishment as well."

"Lord Husband, you suffer too much for me."

"I have suffered worse at Father's hands. Do not alarm yourself." He shrugged, one arm slipping around my waist. "Let us go to Jangare. There we can immerse ourselves in less dolorous matters."

"You tempt with pleasure, but eventually we will surface and these dolorous matters will be waiting."

"Hmm." His eyes cleared to reveal a scandalous image of the two of us. The devil was in his smile. "We shall put off surfacing for as long as your mortal body can withstand it."

※

We put off surfacing until dawn. Clearly, he didn't have to be in his aspect of War to wield his full divinity. The spirit that enveloped me, that rode and entered me was as powerful as it had ever been. When morning came, I wanted only to remain in his arms and damn the world. Alas, duties awaited me. I returned home.

My contentment faded quickly when I saw Jaruma sitting on the floor of my room, her face drawn, posture rigid.

"Jaruma? What is it?"

Her chest heaved, and my heart dropped into my belly.

"For the love of the ancestors, Jaruma, tell me what's happened."

"It's Siddhi."

My body sagged and I reached for the wall. "Is he . . ." I couldn't finish the question.

"Just before cockcrow."

"He's . . ." The words refused to budge.

After a while, she finished the sentence for me. "He's dead, Amina. Gone into the next life."

I slid down the wall to sit with my legs hugged tightly to my chest. I'd known this was coming, but the shock still tore at me. I put my fingers to my lips, where the man I'd once adored had kissed me. That man had been imprisoned behind the eyes of a confused stranger.

I stifled the sobs battering my chest. "Do you know if he was . . . *himself.*"

She shook her head. "He died in his sleep. Peaceful, they say. No fear or pain on his face." Her eyes were moist with tears that did not fall. "I think, perhaps, he died with his mind intact. I prefer to believe it was so."

I nodded emphatically.

Siddhi's death was not the first and certainly wouldn't be the last. One by one, they would go. Everyone we knew. The thought brought my sorrow to a head. Heavy tears rolled down my face.

Jaruma moved closer and put an arm around me. "He was old and his mind was in tatters. It's good that Death came for him before his mind betrayed him completely, before he grew too ill to remember even you."

I was very tired.

"We're also old, Jaruma. In here." My fingers tapping my chest gave off a hollow sound, as though nothing lived inside. "We're old."

"We are." She nodded. "I should have died many years ago."

"A hundred times over."

"Yet we live."

I took a deep breath to slow my tears. Jaruma sighed. We looked at one another.

"It's been too long," she said. "I'm tired of living."

"What are you saying?"

"Don't cry for Siddhi." She used her palm to wipe the tears from my face. "He is at rest. It is you and I who must go on fighting daily. There's no rest for us." With that, she kissed me lightly on the lips, got up, and left the room.

FORTY-SEVEN

City of Zaria, Kingdom of Zazzau, Central Hausaland, circa 1609 CE

Three years after Siddhi's passing, the void he'd left in my life remained. There was no such void in the council, however. His chosen replacement was more than competent and transitioned easily into Siddhi's previous role without so much as a ripple. But he was not Siddhi. I couldn't exchange amused looks with him when the day's court ran long with petty complaints of man against neighbor. And there was an abundance of accusations at this morning's court. Without Siddhi to share my silent laughter, the complaints quickly became tedious.

"He stole an ear of corn!"

"His son seduced my virgin daughter!"

"My crops don't grow because his magic diverts the waters to his farm alone!"

To bicker over an ear of corn was ludicrous, and it was just as likely that the girl seduced the boy. As for the crops, the season had been harsh, and the rains were already late. If anyone had water for farming, it was a well-guarded secret.

After the session of denunciations concluded, it was time for the annual tribute. I sat with hands on knees, tapping my foot impatiently as the vassals brought forth gifts. From time to time, my hand strayed to my temple to rub vigorously at a building headache, but I gave gracious thanks for each gift of grain, yams, butter, corn, livestock, and the like.

Then came Nupeland.

Eight representatives of that land were ushered into the pavilion. I dropped my fingers from my temple, straightened my posture, and bid them welcome. Their usual tribute included sizable gifts of kola nuts, slaves, cloth, and gold.

"Greetings, Fair Queen." The spokesman of the group gave a nervous bow. He was short for a man and thin—with billowing robes reminiscent of my waziri.

My eyes darted to the ever-elegant waziri and back to the Nupe emissary. "Greetings, Sir Emissary. What gifts does Nupeland bring?" Though I could see very well that they brought nothing.

The emissary glanced around furtively then bowed lower. "Ah, Your Majesty." The tremor in his voice betrayed his growing anxiety. "Our master and sovereign, the Great Etsu Nupe has ... ah ... decreed that there will be no ... ah ... tribute this year."

Murmurs echoed through the crowd, getting louder with each passing moment. I raised my hand for silence. The murmurs ceased.

I got to my feet and regarded the emissary before approaching him. He was even shorter than he looked from afar. When I stood directly before him, my line of sight passed over his head.

Unwilling or afraid to meet my gaze, he concentrated instead on wringing his hands while the rest of his party stood by impassively. Each lowered his gaze as I took measure of them. All but two. Those two did not look away, and there was no fear, anxiety, or even a hint of unease in their eyes. There was hatred. Raw, palpable hatred.

My sentiment reciprocated theirs, but I kept a neutral outward demeanor and returned my attention to the emissary. "Why has your master given such a decree?"

His focus shifted from me to his hands and back again. "We are Nupe." The words, which meant nothing to me, bolstered him. He raised his head, though he still refused to meet my gaze. "Tsoede bows to no woman."

Anger rose in my chest, but I maintained the outward calm. "I've not asked him to bow. But he's already sworn fealty. Does he wish now to dishonor himself by breaking the promises he made?"

"Your Majesty, Nupeland's fealty was extracted under extreme duress. Promises made under duress are not bound by law."

"Is that what your master says?"

"It's what the laws of Zazzau say. We are following your laws in this matter."

"Extreme duress, eh?" A cold, mirthless chuckle emerged from the pit of my stomach. "Your master says he was under extreme duress?"

The emissary didn't respond but looked to his comrades as if to make certain they'd not abandoned him.

The war with Kwararafa had drained Zazzau's resources, weakened my army, and Tsoede knew it. In the last two years, I'd twice sent representatives to Nupeland in response to his military fortifications, but I'd not the manpower to force him into compliance. And now this.

"Tsoede was under no duress when he pledged his allegiance," I said, raising my voice for all present to hear. I looked at each of the Nupemen. "He was neither coerced nor threatened into making promises. Your master was free to turn down my offer and do battle with Oyoland on his own. In that, he may have been victorious. We were more than willing to wait our turn."

One of the men with the hate-filled eyes stepped forward. "You make jest at the expense of our great sovereign."

This one was tall. Taller than me, taller even than Jaruma. The dark robes draping him from head to toe shadowed but did not conceal his features. All my rage, my disgust, I leveled on the man in a single look. He met me, contempt for contempt.

No one word could describe what the Nupe were to me. They were a pebble in my shoe, weevils in my grain, body lice, malcontents, rabble-rousers, schemers, and agitators.

I didn't hide my derision. "It was no jest, I assure you. Had I known that Tsoede's word was less than shit, I would have finished what the Oyo king began. I'll soon rectify that." My eyes swept across all eight Nupemen and, again, lingered on the tall one. "I will crush Tsoede. I will dismantle your cities and sell your people to *any* bidders.

And I'll be well rid of you." As I spoke the last word, I faced the emissary.

He took two hasty steps back, jostling the men behind him.

"You and your swine may leave my court." Spinning on my heels, I marched to my chair.

"My Queen?" The waziri gave me a hard look.

The men backed away from the throne.

"Let them go." Louder, I warned, "Whoever waylays these men will answer to me."

There were disgruntled mutterings among my officers, but none dared challenge the edict. The eight made their way out of the pavilion.

❋

Court was ended. Jaruma and Zariya waited quietly as the council members left the pavilion.

Zariya turned to me. "Was it wise to let them go?"

Jaruma strode forward. "Tsoede knew he sentenced his convoy to death when he sent them here with such a message. You should have killed them on the spot."

"To what end?" I asked tartly. "What harm can they do?"

"They could stir up trouble," Zariya said.

"There is no end to the harm they could do," Jaruma added, exchanging a glance with my sister. "I can send bowmen after them. Our fastest riders could intercept them before nightfall."

"No," I said.

"But, Amina . . ." Zariya slid to the edge of her seat.

"I said no, Zariya. Let them go on their way. Tsoede wants a battle—and rest assured I will not hesitate to give him one—but there is no need to execute his messengers as a show of my resolve. Such an act proves only one thing: that I'm afraid." Interlocking my fingers, I held them before my face, eyes closed as though praying. Zazzau could not afford to fight another war. Not right now.

"What makes you believe they'll simply go on their way?" Zariya protested. "Amina, you aren't invincible."

"I'm aware of that."

The Nupe certainly didn't need to kill me to put Zazzau at a disadvantage. My diminished army made us vulnerable. Jaruma's eyes met mine; she had a better understanding than Zariya of exactly how fragile we were right now.

"You're more exposed now than you've ever been," Jaruma threw in. "Letting them go may only reinforce their belief that you're weak."

"Jaruma—"

"You have no protection, Amina," Zariya said, recently aware of my patron's limitations. "Jaruma, send the soldiers."

"Who is queen here?" I asked.

Unspoken words passed between them. I glowered at each. As one, they returned my irate glare, stubborn determination ablaze in their eyes.

Jaruma relented first. "I'll send scouts instead. No executions. If only to ensure the Nupemen leave the region."

It was a reasonable solution to what was otherwise an impasse between me and my two mutinous subjects. It was also a wise course of action. I nodded. "Deploy your scouts."

✻

I stayed the next two nights in Zaria. On the third day, we received word that the eight Nupemen traveled in a southwesterly direction and had already bypassed the former capital, Turunku.

Once again, battle was on the horizon, and my mind would soon be focused on nothing but war— resources, strategy, soldiers' pay. I needed to withdraw, for a day or two, escape from the buzzing cities. But to appease my sister, I stayed several more nights in Zaria. Six nights in total. On the evening of the seventh, accompanied by Jaruma, I began the journey back to my retreat at the stone palace.

The night animals were just rousing from daytime slumber, while the predators of day howled in lamentation at the setting sun. Ordinarily, Demon and I would have made the journey alone, his supernatural speed carrying us from Zaria to Turunku in a matter of minutes. With Jaruma at my side, we traveled at a fair clip but were bound by her horse's mortal constraints.

Travel within Zazzau was the safest it had been in decades, and many travelers passed us on the plains that evening. None recognized us or gave any cause for alarm. Most, riding in pairs or in caravans, were merchants making their way to the next stop on their respective trading routes. With heavy headdresses shielding their faces from the savanna dust, only their eyes showed. In the growing darkness, no traveler stood out from the rest.

Intent on our destination, neither me nor Jaruma gave any undue attention to the people we met on the plains. We took no special note of the two—horses laden with wares—who rode toward and then past us some five kilometers back. Nor did we pay any mind when these same two men, having discarded their wares, turned to follow us.

The riders drew near, their horses' hoofbeats cutting through the evening symphony. A cursory glance over my shoulder showed me two men who looked like any other Hausa traders. They wore dark robes and veiled headwraps. Unperturbed, I faced forward.

While the men were nondescript, their horses were hardly that. Three white socks and a white muzzle on one; the other—all black—had a white star. I paused. Jaruma and I spun around simultaneously.

The rock, flung from a slingshot, hit me before I saw the weapon in his hand. Had I not turned when I did, it might have shattered my skull. As it was, it careened past my temple, grazing the side of my face. Crying out, I fell from Demon's back.

The other man had also hurled a stone but missed entirely. Before I hit the ground, I heard a knife leave Jaruma's hand. After my body thudded onto the dry grass, there went the zip of another knife. *Ivory and bone.* She always kept them with her. Then she was kneeling beside me.

"Amina? Amina!"

"I'm all right." Without touching it, I knew my face was swelling. A biting pain was starting to take root. "Are they dead?"

"I think one is dead. The other will soon join him." She helped me into a sitting position.

On impulse, I reached up to touch my injury but stopped as hot pain stabbed into my head. I groaned. Her eyes darted from me to the two men. One lay on the ground, immobile, and the other was trying to get in the saddle of a fidgeting horse.

"Stop him." I struggled to remain upright after she released me.

Blood veiled the vision in my right eye, but my left saw Jaruma approach the assassin who had managed to hoist himself onto the horse. I couldn't see where the blade had landed, but he didn't look as though he were going to die. Not soon, at any rate.

She reached the man and dragged him off the horse. He howled as he fell to the ground. Heedless of his pained cries, she bent down, jerked the blade from wherever it had landed, and snatched the headdress from his head and face. She went still.

Obviously, she recognized the man, though I couldn't see him. Nor could I hear her exact words. The tone of her voice, however, carried across to me. She spat curses as she wound the headdress around her hand, pulled back her cloth-wrapped fist, and struck him. Seizing his collar, she drew him forward and struck him again. And again.

She beat him until the white of the headdress was red with blood, and even then, she didn't stop. When at last she was satisfied—or spent—she let the man drop and unwrapped the cloth from her hand. Still cursing, she walked over to the second assassin, drew the bone knife from his chest, and used his tunic to wipe both weapons clean before striding back to where I sat with one eye swollen shut and all but overcome by pain.

"Feeling better?" I asked through gritted teeth.

Despite the situation, it pleased me to see Jaruma abashed.

"Sorry." She pointed at the dying man. "He was part of the Nupe convoy."

As she said it, I knew precisely which two men had crept upon us like "assassins on the wind." Perhaps I *should* have killed them at court. My breath escaped in a mixture of cursing, exhaling, and grunting pain.

"Help me up," I said at length. "The scavengers will clear the mess."

❊

After visiting the medicine man, we went to the stone palace. Jaruma had argued that we stay at Gidan Bakwa, but I had insisted that we should not. My will won over hers. In conjunction with the bitter roots that dulled my pain, the blow to my head was severe enough that it compromised my coordination, and the swelling impaired my vision. According to the medicine man, the bone around my eye was likely broken.

Jaruma got me onto Demon's back before mounting behind me, and he carried us to the summit. She hardly ceased complaining all the way up. Still voicing her acrimonious opinions when we reached the top, she dismounted and made to help me. The sound of footsteps brought her drivel to a halt. Knife drawn, she spun around.

"Your world is full of many dangers, Warrior."

She let out a loud breath, and the wargod came forward to pluck me off the horse.

"It is a wonder any of you survive long enough to bear offspring." As my feet touched the ground, he cupped my chin to angle my face and peer at the wound. "I am sorry, my love."

My response was meaningless babble. I locked my fingers around his neck, resting my head on his chest when he lifted me into his arms. He carried me to the palace. Jaruma followed.

Amazed muttering met us at the gatehouse.

"Temple priest," Jaruma said to mitigate the guards' collective curiosity. The explanation only made me wonder, as undoubtedly did the guards, what temple could keep a man of Dafaru's stature so well hidden.

Inside my chamber, Dafaru deposited me on the heavy cushions of my bed. It was a struggle to keep my eyes open, but I managed to stay awake. Jaruma lit the large oil lamp, placed it on a stool, and positioned herself in the doorway. Having received neither leave to go nor request to stay, she simply stood against the doorframe, arms folded.

The wargod proceeded as though she were not there. Sitting beside me, he coursed a fingertip across my cheekbone, below the injury. My face was numb from the medicine, but the heat of his fingers penetrated my skin and sank into my bones. I closed my eyes.

"Kogi cannot give you anything for healing," he said. "He is watched almost as closely as am I." There was a pause before he continued, "I fear, Beloved, that I have failed you."

I groped for his free hand.

He took mine and held it. "Your face will be badly bruised, and the healing will not be quick."

"My face has suffered worse," I said.

The heat spread when he drew near enough to touch his lips to my chin. "Will you come with me?"

"Jangare?" The word squeezed past barely moving lips.

"Yes."

I wanted to go with him, to be anywhere that he was. But at the same time, I wanted to stay where I lay. "Jaruma will care for me here."

Whether he understood my garbled utterance or heard my thoughts, he replied, "I have no doubt." He pressed my open palm to his face, and I ran my thumb across his perfect lips. "I *am* sorry," he said again. The heat retreated when he released my hand and got to his feet. "Rest, Beloved." Then he was gone.

I didn't open my eyes.

After a lengthy silence, Jaruma spoke. "Amina?"

"Yes." My lips were as numb as the wound around my eye. My mind, packed full of cobwebs, was fighting a losing battle against the sleep tugging at my consciousness.

"Do you love him?"

Sleep retreated. I parted heavy lids.

"Do you love him?" she asked again.

"Who?" I knew very well who.

"Dafaru ... Ruhun Yak'i ... wargod. Who else?" In her exasperation, she waved her hand maniacally about her head, gesturing at everything and nothing.

"Now isn't the time for such questions." The medicine in the bitter root kept a simmering apprehension from taking hold. I didn't want to think of my feelings for him or what it might mean when he, in his immortality, grew tired of me.

"Forgive me, Amina. But when is the time?" Her fractious tone pushed sleep even further out of reach.

"Watch yourself." I shoved the words forcibly from my mouth.

"But why?"

"Because I am your queen."

"No, Amina. I mean, why do you lie to yourself?"

Silence as I pondered her intrusive line of questioning.

"Love is not an easy thing to find," she said. "Look at me. In nearly eighty years of untarnished youth, I've only found it once. *Once*, Amina. And he grew old without me." She unhooked her weapons and dropped them on the floor before lowering herself onto a large cushion. "It was good. Even in middle age, I desired him. I *loved* him."

She was talking about Bashiru.

Her relationship with Bashiru had been a strange one. Neither had been faithful to the other. Jaruma had remained as wanton a hussy with Bashiru as she had been without him. And he had been an amorous fellow, no matter the woman.

She gathered up her weapons and arranged them in a tidy row. First her bow and its quiver of arrows, next the ivory dagger, then the bone dagger. She resumed speaking, and I had a feeling she was really speaking to herself.

"Of course, we knew he would grow old. Eventually, like Siddhi, he would have fallen victim to his age. But he died much sooner than we planned." The blazing light of the lamp illuminated a smile that spoke of sweet memories. She heaved a great sigh. "*How* we planned."

Knowing what I did of Jaruma, they'd probably planned a duel to the death before he grew too old to wield his weapon—either of his weapons. I chuckled at the mental image of berserker lovemaking and silently scolded myself for becoming distracted from Jaruma's unusually heartfelt, though one-sided, conversation.

"It was a wonderful thing," she said. "Love. Loving *him*. Whenever I was with him, my heart was filled to bursting. Even now, the memory of him fills my heart."

If nine years after his death, her feelings for Bashiru were as sharp as they had been when he lived, then it must have been true love.

"Amina?" Her eyes flickered with the lamplight.

"What?"

"You haven't answered me."

I groaned. In *my* nearly eighty years of youth, I had found love more than once. First, there was Suleyman, whom I still loved, though he had never "filled my heart to bursting." Not the way Jaruma described it. Then, there was Siddhi. My love for him hadn't had the passion that I'd shared with Suleyman, but there had been strong affection. Both Siddhi and Suleyman were in my heart, though only one being filled it.

The words had never passed my lips, but no matter how I tried to repress it, the emotion could not be fully contained. Always just beneath the surface, it was a fire-breathing beast screaming for release.

I closed my eyes and sighed. "I do love him, Jaruma. Allah help me, but I love him more than I've loved anything. He is the air I breathe."

She nodded. "Is it not a wonderful thing?"

Still facing me, she rested her head on her knees. In silence, we regarded each other. Until my eyelids drooped and the cobwebs began to encroach once more. As the dark of slumber dragged me toward the void, I heard Jaruma settle down to sleep beside me.

Yes, I thought. *It is a wonderful thing.*

FORTY-EIGHT

19 Kilometers North of Atagara, Nupeland, circa 1610 CE

We camped at the same location where we had camped over forty years prior. The village, which had grown from a single family to a collection of families, had maintained the wall excellently. Unlike our previous campaign in the south, the Nupe did not go about their business heedless of our presence. This time, there was a good deal of bustle and wartime activity in the vicinity of Atagara's wall. Also unlike the previous campaign, huge trees, taller than the walls themselves, grew where there were none before. Our long-range archers would be ineffective if we laid siege to the city. Judging from the number of Nupe archers lining the scaffolds behind the wall, the Nupe were hoping for just such a standoff.

I considered cutting down the trees, as the Bornu army often did. But we didn't have the manpower to fell trees as well as defend ourselves against the archers on the scaffolds. The most effective strategy would be to attack them head-on with mounted lancers in the vanguard, draw them away from the city, and weaken their front lines.

After finalizing this plan, my officers retreated to their various huts. Jaruma and I remained in the impromptu war chamber—a frame of thin tree limbs draped over with elephant grass. Palm fronds lined the roof, and stiff woven mats covered the ground.

We sat on the floor, sharing a gourd of coconut milk, the battle schematic drawn on vellum spread out between us, and tried to decipher Zariya's most recent oracular dream. A dream that she had tearfully relayed three nights before we'd set out for Nupeland when she had tried to convince me to forgo the war and release Tsoede from his obligation.

As I had explained to her then, releasing him wouldn't stop the pending hostilities; it would only convince him that he was stronger than us. Whether or not my sister fully understood what I was telling her, she was convinced of one thing: tragedy awaited us. But war *was* tragedy, and if I shrank from it, Zazzau would forever be subject to the changing winds of foreign powers.

Jaruma handed me the gourd. "The dead and dying all around you, eh? I'm ready." Her dark eyes were filled with cold determination.

I took the gourd from her hands. "Ready for what? A battle the likes of the Jamaa're River?"

"No battle could ever match that one. No, Amina. I'm ready for death and dying. I welcome the end."

I froze with the gourd halfway to my lips. "Don't say such things."

Her mouth curved in an oddly jubilant smile.

"Zariya's dreams aren't always accurate," I said. "And she didn't see you among the dead."

"She said my fate was linked to yours."

"I was alive in that vision."

"That's true." She frowned, a perplexed look in her eyes. "But I feel it, Amina."

It was all I could do to keep my anxiety in check. "You feel what, karya?" I slammed the gourd down. Some of the milk sloshed noisily onto the floor.

She glanced at the gourd and back at me, eyeing my outrage. At length, she rubbed the back of her neck. "I will soon see my brother." When I opened my mouth to tell her what I thought of that proclamation, she added, "I know this, Amina. I do."

"Are you mad? Why are you saying these things?"

"Because it's true. I'm ready."

The anxiety rose again; it tugged at my already fragile nerves. "You're ready? Ready for what? To die?" I heard the shrillness of my voice and dropped my eyes to the floor.

Her tone was soft but resolute. "I've been ready for a long time. I'm tired of living and fighting and struggling every day."

"Don't say such things, Jaruma. Death may hear," I pleaded, though I knew the pleading was in vain.

"Death has already heard." A contented expression softened her features, and she moved the gourd from between us. Leaning forward, she put a hand to either side of my face and kissed me lightly on the mouth.

I pushed her roughly back. "What of me?" I wanted to shake her, slap the foolishness out of her head.

Her laughter, as throaty and sinister as ever, could have been amusement or insanity, but her tone remained calm. "Well, my friend, you aren't slated to die."

"Neither are you, karya."

She shook her head as though I was a petulant child. "Abuse me all you like, my queen. You cannot turn the hand of Destiny."

"Jaruma." I took both her hands in mine. "This talk of yours is like the muttering of a madwoman."

"Perhaps." She shrugged. "But have you ever stopped to listen to the words of a madwoman? Sometimes, there is truth in her rambling."

"There is only madness." I squeezed her hands, tamping down the threatening tears.

She pulled me into an embrace. Lean, muscular arms enveloped me, her lithe body pressed to mine. She was the physical embodiment of strength. She was *my* strength. My courage. Carrying on without her was inconceivable.

My arms slid around her waist. "Jaruma, I cannot live without you."

"You know . . ." She released me and took my hands in hers. "Before I came to be your companion, when Suleyman first brought me home, I begged him not to leave me. I told him I couldn't bear to be apart from him."

I stared blankly at her, unwilling to blink for fear of crying.

"Do you want to know what he said to me?" Without awaiting my response, she continued, "He said, 'We have been inseparable far too long if you cannot bear to be apart.'" The manner in which she spoke the words, with her brother's inflections, made it seem as though Suleyman's spirit was with us, speaking through her mouth.

Out of sorts, I asked, "What has that to do with me?"

She regarded me tenderly, her love painted into her very expression. Her hands moved to either side of my face, and she kissed me again. This time, the kiss was hard, decisive. We lingered like that for a while, her lips on mine, my hands covering hers, my tears held back by anger alone.

She withdrew, her hands still on my face. "We've lived as one for far too long if you cannot live without me."

"No, Jaruma." I shook my head as moisture began seeping from my eyes.

With the backs of her fingers, she gently wiped my tears and placed her palms on my face again. "I think, my friend, that our journey has ended." Another kiss. This time on the forehead. "Either you go on without me or we both die here. But I don't believe you are meant to die in this place." Despite her youthful appearance, the eyes looking at me were those of a woman who had seen too much in life and grown old beyond her years.

She had to be wrong. But what if she wasn't? What if she died here in this land of trees and vermin? Would this foul country—these foul Nupemen, who had taken her brother—also take her?

"If you die," I said, "what reason do I have for living?"

"You don't live for me, Amina. I'm your servant. I live for *you*."

"Then go on living for me." Distress cracked my voice. "Please."

Her eyes looked into mine, but she gave no response.

"Jaruma, are you so ready for death that you'll simply lay down your life?"

She laughed, and some of the carefree attitude of long gone youth glowed once again in her eyes. "I'll fight fiercely at your side, as I always do. When I meet my brother, I can tell him I did not go meekly to my death."

Her words were a noose around my heart, and the pain in my soul increased with each word she uttered. I got to my feet. "I need water."

I left the hut.

❀

I did not immediately return to Jaruma. From the banks of the stream where I had lowered my head to wash my face, the god of war whisked me to another world. The sudden change in surroundings left me with a measure of vertigo, which receded after he helped me to my feet.

"Lord Husband." I suppressed the desire to throw myself into the safety of his arms. Along with the prospect of upcoming hostilities, Jaruma's stark declarations filled me with a sense of dread that shook my very foundations. Dafaru's presence helped calm the storm.

"My queen." He bowed.

We stood atop a dune in a barren desert. Above us, the stars sparkled like gemstones sewn into a cloak of black silk.

I shivered at the chill wind. "Where are we?"

"The beginning of time. Or the end of time. It is a place of solitude, quietude, and interlude. A place outside the worlds, yet within."

I hated riddles.

His red eyes blazed like a thousand suns. "I believe you are the first mortal to see this place. Father would hang me inside out if He knew I brought you here."

"Why do you provoke the Creator's wrath? Doesn't He know all things?"

"So you mortals like to believe."

The wind howled, whipping up the sand, which whirled about and stung my skin. Dafaru threw his cloak around my shoulders and I buried my face in his chest. The wind continued to blow violently for a time before it died down and gradually faded to nothing. All became silent.

He released me. "I risk Father's wrath because I want you to feel the power of this place. One sees"—he indicated by tapping his temple—"more clearly when one takes time for quiet reflection."

I shook my head. "I cannot see past my fears."

"You *refuse* to see past them, Beloved."

His chest rose with a deep inhalation, which he savored before silently releasing it. His eyes moved downward. I followed his gaze to the ground where a shiny creature crawled through the sand. In shape and movement, the thing resembled a millipede except it was white. It scuttled onto my naked foot. With an embarrassing squeal, I kicked out, flinging the creature into the golden sands beyond.

"You see?" He smirked. "When you peer more closely, you find that what appears to be desolation is, in fact, filled with life."

"Scorpions and the like," I muttered.

He did not reply but raised an expectant brow.

The silence drew out for a few breaths before I said, "She says she's ready for death."

"She is a warrior, my love. She was born ready."

"But I'm not ready to lose her." I turned my attention to the sand sweeping over my feet.

"All things come to an end. It is selfish of you to think otherwise."

I knew it was selfish and didn't care. My heart was crumbling. Tears again made their way to the surface while the wind increased, threatening another gale.

At length, I raised my moisture-rimmed eyes to his. "Am I going to die in Nupeland?" The wind continued to scream. Louder and louder until I was forced to shout. "She says we've lived too long as one. But I'd prefer to die with her than live without her." My own mortality bared itself before me.

Lowering his head, he raised his cloak until we were enshrouded by it. The noise of the wind diminished within our shelter.

His eyes met mine. "Would you not rather live with me than die with her?"

"My lord . . ." But I had no ready words.

His fingers closed around mine and brought my hand to his lips. He kissed my palm.

Recalling his ghostly servants, I said, "In spirit form, I could remain with you. Could I not?" Under the cloak, I rested my head on his chest and listened to the beating of his heart, which sounded like war drums in my ears.

"It is not so simple, Beloved. Mortal spirits only reach Jangare through great trials. Spirits survive in Jangare only to purge whatever burdens weigh heavy on their souls. Then they move on, far beyond the Crossroads."

Tension throbbed in my temples.

"Even if you believed yourself unworthy, your soul too heavy for ascension, the trials would likely cleanse you before you reached Jangare. Then I would lose you forever." The wind subsided, but he didn't put aside his cloak. "You ask if you will die. To that, I say your path was set before you were born. But there have been many forks in the road. Your decisions—and yours alone—have brought you to where you are today. Another fork is coming, my love. You may die or you may live. I cannot say which end you will choose."

I will not choose life if Jaruma dies.

"But will you choose me?" he asked.

"My lord . . ." Again, there were no ready words.

He kissed my aching temple and let the cloak drop. When he pulled away, we were in his throne room. Brushing the desert dust off his black trousers, he strode over to the black throne, lowered himself onto it, and gestured for me to climb the dais steps.

The wargod might have been without his powers, but that did not diminish him as a god in his domain. Here, he was lord above all. Overcome by the divine aspect radiating from the entity on the throne, I reached the top of the stairs and dropped to my knees, eyes cast upon the ground.

He held out a hand. "Rise, Beloved. You need never kneel before me."

I took his hand and got to my feet, though I was compelled to prostrate myself.

"It is the power of that place outside and within the worlds," he said solemnly. "We of the pantheon absorb it like parched earth absorbs water. The compulsion will pass." Letting go of my hand, he sat back and kneaded his temple with his forefinger. "Tell me your battle plan."

FORTY-NINE

The plan was to march on Nupeland and crush them to dust. The Kaduna River was to run red with the blood of our fallen enemies. We stormed the battlefield, infantry at the fore, pushing back the enemy who fought with equal, if not superior, skill. My lanced cavalry carried out its task well, weakening the Nupe vanguard, while the short bowmen rained arrows on the archers in the scaffolds and on the enemy infantry, cutting down their numbers. Either the thick southern soil or the heavy air—which grew oversized trees and monstrous mosquitoes—had produced a herd of massive Nupemen who did not rely on numbers for their strength.

The Nupe infantrymen were like oxen and carried weapons made for giants. I didn't remember them being so huge on our previous campaign—neither the men nor the weapons. They fought with spears, which they threw with unfaltering accuracy, swords that were longer than the standard Zazzagawa weapon, and battle-axes that could hew a man in half with a single blow.

And their women, an entire contingent for which we had not accounted, fought with short-swords in one hand and knives in the other. They moved fast. Spinning, kicking, rolling in a whirlwind dance of quick jabs and short slashes that opened throats almost faster than the movements themselves. For every woman we felled, they brought down five of my warriors.

Arrows pierced the ranks of my short bowmen, disabling many, but we held our ground, battered by the oxlike infantrymen and the whirling women. Our archers soon lost their efficiency, and the close combat began in earnest.

An arrow buzzed past my ear, nicking it with enough pain that my hand went, reflexively, to the injury. Another arrow missed me and glanced off Demon's hide, hurtling to the ground. I ducked to avoid a spear from a mounted warrior and lunged with my takouba. The weapon, intended for the warrior, sliced into his horse's neck. The horse hit the ground, crushing its rider beneath.

Despite the many horrors of war, it was this accidental death of a horse that filled me with remorse. I bottled the emotion and faced the next warrior charging down on me from horseback. Parrying his longsword, I cracked his face with my bracelet. He fell senseless to the ground.

I looked furtively around and spotted Jaruma, unhorsed. She stood several feet away, shooting off arrows at enemy soldiers before they could get within sword's range. Beyond, a Nupe bowman nocked an arrow and took aim. Forgetting to breathe, I reached anxiously for my bow. His arrow flew but hit the warrior beside Jaruma. I released an arrow as I released my breath. The Nupeman crumpled, my arrow protruding from his chest.

Riding toward Jaruma, I let more arrows fly, hitting my marks more often than not. When the quiver ran out, I drew my takouba and sliced down the enemy.

A spear sailed through the ranks of men, missing all, heading for Jaruma. I dove from Demon's saddle and threw myself into her. We collided with simultaneous grunts and again when our bodies hit the ground. The spear sailed over us. Stunned, she lay on her back, looking up at me.

"I won't let you die," I said—more for me than for her, because she probably couldn't hear past the ruckus.

Eyes wide, she shouted, "Move!"

With one mind, we rolled. A battle-axe came down between us. It swung again, and I jerked my arm out of its path. The warrior started to yank the weapon from the ground, but an arrow tore through his face—in one cheek and out the other. He shrieked and fell forward, a second arrow jutting from his neck.

Jaruma and I were on our feet. She held her bow in both hands, clubbing one man then another. Tossing the bow aside, she drew her sword from its sheath. My blade was already in motion, hacking at enemy soldiers. Everything Nupe felt the sharp sting of metal or the crushing blow of bracelets.

Demon appeared, trampling enemy soldiers into bleeding heaps of flesh. And I was back in the saddle, pressing toward the city gates. Jaruma, now also mounted, was not far behind.

War drums sounded. In the chaos, I couldn't tell what the drums were beating, or even if the drums were mine. But it didn't matter, we were pushing the Nupe back. Battle cries filled the air. Nupe infantrymen fell in droves as we edged closer to the gates. Soon we would be victorious, and the city would be ours.

Or so I thought.

In my vanity, my prideful claim of victory, that two-faced and fickle god of fortune and misfortune turned his hideous mask on me. Rallying in fearless effort, the Nupe swarmed around us and fought back like wild dogs cornered in the bush. It was as though their strength was doubled, so ferocious were they in the attack.

I hacked and jabbed and thrust my sword through Nupeman after Nupeman, yet they came. With blood gushing from open wounds, arms hanging limp, the Nupe refused to die. Theirs was the fight of the hopeless, the fight of despair. Still, they would not yield. My confidence faltered, uncertainty impinged on my determination, but I wouldn't give in either. Not to the Nupe, not to fear, not to death. I turned to face the half-alive warriors clawing at legs, trying to unhorse me. My takouba pierced the eye of one, took off the hand of another, and slid into a third. Triumphant, I sang out my battle cry.

The war song froze on my lips. My breath lodged in my seizing chest when I saw the battle-axe spin across open space and hit its target. *No.* She turned to me with a look of surprise, then blood spurted from her mouth. *No.* The surprise in her eyes transformed into sadness. She brought up more blood. Bile rose in my belly, my seizing chest unlocked. A smile crept over her now serene features, and she tumbled from the horse.

I screamed.

Prayers poured from my lips as I fought my way toward my companion. Tears stung my eyes, but I did not slow. I swung my weapon blindly before me, without a care for whose blood drenched the blade. Mad with fear, I cut into one man after another while Demon charged through warriors, shattering their feeble frames under hoof.

I reached her and jumped to the ground, still wailing my prayers. "No!" Another scream tore from my throat.

Dropping to my knees, I ran my hands over Jaruma's body, touched her chest, her face, and pressed my palms to the yawning wound in her neck. But I couldn't stop the flow. Her blood continued to pour without cease.

My heart died. The battle no longer mattered. Nothing mattered without her. A stream of indecipherable sounds—shrieking, crying, a barrage of cursing—streaked past my lips. I pleaded to and then cursed the gods. I cursed Jaruma for leaving me and cursed Death for taking her. All the while trying to gather her into my arms and stop the damned bleeding.

A spear raked across my shoulder, drawing me painfully back into battle. I bellowed in fury as the spearman, staggering from a vicious wound to his leg, pulled back for another jab. I swung without rising from my knees. My attacker's bowels spilled from his body.

I jumped to my feet, slashed at a swinging sword, and smashed my war bracelet into the side of a warrior's head. He didn't fall. I struck him again and drove my blade into his chest.

As I yanked the weapon out, another swordsman struck, slicing my forehead. The sword swept over me a second time, cutting a channel across my breast. I blocked its third pass with my war bracelet, clenching my teeth against the vibration traveling up my arm.

Blood and tears impeded my vision. I jabbed at the warrior and missed. His long-sword came down. I stepped into him, catching his sword arm beneath my free arm, and plunged my weapon into his belly. An arrow pierced my side. I cried out and fell to one knee. Another arrow missed. I struggled to my feet.

Pain.

White-hot pain raced through me. I looked down. I'd not even seen the lancer. Now my mind was unable to grasp what my eyes could clearly see—the shaft of a spear jutting from my chest. My body folded. Salty blood filled my mouth. I coughed it up, chest rattling from the effort. Silent screams raged inside my head, and the ground came up to meet me. I fell beside her—*this is as it should be*—and reached for the woman who had been my constant companion.

My fingers made no contact.

An inhuman sound formed in my throat but escaped only in a gurgle as I choked on my blood. Broken, I stared up at the reddening sky.

Jaruma was dead. I was dying. I could not breathe.

FIFTY

The cries of vultures reached my ears. The sound of battle receded. Heavy eyelids insisted on closing, but I forced them open, blinking once, twice, trying to clear away the red haze. Still, my vision was a bloody blur. The searing pain in my chest bore down on me like an elephant, crushing me with its weight, squeezing the air from my body in a long, ragged moan. A shadow loomed. I felt its presence as surely as I felt the pain in my flesh. Death. The shrieking vultures grew louder at its approach.

"Death is near but otherwise occupied."

Dafaru.

He stood above me, so very divine in his countenance. I could depart this life with the image of his face upon my eyes. My lips moved, formed words, but no sound came out.

"Easy, Beloved." He dropped to one knee. There was something different about his voice, but I couldn't fathom what it was. "You are gravely injured."

My injury was more than grave. I was staring at Death's door, but I was not afraid. Things had not gone as planned. The Nupe had regained their strength and perhaps the advantage, but my warriors still fought. The sound of battle was distant; the fighting had moved beyond the rise, but I heard it. My people would go on until the last.

Dafaru shook his head. "The Zazzagawa do not fare well. They are defeated, Amina."

There died the last hope for my empire, for my warriors. The moans of the soldiers strewn about me filled my ears even as the despairing thump of my heartbeat filled my head.

Death and dying all around.

"You are in pain." He wiped my eyes with his thumb.

Some of the red haze cleared from my vision, and his face came into focus. It was full of remorse, disappointment. The suffering in his eyes made them dull and stilled the whirling red eddies. I longed to touch the smooth skin of his face one last time but could do no more than raise my fingers.

"Let me ease your pain." *His voice.* The same yet not the same. Different in timbre. Was it grief that made it so?

I tried to speak. Again, nothing came out. The pain in my chest shifted, concentrating in one point before exploding outward. Back arched, I screamed my most exquisite agony. The sound of it sliced through the noises around me, trailing off to mingle with the death cries of the warriors scattered upon the field. I fell back to the ground as Dafaru tossed the spear aside.

There was less pain now, though the weight upon my chest was no lighter. Dafaru's arm slid under me. He raised me up and the weight dropped lower. I breathed a little easier.

"Father has given me a parting gift." Holding me close, he cradled my chin and tilted my head to look into my eyes. "Death is coming for you," he said urgently. "Kogi's water may stay your pain, but Death comes when it will."

"Let me die." This time, the words were audible.

Like his voice, his gaze was flat. His eyes, a shade of red that could not be described, darted across my face. "Will you leave me then, my love? And go with Death?"

His anguish etched lines on a usually smooth forehead, and it was too much to bear. I shut my eyes.

"Will you leave me to wander this world alone?" The off-timbre voice sounded more like a frightened child than the chaotic god of war.

His utterances made no sense. Death, as he already said, was coming. I was destined for the Crossroads. Though I would stay with him, my desires were inconsequential. There was, however, something I wanted to tell him before I left this world. Something he deserved to know, this brutal god who had given me his blazing heart.

Seeing me struggle to speak, he lowered his ear to my lips. In death, I told him what I'd not managed to say in life.

"I love you, wargod." As I whispered the words, I realized it was too late for them to have meaning.

"Long have I yearned to hear you speak those very words." Sadness dimmed his radiance. "After everything . . . I think, perhaps, I do not deserve your love."

If anyone had deserved my love, it was him, for he had loved me in his own fashion. After all, what was a mortal to a god?

He said, "You are everything to me."

A new anguish pierced my soul. Needing to touch him, I lifted my fingers again, but my arm lay motionless at my side, too heavy to budge.

His hand found mine and grasped it. Raising it to his face, he splayed my fingers flat against his cheek. "If you can love me as I am, Beloved, despite all that has befallen you this day, come with me."

The plea in his tone pushed back the darkness creeping across my mind. I took a shallow breath and opened my eyes. His face was twisted in pain, a pain so tremendous that it eclipsed mine, which ebbed with the last of my life. He hung his head and tried in vain to mask his suffering.

If I could leave this place and go with him, I would. And if it pleased him to hear me say it, then I would.

"Always," I whispered, caressing his face with fingers that scarcely moved. My eyes closed of their own accord. Near-empty lungs weakened my voice, speech fragmented and slow. "Always loved you. Love you . . . as . . ." I took several shallow breaths and tried to open my eyes, but could not. "As"—another breath—"you are." It was all I could manage. My hand slipped from his fingers and fell to the ground.

Dafaru spoke, but I no longer understood the words. He pressed his lips to mine. The noise of the dying, the cries of vultures, the distant battle—all were extinguished by that kiss. The only sound was my heart beating in my ears. It slowed . . . slowed . . . slowed . . .

My eyes flew open. I gasped, gulping down a torrent of air, chest heaving, body quaking with the effort of that single breath. Dafaru held my trembling frame for several seconds—or minutes or hours—while I inhaled, throat rasping. My ribs ached from expanding, my lungs were near bursting. When I could take in no more air, I exhaled and went limp in his arms.

The tightness in my chest gradually relaxed. Each breath grew deeper, more effortless. My hand moved languorously to clutch my breast, feeling for the wound. There was a large tear in my armor. Jagged links of broken mail scratched my fingers as I felt beyond them and through the shredded cloth of my battle dress. When my fingers touched flesh, the skin was intact. Sore, but intact.

"That was the last of my power, Beloved. We must leave here now."

In self-exploration, I had not looked at the wargod, whose voice became less and less familiar. I looked at him now and saw his face in full clarity. What I beheld forced another gasp from my throat.

"Your eyes," I breathed.

They were a bright, clear brown.

I sat up and took his face between my hands to peer into eyes whose whites were brilliantly white. Within the brown, a few obscure specks of red still remained but were hardly visible. His eyes, although a shade or so lighter than common, were the eyes of an ordinary man.

"My lord, what have you done?"

"I am immortal no longer." There was no disappointment in his voice, no bitterness. "My life for yours." He rose, pulling me to my feet. "We must leave this place, Amina."

"I cannot leave my people." My eyes lingered on his, still unable to believe what they saw.

"Beloved, your people are beyond your protection." He undid my battle gear. "Your time has passed. You died on this battlefield today, and I could not save her." His eyes swept past me to where Jaruma lay cold and motionless. "Else I might have done it. For you."

I too began to look, then snapped my eyes shut. I didn't want to see her like that. Never again. But even with my eyes closed, the image of Jaruma's death filled the darkness. Tears pushed past my clenched eyelids.

"There will be time for mourning." He stripped me down to my tattered and bloody tunic. "I will mourn with you."

His arms were around me. I lowered my head to his chest. *How does a god become mortal?* He felt as solid and as powerful as he had always been, with skin just as smooth. But his body no longer burned with the fire of War.

He held me only a moment. "Now we must go, for I am but a man." The declaration was a startling reminder of what had occurred in Nupeland that day.

"Where will we go, my lord?"

"I am no lord, but a man." He brushed his lips against the top of my head. "We go east until we reach the Great River Kwara. Then we follow the river into the western Sahel. Beyond that, we go wherever you like."

"What of my sister?"

"You cannot go back to Zazzau." The refusal was final.

Dreams and prophecies had been more accurate than Zariya would ever know. For there I stood in Dafaru's arms, surrounded by dead warriors. Jaruma lay among them. Her fate linked to mine, she had lost her life while I had been yanked back from Death's maw. I would never see either woman again. Not in this life. The realization sent me into a fit of tears.

"Please, Beloved, do not cry."

He sounded almost frightened in his mortality. It was enough to strengthen my own resolve. I wiped my tears.

"There is a village less than three days' ride from here," he said. "I may be mistaken, but I believe it is now called Yauran. They were always a good people. I know they will take us in without questions."

At the mention of riding, I remembered my horse. "Demon?" I stared into eyes that were mesmerizing in their strangeness, in their all too human beauty.

"Free, my love. The moment I became mortal. But there are horses yonder," he added quickly as my tears rose again. He pointed, and I followed the gesture to see several horses in the distance. "Wait here." He made to pull his hand from mine.

I tightened my grip on his fingers. "Do not leave me, my lor—Husband."

So many changes. In a matter of hours, a matter of moments, my world had been altered beyond recognition.

My husband regarded me with a gentle gaze, then cocked his head toward the horses. We made our way over.

The well-trained horses of the Kuturun Mahayi didn't need catching. Some small coaxing with gentle words and we were astride. Both of us on one horse, a second horse tethered to the first.

Underneath me, the horse felt small, but after Demon, *all* horses were small. Locking my arms tightly around Dafaru's waist, I looked at the bodies piled upon the field, and tears filled my eyes again. Once I left this battlefield, no man would ever have to die for me. That was a good thing, except . . . "I've left nothing of myself in Zazzau. All that I was has turned to dust on this field." *I will be forgotten here.*

"You will never be forgotten in this world of men, Amina." He smiled over his shoulder at my surprised expression. "Your mind is still open to me." It was a sliver of normalcy in a world turned upside down.

"But I've left no children. Nothing to show that Amina ever walked this earth."

"The feats of gods are all too quickly forgotten. But the feats of men? These remain legend for generations to come. Your story, my love—the story of a mortal woman who conquered kings and gods alike—will endure."

His claim was almost convincing. I nestled my head between his shoulder blades. He clicked the horse into motion.

"Do not forget who you are, Amina, daughter of Bakwa. You conquered all the lands from the plateaus in the east to the encircling Great River. You have been loved by gods and feared by men. You are the queen of Zazzau—a woman more capable than any man. Your name will be sung by storytellers." He paused, glanced at me again, and returned his attention to the horse. "Even when the names of gods are but motes on the wind, the name *Amina* will be remembered."

With those words, we rode away from the scene that my sister had predicted with painful accuracy, journeying westward to begin our life, *his* life anew. Far away from those things that had shaped me, far away from the people who had known me, from all that I loved— my sister and my home. Far away from my city, my kingdom, my Zazzau.

END

AFTERWORD

The idea for *Queen of Zazzau* came to me in 2006. Like many of the best ideas, it sprang into my head less than fully formed, and I had no clue how to execute it. I completed the first draft in 2007, the second in 2008, another in 2009, again in 2010, 2011, 2012 . . . well, you get the picture.

By the time I finished the many draft revisions, my worldview had darkened. In 2012, Trayvon Martin was murdered by a gun-wielding lunatic, and the information floodgates opened. Myriad reports of the police shooting unarmed black men and black children, like Aiyana Stanley-Jones (2010) and Tamir Rice (2014), quickly came to light. Because I'm a glass-half-full sort of person, I had to believe that the people who claimed they "feared" for their lives (and were exonerated because of it) actually *did* fear for their lives. And if that were true, why did they fear for their lives? Was it because the only black faces they saw on television or in books were depicted as violent, murderous, crooks?

When Black Lives Matters took to the streets in protest of the institutionalized and systemic racism that has led to the deaths and incarcerations of countless people of color, I admired them. When Colin Kaepernick took a knee, I applauded him. The people who risked so much to shine a light on the racial injustices that are still woven into the fabric of the United States forced a dialogue. Although I haven't the constitution to march and be arrested or blackballed in pursuit of racial equality (and perhaps that makes me a coward), I *can* do dialogue.

Afrocentric Books is my silent protest and *Queen of Zazzau* is only the beginning. There will be more black protagonists. There will be more black heroes in the pages of books, on television, and in the movies. We will no longer be relegated to the margins. I truly hope you enjoyed this novel. Stay tuned for the other African monarchs.

J.S. Emuakpor was born and raised in West Africa. She is a married mother of four, a scientist, and owner of Afrocentric Books. She currently lives in North Carolina and is very much allergic to it. Most of her writing draws upon the spiritual beliefs of the ancestors who frequently whisper in her ear and on the superstitions that she refuses to relinquish. You can find her at www.jsemuakpor.com.

Made in the USA
Lexington, KY
13 July 2019